To i

Not a … an end, but this story ends here.



# Tinker's Justice

## Book 4 of the Mad Tinker Chronicles

By J.S. Morin

ISBN: 1939233305
ISBN-13: 978-1-939233-30-1

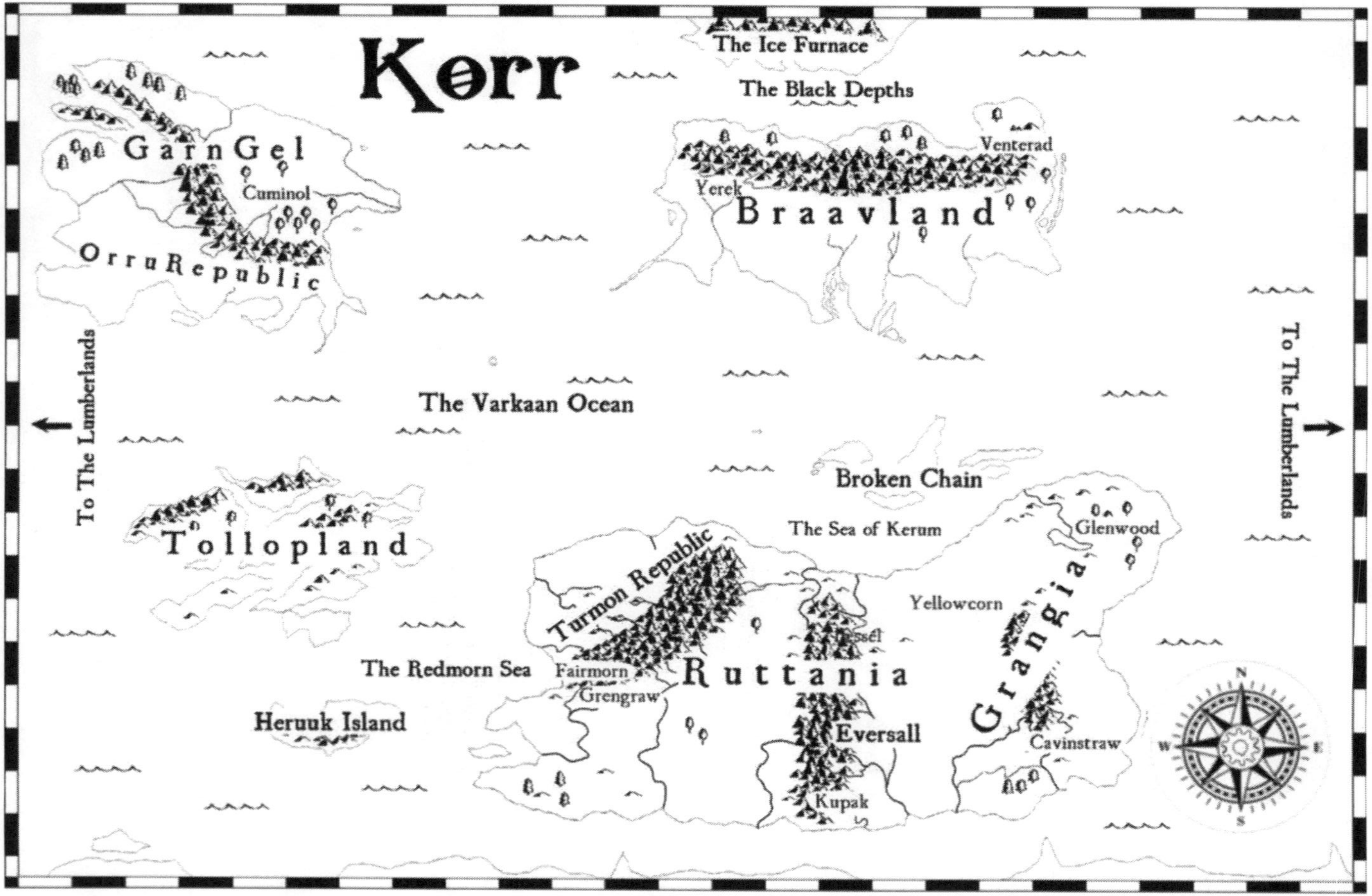
Korr
The Ice Furnace
The Black Depths
GarnGel
Cuminol
OrruRepublic
Venterad
Yerek
Braavland
The Varkaan Ocean
To The Lumberlands
To The Lumberlands
Broken Chain
Tollopland
The Sea of Kerum
Glenwood
Turmon Republic
Yellowcorn
Grangia
The Redmorn Sea
Fairmorn
Grengraw
Ruttania
Heruuk Island
Eversall
Cavinstraw
Kupak
N
W
E
S

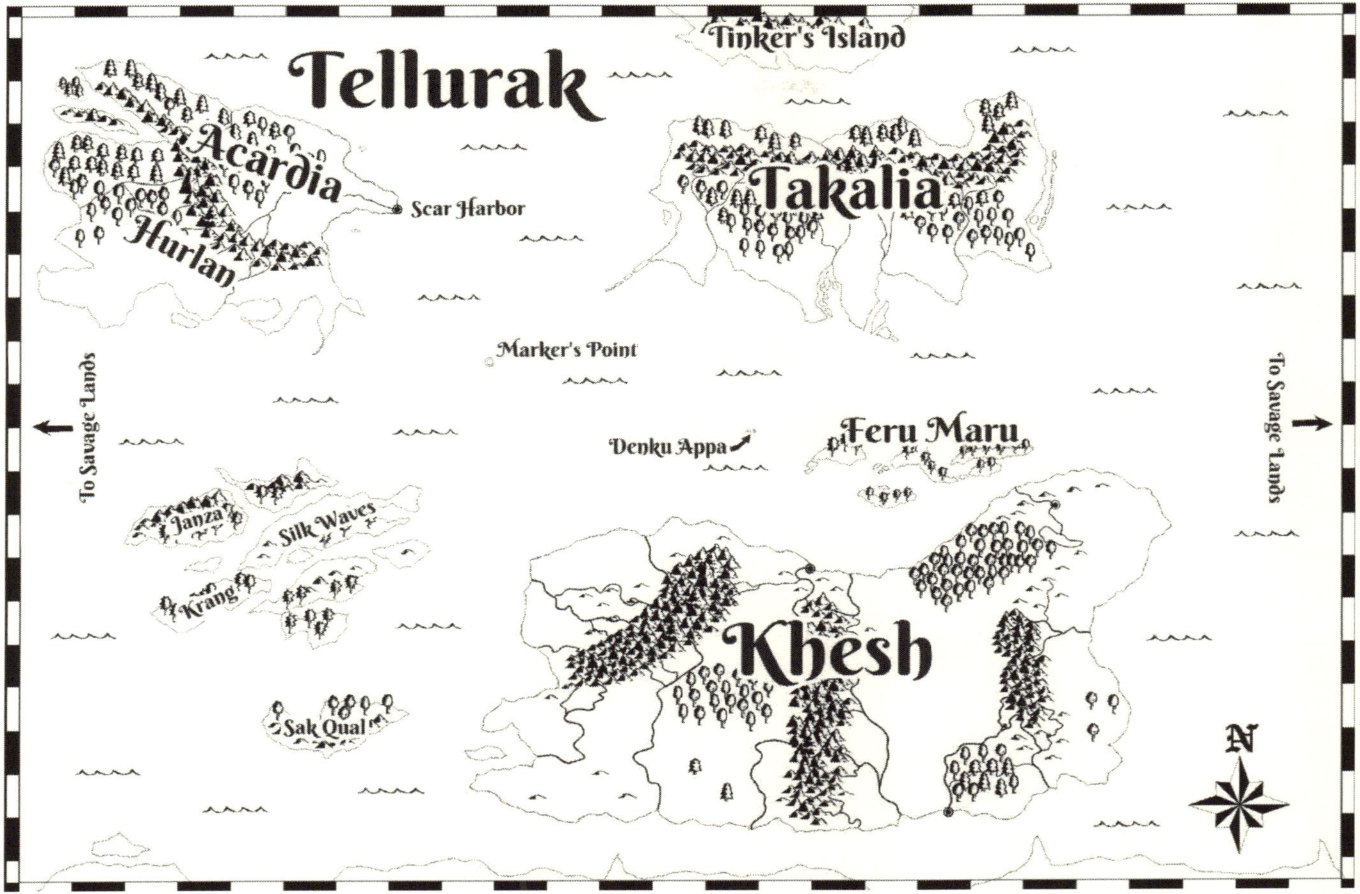
Tinker's Island
Tellurak
Acardia
Hurlan
Scar Harbor
Takalia
Marker's Point
To Savage Lands
To Savage Lands
Denku Appa
Feru Maru
Janza
Silk Waves
Krang
Khesh
Sak Qual
N

# Chapter 1

*"Every time a dragon speaks your name, your life grows shorter by a day."*
*– goblin proverb*

Madlin slipped the spectacles off her face and mopped away dripping sweat with a rag from her belt. The furnaces made the foundry an oven not just for metals, but for the workforce as well. All around her, goblins hustled this way and that, each at some small errand that was essential in the grand operation of what Madlin had begun to call the Valley of Coil Guns. Every square foot of space was dedicated to the sole production of the weapons for which she had become famous. Each day she toured all twenty-one buildings in the complex, culminating in watching the day's production quota packed into boxes and locked away in a warehouse. Technically that was the twenty-second building, but unlike the rest, Madlin was not allowed inside.

She pinched the bridge of her nose and squeezed her eyes shut to force away a headache. It had been a long day of inspecting reports written in notations she could barely comprehend, even after months of practice. The goblin metallurgists were meticulous in their record-keeping, but their handwriting was tiny. Madlin suspected after squinting at so many of them, she was going to need to grind a new refractory angle into her spectacles; the ones she had were just not quite up to the task.

The trill of the shift bell pierced Madlin's ears like a hail of bullets. Thankfully the sound ended after a few seconds, and the goblin workforce flowed to allow one set of workers to exit as the next shift arrived. Even with all the time she had spent among them, she could only pick a few goblins out of a crowd by sight. When she opened her eyes moments later, she could have imagined that the shift had never changed. Goblins manned every piece of equipment, same as they had before she closed them. While she still marveled at their efficiency, Madlin was no longer awed by the goblins.

*Just a bunch of replaceable gears: quick to train, quick to replace, never do anything to surprise you.*

A goblin chuckle drew Madlin's attention. A casual listener might mistake the sound for a stutter of the clearing of a throat, but Madlin had known the tinker long enough to recognize his nervous laugh. "Fr'n'ta'gur wants to see you," K'k'rt said.

The elderly goblin walked with the aid of a stick, too proud to make the daily trek down from the mountain city atop the head of a lizard. K'k'rt hunched over, shoulders heaving as he caught his breath. "Must be important if you ran all the way here," Madlin replied.

K'k'rt glowered at her. "I did not run. And it is always important when Fr'n'ta'gur wants to speak with someone."

Madlin stretched and twisted her neck to the side until it cracked. She was sore and bleary-eyed, sticky with sweat and empty of stomach. "I guess I could use one of those baths the priests insist on," she said with a sigh.

K'k'rt shook his head. "It's not that kind of visit. Last time you had to wheedle the priests into granting you an audience. This time, *he* wants to see *you.* It's an important distinction. You're coming as you are, reeking and disheveled."

Madlin raised an eyebrow. "You notice that sort of thing?"

K'k'rt chuckled. "I'm amazed *you* do. You hardly even know the names of your assistants. Now come along; Fr'n'ta'gur won't like waiting."

"I thought you told me he barely notices the passing of time."

"That's when you're the one requesting the meeting."

When Madlin arrived in Fr'n'ta'gur's lair, the first thing that she noticed was that the dragon was not performing his usual theatrics, hiding in the dark recesses of the cavern upon her arrival. Instead, she found the cavern well lit by aether and the dragon waiting at the edge of the precipice that overlooked his sea of treasure. The second thing she noticed was the stack of crates—crates she recognized from the warehouse she was not allowed to enter.

"Greetings, Madlin Errol of Korr," Fr'n'ta'gur said, his voice vibrating through the floor and into the soles of Madlin's feet. The dragon grumbled something in the goblin tongue, and the priests that had escorted her to the lair departed in haste. "I have arranged privacy for us. There will be no ears listening to your replies, even if my own words rumble through the mountain. Nor will any goblin eyes peer in at us in secret."

"To what do I owe these considerations?" Madlin asked. "Does it have something to do with the guns you owe me?"

Fr'n'ta'gur bared his teeth in what Madlin had come to understand was the equivalent of a smile. "Indeed. These are yours. You may take them home with you tonight."

Madlin did quick math. "Those crates only hold eight coil guns apiece. There's only seventy-two in that whole stack."

"I imagine you must tire of life here among my worshipers," Fr'n'ta'gur said. "You stay among us because of the terms of our bargain, not because you are stranded. Tonight, you return home with these seventy-two weapons. Tomorrow, you arrive to resume your work. Each night, you may take another load of crates, until you have your full share."

"I … well …"

"Do you find this acceptable?" Fr'n'ta'gur asked.

*I find it damned suspicious, you ship-sized lizard. When did you grow a generous streak?* "Yes, thank you," Madlin replied. Was he trying to get rid of her? Did he assume that she would take seventy-two of the guns and count her blessings that she escaped with her life? *Perhaps.* Did he plan to attack, maybe breathe fire through the open world-hole? *Unlikely. What would he gain?* Was he just curious? *Best case, I suppose. Not much to bet on.* There was little else to be done though. Refuse, and Fr'n'ta'gur would take offense—for form's sake, he would have to. Then again, with his promise of privacy, he could lie to his own priests and say anything he liked.

"You may also bring any personal effects you like," the dragon said. "I understand the furnishings and tools are not to your human standards."

Madlin forced a tight smile onto her face. *Gut you, K'k'rt! Do you run to your dragon with my every gripe?*

"I apologize if my worshipers have not the skill of your native craftsmen. Make yourself as comfortable here as you are able. I expect that it will be three seasons before your weapons are all delivered, assuming this paltry amount is not typical of the number made each day."

Every fiber of Madlin's being told her that it was a trick, a trap of some sort, a double-deal, or an outright lie. The problem was that without knowing which, she couldn't think of a way to refuse the dragon's offer. Without a counter in place, angering the dragon would end their deal and her life.

"It'll just take a moment," Madlin said. Rynn was already readying the world-ripper for her retrieval. Madlin watched the dragon's eyes, eager to discern how keen the beast's vision was in the aether. Would it be able to track the viewframe's location as Rynn lined it up prior to opening a hole?

Fr'n'ta'gur settled back onto his haunches, withdrawing his barge-sized head from her vicinity. The reptilian slits in the dragon's eyes widened. Dan had always gotten a distant look in his eyes when he peered into the aether; Sosha and Jamile as well, on the few occasions Madlin had seen one of them look. Madlin's assessment had counted on tracking the dragon's eyes, but at least she was fairly certain that he was watching for the viewframe.

The hole opened not a foot from the stacked crates, angled away from the dragon. A trio of *Jennai* crewmen stood waiting, and immediately began hauling crates through to the airship. Rynn had thrown a blanket over the controls of the world-ripper, preventing any possibility that the creature took note of the settings—whatever good that might have done it. A hooded cloak hid Rynn's face from the world-hole's view. Every precaution was paranoid, distrustful, and precisely what Madlin would have done in Rynn's place on such short notice.

Madlin stopped to bow just before she reached the world-hole. "Thank you again. I will return to the valley in the morning." Before Fr'n'ta'gur could snake his neck around and sneak a peek into Korr, Madlin hustled through and Rynn closed the hole.

"I don't like any of this," Cadmus said, folding his arms and leaning back in his chair.

While Madlin had initially hopped to Korr, the strategy planning session that followed shortly afterward was held in the lunar headquarters. Cadmus, Madlin, Jamile, Greuder, Rascal, and Davlin were all present. The latter two represented the Church of Eziel, which had become the recruiting and manpower end of the Human Rebellion—they had also impressed Cadmus with their craftiness, organizational ability, and experience in deception. They all sat around a planning table in a purpose-built room bored out of the lunar rock specifically for meetings that required secrecy.

"We got seventy-two Rynn-guns out of it," Davlin said, "and the promise of more. We get a bit bolt-footed and don't send her back; we got something out of the deal."

Madlin waved the notion away. "For the time I spent there, that's rat shit. He's trying to string us along like some back-alley root peddler. He's given us just enough to prove he won't stiff us entirely, and not enough that we consider cutting out losses and taking what we got."

"Ain't spottin' the trap the key to breakin' free of it?" Rascal asked. "I mean, anyone who *knows* they're getting' scammed ain't really getting' scammed. They go through with the deal; they get what's comin' to 'em."

"The dragon must underestimate us," Greuder said. The old baker looked around for nods of agreement and found them lacking. "If he doesn't know we're on to him, we have the advantage. We just need to decide how to exploit it."

Cadmus stood, his pent up energy no longer contained by a chair. "And that puts Madlin in the position of bait. No. No, we need to plan a raid on that warehouse. We grab what guns we can, we burn down their factories, kill as many workers as we can, and forget that whole world exists."

"You know, Anzik can probably hear us," Jamile pointed out. The young Megrenn sorcerer still lived within the lunar headquarters, though he was not a part of the rebellion. He kept to himself, and that allowed many of the inhabitants and visitors to forget his presence. Not to mention the fact that he had the magical prowess to hide himself from them, even when he was present.

Cadmus blew a frustrated breath. "His people can have their share from the raid. It's the best deal any of us are likely to get. Veydrus was a fool's errand, and we'll wipe our hands of the place once we've made good."

"You say we'll raid them, like they wouldn't expect it," Madlin said. "Greuder thinks the dragon's underestimating us, but what if it's not? What if it's one step ahead of us? Or two? I know there are wards around the warehouse—"

"World-ripper will get us past those," Cadmus cut in.

"And I don't know what they do," Madlin continued. "They could be simple barriers we could bypass, or they could be explosive, or spark, or turn us all into pigs. It's gutted magic, and we don't know enough about it to even know what to be afraid of."

"We could ask Anzik," Jamile suggested.

Cadmus shook his head. "It would be the perfect time to alley-stab us. Misread the runes, get us all killed, and make off with all the coil guns for himself."

"Why would he—?" Jamile began.

"Because my father is paranoid, and we might need a bit of paranoia to keep us all alive," said Madlin. "But he's still wrong about a raid. We know Rynn can get me out of there faster than the dragon can react. It wanted to see through into Korr, but we outsmarted it—or at least outmaneuvered it. I say we play along; see how many coil guns we can get out of this before we turn it ugly."

"Eziel's blood, kid," Rascal said. "You want to go back under the nose of that thing? We're trying to keep you alive."

"Well, I'm trying to win a war," Madlin replied. "We need the manufacturing, especially now that we're getting reports that kuduks are showing up with coil guns. We're not the only game in the deep anymore. We can't keep up with kuduk factories, not without the goblins' help."

"Maybe it's time we found something better than coil guns," Cadmus said, his earlier anger fading into a tinker's pensive view of the world as a puzzle that can be solved if only one had the right machine.

"Well, until we do, I'm heading back there," Madlin replied. "And I'm going to take that dragon up on his offer of bringing my own stuff along. Be nice to sit on a chair made by someone who knows what it's like to have hips. Even the things they've made custom for me are always too narrow."

"As a baker, I apologize," said Greuder. "Girth is the curse we share and spread."

"Well, spread a little before I go back," Madlin replied. "Goblin food isn't the most filling."

There was no proper day or night in the lunar base. Clocks might say what they will, but neither sun nor moon held sway in the rocky depths beneath the moon's surface. It was easier to maintain a goblin schedule, even with the intra-world shifts in daylight hours. The *Jennai* had been offset from the inhabitants of Fr'n'ta'gur's lair by some five hours, so Madlin had chosen to sleep where an early sunrise wouldn't spoil her slumber.

When Madlin stepped through the hole into the hold of the *Jennai*, all her requested furnishings were there waiting for her, along with enough warm bodies to carry everything through at once. Rynn gave a nod of greeting—which was more than either of them needed—and shut the world-hole.

"All right, everyone," Madlin said, taking charge of the workers who would be following her through into Korr. "This is a simple delivery. We get in; you place everything where I tell you. I stay; you leave. Don't interact with the goblins. Don't talk amongst yourselves. Don't make eye contact if you can avoid it. We don't want them learning anything about this world if we can help it."

Rynn turned dials, and the viewframe swooped in low over the valley, headed for one of the smallest structures in the complex. Madlin's house was built to her specifications, taller than a single-story goblin residence would need to be, and tucked away in a corner of the valley away from the flow of traffic that came and went at all hours. The insides were spare, just wooden walls, poured-stone floor, and three rooms. The main living area was a combination drafting room and hobby workshop, too small to make anything larger than handheld. Off to one side was a room with a goblin-made bed and a chest of clothes. The only other room was an indoor latrine, which Madlin had insisted on. It was an afterthought in the goblins' architectural plan, so it had a separate roof and a second batch of poured-stone, delineated by a seam where older and newer batches met.

"I want every scrap of furniture from that place dragged outside and dumped by the road," Madlin ordered. "Don't worry about the bedding or the goblin-made clothes in the chest, just get it all out."

The workers mumbled and nodded, eyes fixed on their targets. When the hole opened, they sprang into action. The goblin furnishings were the first things to go. The door was a tight fit for the bed and desk, but the flimsy goblin furniture flipped around easily in the hands of burly human workers, banging doorjambs and the ceiling, but doing only cosmetic damage to the house. Madlin's instructions had included nothing that said they were to be gentle with the goblin craftwork, and the workers weren't. She took satisfaction in hearing the crack of broken boards as the bed hit the ground—its days of teasing her with promises of more comfort than it could deliver were at an end. The same went for the chair with its contoured seat that tried to force her backside into a narrower shape than her body preferred. In their places came good, solid Telluraki craftsmanship, salvaged from the ruins of Tinker's Island and brought via the lunar headquarters for Madlin's use. *Finally, maybe this place will start to feel like home, and not a low-rent inn.*

In minutes, the world-hole closed, leaving Madlin alone in a valley of goblins, surrounded by familiar furnishings. She took a deep breath, savoring the familiar scents of Takalish wood polish and the bleach from laundered sheets. Settling into a chair from her own workshop, Madlin could imagine away the rough-cut timber walls and pretend she was on Tinker's Island.

The door opened. If goblins had any customs about knocking or announcing themselves before entering a home, they did not apply them to humans. "What happened here?" K'k'rt demanded. "All your things are outside and broken, and …" The tinker stared into the room, realization dawning when he saw the change in décor.

"Your dragon suggested I bring some things back to make myself more comfortable," said Madlin. "This is what human comfort looks like."

K'k'rt wandered the little house, poking his head around to inspect Madlin's new things. He even looked into the bedroom. "I understood that you would be sleeping off-world from now on. Why the bed?"

"Why not the bed?" Madlin asked. "I might not go home every night. With a praise-to-Eziel bed here, I can get a proper night's sleep without retreating to my own world."

K'k'rt nodded slowly, still looking into the bedroom. "Good … good thinking."

"What brought you here?" Madlin asked. "You the one they nominated to find out why I threw my furniture by the roadside?"

K'k'rt turned toward Madlin and blinked. Then he smiled at her and gave his familiar chuckle. "Not quite. I came by to see if you had come back at all. Fr'n'ta'gur wasn't sure whether you would."

Madlin snorted. "You're not going to buy me off with a few crates of my own guns. You're stuck with me until I've got what's mine."

"You know … you and Fr'n'ta'gur have a lot in common in that respect."

"Comparing me to your god?" Madlin asked, raising an eyebrow. "Isn't that sacrilege?"

K'k'rt chuckled. "Even the dragons know they aren't gods. They just get most of us to pretend, and spend their days surrounded by the most gullible of goblins."

"The priests?"

K'k'rt nodded. "It keeps the hopeless ones out of the workshops and military, so it works out for everyone. So … back to work?"

Madlin nodded and stood, gathering her tool belt and goggles. "Back to work."

That evening, Madlin found herself back in Fr'n'ta'gur's lair. This time, the dragon loomed over a stack of fourteen crates, an improvement over the previous day's delivery. Madlin's hopes rose. *He's going to follow through. This is going to work out.* Yesterday's cries of deceit and treachery seemed like so much fear mongering. Her father had been hammering his own delusions into everyone else's heads for so long that they were beginning to see conspiracies behind every door. The Human Rebellion's bargain with Fr'n'ta'gur made too much sense for both sides for either to risk the arrangement by betrayal. One day that might change, and Rynn would be ready to extract Madlin at a moment's notice—Rynn was at the controls of the

*Jennai's* primary world-ripper at that very second—but for now, things would continue as they had been.

"Your gift for today," Fr'n'ta'gur grumbled. Madlin flinched anew each time she felt the dragon's voice pound through her. It was a sensation she could never acclimate to.

"I take it there are eighty-four guns in total?" Madlin asked.

"Indeed," Fr'n'ta'gur replied. "Summon your minions and carry them away."

Madlin nodded and walked to the stack of crated coil guns. Any second …

The world-hole opened, and the workers spilled through in an instant. The dragon watched, but did not try to peek around to see through into Korr this time. Instead, he muttered something in a foreign tongue, neither Korrish nor goblin speech. Madlin felt a tingle all over her body and knew that the dragon had worked magic on her.

In a sudden panic, Madlin fled through the world-hole. Or at least, she tried. The hole became a solid pane of glass to her, too thick even for her body weight to shatter as she slammed against it. Spots swam before her eyes as Madlin staggered back. She reached up to check a wet sensation on her lips and found blood running from a broken nose.

"This time, she stays," said Fr'n'ta'gur, twisting around to look into the *Jennai's* hold.

Madlin pinched her nose shut to staunch the flow of blood, and watched the chaos through the world-hole. The crewmen had scattered as armed soldiers rushed in, coil guns at the ready. Rynn stood at the controls, one hand on the switch that would shut the world-hole, the other on the dial that would move the viewframe laterally in relations to the dragon's position.

"By all means, attack me!" Fr'n'ta'gur proclaimed. "But your Madlin Errol will die if you do. She is mine now, and she may not pass your gate. You will continue receiving your weapons as stated in our deal, but any other disturbance from this device of yours, and she will suffer. My worshipers will find ways where she will beg them to stop, but leave her still able to work at her inventions." The world-hole closed an instant later.

"Why?" Madlin asked, her voice nasal, her head swimming.

"Because you are going to make me far more than just the weapons you have shown me," Fr'n'ta'gur said. "You are going to create everything I tell you to." He finished by calling out in the goblin tongue, words that, for all her time in Veydrus, Madlin had yet to glean even the simplest meanings from.

A squad of goblins emerged from the hallway. Madlin tried to focus on them, but she could barely stand. She heard chains though. It was a sound she could never forget. The goblins surrounded her, crowding too close for her comfort. They pulled at her arms, sending shooting pains into her nose as she tried to hold it steady and shut. She tried to shake them off, but weaklings that they were, they outnumbered her. After a brief scuffle, they slipped something over her head, and she felt another tingle in the aether of magic working upon her, and then the far more concrete sensation of cold metal around her neck.

With blood dripping down her face, Madlin clutched at the collar, finding two eyelets with chains leading into goblin hands, but neither hinge nor clasp. It was Deliah all over again. She had been captured, collared. She pulled on one of the chains with both hands, yanking one of her goblin captors from his feet, but then a jolt of spark shook her body and she collapsed to the stone floor. Three more jolts followed, each sending a spasm through her every muscle. Fr'n'ta'gur spoke a brief command to the goblins, and the jolts stopped.

"They will take you to the healer, then to your new quarters," said Fr'n'ta'gur. "In time, you will learn that you have received a great honor. I do not trifle with forces like your allies lightly. You are very valuable."

The goblins holding the chains tugged Madlin to her feet. Thankfully, they did not object when she resumed quelling the flow of blood from her nose. Still reeling and unable to focus her thoughts, she allowed herself to be led from the dragon's lair and up into the passages to the surface.

The journey to the goblin healer was not a long one. Perhaps two blocks filled with gawking eyes were all it took to bring her to a tidy, whitewashed building that smelled of antiseptics. *At least they seem to have some concept of medicine.* She had not run into any goblin medical personnel in the valley during her stay, so she could only guess that they were more primitive than Tellurak's physicians. Once her handlers ushered her inside, she was only mildly relieved.

The hospital room was centered on a knee-high table with a polished shine that told her that the wood was well-sealed. Shelves along one wall were filled with glass jars bearing illegible labels. Cabinets dominated another wall, and a third bore hooks holding tools of every description. Many of them had familiar appearances, similar in form to ones that Jamile had described from her medical training. Others, Madlin's imagination could only make macabre guesses as to their function. She could only hope that a simple broken nose wouldn't require any of them.

One of the goblins spoke up and conversed with the flummoxed physician, who was clearly unprepared to receive a human patient. Madlin was guided to a seat on the floor while the physician climbed onto the table to examine her. She allowed her hands to be pried free of her face, restarting the flow of blood. The physician chittered orders to an assistant, and in moments Madlin's face had been daubed clean with alcohol. Rolled bits of liniment-soaked cloth were stuffed up her nostrils, stemming the flow of blood. A pair of thin, metal bars flared to life with aether in the physician's hands. Madlin flinched away, but the handlers forced her forward and still once more. The physician pinched the bars to the sides of Madlin's nose, forcing it straight with a stabbing twinge; then they felt cold, far colder than bare metal should have. In seconds her nose began to numb, the sensation spreading across her cheekbones and up to her brow. A slathering of paste was then applied, holding the bars in place. The assistant packed cloth at both sides of her nose and wrapped a bandage around her head, packing everything tight.

The cold numbed the pain in her face, but brought her wits back to her. Madlin began taking stock of her new situation as the goblins brought her a wash bowl and soap, and helped her cleanse herself of blood. *I'm collared again.* She was still too shocked and disoriented for that to have finished sinking in. For now, it was a fact, nothing more. *The dragon wants me, which means he wants me alive. That's good. He might find ways to make my life miserable, but as long as I can survive, I can figure a way out of this. Eziel's blood, he even said he'd keep delivering coil guns.* Madlin paused in her thoughts as the handlers prodded her to her feet. She followed them out of the hospital and back toward the mountain. *Of course he'd promise to keep the deal. He needed to buy time, and to stop them thinking of ways to rescue me. As long as they keep getting the guns, he must assume they'll play things safe.*

Madlin sighed. *He's probably right, too.* In a strange way, it was a relief. The expected treachery had come, albeit in a form none of them had predicted. And she was still alive.

Madlin's new quarters were within the dragon's complex. It was not a part of the lair itself, but rather a newly excavated chamber not far from where Fr'n'ta'gur's priests lived and worked. Life in Korr's deeps had taught her what new stonework looked like. It galled her to think that the goblins had been planning ahead for weeks for this betrayal. Almost as galling was the fact that by the time she had arrived back from the goblin hospital, all her belongings had already been set up within. From desk to dresser, everything from her cottage in the valley was set up just as she had left it. The sheets were even tucked, and the pillows fluffed.

Her captors had proven to be an enigma. Two goblins were assigned to the ends of her chains, which clasped around their wrists with hinged bracers. The goblins could remove these easily, but they also bore runes that would send one of those jolts of spark through her whenever they liked. Neither of them would admit to understanding the least bit of Korrish, but when she had pantomimed a desire to change out of her blood-stained clothes, they had been surprisingly accommodating. Both had removed their bracer, allowing Madlin to pull a fresh shirt over her head by threading the chains through one at a time. Changing in front of the goblins was somehow less intimidating than being naked in front of a kuduk. Kuduks looked almost human, and she could project human motives onto them. The goblins … well the ones that didn't speak Korrish were little more than trained monkeys to her.

It occurred to her to run when she had herself free from the handlers briefly. *Run where?* That was the problem. For the time being, she had no solution to the impassable world-ripper. Working with Anzik on a solution to that would be a priority for her. She was also in the dragon's lair, and would have to sneak past untold numbers of goblins just to reach the surface. That left a more old-fashioned escape a dubious prospect, not to mention that she would be dragging her chains the whole way.

The chains. Drat them for a sense of irony, but the goblins had used knowledge she had taught them to help free Korr's humans, and turned it to her capture. The chains were forged of brightsteel, and were frankly one of their metallurgists' better efforts.

*I'm too tired to escape, anyway.* The day's events had drained Madlin, both of willpower and of blood. Whatever plans she came up with, they could wait for a bit of convalescence first. Broken noses weren't the sort of thing that took months to heal. She collapsed onto the bed amid a clatter of delicate chain.

"K'k'rt," she muttered. Surprisingly, being unable to breathe through her nose made goblin names a bit easier to pronounce. She repeated herself, lifting her head to see if she got any response from her keepers. One of them shook his head.

"K'k'rt?" Madlin asked, trying the human method of raising the last syllable to make an inquiry. The other keeper nodded, but the first one muttered to him, and then both looked to her and shook their heads.

Madlin collapsed onto her back and looked up at the stone ceiling. She was feeling queasy from having more of her own blood than food in her stomach, and exhausted from the turmoil. *Rynn's problem*, she decided, and gave in to sleep.

# Chapter 2

*"Aim to become High Sorcerer one day, not Warlock. You get to work indoors and the only people trying to kill you are friends and colleagues."*
*–Axterion Solaran, to Danilaesis Solaran*

Axterion Solaran sipped at a tea that reflected his mood—cold and bitter. The reports strewn across his desk held too little good news mixed in with all the bad. The Kadrin Empire relied little on the outside world, but since the war with Megrenn had begun in earnest, their foreign trade had dried up entirely. Their ships were lost at sea; their caravans disappeared from the tradeways. The old sorcerer shook his head in dismay. Letting a trickle of aether into his cup, he heated the tea back to a potable temperature.

The best news, as always, came in the form of missives from his grandson. For all the boy's faults, Danilaesis Solaran was making a name for himself as a proper warlock, nipping at Megrenn raiders and giving pause to supply convoys, bottling up the forces arrayed along the borders of the empire wherever he could. Axterion was proud, in a wistful way. *Boy's got his uncle in him, that's for certain. He'll meet no good end, but he'll end his share of the empire's enemies first.* It was the curse of a warlock. There was no *actual* curse, but the Kadrin Empire used them like battering rams, smashing them into their foes until one or the other broke. If the warlock survived, it was only a matter of time before the next war.

*Well, this is the next war.* Axterion sighed. There was always a next war. One hundred forty-eight years of living in Veydrus had shown him that often enough. There was no final war. Wipe out every living thing in the world, and the rocks would start fighting amongst themselves. Axterion scratched at his chin, wondering whether he could spare the time for a shave. The war wasn't going anywhere.

A knock at his office door provided Axterion a respite from his own company. "What?" he snapped at whomever lay beyond. The door cracked open and an eye peeked through.

"General Varnus sent me to find you," said Tolomey, one of the Tower of Contemplation's many guards.

"Congratulations," Axterion replied. "But I wasn't lost." There was a blank stare from the eye in the doorway. *Imbecile.* Axterion rubbed his eyes, wondering if the headache was from too many hours of staring at words on paper or from the vexatious underlings that surrounded him. "What does the general want?"

"We've got visitors. Said you should meet them."

Axterion gestured and the door to his office swung wide, revealing Tolomey fully. "General Varnus has never been prone to wasting my time. Either he has taken up a new hobby, or you are leaving out some important detail as to why, precisely, I should care that we have visitors. If they are dignitaries, they ought to see Empress Celia or her staff. If it's a military matter, he ought to take care of it his blasted self. And if the issue was of a magical nature, I'd bloody blasted well hope that I'd hear about it from one of my own underlings, and not from that ox-head General Varnus."

"They're … um … rock people," Tolomey replied, edging out of the doorway.

Axterion let his vision slip into the aether, looking for answers that eluded him in the light. He sighed. "Let me guess, they don't speak Kadrin."

"No, High Sorcerer," Tolomey confirmed. "The general was hoping that you might, you know, understand their language, what with you being High Sorcerer and all. Do you? Happen to speak their language, that is?"

"No, I don't" Axterion replied. He stood and began rummaging through the clutter in his office. Tolomey looked on, edging farther from the door by the moment, as if waiting for the perfect opportunity to slink away unnoticed. Axterion made a point of glancing in the guard's direction often enough to keep him close by. "Aha!" The old sorcerer exclaimed, pulling a book-sized slate board from beneath a stack of historical texts. "I doubt I can speak their language, but I can write it."

Kezudkan tried to stand as still as he could, but his eyes kept pulling his head to one side or the other, taking in his environment. He was aware that there were skies where the majority of the population was human. There had never been reason for him to visit one, but from all that he had heard, they were dusty, grimy places that baked beneath the relentless sun. Never in his wildest imaginings had he envisioned anything like the human city of Kadris. Farther than the eye could see, buildings kept popping up from the landscape, clear to the horizon. Individually, they were primitive, homely structures, but taken en masse, the effect was humbling. *This is the race that mops our floors and hauls coal out of our mines. These are the ones my kin turn to for aid.* Not only were there buildings everywhere, but humans swarmed around them like maggots on raw meat. And from their vantage on a low hill on the outskirts, Kezudkan could only see the very edge of the city.

"How many of them live here?" Kezudkan asked in a hushed tone.

"Reports say anywhere from half to three quarters of a million humans," replied Lunjak, the successor to King Dekulon. It was just the two of them, along with four soldiers of the Iron Guard who were acting as an official escort. The Iron Guardsmen stood in a square formation around the two daruu dignitaries, keeping the spear-toting Kadrin soldiers in their ratty chain shirts at bay. None of the humans spoke the daruu tongue, and King Dekulon had no one in his kingdom who knew how to speak the Kadrin dialect. By primitive gestures, the humans had conveyed that Kezudkan and Lunjak should wait where they stood.

"What are the odds that any one of those half million or more humans speaks our language?" Kezudkan asked.

Lunjak shrugged, causing a jingle in his gold-chain shirt. "I'm sure we'll manage something. They have scholars."

Kezudkan weathered the looks of the human soldiers as they waited half the morning for someone to come retrieve them. *City this size, they might not even have gotten across it yet to ask around for daruu speakers. We should have brought chairs.* At length, a delegation arrived, looking far more formal than the contingent of soldiers who happened to have been guarding the city gates that day. The soldiers acting as escorts wore plated armor, with swords dangling from their hips and shields in hand. In their midst, a monstrous human in gold-trimmed armor strode along, his shaved head and bushy grey beard not covered by any helm. Beside the giant was a slim human nearly the same height, clad all in black. With unkempt hair and a grit of unshaven beard on his face, the slim human reminded him of someone. When the entourage approached closely enough for Kezudkan to see the slim human's eyes—set into a scowl beneath a furrowed brow—he knew who that was: Erefan. Though taller, the Kadrin human had the same look to him. As initial impressions went, the Kadrins could have done better than someone who looked like Kezudkan's least favorite human.

"Greetings," Lunjak said as the group drew close enough for introductions. "I am Lunjak, successor of King Dekulon of—"

The slim human in black waved him off, cutting the successor short. Taking a slate board in hand, the human jabbed at it with a stick of chalk, squeaking and tapping until he held up the finished work for their inspection. Written in daruu runes were the words: CANNOT UNDERSTAND. MUST WRITE. COME WITH ME.

Lunjak nodded, gesturing to himself. "Lunjak."

The slim human hooked a thumb at his chest. "Axterion Solaran." Then he muttered something in his own tongue to the giant. With a snap of the giant's fingers, the human soldiers fell into formation around Kezudkan and his fellows.

"Hope it's not far," Kezudkan muttered to Lunjak as they started the trek into the city.

The conversation had moved at a glacial pace. Kezudkan, Lunjak, and the human sorcerer Axterion had passed around a slate board, scuffing out and rewriting messages to one another throughout the afternoon. The Kadrins had scant information about the destruction of their outlying city, and even the little that Kezudkan and Lunjak knew was treated as military intelligence. Perhaps five minutes of proper conversation on the subject was stretched into hours by the tedious chalk scribbling and undertone translations to the rest of the two contingents.

Axterion's people crowded his side of the long table and arrayed themselves along the wall. Several were clearly soldiers, but most dressed similarly to the sorcerer and presumably shared his occupation. Rune throwing—and the concept that aether could be unbound from objects—was an idea that the Kadrins seemed comfortable with. When they all gathered together around him, Kezudkan wondered just how easily he could be torn to tiny shreds by the first of them to get offended by something one of the daruu wrote. Kezudkan had always possessed a strong feel for the life within stone, but had never felt the sensation in the presence of people before. To feel that sort of life among humans … it made him question Korr's vibrancy. The thought nagged at him as Lunjak eased the conversation into talk of alliance.

Kezudkan grabbed the track switch lever and heaved, hoping the thunderail stayed on the tracks. "Do you know what a kuduk is?" he wrote.

Axterion read the slate and looked up, a puzzled look on his face. He muttered over his shoulder to his compatriots, and clearly made out the word "kuduk" amid the blabbering. *So they can speak the words.* It was a simple failing of conversational understanding at work. Kezudkan was not about to let the observation pass without comment. He took the slate back. "You can sound out these words?" he wrote.

Axterion glanced at the slate and shrugged, nodding. Kezudkan reached across the table and tapped the slate with one thick finger, then pointed to Axterion. The human sorcerer narrowed his gaze and looked sidelong at Kezudkan, but sounded the words out like a schoolboy with his first-year primer.

"How did you know those sounds?" Kezudkan wrote.

Axterion took the slate. "They are the same runes that our sorcerers use," he wrote in reply.

"Lunjak," Kezudkan said aloud, "What if we brought the Pillar of Runes? Think that he could talk their rune language."

"I don't know," the successor replied. "But I don't see how that helps us right now."

"Look around the table," Kezudkan continued in an undertone. "The humans are wearing down; I know the look. They'll call an end to the talks soon enough, and tomorrow we'll see if we can't find ourselves a proper translator."

The talks carried on for another hour, but Kezudkan had been right about the growing fatigue among the human contingent. The final few minutes of passing the slate board back and forth revolved around accommodations for the night. Lunjak accepted an offer of rooms for each of them, and human servants escorted them through the halls of the palace.

Kezudkan had been preoccupied on the way in, paying more attention to the people than the stonework. He had taken his initial impression of the Veydran humans at the city gates, and had not bothered to revise it as he was presented with new information. The imperial palace was, to say the least, impressive work for humans. It was black marble, shot through with thin veins of copper that had oxidized to form a green patina. Unlike every other human structure Kezudkan had seen, there was no trace of mortar—"fools' glue," his people called it. Nor was there any sign of seams between stone blocks. It was as if the palace had been carved from a single monolithic block of stone. To a daruu eye, however, there were hints of the true process of creation. Misaligned grains in the rock and odd veining at corners and around arches hinted that the stone had flowed from its original shape. The palace was still rough in form, lacking the fluid beauty that the daruu city had displayed, but the craftsmanship was better than kuduks could manage.

*These … these are humans I might work with.*

The room Kezudkan was provided had everything a human might need, and it was passable for a daruu. The bed was plenty large and sturdy enough, but too soft for his old joints. The stone floor was obscured by thick carpets, which Kezudkan was not rude enough to pile in a corner for the duration of his stay. A pair of floor-to-ceiling windows dominated one wall, incessantly reminding him that he was not only above ground, but well above ground level. No amount of drapery was going to fool him into thinking otherwise. Of most immediate use was a writing desk, complete with a small provisional stash of paper and ink. In quaint fashion, the ink was the dipping sort, and an assortment of bird feathers was provided in place of pens.

Kezudkan seated himself and took up one of the quills. It felt like nothing in his hand; his fingers pinched together with only a thread of resistance between them. Squinting in concentration, the old daruu dunked the tip in the inkwell and began scribbling a note. By the time he finished, there were droplets of ink across half the page, and his fingers were stained a deep violet color. He held up the note, holding it nice and still so that Gederon and whoever else might have been watching could read it through the viewframe:

*Have the Pillar of Runes outside the city in the morning (local time), same place you delivered us. We may have need of his services. All well.*

*Best wishes,*

*-K*

The following morning, after a sampling of bland local delicacies, the negotiations reconvened. All the principals from the previous day's session had returned—Kezudkan recognized faces, even if he could not recall their names—

and a number of newcomers crowded in as well. Sitting between the monstrous human general and the sorcerer Axterion was a human woman of child-bearing years. It felt demeaning to think of these humans in the terms by which he judged his human slaves, especially once Axterion introduced her, passing the slate across the table with the note: "Allow me to present Empress Celia, ruler of the Kadrin Empire."

Kezudkan had gathered that Axterion was someone highly placed in the empire, not merely the first scholar they could find with a working knowledge of daruu text. But there was no doubt now that they had the attention of the highest levels of the Kadrin government.

As Lunjak inclined his head in acknowledgement and tapped out a formal reply on the slate board, Kezudkan's mind wandered. *We've got their ruler right here. Who are we to bargain with her?* Kezudkan had stood before committees and councilors, negotiated with industrialists and entrepreneurs, employed scientists and thugs. None of that had prepared him to interact with royalty. There was a whole protocol around King Dekulon that went amiss in Kezudkan's presence, and he knew deep down that only the king's curiosity and good nature kept it from being an issue. The young woman who Axterion claimed as his liege sat still as a sculpture, but had rifle barrels for eyes. She could pull the trigger with a single uttered word to her sorcerers, he did not doubt.

Kezudkan leaned subtly to Lunjak and spoke from the side of his mouth. "Perhaps we need to call in reinforcements."

"Not to worry," Lunjak replied beneath his breath. "Zepdaan will be discovered at their gates any moment. I was about to mention his arrival."

*Not the Pillar of Runes, you fool!* Kezudkan wanted to shout. *It's time for King Dekulon to meet his counterpart.* But curious eyes from across the table made him think better of getting into an argument right then, even if he could manage a civil tone as Lunjak's unrelenting politeness plowed along into the day's talks. He kept his tongue still and listened with his eyes, reading exchanges chalked on the slate board like they were a transcription rather than the communication itself. The morning passed like mud drying as Lunjak and Axterion went over plans to repatriate the refugees from the goblin slaughter.

Things perked up once the Pillar of Runes was escorted into the conference. After a brief verbal tussle, which Zepdaan won, the Pillar of Runes took over at the center of the daruu contingent. The slate board was pushed aside, and Zepdaan acted as translator, familiar with the variant rune language that was apparently common to both human and daruu rune-throwers. After revisiting the introductory pleasantries with the new arrival, they skimmed the dross from the pot and delved into more pressing matters.

"So," Axterion asked through the translator, "how is it that you arrived here? You brought no animals, and your kind aren't known for fleetness."

"That was a matter of secondary importance to the fate of your survivors," Lunjak replied in kind. "We have a great deal to discuss on the topic, but let me first dig a side tunnel into a most peculiar discovery that we made, not long ago."

*Here it comes.* Kezudkan watched the reactions of the Kadrin humans. He noticed as soon as Zepdaan began translating that Axterion was far from the only one in the room who understood the alternate rune language. All the dark-clad officials in the room, as well as the empress, seemed to follow the pillar's words without waiting for translation. In fact, Kezudkan guessed that it was only the general and his soldiers around the periphery of the room who warranted Axterion's trouble in repeating the words in the human language.

"You see, our friend here, Citizen Graniteson, is not from this world," said Lunjak. Several whispered conversations broke out around the periphery of the world, and Axterion hesitated before translating for the rest of the Kadrins.

"So … where precisely *is* he from?" asked Axterion. Despite having to wait a moment for the words to be translated, Kezudkan could tell by the smirk on the sorcerer's face that he knew. *The muddy bastard. This one* knows *about the other worlds.*

"A world called Korr," said Lunjak, who waited just long enough for the words to be translated before chugging onward, full coal to the furnace. "Now before you decide that I have taken leave of my senses, please allow me to assure you that we took convincing as well. The very notion that our world is not the only one in existence was, to say the least, implausible. However, Citizen Graniteson was able to make a compelling case, which—" Lunjak stopped, glaring at Zepdaan, who had stopped his translation midway through the rant.

"Let's just show them the muddy thing," said Zepdaan, turning up his palms. "That's what you're leading up to anyway. Quit angling your chisel and hit it."

Lunjak offered a forced smile to their hosts. "My colleague was just suggesting that I skip ahead and show you our proof. Please do not be alarmed by what you are about to see; it is completely harmless."

*You obviously haven't given that much thought to it yet. "Harmless" is one of the last descriptions I would offer for a world-ripper.*

"Kezudkan, if you would please give the signal," said Lunjak. To Kezudkan's mild surprise, the Pillar of Runes translated the request. There was an uneasy shifting in the seats of the humans across the table, and a few of the guards gripped their weapons tighter. *Gravel-headed old dimwit. Make them edgy right before we surprise them, why don't you?*

Kezudkan hoisted himself from his chair with nods to the empress and Axterion. The empress gave a nod in reply, which was a welcome reassurance before the shock he was about to give them. Hefting his cane, Kezudkan gripped it halfway up and held it aloft. Within seconds, a world-hole opened behind the daruu contingent. The Kadrins gasped, gaped, and wondered aloud at the sight. All but Axterion.

The old sorcerer cackled. He threw his head back and laughed like he was at a comedic play of the finest caliber. Even his own attendants and his empress looked at him with questioning eyes, diverting them from their wonderment and hushed debates.

"Something amuses you?" Lunjak asked.

Axterion wiped tears from his eyes. "I've had the most miserable season I can remember. I'm beset with foes who are more prepared for a war than we are, and a grandson who's mad as a pig in a blindfold. And here you come, dropping one of those machines right in front of me. Gut me, but the gods must be returning, and they've got a sense of humor."

Axterion straightened himself in his chair, took a deep breath to compose himself. "Gentlemen, let's work out an arrangement."

# Chapter 3

*"Overcoming the fear of the skies proves that we are capable of overcoming our natural inclinations." –Wendrus Olkant, kuduk philosopher*

The *Jennai* was a rune-lift airship, the only one of its kind in Korr. Its hull was cobbled together from the wrecks of four vacu-dirge airships with the enormous vacuum tanks repurposed as crew quarters. The central space between the gondolas that hung beneath the vacuum tanks had been turned into an aerodrome with a runway of steel plating the full length of the ship. Each of the four quadrants of the *Jennai* housed a world-ripper for resupplying and for conducting raiding and recruitment actions.

It felt cramped.

With a standing crew numbering close to two thousand and featuring all the amenities of a small city, Rynn still felt trapped aboard the *Jennai*. It was Madlin's fault; she knew in her head. But every morning Rynn woke with a fresh memory of a collar around her neck and two goblins chained to her. The airship wasn't swift enough, large enough, or open enough to get rid of that feeling before she was plagued with memories of her time in Deliah's custody.

She had tried spending more time in the workshops to give her mind a respite both from Madlin's dilemma and from the rebellion's demands in general. Davlin had been a boon in helping with the organization of the military side of the rebellion, and Vaulk, Rascal, and Hayfield had taken up management of the civilian aspects of life aboard the ship. Rynn had squirmed her way into an oversight and figurehead role. *What I really want is Kupe's job*, she chided herself. *Show up, blow glory smoke in everyone's faces, and get them to join up with us.* Even in the privacy of her thoughts, she couldn't convince anyone of that lie. She hated recruiting.

Humans were stubborn beasts, more worried about the unknown future than their deplorable present. Every visit was a variation on a theme. "We just want a bit more meat is all," "Just a few hours with my little ones all I'm after," "They oughtta quit beatin' us when's all's we're doin's what we're told." They lacked ambition, vision, hope. It was strange how the right infusion of the three could turn bedraggled workers into killers. But humans were greedy creatures as well, and once you convinced them—deep down, and not just the reluctant acceptance that slaves gave so easily—that they could have more, they wanted more. Kupe had a gift for that sort of convincing. Rynn could manage it, but it wore her out each time in a way that never seemed to weigh on Kupe. It was as if he had reserves of personality that weren't depleted by giving alehouse speeches and holding mine-shaft rallies.

No, Rynn didn't really want to be Kupe, though she occasionally envied how little real responsibility he had. She would deny it to anyone, even Sosha and Jamile, and *especially* to her father, but she wanted to be Dan. Dan hadn't ducked behind building corners during the fight for Tinker's Island. He wouldn't have run from the knockers if he had been in Rynn's place for the heist that got No-Boots killed. He stood and fought, unafraid of any foe. Admittedly he took that bravado off a cliff with him, but it was the ability Rynn envied, not the mad bloodlust.

Looking down at her latest personal project, Rynn saw a step in that direction. It looked like something out of Anzik's world, a suit of plate armor that only went from arm to arm across the collar. Of course, the insides looked more like the right half of her tinker's leg, with its spring reinforced joints and hinged articulation. It was time to test it out and see what it could do.

Rynn slid the contraption over her head like a pullover shirt, with padding around the opening settling on her collarbone. Though the device weighed half as much as Rynn did, judicious use of levitation runes rendered it feather-light. It still swung around like she was pushing it through water due to its mass, but there was no discomfort in wearing it. Left-handed, she began buckling the straps for the right arm and securing the device in place. Unlike her tinker's legs, she had designed the arms to fit over her clothing, not against bare skin, and the outer coverings hinged into place without having to be fitted as separate pieces.

With the right arm encased to the wrist, she checked the articulation, pleased to find that she had nearly her full range of motion. She proceeded to strap into the left arm, which included a fingerless glove with a plate assembly fixed to the back. That plate assembly was the real trick of the device.

Standing and flexing her arms, Rynn checked her physical dexterity with a few calisthenics. No one was watching, so she twisted and couched, swung her arms overhead, and bounced lightly on her tinker's legs. Everything seemed slower than she was used to, but nothing impeded her motion. With an imagined foe popping out from behind one of the workshop's machines, Rynn quick-drew her coil gun, fumbling briefly as the bulk of her tinker's arm made the grab awkward. She aimed at one phantom kuduk, then another behind a crate of ball bearings, then a third who had snuck behind her. With how muddy her motions were, she was going to have to trust in the runes scrawled across the plates of her new armor for her defense.

There were a number of innovations she had implemented, but none felt as satisfying as scavenging Kadrin runes from the wall at the city of Raynesdark. A chunk of that wall still sat on her desk, displaying an intact series of runes which she had copied in miniature several hundred times over the surface of both arms. It had been the most time-consuming part of the work, but when she had emptied a hopper of ball bearings from her coil gun into the runes, they had splashed ringlets of aether but held firm.

The table at the side of the room wobbled and had several chunks that had been gouged out by inexpert woodworking. Rather than pitch it through the world-ripper or off the side of the ship as the crew did with most of their rubbish, Rynn requisitioned it as a test subject. She lifted her left hand above the table, palm up. *Here goes …*

She dropped her hand to the table, the plate on the back of her glove hitting the surface first. Inside, between plate and glove, a spring compressed, and a smaller plate bearing part of a rune was pressed into position, completing an arrangement of runes similar to the ones that reduced the recoil on the coil guns to almost nil. Instantly, the mass of the plate jumped a thousand-fold (Rynn had calculated it to an equivalent weight of nearly five hundred pounds), and the table shattered. All Rynn felt was the pressure of the spring plate on the back of her hand. As soon as the resistance from the table was gone, the spring separated the rune and her hand returned to its proper weight.

Turning the battering ram of a gauntlet over, Rynn checked for damage. The reinforcement of the runes had prevented even a scuff from marring the surface.

Grinning, Rynn worked to put on the rest of the armor she had fashioned. The other pieces were nothing extraordinary by comparison. A breastplate and back plate clasped into place with fittings that matched the tinker's arms where the joining piece crossed Rynn's collarbone. Filtration tanks attached to the back plate had hoses leading to a helmet custom fit to Rynn's head, with a gasketed fit based on the military gas filtration masks the kuduks invading Tinker's Island had worn. Though they hadn't run into it yet, they were bound to blunder into forces armed with poison cloud canisters sooner or later.

Rynn took off her spectacles and donned the helmet. Goggles built into the face mask carried the same refractory correction she was used to, though the mask itself blocked much of her peripheral vision. She twisted her neck to either side, feeling the tug of the hoses' weight, but otherwise unimpeded. Her breath echoed back to her, making the helm feel claustrophobic, and there was a rubbery odor inside, but nothing intolerable. She made a mental note to wash out the hoses with peppermint or lilac perfume, or perhaps lime juice.

There was a spring in the step of her tinker's legs as Rynn made her way to the world-rippers.

Jamile put her arms around Cadmus as he sat gazing lazily through a viewframe overlooking a factory town in western Ruttania. He leaned his head back against her shoulder and sighed. There was a whiff of shaving liniment on his face, which felt smooth against her cheek. If nothing else, her attentions had gotten him to start taking better care of himself again.

"What news from Madlin?" Cadmus asked.

Jamile pushed herself away, leaving her hands on his shoulders. "That's your third foul of the day. No dessert tonight, and don't you think Greuder's not with me on this."

The Mad Tinker twisted his head around and smiled at her, but it faded quickly. "She's fine, and I got a drafting square thrown at me last time I asked, so you're not getting any more detail than that."

Cadmus leaned forward to the control console, his hands stretching out for the dials. "I've got to check."

Jamile pulled him against the backrest of his seat. It had been a revelatory experience when she realized that, for all the strength in the tinker's arms, she had enough leverage to manhandle him on occasion. She was a full three inches taller than the tinker, and probably out-hefted him as well. "You'll do no such thing. We *know* the beastie can see our viewframe, and Rynn says Madlin's being held so close she can feel his breath rumble the floor. You'd open a view just in time to see her get eaten."

"I'm no good at doing nothing," Cadmus grumbled.

"You're not doing nothing, you're doing the right thing. It's called waiting, and it's one of the harder things to do, I think," Jamile said. "Especially for you and your daughter. Daughters?" She planted a kiss on the bald spot on his head. "I saw your sketches for the medical station on the *Jennai*. It's a big improvement over the closet we're in now. Why don't you work on that for me?"

Cadmus furrowed his brow. "I tossed those in the bin. They were rubbish."

"Well, I found them there and I liked them. Un-rubbish them, if you're as good a tinker as everyone says." She reached over his head and flipped a switch to shut the viewframe off.

Cadmus grumbled beneath his breath. Jamile wasn't even sure they were words, just noises meant to convey his annoyance.

"What was … oh *poo*!"

"Hmm?"

"It's Rynn," Jamile said. "Madlin may be pillowy safe in Veydrus, but Rynn's just signed up for a raid. She's … well, she's made herself into a tinker knight … or something."

A standard raiding squad had twelve soldiers, a commander, and a medic. Twenty or so crewmen waited to haul supplies and wounded through the world-hole once the shooting was done, and all available medical staff were on hand, including their chief medical officer, Doctor Sosha. When Rynn walked into the staging room, clad in her tinker's armor, minus the helm she carried under her arm, the personnel on hand shifted from stoic readiness to gawking gossip.

"Rynn!" Sosha exclaimed. "What are you …?"

Rynn smirked. *Wearing? Thinking? Doing here?* "It's time to field test this new gear."

Sergeant Hemock stepped forward. "General, is this the time?"

Rynn shrugged with a clank of metal. "Your lucky day. It was going to be one raid or another, and this one was next up when I was ready to put this stuff through its paces."

"Yes, ma'am," Hemock replied with a salute. *Eziel, I love soldiers. One question, one answer, and that's that.* Soldiers might not have been the thinkers in the rebellion, but there were times where all Rynn wanted was to act, not spend days or weeks debating options. Soldiers were all about taking a plan and performing an action. She snorted, amused at a thought she had no intention of ever sharing. *They're a little like the goblins, actually. Except instead of building me factories and parts, they go kill kuduks for me. Happy little gears in this big old machine.*

There was a viewframe in the staging room, but none of the incidental equipment that went along with a world-ripper. These were the latest design, a two-room system where all the controls and spark systems were housed on the other side of a wall from where Rynn stood with her troops. A periscope and a series of mirrors relayed the viewframe's image to the operator at the control console. In the event of anyone counterattacking or looking back through the world-hole, there was nothing sensitive for them to see or damage. Well, aside from personnel, of course.

Sosha separated herself from her medical team and rushed over before Rynn could join her troops. "What do you think you're doing?" she whispered. "This is no place for a general. You belong on the *Jennai*, where you're safe."

"If I don't test things myself, how can I expect my troops to trust me?" Rynn asked, loudly enough for Sergeant Hemock to hear. "A month from now, all the squad leaders will be armored, and in six months, I can see all the troops that go through that viewframe to be outfitted like this. How would you like to get *bored* waiting for troops to patch up? I want standing here waiting for casualties to become a waste of your time." Rynn laid a hand on Sosha's shoulder—not the gloved hand, just in case—and smiled. "And I always build the prototypes to my own measurements."

There were no further objections. Sosha fumed behind pursed lips, but Rynn knew she had thrown a grenade into any arguments a doctor could make. She was doing this for them, for the troops she kept sending into harm's way, and for the ones who had gone but never came back.

"Come on, boys … and girls," Rynn said, noting that two of the squad were women. There was nothing that prevented women from toting rifles around, but the reduced weight of the coil guns seemed to have convinced more of them that they could soldier right along with the miners and freight handlers.

Rynn pulled on her helm and took up a position at the front of the formation.

"You familiar with the op spec?" Hemock asked. *Soldiers' jargon. I wonder if my tinkering sounds as strange to them.*

"I wrote the mission plan," Rynn replied. She didn't care for the sound of her voice in the echoic confines of the helm. There was no getting around that for now though. She made a mental note to think of ways to fix the echo. "We match speeds with the thunderail, take over the engine, and work our way front to back. Full clear. I want no human casualties, civilian or otherwise. Is that understood?"

"Yes, ma'am," the squad shouted in unison.

"These supplies are going to shore up spots we've already hit, and they're going to be used against our brothers and sisters in retribution. Every bullet we dump in the Sea of Kerum, every crate of bandages that patches up one of ours instead of one of theirs, every box of coal ash crackers we take out of those kuduks' mouths is one step closer to beating them."

*Piss off, Kupe. I'm what you pretend to be.* Rynn felt a pang of guilt even thinking it, but it made her feel better, too. She couldn't do anything to help Madlin, but she could fight for the cause.

"Form up!" Sergeant Hemock ordered. The medical staff scrambled clear as soldiers lined up in two rows, leaning forward to be ready to run on the order.

Rynn held up three fingers for the operator of the world-ripper to see … then two … then one. She made a final check, watching the view jitter as the operator kept pace with the engine room of the moving thunderail. When Rynn dropped her arm, the world-hole opened.

"Move out!" Rynn immediately followed her own advice and was first through the hole.

Private Juliana had the distinct impression that she was the only one in the squad who was enjoying herself. Clutching her coil gun, she followed Sergeant Hemock through the world-hole, setting foot on a thunderail for the first time in her life. The wind rushed through her hair from the open window in the car, and she ducked to the side, toward the break between the engine and coal car, to make room for her fellow soldiers to pile through. The shouts of the kuduk engineer and coalmen were lost amid the whoosh of the wind and the noise from their own engine.

One of the coalmen pulled a pistol—it was a military thunderail, after all—but the rest of the crew were blasted full of holes before even drawing a weapon. The world-hole closed, and General Rynn shouted instruction. "Leave the engine running until we sweep the cars! We don't want escapees."

With that, General Rynn hopped the gap to the coal car and led the charge through the thunderail.

Juliana liked what the general had done with her outfit. The runed plates looked like they would offer plenty of protection from the guns that the kuduk soldiers might be carrying on board a vehicle this cramped. While Private Juliana was no expert on guns of any sort, she was a fair hand with runes, and had more informal soldiering experience than the whole rest of the squad. So she was confident that she could let the general go ahead without her when Sergeant Hemock ordered her onto the top of the thunderail.

*It's my natural grace and poise he must see.* When she saw the straggly tunnel-urchin-turned-soldier who followed behind her as she climbed the ladder to the roof, she revised her guess. *Wrong place, wrong time, I suppose. I should have figured it was blind luck.*

Kuduks didn't seem to be the most nimble of creatures, so aside from a wobbly track, there was likely to be little danger in covering the approach from above. Someone had to do it, of course, just out of sound military thinking. You didn't let your enemy flank you, even if you thought he didn't have the balls to climb onto the roof of a moving thunderail. Juliana checked behind her to see that her fellow roof-guard was crawling on hands and knees, with his coil gun still in hand.

"You afraid of heights or something?" Juliana asked over the wind.

"Get low, you blasted fool," the scraggly soldier snapped back.

Juliana smiled, fighting back a chuckle. "There's no one up here but us. No one finds their thunderail under attack and climbs onto the *roof* of it to see what's wrong. Especially not if they've got people shooting at them in the cars already."

The coil guns made so little noise compared to the engine of the thunderail that the shots couldn't be heard from the roof. The only sign of the gunfire was the splintering sound of ball bearings tearing their way through the walls of the cars on their way out.

"Yeah, well, you're gonna fall off, if you're not careful."

Juliana just shook her head and walked away, heading down the center of the roof and hopping lightly to the next car. She didn't worry that anyone inside would hear her footsteps, or the thump from her landing. Juliana had always been light afoot, and she wasn't overly concerned with what might happen if even anyone did hear her.

Just then, to her surprise, a head peeked over the edge of one of the last cars of the thunderail. The head's owner brought a pistol over the edge as well, and aimed somewhere in Juliana's vicinity and fired.

*No interference*, she reminded herself. Drawing her coil gun, Juliana fired off several shots in rapid succession. None hit the kuduk with the pistol, but a few blasted chunks of roof free near his head, forcing him to retreat back down.

"You see?" she asked, turning to the crawling soldier behind her. "Nothing to it."

The scraggly soldier shook his head. "You're a nutter."

She shrugged, firing another two shots off behind her without looking. "I've been called worse."

Rynn pulled off the helm of her tinker's armor, shaking her sweat-soaked hair to get it unstuck from her face. The world-ripper was once again just an image, not a hole, and they had made it back with only three injured, none dead. Sosha and her assistants had already carted the injured soldiers off to the infirmary, leaving Rynn to oversee the plundering of the thunderail.

Turning to look back at the viewframe before ordering it shut down, Rynn had a puerile thought. What would happen if they took the World Ender Cannon and aimed it down the length of the thunderail? How far could they penetrate with a single shot before a deflection or the sheer mass in its way stopped the shot? "Close it down," she shouted before her impulse got the better of her. The sooner the kuduks got their thunderails back up and running, the sooner Rynn and her rebels could plunder them once more.

"Good job everyone," she said to her squad. "We put a hurt on them today, that's for sure. Tell the barkeep drinks are on me tonight, you hear?"

There were good-natured jokes and a mock cheer in the wake of Rynn's pronouncement. She couldn't tell anymore who was who, but she knew that the soldiers who grew up in Tellurak got the joke. Booze was free on the *Jennai*, and some commander or other made the same coin-fisted joke when they got back from a successful mission. Rynn took it as a responsibility to make the same inane jest, even though the Korrish troops didn't get the joke.

Sergeant Hemock gave the official dismissal, and the squad dispersed. Rynn went her own way, heading back toward her quarters and her private workshop where she could remove her armor and relax. It had done everything she thought it would. She had taken three bullets off the runed, brightsteel plates of her chest piece and arm, and the gauntlet had bashed through locked railcar doors like they were made of foil sheet. Of all the improvements she had thought of while testing out the tinker's armor, the issue of heat was the most pressing. She was baking. Part of her looked forward to Madlin's nose healing just so she could see what runes the goblins had used to create the numbing cold. Applied judiciously, they could make the tinker's armor far more comfortable.

Halfway to her quarters, she noticed that someone was following her. She tried to be subtle and use Dan's trick of looking in the aether, slowing her pace so that she didn't walk into any walls that she would be blind to without seeing light. There were crewmen and women on the floors above and below, and a few scattered in nearby rooms, but she could find no one following. *It's that paranoia again. I'll get to be like Dan if I go looking at shadows for assassins.*

Just as she reached the door to her cabin, she caught another glimpse, but this time it was not fleeting. It was one of her soldiers from the raid, the taller of the two women.

"Oh, I'm sorry!" the woman apologized, holding up her hands in a gesture of surrender. *We pick 'em brave, that's for sure.*

"What is it?" Rynn asked, not bothering to disguise the weariness in her voice.

"If you have a moment, I have something I need to talk to you about," the woman said.

Rynn reached for the door handle. "I really don't. I'm wearing a boiler and I'm about out of coal."

"Well, I still have something to talk to you about, so let me give you a hand."

The woman followed Rynn into her cabin, failing to take a hint that Rynn had gone to some lengths to leave blunted.

"Listen, you did good today," Rynn said. "But I need some rest. If you have something to report, talk to Sergeant Hemock and he'll pass it along if I need to know it. Dismissed."

The woman snickered and shut the door. "You act like I'm actually one of your toy soldiers."

Overheated or not, Rynn's blood ran cold. "Who are you?" she demanded, reaching for her coil gun.

"My name's Juliana Hinterdale. You won't be needing that." She nodded toward Rynn's weapon.

Rynn backed up a step, but kept a hand on her gun. She was still wearing armor that turned aside bullets, and Juliana didn't even have a hand near her own coil gun, but Rynn couldn't shake a feeling of being cornered. "Who sent you? What do you want?"

"I'm here on my own initiative, and I'm here to return something that was taken from you." The woman who was not one of Rynn's soldiers held her hands forward, palms up, and a stack of books appeared in them.

"What are those?" Rynn asked. She could have asked where they came from, but the involvement of bald-faced magic seemed to render that question moot.

Juliana grinned. "Books."

Rynn swallowed. "Fine. You said you had something you needed to talk to me about. Talk."

"These are yours. They were found lying around on Tinker's Island after it was abandoned but before you went back to salvage your belongings."

"Are those what I think they are?"

"If you're not stupid, then yes. If you are, then probably not."

Rynn scowled, unaccustomed to having her intelligence called into question. "What were you doing with them?"

"My husband's doing, actually," Juliana replied. "But he's not here right now, is he? And I think he made a mistake. He preaches neutrality, but he took a valuable resource from your side. Your whole rebellion has been born out of this book."

"That's where my father learned how to make world-rippers," Rynn said.

Juliana snickered and scrunched her nose. "I love your name for them. The book calls it a transport gate, in case you were curious."

Rynn perked up. "You can read them?"

"Of course," Juliana replied. "I learned to read that language as a little girl. All Kadrin sorceresses do."

Rynn stared, her tongue too heavy to move. *This is it. She's here to finish me off. Dan found a way to build a world-ripper and sent a sorceress through.*

"Oh sweetie, you look like you think I'm going to kill you," Juliana replied. "I've killed a *lot* of people in my time, and let me tell you, I'm not in the habit of delivering books to them first." She set the stack down on Madlin's bedside table.

Rynn let out a breath. "All right, then … if you can read them, what do they say?"

Juliana rubbed at the back of her neck. "There's a problem, see? Like I said, my husband preaches neutrality, doesn't want us interfering with your war. There's no helping the other side, either, and I agree that everyone's better off without us kneading your dough with our dirty hands."

"Who are you?" None of this was making sense. Or at least, it was carefully circling around the edges of making sense, dangling sense overhead where Rynn couldn't reach it.

"I can't say," Juliana replied. "And in keeping with the spirit of neutrality, I can't tell you that every sorcerer in Veydrus can read these books, or that there's a one-worlded twin of one named Harwick running half of Acardia. I'd be in violation of the spirit of the rule if I hinted that oppressed humans are a bit of a cause of his, and that he might be willing to help if he knew what you were doing. I'd also be dodging some uncomfortable questions if I told you that he could also teach you magic if you asked nicely. Now, if I were to have taken that thunderail of yours and heaved it clear off the tracks for you, well I might actually be standing in a serious pile of shit. But as for all that other stuff I told you, well, the other demons can just piss off for all I care." With a wink, Juliana vanished.

Rynn stood staring at the stack of books, sweating like a crashballer in her tinker's armor, wondering what had just happened.

*I guess it's time to find a man named Harwick.*

# Chapter 4

*"Crackle doesn't separate the men from the boys; it separates the men from their money."*

The thing about cards and ships was that cards didn't fall over in rough seas. You could play a hand with the ship pitching like a bucking horse, which couldn't be said of dice or chess. Tanner had never grown accustomed to the worst that the Katamic Sea offered to a ship the size of the *False Profit*, and he could only imagine how much worse it would have been in a smaller vessel. But with cards in his hands and rum in his belly, he was willing to overlook a great deal. The outside world faded away, leaving just a circle of lantern light over a table hazy with pipe smoke, surrounded by killers.

The killers didn't worry Tanner; he'd been around their sort most of his life. Cutthroats, alley-stabbers, soldiers, and coinblades, those had been Tanner's people. A pirate was a bit of an odd duck; most of them just sailed a ship, while some did little between boarding actions but drink and lose their share of the plunder at cards. It took a hard man to fleece a crew of murderers at Crackle, and Tanner was just that sort of man. He didn't go in for alley work, but he'd been a soldier and a coinblade since he was old enough to hold a real sword. Any scum with a sharp blade could sneak up behind someone and slit a throat, but it took real skill to kill men who knew you were coming. Despite all that, Tanner lost more money than he made at Crackle. It wasn't for lack of trying, but because Denrik Zayne seemed to attract the sort of sailor that knew his cards.

So there was a bright spot in Tanner's heart as he looked at his cards and saw that he held two kings and a four. The four he would toss to some unlucky sap at the first pass, but he could hold a pair of kings all hand. The coins in the waning pile in front of him were about to gain new friends. "I raise," he said. He lifted a bottle of eight year old Takalish rum to his lips lest he grin and ruin his chances of getting calls.

One scruffy, alcohol-soaked sailor after another tossed in his cards, until one held up the game thinking over his play. Tanner's mind started working out how much coin he could squeeze out of the pirate, a man named Skapp.

"Ya in or ya out?" one of the other players griped.

Skapp looked up from his cards, firing a scowl at the offending player. "Gimme a minute."

*Take all the time you need.* Tanner took another swig of his rum. *I ain't goin' nowhere.*

Boots pounded down the steps from above. An interloper was joining them from the deck, and it was someone in a rush. Tanner squeezed his eyes shut. *Not now …*

"Mr. Tanner, Cap'n wants you."

"Just as soon as I'm done this—"

"*Now*, Mr. Tanner. Cap'n doesn't like being kept waiting."

*I've known him years longer than you, Smickens.* Tanner drained the last of his rum as he stood. "I know how much is there," he said, pointing to the pile in the table. With a pat on his sword hilt, he let his eyes sweep over the players, letting them know he'd remember who he was gambling with.

The floor had a little extra wobble in it as Tanner followed First Mate Smickens up to the deck. "He say what he wants?"

"Does he ever?"

Tanner sighed, wishing he'd brought a bottle with him.

Captain Denrik Zayne was known as the Scourge of the Katamic, and had been for nearly thirty years. He had sunk more ships than most navies during that time, and killed more men than a fever plague. It was easy for Tanner to dismiss the man's reputation as overblown, now that he knew him, but facts were facts. He was going to live as long as Denrik Zayne had a use for him … and if it weren't for the pirate's sorcerer son, Tanner probably would have run the scoundrel through years ago.

First Mate Smickens hustled ahead and knocked on the captain's door, knowing that Tanner would just barge in if he got there first. "He's here, Cap'n."

"Very good, send him—"

Tanner pushed through the door, stumbling as the ship rocked beneath his feet.

"… in."

"How's the weather?" Tanner asked. He hated bland greetings, but he could have used the reassurance that the present angry seas might subside before he needed solid food in his gut.

"I don't have time for your usual nonsense, Mr. Tanner," Denrik replied. He sat at his writing desk, a pair of spectacles, a visible concession to age catching up with him. "I need you to pass along a message."

"Bloody eyes, can't a man just drink his days away on a couple of boats, without getting himself shipped all over everywhere, carrying letters?"

Denrik Zayne forced a smile. "Well, you'll be happy to note that this message is for your whoring compatriot."

"You mean the one with the *fun* ship, not the one where I lose hands of Crackle because I get alley-clubbed and dragged in here whenever you get a notion?"

"Mr. Tanner, you are aware that we are at war."

Tanner blew though loose lips, making a rude noise. "You and me ain't. And me and Stalyart ain't. It's the boy's war; let him fight it out."

"You may enjoy this particular missive, since you may—inadvertently, I assure you—find some pleasure in it."

The ship swayed, and Tanner stumbled against Denrik's desk. He blinked as he stared into the face of the suddenly-too-close pirate. "Whazzat?"

"The message I need you to relay to Mr. Stalyart is that I need him. Anzik needs him. The Megrenn Alliance is short of airship captains, and I want to put him in command of one."

Tanner whistled. "Nice and tidy, but you know old Stalyart likes to keep his head low and his sails up. Why would he put himself in front of the Kadrin air fleet now of all times?"

"Because at the end of the war I fully expect him to steal the ship."

Tanner paused and stood straight. Denrik had a point. Stalyart might have been more of a smuggler than a cutthroat, and more of a cutthroat than a navy man, but the promise of *owning* an airship … well, that might just be enough to tip the boat.

Tanner nodded his agreement. "Fine. I'll deliver the message tonight, once I get some sleep."

Denrik reached into a desk drawer and withdrew a bottle. Tanner squinted to read the label. "Bekairon, Black Label," Zayne said. "Might as well drink yourself stupid in style." He lobbed the bottle across the cabin to Tanner. Despite the world tipping around him, Tanner still had the reflexes of a swordsman and snatched the bottle from the air. "Now, go deliver my message."

The sky, blue as a baby's eyes, spread off to infinity, cloudless and pure. The rush of wind blew through thinning hair—invigorating. Masts creaked as the *Northern Squall* banked in a turn, trying to outmaneuver the Kadrin vessel that was closing in on them. The airship ducked low, entering a mountain pass and approaching the bridge that connected the two halves of the Kadrin city of Reaver's Crossing.

"They using the same wind as us?" the first mate griped as the Kadrin vessel matched their turn and continued gaining on them.

A second Megrenn airship, the *Bluebottle*, crossed over the bridge heading in the opposite direction, diving for the Kadrin vessel and firing its forward ballistae. The *Northern Squall* sped beneath her, crew cheering their apparent rescuers. The *Bluebottle* loosed grappling lines, the sharpened hooks meant to catch rigging and sails and shred them. Several of the lines caught, but the Megrenn had not counted on rune-strengthened spars; after the grapples sliced through rope and canvas, they caught hold on wood and could neither cut nor snap their way free. The *Bluebottle* pitched forward before the lines snapped and freed them from the Kadrins' embrace. A sorcerer aboard the Kadrin ship let fly a volley of fire bolts, scorching the *Bluebottle's* sails and leaving them helpless to turn as their momentum carried them into the mountainside.

The Kadrin vessel fared little better. The damage to their sails had cost the ship its wind, along with any hope of catching up to the *Northern Squall*.

The vision grew blurry at that point. Anzik removed his hand from Captain Aigrin's forehead. "You're blocking me."

The captain of the *Northern Squall* looked abashed. It was just the two of them in the royal sitting room. They both knew the factual account of the airship's escape already. "My apologies, Sorcerer Anzik. Just not proud of what we did, leaving them like that."

"Your memory of the events bears out your report," Anzik replied, "They bought you a chance to escape, and you took it. There is no shame in losing a battle."

"Thank you, sir."

"Now, if we might continue?" Anzik raised an eyebrow.

Captain Aigrin squeezed his eyes shut and gave a tight nod. Anzik resumed his memory vision spell and placed a hand on the man's sweat-slick forehead.

The *Northern Squall* lost sight of both of the other airships as they swung around the mountain. There was a crash of timber in the distance behind them, quiet in the vast open air but unmistakably the sound of one of the airship's crashing. Though Aigrin could not be certain, he suspected that it was the *Bluebottle*.

"Ready the port catapults!" he shouted. Their target was in sight, the narrow, winding mountain road that ran up to the city, the main trade route with the rest of the Kadrin Empire. While the city was nigh impregnable except from the air, the inaccessible mountain pass made cutting the city off from aid all the easier. "Fire!"

Catapults cranked and thunked, lobbing their payloads into the sky to smash into the mountainside. Each hit was accompanied by an explosion, as the mysterious black sand detonated on impact. The mountainside shattered, dumping tons of rock across the pass.

Anzik removed his hand once more. "Good enough. I don't need to see the details of your return. You obviously suffered no ill fortune, else you would not be here. The pass appeared thoroughly impeded; it will take the Kadrins considerable time or magic to remedy, and at this point I'd rather they waste their sorcerers on menial labor than in counteracting our plans."

Captain Aigrin nodded. "Begging your pardon, sorcerer, but this was my third encounter with Kadrin vessels, and the third time I was lucky to crawl off still breathing. They've just got us out-shipped. Those boats of theirs take a beating, and we hardly ever crash them, just ground them if we're lucky. Any chance we might get some improvements to help keep us punching back?"

Anzik closed his eyes. "You may go."

The captain muttered his acknowledgment and departed, leaving Anzik alone in the room. He waited a count of one hundred, using the time to think through the possible complications of his fledgling plan. There were always pitfalls in any endeavor, and enumerating them as thoroughly as possible beforehand always put his mind at ease. By the time he finished his silent count, he had come up with eight possible ways his request could result in misfortune, none of which promised catastrophe. The worst outcome he could imagine was if Cadmus became involved, and his interference unraveled the alliance between Megrenn and the Korrish rebels. Even that scenario seemed improbable.

Having reached the limit of the time he was willing to force Jamile to wait, Anzik raised a hand and made a beckoning gesture. Within seconds, a world-hole opened, showing him the central chamber of the Korrish moon hideaway.

"Things going well back home?" Jamile asked as Anzik crossed the threshold between worlds. She shut the machine down behind him and zeroed the controls.

"No," he replied, taking her aback. *Why do they ask if they expect a comforting answer instead of a truthful one?* "Our airships are proving inadequate compared to their Kadrin counterparts. Please reactivate the machine and take me to see Rynn."

"Now wait just a tootin' minute!" said Jamile. "I let you check on your people as a favor. I don't take orders. Rynn's a busy woman; you can't just go barging in whenever you like."

"I've been patient in regards to our share of the coil guns," said Anzik. "Now I would like to speak with Rynn. I have other matters to discuss, and the fate of my people may swing on the timeliness of my actions."

"Things are that bad?"

"No," Anzik replied. "I don't want them to get that bad before I act. I think that was one of my father's failings. He waited until we had crested the peak of disaster before he dug in his heels. Only Kadrin in-fighting saved us in the last war. I won't wait until our last airship falls from the skies before I seek to overcome our deficit in aerial naval power."

"Oh."

*She doesn't understand. She is a physician, not a strategist.* "I need to take Korrish knowledge of airships and apply it to ours. Rynn would approve, as it will show that tinkering and magic can overcome magic alone. Please open a hole so that I might discuss terms."

Jamile frowned. "I'll make you a deal. Rynn's had herself a bit of a day, and I'm not going to wake her. She wasn't quite putting words together in a straight line, last I saw her, rambling on about Eziel-knows-what. You let her get a sleep in her, and I'll have her come find you in the morning."

*A bargained position, better than I might otherwise get if I don't enlist her aid. I might be able to rouse Kaia to use the machine for me, but this plan has a higher likelihood of success. Cadmus is out of the question. I don't know whether Greuder can work the machine. Kupe cannot. I might be able to manage the controls on my own, but I would cost myself this alliance if I was discovered.* "Very well. Tomorrow."

"Please repeat," said Stalyart. "He wants *what?*"

Tanner and Stalyart—who went by the same names in Tellurak and Veydrus—sat together on the pillars of a pier, overlooking Zethin Harbor in Safschan. The *Wind's Shadow* was moored nearby, taking on crates of goods with contents Stalyart would steadfastly deny any knowledge of.

"To make you an airship captain in the Megrenn sky army," Tanner said. "Though I admit I might be hazy on the title. Says he needs men who can sail, and ran out of names."

"I am touched by his consideration," Stalyart replied. "Touched in a rude and most inappropriate manner. I have told him I have no interest in his wars. He has, until now, respected my wishes. There are causes worth killing for, but none worth dying for. This very much has the feel of a cause of death. He seeks to dangle the promise of a ship before me, hinting that I could steal it after the war. What manner of fool does he think I have become? I answer you: none."

"So … then … I take it you want me to pass along a refusal?" Tanner asked. "We go on doing what we do, and you and Zayne keep sailing together in Tellurak?"

"Oh, no," Stalyart said, his face suddenly blank. "Not at all. Denrik Zayne would never let such a slight pass." Stalyart's ever present grin slowly crept back onto his face. "I have told Captain Zayne for years that his mind will go soft if he is not lied to and deceived regularly. It seems that this has finally happened. I have followed him for … hmm … over twenty-two years now. I think it is time that he was reminded that I am, after all, a pirate."

"How's that, now?" Tanner asked.

"We are going to steal his airship, and we will *not* wait for the war to end."

# Chapter 5

*"Train soldiers to fight for a cause. Hire them when you need foul deeds done without question."*

Half a dozen filthy humans rummaged through the shelves of a general goods store, shoveling merchandize into sacks without even looking to see what it was they were stealing. Similar scenes were playing out across Enmer Deep, the second largest city in Tollopland. The rioting had entered its third day, and kuduks who had the means were leaving the city in droves. Enmer Deep was quickly becoming a human slum, top to bottom. Military patrols concentrated on shepherding civilians to the thunderails and up to Enmer Sky, where airships packed to barely buoyant floated off with refugees.

General Yurgen spat on the floor in front of the world-ripper as he watched, tugging at his freshly braided beard. He looked like a proper general now, he knew, but the braids tugged at his chin in tiny bunches, and the weight of the rank beads threatened to tug the hairs from his face. "All right, you block-fisted oxen, you seen what's what over there. Them Enmerites need us, and them humans ain't gonna want us, and that's the way it's gonna be. You see a human what ain't cowerin' with his hands over his head, you pull the trigger. You see one of ours in trouble, you put yourself between them and the trouble. That's bein' a hero, and that's what you boys're gonna be. You ain't heroes yet, but I'll be blasted if I don't make a hero of every last one of you lot. Now most of ours is already shoveled coal out of there, but that don't mean you can get sloppy. I find a hole what don't belong in one of ours, there's gonna be discipline."

Hard eyes and set jaws all pointed in General Yurgen's direction. He looked them over and gave a nod. It had sunk in. "You boys go do the good work. Corporal Oggit, open 'er up."

"Yessir!"

A second later, the viewframe became a hole to Enmer Deep, into the middle of Daljean's Fine Goods. The squad was sixty strong, and led by a grizzled army Sergeant named Zeetler, who hated humans since losing his brother in a mining accident that was blamed on human incompetence. Every man was armed with a fresh-made coil gun, never fired except in the test range. The soldiers poured through the world-hole like an angry river bursting a dam, cursing and shouting as they fell over the astonished human rioters.

"Keep it open," General Yurgen ordered, "and follow 'em good. I want to hear what's goin' on, smell it." He ambled around to join Corporal Oggit behind the bullet-thick glass wall that separated the control console from the viewframe.

It was exhilarating to watch, probably even better—and certainly safer—than actually being there in the deep, felling humans like rats. There were too many kuduks in the squad to keep track of all of them as they dispersed into the city, so he had Corporal Oggit zip from one skirmish to another. Most of the humans fled as fast as their gangly legs could carry them, but some made a fight of it. They threw rocks and bricks; a few had pistols and returned fire. All were quickly dispatched by the sheer number of Yurgen's men and the power of the coil guns they carried.

They had a few close calls. Some rebel element among Enmer's humans seemed familiar with the world-ripper, and directed their stones and bullets toward the controller. The bullet-thick glass held, but the dings where shots had struck just in front of his face kept drawing Yurgen's eye.

Corporal Oggit kept pace behind a knot of soldiers as they chased a gaggle of humans down a sloping tunnel. Yurgen shouted encouragement. "Keep on 'em, boys! Fire on the run; they'll be slower if they're duckin' the whole way." One of the soldiers caught a boot in the ruts of the trolley rails. "You imbecile! Get up!"

Despite being safe behind cover and standing still, Yurgen found his breath coming quick. "There!" He pointed, though none of the squad looked back. "Two of them broke off to the left. In the silverworks! In the silverworks, you blind, suckling piglets!" Yurgen clenched both fists until it felt as if his knuckles would burst from the strain.

"I'm not sure how well they can hear you, sir," Corporal Oggit said. "Might need to lean around the glass."

Yurgen narrowed an eye at the corporal. "You'd like that, wouldn't ya? Easy promotion, draggin' my keester out of the line of fire if a human gets ideas, seein' me peek out?"

"No, nothing like—"

"Or you just coverin' for them coal-eyed inbreds who just let two humans get away? Prob'ly rebels too, just our luck."

"Sorry sir, it was just a suggestion, that's all," Corporal Oggit insisted.

"Well, you just mind that I don't write that bit into my report," Yurgen said. "Bad enough writin' 'em in the first place, without havin' to write 'em longer on account of yammer-mouths like yourself."

Yurgen turned his attention back to the action in the world-hole, where Corporal Oggit was still following behind the chasing soldiers. "Better'n crashball," he muttered to himself, feeling his heart begin to race once more.

In another viewframe, a far different scene played out. Kuduks lined the walls of a lavish antechamber, expensive furniture shoved into a corner so that they might all be bunched together under the watch of a single guard. They were bound at the wrists and gagged, the beards of the men shaved down to bloodied skin. By the door, two more humans stood with rifles in hand, peeking down the tunnel outside. Even through the viewframe, the fear in that room had a stench to it.

General Bradet paced in front of his troops, standing between them and the scene in the Council Hall of Kupak Deep. Though Draksgollow's army had given him a promotion to general, he was still a sergeant at heart, his beard frazzled and less impressive than any of the men in his command. He scratched an itch under his chin as he decided how long to let them stew, getting them riled up watching a bunch of helplesses being roughed over. With a curt nod, he decided that it had been long enough.

"Listen up, washcloths, because I don't want to go over this twice," Bradet said, projecting his voice so that the soldiers in the back could hear him. "This is a rescue mission. Dead humans are acceptable; dead kuduks are *not*. Our number one priority is the safe retrieval of nine councilors from Kupak Deep. Not eight, not seven, and sure as shit not six. Nine. Count them up, if you sniffing flowers can count. I see nine, right plain as a plate in front of me. You're going to go through there, put a bullet shield between those hostages and anything that might harm them, and get them the cracked, rusted bolts out of there. They ask you any questions, just tell them you're here to rescue them, and that they've got to move. They get panicked or stupid, and don't want to move, pick them up and carry them. Mind your hands with the lady councilors. I want two of you on the heavy one there at the end. Once they're through, you bring them down to the barracks, get them something to eat and let them have a piss, whatever they need. We're a hotel from that point, and they're dignitaries. Until then, they're sacks of the most expensive meat you're ever going to haul, and I don't want to see bruise nor blood on any of them. Any questions?"

There was silence.

"Phase two," said Bradet, pointing to the console operator, who took the cue. The view shifted to the next room, where two dozen human rebels, armed for a war, were packed together, fidgeting, waiting for someone to answer their demands. Bradet knew that, because he read it in the newspaper; it had been the lead story. "We will re-open the hole, once the councilors are safe, and we will eliminate the rebel force. That part, at least, I think you whistle-ears can manage without too much fuss." He grinned, and his soldiers chuckled with some reservation. They were good lads. Still had a bit of a shine on them, but they would scuff with experience.

"First ones through, I want bullet shield mashed into the faces of those gun-toting humans, and I want both doors blocked off. Ready?"

"Yes, sir!"

Bradet grinned. It was good being general. "On the count of five!"

At the end of Bradet's countdown, the world-hole opened, and his troops sprang into action. He couldn't see what went on outside the viewframe's vantage, as they had brought it as close as possible to the hostages to speed the rescue without impeding the flow of troops to do the rescuing. Bradet kept out of his men's way, standing at the world-hole and ushering frightened councilors through as his men shepherded them.

"Come on, come on; get through. Make way for the others; you're all safe, but get those arses of yours hustling. No time. I'll explain later. Are you all right? Get going then. If that was a thanks, then you're welcome, now *move*."

In all, it took less than a minute. The three armed humans in the room were dead, nine hostages safe and cut free from their bonds, and a world-hole closed behind them.

"Who are you people?" one of the councilors demanded. She was grey of hair and sideburn, with a scowl that looked congenital. If it weren't for the frazzled hair and a busted spectacle lens, she might have even been intimidating.

"We work for Draksgollow. I'm General Bradet." He saluted, mindful of his orders from Draksgollow. They were supposed to make a good impression and leave it there. Much as he would have liked to backhand the ungrateful mule of a councilor whose first words free of a gag were anything but a thanks—it hadn't been her who had mumbled gratitude through a burlap cloth.

"I've never heard of any Draksgollow," one of the other councilors said, a man in his middle years with a mangled face that might never grow a proper beard again. "Who does he work for? And … what the quakes is this place? Where are we?"

Bradet held up his hands and gave a gentle smile. "You're among friends. Go freshen up, grab a bite, and relax. We'll figure out someplace safe we can deliver you, and you'll be home by dinnertime. And don't worry about Mr. Draksgollow; you'll get to meet him before you go. It'll be something you can write about in your memoirs, brag to your drinking mates about. And he'll answer any questions."

"All well and good, but *who* is this Draksgollow fellow?"

"He's Korr's solution to the human problem."

General Knorlen clasped his hands behind his back, staring into the viewframe. Five minutes ago, he had ordered his troops to raid a church in the lowest layer of Kupak Deep. The city had been hard hit by the rebels, who had dug in and taken control of the lifts and stairshafts, cutting off all travel from layer to layer except those they permitted. Kupak was under siege from within. There hadn't been a thunderail through in a week, and the two that tried were looted and derailed. Draksgollow had ordered a stop to it.

But the scene before him was anything but encouraging. The ragtag assemblage of human fighters was well-armed. Early intelligence sweeps through Kupak had given no indication that these rebels were coil-gun armed, but clear as the bullet-thick glass protecting Lieutenant Fedrin at the controls, there they were, firing back from around corners with guns that punched holes in stone. It didn't help matters that the church was human-made brickwork, barely fit to stand under its own weight. The balls from the coil guns tore through the masonry like it was made of crackers—and not the rock-hard sort served in the cheap cars on the thunderail.

"I don't like this," Knorlen muttered.

"Yessir," Lieutenant Fedrin agreed dutifully.

Knorlen fingered the coil-gun holstered at his hip, itching to order the machine on so he could offer support fire. Draksgollow would pitch a fit, risking himself like that, but Knorlen was rapidly approaching the point where he would either have to intervene or make the call to abort the whole operation.

"This should have been a two-machine raid. We could have hit them from multiple angles, right off." He knew Lieutenant Fedrin was listening, but he didn't care. Fedrin was no fool, and must have been thinking the same thing. Most of the operators were clods, simple dial-turners who happened to be quick with their hands. Fedrin was an officer, a bit quiet and bookish, but he had a head for strategy. He kept the viewframe on the most critical areas, shifting angle and location to match the flow of the battle.

"Sir!" Fedrin shouted. "Reinforcements!"

"Those rat bastards," Knorlen grumbled. "How many of you are there?" He closed his fingers around the grip of his coil gun. It was now or never. To Fedrin he shouted, "Open the hole. Grab your sidearm and help me hold them off."

Fedrin, to his credit, did not hesitate. The young Lieutenant threw the switch and rushed to the dangerous side of the bullet-thick glass, weapon drawn. The human reinforcements screamed to one another and dove for cover, but Fedrin had left them a prime firing angle. Knorlen and Fedrin were both taking cover and reloading before the humans found anyplace safe from their withering fire.

"Don't worry, lads. We've got your covered," Knorlen leaned around to shout through the open world-hole.

That was when the first canister came through, plinking onto the stone floor of the world-ripper chamber. It bounced erratically, the oblong cylindrical shape hitting the ground with a mind of its own. After bouncing harmlessly off the bullet-thick glass, the canister came to rest between Fedrin and Knorlen.

"Gas!" Knorlen shouted. He sucked in a deep breath of clean air, then buried his nose and mouth in the crook of his elbow, letting the wool of his uniform act as makeshift breather cloth. He and his squad didn't have gas masks on hand; humans just hadn't shown a propensity for using gas canisters, by all reports. Dropping his coil gun, Knorlen dove for the canister, hoping to throw it back into the midst of the humans—who also wore no masks—before it went off.

Just before he scooped the canister from the floor, two more joined it, clanging along the ground in an ominous chorus. "Throw them back," he ordered, his voice muffled by his own sleeve.

But Knorlen had been right in his initial assumption. The humans did not have gas canisters, nor was that what he held in his hand. Crackling spark stung his hand, coming from runes etched all around the canister. His introduction to the exploding rune dynamo was very, very brief.

The sun was nothing short of an open furnace door hanging in the sky. Draksgollow thought he had been prepared for it. He wore a wide-brimmed hat, and along with all his men he wore tinted goggles against the glare. But there was no escaping that blast-wave heat from above, not without retreating back to the consistent cool of the deep, not without losing face. Certainly, he was not letting his men off so easily. If half the human population of Korr could take the outdoor heat in the growing season, so could fifty kuduk soldiers for a few hours.

The ground was spongy beneath his boots, lacking the comforting solidity of rock. With every step, he half expected it would give way and let him sink in to the knee or worse. Nothing grew in rock though, and to find farmers he needed to go where the ground was arable soil, not stone or even clay. An unfamiliar stench wafted everywhere, coming from all directions. Asking around had gotten him no answers to its source, since none of the kuduks knew, and none of the humans seemed to have the first clue what he was saying—not that they were inclined to be helpful anyway.

His soldiers tromped through wheat fields and orchards, pastures and sties. They were on their eighth world-hole of the day, the Telluraki humans spread maddeningly over half the continent. They congregated in cities, but city humans weren't the ones he was looking for. City humans of this world were spoiled, soft, and either scrawny or fat, with too little in the brawny middle ground that he wanted. Countryside humans, even the scrawny ones, were built for hard work, with muscle on their bones and muscle in their heads. A thinker was the last thing he needed in a human.

Kep stood at his side, a clipboard in hand, taking the tally. A squad of four approached, two holding either end of a line of chained humans, two others flanking with leather-wrapped clubs in hand. The humans had put up a fight, but his men had it beaten out of them. Bruises, bloodied faces, welts all over, the menfolk had been almost too much trouble to keep. But now all of them were trussed up, wrists chained up behind their backs, tethered to their collars so that they had to strain to keep from choking themselves. They stumbled along as best they could, no doubt imagining bloody vengeance enacted on his person.

Draksgollow chuckled at one thuggish farmhand who had the gall to glare at him on the way by. He took his own club from his belt and reoriented the farmhand's eyes in the direction he was walking. "Yeah, you don't know what I'm saying, but you're going to learn some manners." He turned to Kep and lowered his voice. "Muddy piss, we've got to get someone to translate to these savages."

Kep snickered, holding up the clipboard. "Don't look at me, I just count 'em."

"Speaking of, what's the count?"

"This one, or the day's?" Kep asked.

Draksgollow removed his hat and fanned his head. For once he envied the humans their innate cooling system, wet and stinking though it might be. "Both."

"Well, here we got eighteen males, twelve females—nine breeding age and two of them already bred—and twenty two children. We culled six—five for age, one as a cripple," Kep reported. Draksgollow clenched his mechanical fist. He knew that cripples were the last thing Korr needed in new human stock, but for some reason it still hurt deep down. "On the day, one hundred eleven working males, ninety females, one hundred fifty one children, with a couple of the older females close to breeding. Sixty-one culled in total."

Draksgollow nodded to let the squad know they were counted and cleared to take the new slaves through. There was only one squad left out in the fields. They would be back in the cool deeps before long.

"Not a bad haul," Kep commented.

"A gesture, more than anything," Draksgollow replied. "A proof of concept. We'll need a huge operation to replenish Korr's stock."

"You don't mind me sayin', but these here seemed like more trouble than the ones we're getting' rid of."

"Oh, they've got fight in them for now," Draksgollow replied. "But that kind of anger fades quick enough once reality sets in. They've got closer ties to their kin, and won't want to see them get hurt. They're not used to getting beat if they don't work, not used to getting a half ration if they don't work themselves to collapse. Korr can break these. What they lack is organization, and that's the real trouble with the rebels. A few troublemakers here and there, you can snuff them out like candles. You can't snuff out a grease spill, once it catches fire. You gotta bury it good."

Kep pointed down the rows of wheat. "Here come the last ones."

"About rusted time," Draksgollow grumbled. "Let's count them up and get out of here."

Back in the cool of his own office, in a desolate stretch of tunnels that Kezudkan had never seen, Draksgollow let the heat of the foreign world bleed out of him like pus from an infected wound. His desk was piled with reports, and his generals and officers stopped by to get advice, check in with him, or see what he might need. Despite all that, he kept his muddied boots off, letting the stone leech heat through the sole of his one good foot. He should have changed into fresh clothing, he knew. His guests were the delicate sort, with sensibilities belonging in the deeps, not the open skies, and especially not skies from another world. Draksgollow still smelled of farm, which, after conferring with his troops, was a mixture of dung, animal sweat, human sweat, and fertilizer—which was also dung.

Report after report, all glowing victories; it was enough to cool his sun-soured mood. They were biting into the neck of the growing human rebellion and shaking it. The details were just details; let the generals worry over those sorts of things. Draksgollow could spend an hour poring over a schematic with a hundred interlocking parts, and find the one number that was in error, but that was his stock in trade. For all the military airs he had put on of late, he knew he was still just a tinker, albeit one rich enough to buy armies. He enjoyed the big picture, and to a lesser extent, planning the raids. Then the generals got involved, turned the plans into something they could accomplish with the men they had, and generally mucked things up. It was good to see that for once they had skipped the mucking up part.

"Kep, where's the report from General Knorlen?" Draksgollow shouted out his office door. "Those Kupak Deep rebels were the worst of today's bunch. I want to know how it went."

Kep poked his head in the door. "Ain't got one from him." The head disappeared.

"Get your arse back in here!" Draksgollow shouted. Kep reemerged with his head low, not meeting Draksgollow's eye. "What do you mean? Get Knorlen and get his sorry beard in here, and I mean yesterday." Kep was gone before Draksgollow finished his sentence.

Draksgollow sighed, checking the gibberish label on the bottle of booze he had taken with him from one of the farms. There was a picture of a waterwheel and a patch of grass riverbank, but the rest was human script. It looked like someone had shattered a pile of runes and sprinkled the pieces into rows of simpler symbols. He popped the cork and sniffed the contents. The overwhelming scent of alcohol stung his nostrils, but he guessed that the subtler smell beneath it was grape. The humans hadn't known they would be the target of a world-ripper assault, so there was no reason to think they would have poisoned it. He took an experimental swig. Once the initial sting wore off, it was sweet. Not good, but palatable. He leaned back in his chair, throwing his good foot up on the desk as he drank the rest and waited for Knorlen to report in person.

Half an hour later the bottle was empty, and a light fuzz settled into Draksgollow's head. Kep returned alone. "He ain't coming back."

"Aww, piss," Draksgollow said, though he couldn't muster enough anger to shout about it. "What'd that brickwit do?"

"Can't be too sure, but I had the boys peek in on his world-ripper with ours, and the place is wrecked."

"Underestimated 'em," Draksgollow said, nodding. "Shovel it, get a team in there. Get survivors out, and anything we can salvage. Plant charges and collapse the place when you're done."

"You got it, boss," Kep said. Once in a while, it was nice to be treated like a businessman, instead of a soldier.

"Hey, before you go kicking the dogs, send in that lady councilor, the one in charge," said Draksgollow. He worked his tongue around his mouth, trying to get rid of the clumsy, filmy feeling that made talking more work than it ought to have been.

"Her name's—"

"Yeah, I know. Gerkie Steelsmith. Just tell her it's time we had a talk."

Kep departed with a vigorous nod.

Draksgollow had never been to sea, so he was only guessing that the swaying motion of the room was the same. He knew it was the waterwheel grape booze having its effect on him, which told him that his thoughts were clear enough to be meeting with councilors. Despite an unsteady view, his brain was still in there, tinkering away.

"This is him, councilor," Kep's voice preceded him into the office. Right behind him was a woman of late middle years, wearing a pair of spectacles with a freshly ground lens in one side. She was a sharp one—knew her optical refraction off the top of her head. One of Draksgollow's glassworkers had taken care of it inside an hour. That was what a good man called "politeness," and what a politician called an act of goodwill.

Draksgollow set his feet back to the floor and stood to greet his guest. "Councilor Steelsmith. It's a pleasure." He stuck out a hand, not sure whether councilors were above that sort of thing or not. Anyone he'd dealt with in business had always expected it, but Kep and his generals had warned him that politicians weren't businessmen—at least not that they admitted publicly.

Gerkie Steelsmith did not take the proffered hand, but inclined her head in Draksgollow's direction. "Mr. Draksgollow, I understand that I have you to thank for our rescue."

"Yes, ma'am," he replied with a tight smile. "Have a seat." Draksgollow eyed the chair in the corner of the room, and Kep took the hint, sliding it over for Councilor Steelsmith.

"Let me be blunt, Mr. Draksgollow, since you appear to be a blunt man," said Councilor Steelsmith. "What are the terms of our presence here?"

"Terms?"

"What is it you want, in exchange for our return?"

Draksgollow laughed. "We just pulled you out of a city overrun by humans that got themselves guns. You want us to send you back where we found you, we can do that now. But I'd rather you didn't get rounded up and tied like a roast ham the minute we leave you on your own, so we're looking for a place you can run things in exile. You got any suggestions, we're open-eared."

"So, you have no demands? No requests for a reward before we are returned?"

"Reward?" Draksgollow asked. He looked to Kep. "Kep, are we some sort of bandits or mercenaries?"

"Nope," Kep lied for him. Draksgollow and Kep might not have been fighting for money, but most of their soldiers certainly were.

"Very well, then," Councilor Steelsmith conceded. "And what was that machine we came through? I and the other councilors are quite keen on knowing how easily that security was breached."

"Aw, there's a lot you don't know in this world," Draksgollow replied. "Just let that be another on the list. Let's just leave it that I can get places I need to get, and I'm using it to get there."

"And what are you getting in this arrangement?" Councilor Steelsmith asked.

"Respect," Draksgollow said. "We're doing good work here, and hardly no one knows a button about it. People see humans wrecking everything they can get their hands on, and the government can't do a rusted thing about it. I want them to know that I can, and I am. The name is Ganrin Draksgollow, and I want people to know that I'm working to save them from the human menace."

"Human menace?" Councilor Steelsmith asked, furrowing her brow. "Even being held for three days by those brutes, I don't think that the whole species is to blame. Most of them are docile enough."

"How do you know which ones are docile, and which are just faking it until the time is right?" Draksgollow asked. "No, I've got a better plan. We killed thirty-five humans from Kupak rescuing you. We're going to give you thirty-five new humans to replace them."

"Replace them? From where?"

"We found a place with wild humans, still living on their own, talking their own languages and everything. They've never heard of the rebellion, couldn't understand a word if you tried to tell them. Me and mine are rounding them up in chains, and we're going to give them out as reparations for the war. That's what we're calling the Human Replacement Plan, which is an adjunct to the Human Extermination Project."

"Extermination? That sounds extreme."

"Once we nip the danglies off this rebellion—er, pardon the language—we're going to root out the core. Get rid of just about all the humans; leave the ones who got special skills, and enough to show new slaves how to act. Rest go to the furnaces. With the council's consent, I'd be willing to start with Kupak. Fresh slaves for the slave owners, and slaves to the patrons of the freeman we exterminate. You lot have all the paperwork of who owns who, who works for who. You just let me handle the replacements."

Councilor Steelsmith stood. "Mr. Draksgollow, I don't see that I can condone this sort of—"

"Yellowcorn's a bit warm this time of year," Draksgollow cut in, "but the humans haven't rebelled. Probably because they practically run the place already, but it's peaceful there. Kep can take you and the other councilors there right now, if you like. Safest place I can think of for you, if it comes right down to it. Or … you can let Kep take you down to the cages, you pick out thirty-five new humans, and you can get back to Kupak Deep and your own nice soft bed, soon as we get done clearing it out."

Councilor Steelsmith locked gazes with Draksgollow, and held a glare on him for longer than most could stand to look at his maimed face. Without a word, she turned and left the room, Kep following close behind. Draksgollow didn't think she was heading for the world-ripper.

# Chapter 6

*"You cannot hide a sorcerer beneath a farmer's hat." –Kadrin proverb*

Jamile eyed Anzik up and down, making sure no detail was out of place. The clothes he wore were new, but Jamile had dragged them though the underbrush of the Veydran jungle just outside the lunar headquarters, laundered them, and repeated a handful of times. The wear made the outfit believable for a freeman human worker down on his luck stowing on thunderails city to city looking for work.

"I don't see how a tavern in Korr makes any sense for a meeting," Anzik said as Jamile circled him.

"Me neither," Jamile replied. "But Rynn's cranky enough these days that I don't ask questions just out of curiosity. I save them up like bank notes, in case I want to ask something important."

"A deserted island in Tellurak would be most secure. The remote location and paucity of both technology and magic in Tellurak leaves fewer opportunities for someone to stumble onto us browsing with a world-ripper, or overhearing our conversation. I can give her locations for seven small islands, any one of which would be suitable. If you could relay the options to Rynn with a request for her to select whichever she prefers, I think we can settle on a more appropriate meeting venue. I can change into my accustomed attire while you send Sosha."

Jamile stopped her inspection and folded her arms, fixing Anzik with a raised eyebrow. "No. I think a tavern will do you some good. Get to see some right-as-Eziel people for once, instead of being stuck with sorcerers, tinkers, and twinborn all the time."

Anzik said nothing, but Jamile noticed a knit to his brow. He wasn't the statue-face everyone seemed to think; he just underdid it a little. A twitch of his lips could be a smile or a frown on most people, a single blink a look of perplexity.

"What's wrong? Don't tell me you *like* being cooped up alone all the time," said Jamile.

Anzik cocked his head a few degrees. *Blessed mercy, I told him not to tell me.*

Jamile stood straight and tall as she could, lessening the degree to which Anzik towered over her. "I'm giving you an assignment. Once you're done your business with Rynn, your mission is to get drunk. Extra marks if you talk to a pretty girl while you're there—not counting Rynn. I'll even give you some time after the meeting, if you need it."

Anzik's eyes shot wide. "You will *not* leave me there. I have important matters to attend."

Jamile clucked her tongue. "You stare at your own walls all day. If there's thinking to be done, let that twin of yours handle it, or try a little of it between drinks. A bit of ale in the head might give you a new perspective. Might also make things a bit easier with the girls."

"I have no interest in talking to girls in a tavern," Anzik said.

"What'll you do when you've got yourself a princess … what's her name again?"

"Anju."

"By the time she's old enough to marry you, she'll be right to expect *you're* the one who's got things figured out. And how you going to know how to woo a girl if you've never tried?"

"We are arranged," Anzik said, taking a pedantic tone. "Thus there will be no need for such speculative courtship as you recommend."

Jamile let out a long breath and looked to the cavern ceiling. "Not going to be any royal heirs with *that* attitude, arranged or otherwise."

"I think there may be a cultural gulf here," said Anzik.

"Oh, don't pull that twinborn nonsense on me," Jamile replied. "Girls are girls, same in Korr and Tellurak, and bless my boots if they aren't the same in Veydrus, too. But fine, I'll let you off the good-time trolley, if you promise me one thing."

Anzik angled his head to glance sidelong at her. "What promise?"

"Ask Kaia to dinner tonight," she replied.

"I had the impression that she was the object of Mr. Kupe's affections."

Jamile sniffed. "Her and anything else in a dress. Boy your age should be more like that, actually. It's healthy; proves all the glands are working. As a nurse, and as someone who spent years taking care of orphan boys younger and older than you, it's time you looked after those glands of yours."

"Are my garments satisfactory or aren't they?" Anzik asked. Jamile was shocked to notice a flush to his cheeks.

Jamile held her hands up in surrender. "You win. Go be Mr. Crafty Sorcerer and bargain for kingdoms and worlds. Just … if you happen to talk a barmaid into your lap, you'll feel a lot better."

"I'll take it under advisement," Anzik said in a deadpan.

Rynn slunk into the Hammer's Harm Tavern, careful to avoid any sudden movements that would cause her tinker's legs to make noise. The latest model was inconspicuous beneath baggy coveralls, with a tighter pair of trousers underneath to keep edges from showing through when she sat down. Her hair was tied up in a handkerchief to hide the fact that it was brushed and washed regularly. Spectacles would have made her stand out in a crowd of humans, so Rynn had left them on the world-ripper control console with Sosha. Before the rebellion, Rynn had gone without optics of any sort except when she was working. She had forgotten the hazy blur the world took on past a few paces when she didn't wear them. After months of never being without them, she had lost the habit of squinting to make out details, and noticed the strain every time she caught herself trying to read.

The Hammer's Harm was humans only, located on the eighth layer of Venterad Deep, one of the deepest cities in Korr. Aside from the odd knocker patrol or some poor slob with a business errand he couldn't pass off, there wasn't a kuduk within three layers of her. The standard work shift wouldn't be out for more than hour, so she had her pick of tables, taking one against the far wall, farthest from any other patrons.

"Ale me," Rynn called out. An aleman came by within seconds, whisking a one-tenar coin from the table and replacing it with a tankard and eight gorms in change. Rynn left the coins there to save the trouble of fishing in her pockets to pay for Anzik's drink.

She could have held the meeting almost anywhere. With the world-rippers, anyplace that wasn't overrun with hostiles was just a few twists of the dials away. Sosha had given her a strange look when Rynn picked this location, but had managed to keep her mouth shut about it. Give the girl credit; at least she learned. Time was, Jamile and Sosha used to yammer constantly whenever they were around her. When she was little, and working with her father in the workshop, the two of them could go hours without saying anything to one another, even sitting side by side at a workbench. Sosha just felt a need to fill quiet air with the sound of her own voice. She was like Kupe in a dress sometimes—an image that had Rynn chuckling to herself as she sat by herself at the table.

The ale was everything her crewmen had boasted of—rich, thick, with a bitter jolt that didn't linger between swallows. She still had yet to find any place in Korr that could make an ale to rival the better Acardian brews, but the Hammer's Harm made a good effort. She closed her eyes, and tried to imagine that she was still Chipmunk, drinking with her friends at the Tap'n'Chug. Of course, she could go there whenever she liked, but she could never be just Chipmunk again. No simple disguise would pass muster there, and her old gang were all on the *Jennai* now. All except Tabby. And Buckets. And of course, No-Boots. If Rynn wasn't careful, she'd end up as one of those maudlin drunkards who sat around mourning lost friends.

"Table's lookin' awful empty," said a man in a plain brown shirt and an equally plain smiling face. His neatly trimmed beard glistened with oil, and his teeth shone white amid the coarse black hair. Rynn glanced at his hands; they were slender and pink. He worked for humans, in some job that a kuduk would have if it were on another layer.

Rynn gave him a tight, forced smile. "Thanks, but no thanks. I'm waiting for someone."

He slid into the seat across from her anyway. "I'll keep a place warm for her," he said with that same smile.

Rynn pulled a pistol—the common black powder variety that seemed so quaint now—and laid it on the table between them. "It's a 'he' and I'll wait alone, thanks."

The man stumbled over his own shoes as he scrambled to his feet. "Eziel's eyes, girl! You one of those rebels or something?"

Rynn looked up at him wide-eyed and innocent, face impassive. She took a sip of her ale. "Naw, I just own a pistol." *And an airship with a cannon the size of a six-car thunderail.* "Now scoot. You're blocking my view of the door." *Scoot? When did I become Jamile? And so much for keeping a quiet corner to myself.*

No one else approached her as she waited, with the exception of the aleman who brought her a fresh tankard. She wasn't sure whether the aleman was the brave sort, just used to armed patrons, or counted on the fact that no drinker ever punched an aleman, let alone shot one.

Anzik's arrival was both a blessing and a curse. Rynn couldn't sit there all night letting the rebellion coast off in whatever direction she last pushed it, but she was enjoying the quiet and the drink. The Veydran sorcerer walked through the door like he had just entered a pipers' den, wary of touching anything or anyone as he threaded his way over to the table. Someone—it was hard not to see Jamile's hand at work—had dressed him in dreary brown trousers and a pullover shirt. If he was supposed to be a down-on-his-luck worker, like they had planned, Jamile ought to have had him stop shaving, or magic himself a beard to better fit in. Everyone in the tavern had either breasts or a beard except for Anzik. It wasn't a shavers' sort of establishment.

Rynn nodded to the seat across from her. With a furtive glance around the room, Anzik joined her. Without her spectacles on, it was hard to be sure, but she thought she saw a gap between his hand and the chair as it slid back far enough for him to sit. It could also have been the ale.

"This place is strange," he said, his voice low, speaking Kheshi. "Such weak Sources all around. Is this typical, or was this part of your reason for selecting this peculiar location?"

"I picked it for the ale," Rynn said, hoisting her tankard. She signaled for the aleman to bring one for Anzik. "Dunno about the rest. I can see aether when I need to, but I hardly bother most of the time."

"I sometimes wonder what that would be like, seeing light and aether separately."

Rynn paused, lowering the tankard as she was about to take a drink. "How's that?"

"It's not important. I have true business to conduct."

"Half what we get sound fair?" Rynn asked.

Anzik blinked. "Yes, actually. More than fair. I had expected a harder bargaining position on your part."

"We'll be piled with them before long," Rynn said. "Dragon's got a fertilizer factory for a tongue, but he's kept his deliveries going. We're keeping up arming new recruits; we've got more in the field now than aboard the *Jennai.* It's not going to hurt us to split the share even."

"Excellent news," said Anzik, sipping at his ale like a steam soup. "But I have another proposal to make."

"I'm listening."

"The Kadrin airships outmatch our own," said Anzik. "Can you build us Korrish ones?"

Rynn regarded him a moment over the rim of her tankard, ale sloshing against her lip. "You're serious."

"Yes."

"And what do I get if I can?" Rynn asked. "Not that I'm saying I can, mind you, because it's taking me months to get coil guns from a goblin workforce. I can't exactly steal you airships and shrink them to fit through a world-hole." She furrowed her brow. "Unless *you* can shrink them."

Anzik shook his head. "Too large. But what price would you want for them if you can?"

*I want you to translate 12 books into a language I can read.* It was tempting. Any sorcerer supposedly knew the language. A freak like Anzik would probably manage it in a day or two, not blinking the whole time. But the knowledge was more valuable than anything she could imagine. Anzik ought to pay *her* for the privilege, knowing that he'd learn the contents in the process. Plus … there was still something disquieting about him. His oddities disguised his character in a way Rynn couldn't begin to unravel. He worked with his pirate father in one world, and was running a war in another. Simple pragmatism might keep him to his agreements while he needed her, but the moment he had all that he needed, Rynn suspected he could turn on them.

"How about you figure a way so Madlin can get back through the world-ripper?" Rynn asked. "The rotted dragon figured some way to keep me from passing. You find a way to undo it, and I'll find a way to get you your airships."

Rynn slumped into the chair at her bedside and took up a pencil. The images were still fresh in her head, and she wanted to transfer them to paper before sleep took her. The pitcher of ale she had brought back with her from the Hammer's Harm had not been her best idea, nor had absentmindedly draining it as she sat alone studying Megrenn airships through a viewframe. They were just boats with runes, floating on the same aetherial buoyancy that kept the *Jennai* aloft. The key difference was that the Megrenn still relied on wind for both propulsion and steering.

Rynn's pencil flew across the page, scribbling a sailing vessel in a bird's nest of overlapping strokes. Next she sketched a liftwing airship, using the Gradlek P-103 as a guide. Chassis, cockpit, wings, wing-struts, propeller, tail, she added features as she remembered them, more to fix the images more firmly in Madlin's mind than for what value they had on paper.

Shoving that page aside, she drew another sailing vessel, this time from an overhead view. She took more care this time, trying to represent proper proportions. The masts and spars were the key, and when she finished drawing those, she sketched the liftwings attached to the spars. They were already built to take the force of the wind on the vessel and transfer it to the hull of the ship for propulsion. With the liftwings attached, they could ditch the sails and use propeller power. She continued on to draw front and side views, continuing to recall the dimension of the Megrenn sailing ships as best as her drowsy mind was able. *This looks ridiculous.* From the top the liftwings had looked odd, but plausible. From the front and side, they looked like oversized birds stuck up in a tree. The forces looked like they would align poorly as well; the liftwings would pitch the vessel forward without some other force to balance it. The Megrenns must have changed the cut of their sails to compensate. Doing the same with the liftwings sounded like too much trouble. Rynn crumpled the page and tried again.

The next attempt showed two liftwings attached to the sides of the vessel, each one missing a wing where it was bolted onto the hull. They could work out a center of mass for the ship and align the liftwings accordingly. The wing flaps would be on the small side to move something the size of a sailing ship, but they would work. Piloting the ship would be an act of coordinating two operators in the cockpits.

Rynn was sketching alternate views, checking for flaws in the plan, when there was a knock at the door.

"Come on in," she called out.

The door opened. "What did you need me for?" Vaulk asked.

Rynn pushed her pencil away and leaned back, cracking her stiff neck. "You were my father's agent in Acardia since before I was born."

"Well, Greuder was, but yes."

Rynn motioned for Vaulk to have a seat. "I need some of that local knowledge you've built up. Do you know a man named Harwick?"

"I know two, actually: father and son, lord and lordling. Why?"

"I need to get in touch with whichever of them is a one-worlded Veydran sorcerer," Rynn replied. She pointed to the shelf where she had stored the twelve books. "The one who returned my father's books said that Harwick could translate them. They're written in a Veydran language that sorcerers know."

"If Veydran sorcerers know it, why not just ask …" Vaulk slowed as Rynn offered him the best patronizing glare she could manage while drunk. "I see. No getting help from the boy. But what makes you think you can trust this Harwick fellow? I don't know that I'd be inclined to go to either of them for aid."

"She said he was a reformist, someone who would sympathize with Korr's humans."

"She? She who?"

"She said her name was Juliana."

Vaulk stopped, his eyes wide. Rynn couldn't even see him breathing. "Thin girl, taller than I am, swaggers like a coinblade?"

"You know her?" Rynn asked, blinking to try to wake herself fully. This was promising.

"Know her? Not well, but yes, I've met her. Blazes girl, she's married to Kyrus Hinterdale, a good friend of mine who's been gone for years. It's *him* you want helping us. If we can convince that one to help us, we won't need Anzik, or goblins, or any of the allies of convenience we might dredge up."

"Oh?"

"He's a sorcerer, lass. It was all rumor and speculation until I put the pieces together, but that Kyrus is responsible for the Marker's Point incident some years back."

"My father said it was black powder that was improperly mixed," Rynn said.

"Cadmus left it at that. It was his man's best guess at the time, but he didn't believe in magic outside of runes back then. I had a chat with Kyrus and his wife the day they dropped off the face of the world. He hammered everywhere but the nail, but he hinted that he had stumbled onto some big secret. It didn't take much to piece together that the two of them were both twinborn."

Rynn sighed. "So he's a sorcerer, she's a sorcerer. She told me that they couldn't help us directly, that giving the books back was just to make up for taking them in the first place. She's the one who recommended we see Harwick."

Greuder scratched at the back of his head. "That's all well and dandy, but the Harwicks and I … well, let's just say they're the ones who chased me out of Acardia."

Rynn squeezed her eyes shut and clenched her jaw. She might have guessed. Nothing was ever easy. Send a man to spy in Acardia for over twenty years, and the one name you needed was the one who ousted him. Rynn needed another pitcher of Hammer's Harm Stout.

"Fine," she murmured. "Can you remember my plan long enough to have Greuder tell my father? If you can't go see an Acardian lord, he can."

Cadmus Errol had been a warmonger for less than a year. Before that, for over twenty years, he had been known as the Mad Tinker, his reputation spreading from Tinker's Island to the southernmost reaches of Khesh. He had met kings, mayors, governors, councilors, prelates, generals, and more lords than he cared to count. Among the latter was a heavyset drunkard named Dunston Harwick. Greuder's mere mention of the man conjured an image of a conniving sneer, emanating from a pudgy face flushed with recent drink. He had met the man only casually, while he had been in Golis working on the installation of a clock tower, but the Acardian lord had left an impression.

The occasion called for a shave and a change into laundered clothes. That gleam in Harwick's eye made so much more sense now; it was the look of a man who knew something he wouldn't let on. Cadmus wasn't sure the impression he had made last time they saw each other, but if the man could read Kezudkan's books, it was worth the trouble to make a good re-impression.

"Anything amiss?" he asked, surveying himself in the mirror like a girl in her first ball gown.

Jamile tugged his collar, holding onto it as she looked first to one side of him, then the other. "You'll be fine. You've got a speck of grease on your left lens though."

Without hesitation, Cadmus pulled off his spectacles and wiped the lens on the front of his shirt.

"Well, there goes that now," said Jamile. "You've gone and wiped grease on your shirt. Here, let me get you another one."

Cadmus took hold of her arm, careful not to hurt her with his grip. "No time. It's small enough."

"No time? He's not even expecting you. And just a minute ago you were worried about impressions."

"There's no time because there's no time to waste. That bastard daruu and I tried for years to puzzle out the words in that book. All the right runes, arranged into gibberish. We tried every code we could think of, but we didn't need a code-breaker. We needed a translator. And now we've got one. Or we will, once I convince him."

"Your gears are freewheeling, tinker," said Jamile. "Put a brake on and slow it down."

"Working from rusted *pictures*, we built the most dangerous device known to Korr," said Cadmus. "The sooner we find out what's in the rest of it, the sooner we can end this war."

"What makes you think the rest will be weapons?" Jamile asked.

"I don't think the world-ripper was ever meant as a weapon. But drive a steam-shovel through a village of savages and it will be a good enough weapon. These books are so far beyond us; whatever wonders they contain will have power greater than Korr can sustain. And *this* time I won't be sharing those secrets with any daruu."

The world-hole opened in a vacant hallway of the Ministry of Law in Golis, capitol city of Acardia. Cadmus looked both ways just to be sure, then stepped through into Tellurak. As the world-hole closed behind him, he shrugged off his jacket. The building was warmer than he had expected. Despite some similarities of climate with Tinker's Island, the kingdom did experience a proper summer. Even in the evening hours, the air was thick to breathe. He broke out in a damp sweat within moments of his arrival.

There was not much to his plan. Dunston Harwick was King Gorden's chief jurist and one of his closest advisors. If Harwick was the sort of man who was that close to a king, he was the sort who lived his job at all hours of the clock. Cadmus walked the halls, wishing he had just scanned the building until he found Harwick, but caution had stayed his hand. The dratted dragon could see the viewframe, even when a hole wasn't open—some of the goblins as well—and it wouldn't have surprised Cadmus to find that Harwick was enough of a sorcerer to be put on his guard by one opening nearby. Once the Mad Tinker showed up at his door, he hoped that Harwick would be too preoccupied to notice. It was a risk he was willing to take, with it being his only option for escape.

If there was a trait he admired in the Acardians, it was in their fastidiousness. When he came to the top of a flight of stairs, there was a plaque listing all the offices on the floor, with directions to each. A separate plaque listed general categories of offices on other floors. There was no mention of a Harwick on his current floor, but the top floor had a listing for "Chief Magistrate."

Age had its advantages: experience, reputation, perspective. Cadmus had all these in greater abundance than when he was a young man. But as he tromped up two flights of stairs, he considered signaling for Jamile to open him a world-hole and save him the exertion. By the time he reached the top floor, his shirt stuck to his back and his brow was dripping; the heat had risen with each successive floor as well, due to some defect of ventilation. His only consolation was a plaque that told him which way led to the Chief Magistrate's office.

The halls were lit only by the moonlight from windows down one wall. As he made his way to Harwick's office, a glow of lamp light shone beneath a door here or there. A wash of light spilled into the hall from an open door just before the end of the hall.

"Excuse me, sir, but the Ministry offices are closed for the day," a woman called from the open-doored office. Cadmus had made no attempt to quiet his footsteps.

Cadmus glanced at the plaque outside the door, squinting in the moonlight: Elleigh Crownley, Chief Prosecutor. "I'm here to see Lord Dunston Harwick."

Lady Crownley looked Cadmus up and down. "I don't know who you are or how you got in here, but—"

"I'm Cadmus Errol," he said. It answered both questions, as far as he was concerned.

The woman blinked, donning a pair of spectacles that hung on a silver chain around her neck. She craned her neck toward him. "Of course you are. I can see why a man with Cadmus Errol's wealth and connections would skulk around the ministry offices after dark. Now get out of here this instant, before I must suffer the indignity of shouting for the guards."

Cadmus scratched at his face, even though there was no stubble to itch. "Do what you have to. Harwick can send them away," he said after a moment's reflection. He turned and headed to the end of the hall, and there was no shout of alarm from behind him.

As he raised his hand to knock, a voice from inside called out. "Just let yourself in. I'm not half as deaf as you'd expect of a man in my advanced years." Cadmus hesitated a moment and let himself in.

"You don't seem surprised to see me," Cadmus said by way of greeting.

"I try not to seem surprised by anything," Harwick replied. "It's bad for my image. Close the door and have a seat. Care for anything to drink?" He fussed over a side table cluttered with bottles before deciding on one and pouring himself a glass.

"Water?" Cadmus asked as he slid into a chair across from the Chief Magistrate. The man was everything he remembered, albeit older and less rotund. The office was decorated to convey gravitas, lined with walls of bookshelves filled with legal treatises and histories, with velvet upholstered chairs and old polished wood.

"Nasty stuff. Don't touch the swill myself," Harwick said, giving no indication he would provide any. "So what brings a dead tinker to my office in the dark of twilight?"

"Dead?"

"We got reports from crews that had been to Tinker's Island, found the place in ruins, empty, abandoned. You're presumed dead, my good man," said Harwick. He held up his glass. "Congratulations on defying your reputed death."

"We have business to discuss."

"Business?" Harwick asked with a smile. "Are you operating out of the back of a wagon? You *have* no business. Your business went belly up, tossed in the fire, scattered like dandelion fluff on the wind. What kind of business are you in any position to conduct?"

"I have need of a Veydran sorcerer," Cadmus said. Harwick's brow knit.

"A what, now?" Harwick asked, his eyes darting toward the door.

Cadmus leaned across the desk that separated them. "You are a one-worlded Kadrin sorcerer, and you're just the man for a job I have."

"I think you have mistaken me for someone," Harwick said, shaking his head.

Cadmus nodded. "I understand. Ears all over." He raised a finger in the air and waggled it. "Let's take this someplace private."

Behind his chair, a world-hole opened. Beyond lay the lunar headquarters of the Human Rebellion of Korr. The effect on Harwick was astonishing. A childlike grin broke out on his face. The old magistrate stood and put his hands on his desk, leaning to look past Cadmus as if he had ceased to exist. "Remarkable."

"Come on," said Cadmus. "We'll have you back soon enough. For now, come see what our business is going to be about."

Harwick followed Cadmus through the world-hole like a kid riding the thunderail for his first time. Years melted away from the old man's gait as he wandered along the banks of a river that started in one end of a room and ended in the other. The control console fascinated him. He looked back through the world-hole to his own office.

Cadmus put a finger to his lips lest Jamile say anything to spoil the moment. He was willing to let the one-worlder enjoy himself, if that meant he would be easier to deal with.

"Fine," Harwick said. "You have it out of me: I've worked a bit of magic in my day. But if you can manage *this*, what do you need me for?"

Cadmus nodded to Jamile, who returned the hole to just being an image. "If you'll join me in the kitchen, I can explain."

"I have so many questions," Harwick said. "I … I'm a man rarely at a loss for words, but I don't know where to begin."

"For a wordless man, you use a lot of them," Cadmus observed. "If you've got the time, I can answer a great heaping pile of questions, but I'll start with one you haven't asked. You've already figured out that I'm probably twinborn, but *this* isn't Veydrus or Tellurak."

Harwick's head snapped around; the statement was enough to drag his attention from his surroundings. "Then where *are* we?"

"Korr," said Cadmus. "It's a world with a rotted core, where humans are fighting for their lives and freedom."

Harwick's eyes narrowed. "Wait just a minute … you're raising an army. *You're* the one taking farmers from their fields, aren't you!"

Cadmus was taken aback. "What are you talking about?"

"For a week, I've been getting reports of farms ransacked. There are bodies left behind, but far more just vanish. You're conscripting!"

Cadmus held up a warning hand. Old as he was, Harwick was a large man, and a sorcerer as well. He didn't want to be the target of his ire. "I hadn't heard, but I can assure you, it wasn't our side."

"Your side?"

"The Human Rebellion. I'm fighting to save our people."

"Gut me, and choke me with my own entrails," said Harwick. "Your bloody war is spilling into my world, isn't it?"

"Yes," said Cadmus. "It would appear so."

"I still don't know where I fit into all this."

"You're going to help us win our war," Cadmus said. "Because from the sound of things, it's become your war now, too."

Harwick waved his arm around the cavern. "You can do all this, and you need my help? What can one dried up sorcerer do?"

"He can read the instruction manual."

# Chapter 7

*"Do not despair at finding yourself in an unfamiliar world. These simple steps will help you survive until help arrives."* –*Traveler's Companion: Basic Survival, Introduction*

The countryside spread out before Bvatrain, a blanket of green to warm the slumbering earth. The air had a different smell to it than he remembered, more fragrant, less wild. But it had been so long, it would have been stranger had things stayed as they were. He carried neither weapon nor pack. No beast carried him nor followed behind with his belongings. He simply strolled the land barefoot, following no road, enjoying the feel of sod and wild grasses between his toes.

Overhead, a pair of birds frolicked in the air, descendants of the avian creatures he once knew, striving for yet a new generation. Stretching out his arms, the birds took note and alighted, distracted from the mating chase. "Hello, old friends. I have returned."

The birds were simple creatures with no capacity to understand the demon's words. The magnetic draw that had summoned them petered away, and they resumed their courtship. Bvatrain stood and watched them for a time, smiling, before he took up his journey again. He had no destination. This place, all of it, was where he wanted to be. The natives called it Takalia, and the residents had taken good care of his old homeland.

Ancient feet, supple and strong as those of any infantryman or wandering minstrel, set their own path across the land. As night approached they carried Bvatrain to a settlement. Neither wall nor fortress protected it, which struck him as fanciful. What manner of people had his lost kinfolk become, that they did not fear armies or bandits any longer?

He paused in sight of a road, his keen eyes stronger than those that might spy him wading amid the wild grasses. The clothes he wore would never go unnoticed. His sash and pantaloons belonged in another age, and no other traveler bared his chest to the sun. After watching a dozen small groups entering the city, he clothed himself in similar style—colorful shirt, drab jacket and trousers. Bvatrain chose lavender for his shirt, a charcoal grey for his other attire. He conjured boots that lacked the telltale shine of a new purchase, letting them look worn from years on the road.

The city blended with the countryside, and Bvatrain could not quite tell at what point he entered its border. The farmhouses grew more frequent, the farms smaller. Roads converged, grew wider; the ruts of wagon wheels were replaced with packed dirt, then cobblestones. Stores and workplaces interspersed … that was probably the point at which it became a city, when the workplaces mixed with homes. The babble all around him was a language he had never heard, though a note here or there recalled dead tongues he spoke fluently. He could hear the emotion in the words, the brusque conduct of business, the casual greeting of acquaintances, the laughing calls of one child to another.

Smoke rose to the sky in a plume like a feather in the city's hat. It was summertime, and there was little need for fires besides cooking. Bvatrain followed the smoke, as many of the inhabitants seemed to be doing. People flowed likes streams into a river, the tributaries joining, seeking the sea together.

Music. There was music ahead. It was a festival, one whose origins no doubt held ancient roots that Bvatrain predated by ten thousand years. He grinned.

The smoke came from a bonfire in the central plaza of the town. Musicians filled the air with a jaunty melody, all fiddles and drums. Smaller fires scattered around the plaza cooked spitted meats, and barrels of spirituous drinks provided merriment to those who did not come by it naturally. Bvatrain wended his way through the crowd, greeting smile with smile, and answering words with a nod. A man with a crippled leg leaned against a table, and pressed an ashwood cup into Bvatrain's hand. The demon took it gladly in both hands, accepted it as a gift, and gave a shallow bow.

While mostly alcohol, Bvatrain smelled strawberry and vanilla, with a hint of potato lying beneath. He sipped it, savoring the gentle tingle on his lips and tongue, the scratching burn as he swallowed. Though as a demon he had reshaped his body over the countless centuries of his life, he could still allow the drink to take a semblance of hold over him.

A stout man clapped him on the back, leaving the hand there as he spoke. Bvatrain heard the words as gibberish, but chose instead to listen to the man's thoughts so that he might converse. "Don't recall seeing you around here before, friend. And I know people. It's my business."

"And what business might that be?" Bvatrain asked. Though his words were in a great-grandfather tongue to the one the modern Takalishman spoke, he lent the ideas to the man's mind directly.

The man took his hand from Bvatrain's back and offered it for shaking. "Ganshii dar Sullin, Mayor of Faijun, at your service."

Bvatrain knew the custom, which had once been a test of grips between warriors who met upon the road. He could have crushed every bone in the man's hand without effort, but gave a firm squeeze instead—enough to show respect, and earn it. "I am Bvatrain."

"What brings you to our midsummer festival, Bvatrain? Where you from? You don't mind me saying, I expect I wouldn't have missed a man like you living in the villages."

"The smoke summoned me," he said. "And I am from very close to here. I have spent my time abroad, gone places and seen things I would never have dreamed as a boy. But I thought it was time to come home and see some old friends."

"You have family around here?"

*You are probably a descendant of mine. A drop of blood in the ocean, but you must bear some trace, living here. I came to see the mountains, the only ones who would remember me, but you would not understand that.*

"Not any longer," Bvatrain said. "They have passed on. I had been gone so long, in fact, that I feared to come back."

"What's there to fear? You run from some sort of trouble?"

"No, nothing like that," Bvatrain replied. "My grandfather once told me that if you leave a place for long enough, it will have changed by the time you return. You will have changed while you were gone. Two pieces removed from one another, reshaped, cannot be fit together once again." He gestured with two hands to show ill-fitting pieces.

"And was your grandfather right?"

Bvatrain smiled. "Yes. And no. You see, the pieces can be shaped to fit again. They remember. Turn the piece on its side, and you may find that the old shape is still there, but you did not see it."

The mayor smiled and shook his head. "You're a philosopher then."

"I am a demon," Bvatrain said, but he let the mayor think that he had simply agreed.

Viyax had changed his form to match the surroundings. Instead of bronzed skin, he turned it a pasty grey, with just enough color to keep him from looking deathly ill. All around him he saw beards braided and plaited in fanciful styles. He did them all one better by weaving a beard of his own in the style of an ancient Garnevian tapestry. Curious eyes followed him wherever he went, and the gossip amused him to no end. The creatures spoke daruu, a language incapable of change, and Viyax spoke it like a native son. Languages were a hobby of his. When you needed to cross-reference two dead calendar systems with a modern one to determine your age, you tended to acquire a great many hobbies.

Another of his hobbies was instigation. Demons, as a general rule, were static creatures. Most of them hated change that moved faster than continental drift, but not Viyax. Living among them, he often found ways to prod them into action, to force them to be interesting, to trick them into providing him entertainment. He knew the questions to ask, the pranks to play, the topics to mention in passing to rile any of his fellow immortals. Torvarin would argue for days that mortals were a great experiment by the gods, left to run amok. Zi Yik Lai would be out of sorts for days if the wrong bee pollinated a flower in her garden. Illiardra kept a secret lust for mortal love to replace the life she never lived. When he grew bored—

which happened all too often—he simply chose a demon and teased forth some amusement.

The transport gates offered a whole new solution to his yearnings. No longer was he stranded in a single, stale old world. Korr had changed since his last visit, and he had never paid it much mind when it had been easily accessible. It had been there; that was the best he could have said for it. Now? Now it was a playground.

He fell in with a pack of kuduks—creatures whose existence was new to him—and followed along to see where they were going. They wore colorful shirts, more likely to be festival garb than any sort of uniform, but they were dressed similarly to one another, and far differently from the conservative clothes most of their kind wore. It held the promise that they were planning something fun.

Their destination was an underground amphitheater, surrounding a rectangle of flat ground, painted with lines and numbers. Someone at the door collected tickets from each of the kuduks in line, but let Viyax pass with a befuddled look. Hordes of kuduks funneled through the doors and filtered into seats, preferring the lowest sections, closest to the stage. The walls were hung with banners and signs of all manner, mostly touting the merits of commercial products. A different sort offered bold encouragement to a group known as the Cuminol Rockslide, with colors that matched those of his tagalong companions. He took a seat among them and hoped to blend in.

"So, excellent night for a performance of the Cuminol Rockslide, wouldn't you fellows say?" Viyax asked, smiling as he squeezed himself between two of them and put arms around their shoulders.

"Who's the leaking pipe?" one of his newfound companions asked the other, talking past him as if Viyax wasn't there.

"Dunno," said the other. "Pound screws, fella. These are our seats."

"Pardon me, but this is my first time attending such an event," Viyax replied, nonplussed. There was a certain bravery that came with the knowledge that he was speaking with the equivalent of precocious children. "Would you mind giving me the looks-around?" He had heard the term in passing from other kuduks in the tunnels and used it to sound native.

"Listen, pal," the first companion said. "I punched nine hours today grinding trolley wheels, and paid half a day's wage for my ticket. I don't see me flushing my night to explain crashball to a country yokel."

"Hey, where you from, anyway?" the second companion asked. "Ain't heard an accent like that before."

"That's because I speak properly, and don't torture the language until it howls in pain, as seems to be the local custom."

"Hey buddy," the second companion said, taking Viyax by the collar. "You spoilin' for a fight?"

"Spoiling," Viyax corrected him. "You're clipping the end. Takes practice, but it'll make you sound more intelligent."

Viyax ducked the punch that followed with a grace that belied the stocky form he wore. The lack of a solid destination for the blow left the kuduk who threw it even angrier, and within moments, Viyax parlayed that reckless abandon for satisfaction into a full-fledged brawl. Kuduks who had no quarrel a moment ago took umbrage to being jostled and shoved, having their drinks spilled, and generally being collateral damage in a conflict that didn't involve them. Viyax made sure that it came to involve them.

Strolling out of the amphitheater against a flow of peace officers with clubs in hand, Viyax whistled a tune meant to be played by a daruu bassoon. It was the first melody that sprang to mind. *War Among Brothers* was its title, and though it lacked lyrics, Viyax had always imagined that it described such a scene.

"Pardon me," Viyax said, catching a passing woman by the arm. "But where might I find the humans? I heard that there were humans around here."

"What do you want *humans* for?" the woman asked, aghast as she yanked her arm free. When Viyax just shrugged, she replied. "Get down two layers, and learn some manners."

Viyax frowned, regarding the woman as she backed away from him. *Killing them would be interfering. Of course, who's* really *paying attention? It's not like I'd be starting a war.* He decided that he did not much care for kuduks.

The royal palace of the Kheshi Empire looked much like Illiardra remembered. The whole empire was new as a fresh snowfall to her, but she had been off world far more recently than most of her fellow demons. The structure had worn with age, but in the graceful manner that hinted at great care and maintenance. Understandable, for the building was home to the rulers of a sizable chunk of Tellurak.

A courtyard dusted white with fresh-fallen flakes separated the palace from the road that encircled it like a moat. Despite the wintery weather in the southern hemisphere, she wore only a light dress, and let her barefoot feet feel the nip of cold with each step. Like the others who looked inhuman, she wore a guise more comforting to the eyes of local mortals. Her now-golden hair fell in ringlets, but her horns were gone and her ears shrunken until they hid beneath her curls. The skin of her face was pale as alabaster, a mark of purity to the insular Kheshis of the southernmost reaches of the empire. That much had not changed at all in her absence.

The guards at the gate were smitten with her. They stumbled over their own tongues before letting her pass without learning either her name or her purpose. She felt no guilt for bewitching their wits; she considered it a courtesy that she even allowed them to see her. The encounter with the enchanting stranger would be the talk of taverns for months, and the story would serve as fair repayment for their dereliction.

The guards at the palace door were the formal sort. They carried swords at their belts instead of the smoke-powder cannons carried by the soldiers at the gate, and their uniforms were starched until they could be used as cutting boards. Both were fine specimens of the old Kheshi bloodline, tall, broad-shouldered, square of jaw. Despite the fresh-shaven faces and a sniff of perfume to the air around them, they were the sort who had earned their positions by military prowess.

"State your business," the leftmost guard said.

Illiardra noticed his gaze drifting down her, and lifted it with a finger beneath his chin. "I am here to speak with your emperor."

The guard flinched away from her touch, which he seemed not to have minded until she spoke. "We have no emperor, who are you?"

"Empress?" Illiardra realized she might have done well to have researched the empire before visiting its ruler. It just seemed that she had the right to speak with whomever she chose.

"You should go."

Illiardra smiled, and the guard's stoic demeanor softened. "State your business." He was suddenly oblivious to having spoken to her just a moment before.

A harp appeared from nothingness, tucking itself beneath Illiardra's arm. "I am a musician, here to play at court."

"I'm terribly sorry, miss," the guard said. "You should enter through the servants' tunnels, around the north side of the palace. This is for official guests and dignitaries."

"Thank you so much," she replied. "If you would be so good as to escort me in?"

"Of course," the guard replied. His companion moved from a flanking position to a central one behind them, as if nothing was amiss. Illiardra could have been a princess or a warlord for all either of the guards cared at that moment. In truth, she was far greater than they could imagine. It was only fitting that she be treated accordingly, even if they didn't know better.

The halls had been redecorated since her last visit. She supposed that it had been over a hundred years since her last visit, so it stood to reason. Here or there she noted a painting or a vase that looked familiar, but everything had been repainted, reupholstered, and refurnished in the interim. The eyes of palace staff members were drawn to her; she had always had that effect on mortals, she found. They were just perceptive enough creatures to note that there was something extraordinary about her, but not enough that they could put words to how they knew, or what in particular caught in their minds.

The imperial audience chamber was so much like the one in Kadris, seat of the Kadrin Empire of Veydrus, she knew that some architect in bygone days had been twinborn. There was no other explanation for the similarities in style and adornment. The vaulted ceiling, the placement of the support pillars, even the number and width of steps up to the dais upon which the throne sat, all were identical.

Illiardra slipped away from her befuddled escort, and allowed him to return to his duties with a hazy recollection of having performed some needed task. With no introduction, she started to play her harp. There had been no plan in her mind when she had conjured it, but now that she had the instrument in her hands, she felt the need to sing.

"Who are you, and—" a royal advisor of some sort managed to spew before his jaw went slack, and his eyes glazed over. Illiardra was kalanoi by birth, a spirit of the forests, fey and magical by nature. Her words held the court in thrall. The song told the Kheshis of their own ancestors, of times long past and heroes and villains whose legends had faded into myth before being forgotten entirely by mortals.

That evening would prove to be one that none of the court could recall. They would remember the songs, and the emotions they stirred, taking with them a feeling of being a part of something greater. It was a legacy that they deserved, to know who they are by who they had been. Her stories told of strange creatures that had once shared the world with humans, and over whom humanity had failed.

There was one name that she made sure she left them. Neither subtle hint nor vague allusion would hide the name of Tallax from them—the man who had won Tellurak for humanity, and left the world to search out others. His was a myth while he was still a man, and an unbelievable fiction since his passing. Illiardra knew Tallax, and this fact of knowing she instilled in the Kheshis.

"This place makes Korr look primitive," Juliana whispered as she leaned across the table. She sat across from Kyrus, each with a cup of steaming coffee and a plate of pastries in front of them. The seats of their booth were covered in a shining red material that was neither leather nor fabric. The table had a painted pattern trapped beneath a layer of some clear substance that wasn't glass. In fact, nearly everything seemed not to be made of what it first appeared to be. The restaurant around them was packed with people, many of them vying for spots near the window that took up an entire wall. From their booth, the two of them could see the efficient core of government workers, fighting back a tide of chaos. Red and blue lights flashed atop self-propelled metal carriages, disgorging more uniformed officers to keep the crowds at bay.

Their arrival had garnered some attention.

"Hey, how was I supposed to know they'd have machines that could detect a transference spell?" Kyrus asked. "At least they can't seem to use them to find *us*. If they could, they'd be in here already, instead of sending people into the lobby of that massive inn."

The buildings were something that Kyrus could just not get over. The Tower of Contemplation in Kadris had been eleven stories tall. The inn they had arrived at was thirty-five stories, and there were buildings in every direction that dwarfed it. Not only that, but it seemed to be built entirely of metal and glass, without even the simplest of magics for protection. There was nothing but clever architecture holding it up, which he couldn't say for the Tower of Contemplation.

A woman in an apron stopped by their table, carrying a glass carafe filled with coffee. She babbled a question in the local language, and Kyrus answered her with nonsensical noises. She never heard a word of it, assuming he had just confirmed that he did indeed want his cup refilled.

"I had hoped they'd speak arcane at least," Kyrus said as the woman left.

"Well, maybe some do, but I'd stick to Kadrin until we decide who to talk to," Juliana replied.

Kyrus chuckled. "You actually sound worried. What are they going to do to us? Lock us up as madmen? I'd like to see them try."

"I wouldn't," Juliana replied. "This place would seem a whole lot safer if half the truncheons in the world hadn't just shown up to figure out what happened when we arrived."

"I get the feeling that this city could take in the population of Kadris and just call it a festival day. Look at the size of everything. And are you looking at the skies? I've seen three airships go by flying faster than a pistol shot, and twice the size of anything Korr ever put aloft."

"All the more reason to be careful."

Kyrus waved her worries aside and took a sip of his coffee. It was a strange flavor, but not a bad one. He was willing to have a try at developing a taste for it. "I think it's a people like this that wrote those books. Rudimentary understanding of magic at best. They can tap into the aether, but they use machines to do it. I don't think they can hurt us."

"I'm counting on you, Mr. I'm-Not-Tallax. If these people turn against us, you're dealing with them."

"I haven't figured a way to tell for certain, but I'm guessing that you've got a stronger Source bottled up inside you than all but a few of those demons in Podawei Wood. You'll be fine."

Juliana pursed her lips. "You sure about that?"

"Nope," Kyrus replied with a grin. "But we won't let that keep us from enjoying ourselves here for a few days."

"A few days?" Juliana asked. "After the trip we just took to get here?"

"Hey, it was me doing the hard part finding our way. And yes, for now just a short visit. Until the war of three worlds is ended, I need to make sure none of the others do too much harm."

"What do you think they're up to?" Juliana took a sip of her coffee.

Kyrus shrugged and reached for a cinnamon pastry. "Most of them are probably sitting around that far-seeing pond, watching like it's a theater show. A few of the brave ones might be sneaking around in mortal form, trying not to reveal themselves."

# Chapter 8

*"If you find yourself in a world with class five technology or better, just find paid lodgings." –Traveler's Companion: Finding or Building Shelter*

Harwick's manor home was tucked away behind evergreen shrubs and a wrought iron fence with stone pillars. For a man of his prominence it was quaint, not even a quarter the size of the Errol home on Tinker's Island. The gate stood closed, manned by a pair of sleepy guards keeping one another awake with idle chatter. They defended a well-liked and respected man of modest outward means, a public servant who held a reputation as a man who looked out for the people. Their job was mostly for form's sake.

On that night, they had no way of knowing that they allowed an intruder past them without the faintest hope of stopping her. Had Rynn stopped by the gate, a brief exchange would have resulted in her being allowed entry, but she was a busy woman, and even a brief exchange was more time than she was willing to fritter away. She had scanned the whole structure before departing. There was a guest bedroom and two smaller, lived-in rooms that appeared to be servants' quarters, but that night all were vacant. The only one at home was Dunston Harwick, expert translator of Veydran texts. He sat by a cold fireplace, a glass of dark liquor in his hand. He didn't perk up at the presence of the viewframe until it opened.

"Hello there," Harwick greeted her, raising his glass. "You must be Madlin Errol. Haven't seen you since … oh you were probably seven or eight years old, tagging along after your father at the clock tower."

"You must be Dunston Harwick, the man who's going to tell me what these books say," Rynn replied. She saw no reason to get into the nitpicking details of her identity. The man had been twinborn, and was likely one of the ones who conflated twins.

"So what's that place?" he asked, gesturing with his half-full glass. "Doesn't look like where your father took me last night."

"We keep our operation dispersed. Our enemies have the same devices, and if they discover the location of one, it's as good as wiped out. We can't keep all our key personnel together. That's my airship through there." She turned to the world-hole. "It's all clear. Come on through."

Sosha stepped into view, arms piled with books. "This is my friend Sosha," Rynn said as Sosha set the stack of books down on a decorative table, gently shoving aside a vase.

"Charmed," Harwick said, leaning forward to bow in lieu of standing. He narrowed one eye at her. "Takalish … maybe a bit of Kheshi blood."

Sosha shrank back. "How could you tell?"

Harwick shrugged. "Simple observation, applies to years of experience. Your skin isn't dark enough for you to be pureblooded Takalish. Cheekbones were my best guess at the Kheshi in you. Now, how about we have a look at those books?"

Rynn took the first book from the pile and handed it to Harwick, who held it at arm's length until he fished a pair of spectacles from his vest pocket. "What's the title?" she asked.

Harwick chuckled. "Is this a jest? It says *Traveler's Companion – Basic Survival.* Is this what Cadmus Errol thinks will win him a war?"

"Try another," Rynn said, picking the next book from the stack.

"*Traveler's Companion*—I suspect it is the name of the series—*Finding or Building Shelter.*"

"Wait, this one I know is important." Rynn dug through the pile and handed Harwick the book that had given birth to the world-rippers.

"*Transport Gate,*" said Harwick. "Now that one sounds a little more promising."

"It ought to," Rynn replied. "That's what we used to cobble the world-rippers together."

Harwick leafed through the pages. "I may have judged prematurely. Maybe those first two books are rubbish, but this one … they're written as if they expect a traveler between worlds to end up stranded. This one is to try to find a way off-world. It advises that it may not be possible with local resources—top marks to your father, then—but that the machine it describes ought to get you back to your own world—which presumably is neither yours nor mine."

"Presumably. Point being though, you can read this."

Harwick flourished a languid hand. "As if it were Acardian. But I find it strange it you had to go to such troubles to find someone who could read arcane text. Any Academy student could manage it."

"Let's just say that you came recommended, and we've had worries about who to trust with it," Rynn replied.

"Oh?" Harwick asked. "Who sent you my way? I've been dreadfully out of touch since my network of twinborn was dashed against the rocks. I'd almost managed to convince myself that Veydrus was some vivid dream."

"She said her name was Juliana," Rynn replied. "I assume you know her."

"Know her? She was married off to my nephew. Clever girl, not much of a lady, but willing to roll up her sleeves and put a blade in someone. She was a coinblade on this side. Temper like a volcano. So yes, I know her."

"Well, she's the one who said you could help us," Rynn replied. "I'm sure you're still willing."

"Hah! If Juliana is still around and watching me like a vulture, I'd *best* help you … if I know what's good for me," Harwick said. "I used to have some leverage with her in Kadrin, me being part of the Inner Circle and all, but now I'm just an old, old sorcerer, too feeble to be putting myself between her and what she wants. Have you, perhaps, heard anything about Kyrus?"

"Who's Kyrus?"

Harwick shrugged. "No relation in this world, but his twin was another nephew of mine in Veydrus. Might have liked to know how the boy was doing. If Juliana was around, I suspected he might be as well."

"Juliana mentioned a husband."

Harwick sniffed. "Figures. The two of them weren't likely to part short of death."

"How long is it going to take you to translate these?" Sosha asked. "It looks like an awful lot of work."

"Oh, a few days, I imagine. I fully intend to cheat."

"Cheat?" Rynn asked.

Harwick lifted a finger and beckoned. Another book from the pile rose of its own accord and drifted into Harwick's waiting hand. "It's one of the benefits of sorcery."

Madlin sat at the desk of her goblin-run prison, scribbling humdrum Korrish conveniences across a sheet of shoddy vellum. She had started them with basic tool-making, which would make subsequent work easier. Ratchets, wood screws, hand-cranked drills, and toggle pliers all scattered about the surface on their own sheets. Her current page contained her best recollection of Jamile's surgical tools; it seemed like years since she had drawn those for her machinists to fabricate, but the shapes and functions came easily from hand to paper with little thought.

In the privacy of her own head, Madlin worked out more complex details. Rynn had made a promise, and Madlin had the time to keep it properly. In her head she altered the concept to use a modified Yokker A-179 liftwing to suit Anzik's needs. It was a dual-wing design, and the upper and lower wing attachment points would give the hull the stability it needed to bolt to the side of one of the primitive Megrenn sailing ships. It would take two of them at a minimum to get an airship moving under the power of the little liftwings, and the speed would be nothing like what the Yokker A-179 could manage on its own, but it could outrun the wind. That was something that the Megrenn airships couldn't do except for short bursts aided by magic.

The best part about using the Yokker A-179 was that they were no longer seen as fit for military use. The design was a failed attempt to build an armored liftwing. They were bulky and sluggish to turn, and the guns they carried had to be lightweight to compensate. It had never been good enough for Ruttania or Grangia to have a bunch of airborne bricks plinking shots off one another's hulls. Ever since the introduction of the Yokker D-19, the A-179s had been relegated to civilian uses, where sturdiness and reliability were valued over the ability to take armaments aloft. For Madlin's purposes, civilians were easier to rob.

Rynn had her hands full, so Madlin was glad to have found a raw ship hull that was easily obtained. Someone else could plan the raid to boost a few. Hayfield could handle something so straightforward. The former crashballer would just need a few soldiers for crowd control as the civilian aerodrome staff scattered. The rest of the squad could be mechanics, disassembling the wings to fit the lift-wings through a world-hole. After the disaster of their only prior liftwing heist, Madlin had resolved not to try to fly stolen airships to the *Jennai*; there was simply too much risk involved. One day, she would work out the parameters for upscaled viewframes, and bring liftwings through intact. In the meantime, the heist might be a perfect opportunity to get a certain someone a bit of practical experience with little risk.

*Kupe, you can finally get on a heist that's more than just filling up the larders.* Madlin chuckled, drawing the attention of both her guards. One chittered to the other in their own language, and jerked on her chain. Her mood soured in an instant, and she had to fight back the urge to yank the offending guard from his feet. Of course, the other could still use the chain to shock her, and no one would be happy in the end. She sighed and turned her attention back to the page, trying to ignore the two goblins.

For the most part, ignoring them had been easy. While the shifts changed, she seemed to get the same pairings each day, and the novelty had worn off for everyone involved. Of the current pair, the heavier of the two always brought a book, and spent most of his time reading. The other was a woman who dragged over a stool and perched to watch Madlin's work like she was a Kheshi street artist.

Madlin whiled away the hours, refining her design iteration by iteration. She lit the discarded pages aflame, using Dan's trick of heating objects with aether. It was good practice, as well as cathartic. Getting something hot enough to light on fire took effort, but it only took a tiny corner to catch for the fire to spread across a whole page. For all the guarding they were supposedly doing, none of her guards seemed to think anything of the burning. A lit paper drew less interest than a sneeze, an event which had her guards diving for cover, and had gotten her shocked more than once.

With a satisfactory design in hand, she had a new dilemma: how to get the drawings to Rynn. While her twin could remember doing everything as if she had done it herself, there were measurements and calculations scrawled across the vellum that she would never remember fully. Reproducing it seemed like a waste of Rynn's time. She turned to her guards for help.

"Kookaroot?" she asked.

The goblins looked at one another. One spoke, the other shrugged.

Madlin seethed a breath through clenched teeth and tried again. "K'k'rt."

A brief conversation ensued. The book-reading guard knocked at the door and spoke through it. When it opened, he said something to one of the priests stationed outside. Madlin strained her ears to pick apart the chaotic language, and thought she heard K'k'rt's name repeated. Madlin checked her pocketclock. It was still set to Lunar Standard Time, the joking demarcation that Cadmus had chosen for their timekeeping, but it was accurate to the second.

Two hours, thirty seven minutes, and eleven seconds later, the goblin tinker was shown in to see her. "What took you so long?" she asked, crossing her arms.

K'k'rt chuckled. "You know what trouble you cause with these little requests of yours?"

Madlin shrugged.

"I've been escorted here by five of Fr'n'ta'gur's personal guard, told that you urgently need my assistance. No one else would do," K'k'rt said. He shooed the female guard off her stool and took her place. "What did you tell them?"

"Sorry, but they don't speak Korrish. I just said your name."

"You just said my name, and they went to all that trouble to bring me?"

"Well," Madlin admitted, "I did have to repeat myself so they could understand me."

K'k'rt squeezed his eyes shut and rubbed at his temples. "She repeated herself, she says. Sorry, she says. They must have understood you the first time, because by repeating yourself, you made it clear that you would do nothing until I came to see you."

"No I didn't."

"Yes," said K'k'rt, "You did. You as much as told them you wanted nothing but me. Otherwise, you would have said something other than just repeating my name."

"But I don't know more than five words of your language, plus whatever I accidentally say coughing."

"Well, those sticks have burned," K'k'rt said with a resigned sigh. "What do you need me for?"

"I need you to deliver something for me," Madlin said. When K'k'rt's eyes widened, Madlin quickly continued. "Nothing difficult, just slip it into a crate with the next shipment of coil guns." She folded the sheets with her airship modifications and pressed them into K'k'rt's hand.

"I can't—"

"If you want out with me when this is all over, you're going to need to help me out."

K'k'rt glared at her, but slid the drawings inside his coat. "There may not be an 'over' for you, you know. Your chance was when he let you go home. You are stuck here now, and have to learn to accept that."

"I only came back because I had a plan," Madlin replied.

"I will certainly not deliver whatever this is," K'k'rt said, patting his coat. There was crinkle of paper beneath it. "I must decide whether to show it to Fr'n'ta'gur, or simply burn it. Good day, tinker."

"You little—" Madlin dove for him as she cursed, but the guards were too quick. Madlin hit the ground, her muscles spasming uncontrollably. The pain of the spark jolt was nothing compared to the pain of betrayal.

"Let this be a lesson," K'k'rt said, wagging a finger as he stood above her. "No more talk of escape, or plans, or deliveries. You belong to Fr'n'ta'gur now."

He rapped at the door and the priests let him out. Madlin couldn't work the rest of the day, and fell asleep that night imagining painful ways to repay the goblin tinker for his treachery.

Rynn stood by as workers opened the latest goblin shipment with pry bars. The nails squeaked as they fought back against being removed. It was a hopeless battle; they were doomed to lose to the pry bar, but they gave everything they had in the resistance. The nails were good soldiers. Rynn had always imagined the rebellion as a similar battle, back when she had gone by the name Chipmunk. Chipmunk's world was simpler, filled with friends and foes, and she always knew which were which. It didn't matter if she and her friends were the nails; they fought because it was the right thing to do.

Now, Rynn struggled with foes becoming allies, and allies betraying her. The Human Rebellion had grown so large that it attracted the sorts who liked the *idea* of a rebellion more than the actions that were involved in rebelling. Rusted nails, ready to snap at the first blow. Davlin and Rascal helped in their own way, but it had been Rynn's rebellion; the ultimate responsibility lay with her. Every lax soldier felt like a judgment on her leadership. Cadmus questioned her choice of allies. Maybe he was right. Aside from the trickle of much-needed coil guns, her bargain with Fr'n'ta'gur had been a disaster. K'k'rt's betrayal didn't hurt her chances of escape, but it could hurt her relations with the Megrenn.

"General, there's something in this one," one of the workers called out to her.

Rynn walked over to where the last crate was being unpacked. The worker who called her over stood and scrambled out of her way, pointing into the crate. Rynn leaned down and pulled out a familiar packet of folded pages. Her heart raced.

Unfolding the vellum sheets, she scanned them to make sure someone hadn't played a cruel joke on her. But there they were: her drawings for the Megrenn airship modifications. At the bottom was a note, scratched into the page without even using ink or pencil. Rynn had to angle it in the light to read it.

*Sorry.*

Rynn smiled. Madlin hadn't been wrong after all. "That little bastard did it."

Hurrying to the door out to the plaza, Rynn stuck her head out and shouted. "Someone find me Hayfield. I've got a job for him."

# Chapter 9

*"Most non-sentient animals are afraid of fire. Use it liberally if threatened."*
*–Traveler's Companion: Dealing With Wildlife*

"War makes the world make sense," Danilaesis said. "We know who our enemies are. We know our job is to kill them." His men lounged in bunks and leaned against the walls as the warlock held court in the hold of the *Sudden Blade*, the latest airship he had taken as his own. He took a swig of wine and passed the bottle to his first mate. "Men like us, we don't belong in peacetime; we're just swords rusting on the wall. This? This is living." He held out his arms.

There were murmurs of agreement, but he was used to that following anything he said to a group. Danilaesis was no fool. He talked because he enjoyed thinking out loud, and they listened because he was in charge. It didn't matter whether they agreed or not; most of them would probably have been happy sailing on the seas, hauling bales of hay or whatever worthless cargoes sailors shipped. He might convince some with his words and some with the wine but most would keep their counsel and agree for form's sake.

Wars were fought by two sorts of soldiers, motivated by either duty or obligation. Danilaesis took his duties seriously, and would not dream of pretending he didn't enjoy performing them. Most of the sailors of the *Sudden Blade* were obligated; they served because someone was forcing their hand. As much as anything, Danilaesis needed to weed out which were which, because when things went badly, the obligated ones were the ones who faltered, the ones who surrendered, the ones who retreated with no order given. And if they were not fools, this crew knew that they were doomed men.

Danilaesis had never cowered from battle, and he was commanding his eighth vessel because of that fact. Only his first command, as a child during the last war, had ended with the return of a mostly intact crew. He had used his next six airships until they broke. Serving him, the sailors of the *Sudden Blade* could expect a good death, and soon.

The ship lurched, causing the wine in Danilaesis's stomach to slosh. They were banking; something had happened. Danilaesis rushed for the stairs to the main deck only to run into a sailor headed down. "Warlock, a ship!"

Danilaesis turned to the sailors in the hold. "Time to work, men." He bolted up the stairs two at a time, despite the ship's angle and the force of their turn.

On the deck, Danilaesis headed straight for the helm. "What do you see?"

"Megrenn bird, doesn't look like it's spotted us," the helmsman replied. He pointed to the horizon, where a fleck in the sky drifted across their path.

"Good work," he said with a nod to the helmsman. Raising his voice, he called out to his crew. "All right men, two days' shore leave when we down that ship."

The *Sudden Blade* leveled out, cutting through the sky on an intercept course. The clouds were sparse, the sun still on the rise, and no mountains or hills below for the Megrenn ship to lose themselves behind. There was little chance of their escape. Danilaesis summoned a stronger wind, and the sails strained at their rigging. Wood creaked as the ship sped forward.

Danilaesis hungered for the day when the Megrenn Alliance would be stripped of its defenses, its stronghold in Ghelk exposed. He would relish killing Anzik Fehr. In the meantime, he would feast upon their fleet of weakling airships, poor copies of the ones Kadrin built. There would be a new trick this time—there always was—but he looked forward to seeing how they would test him.

Taking up his preferred perch at the prow of the ship, Danilaesis watched the Megrenn airship grow in the distance. Their lookout had sharper eyes than he did, for initially it had looked like nothing but a speck, easily mistaken for a bird. But it was a ship, sails and everything. It had spotted the *Sudden Blade*, and was turning … towards them.

Danilaesis frowned. While the Megrenn had prepared traps for him before, they had always been more trap-like, more about trickery than confrontation. A second ship hidden in the clouds, siege engines stationed along a planned route of escape, something clever to balance the fact that Danilaesis was more powerful than any sorcerer they could find to oppose him. This was the first ship to have turned to fight head on at even odds. *Maybe their spies have lost track of which ship is mine.* It was certainly a yeoman's task to follow the trail of mangled wrecks that he had left in his wake, both friendly and enemy. *Could it be that Anzik has decided to come face me?* He grinned at the thought, but could not sustain it. *No, he would never, even if he thought he might win. He'll trick and trap and hide and run until he manages to kill me or I find him first.*

The Megrenn weren't stupid. It was a thought that Rashan had forced between Danilaesis's ears. You could not underestimate an opponent; nor could you overestimate them. You needed to know them, understand them, and react to them. Megrenn wouldn't have been attacking head on if they thought it was suicidal.

"Pull up," Danilaesis ordered. "Climb above them."

"But warlock," the captain replied. "We won't be able to attack them. They'll be below the catapults and ballistae's reach."

"They're up to something. They know better than this. Forget the ship's weapons, I'll handle this one." Downing an airship by magic alone was daunting, but Danilaesis had the aether for it. He drew yet more, until he was ready to burst at the joints from the burning pressure within him.

The *Sudden Blade* rose, its runes of levitation flaring bright. Danilaesis clung tighter to the rigging to maintain his perch as the bowsprit pushed against the soles of his feet, threatening to overbalance him. The Megrenn airship continued its approach, veering to the left to bring it on a course to go directly beneath them.

*What are they thinking?* Neither ship would be able to bring any of the standard weapons to bear. That left combat between the ships' sorcerers, and whatever bows the crew had—bows that could do little to sink an airship from the sky. A contest of sorcery favored Kadrin nine times in ten, and Danilaesis was certainly not the tenth. *This isn't right. A new weapon? A better sorcerer?* The tangled puzzle was approaching the *Sudden Blade* faster than Danilaesis could unravel it. He needed a decision.

"Dive!" he ordered.

"What?" the captain shouted in reply.

"Ram them! That's an order." Whatever plan the Megrenn had concocted, he could sift it from the wreckage. If the hostile ship's sorcerer survived, Danilaesis could deal with him on the ground.

The ship continued on course.

"I am ordering you to ram them!" Soldiers were meant to die, and sailors were just soldiers on a boat. Blast them all to ruin if they wouldn't follow orders. Danilaesis leapt to the deck, ready to wrest the ship's wheel and steer it himself.

A crack of wood made Danilaesis pause, mind racing. He wasn't watching the aether, but he ought to have felt a magical attack strong enough to damage the ship. Another crack and he began to worry. He ran back to the bowsprit to see for himself what the Megrenn ship was up to. That was when he noticed them. Cobbled onto the sides of the ship was a pair of liftwing hulls, just the bodies of the vessels with the propellers sticking out the front, blurred to translucent discs. The Megrenn were speeding up now that their trick had been revealed.

The liftwing engines proved not to be their only tricks. Cracks started coming more quickly. Danilaesis squinted down at the onrushing vessel as it prepared to pass below them. He was thrown to the deck. Something had struck him in the chest like a sword blow. Blinking to clear his head, he found himself staring up at the sails, struggling to draw breath. The shielding spell that was his constant companion had just saved his life, and it was reduced to a flicker in the process. He drew more aether, but did not use it to renew his shield. He had to do something about that ship.

He crawled to the gunwales and peeked over the edge. The ship had gone, passed beneath them in a hail of what Dan now realized was coil gun fire. It was Madlin's doing, all of it. He hadn't been certain, when Anzik Fehr had killed Dan, whether Madlin was complicit or had been duped by the Megrenn weasel just as he had. The presence of new Korrish improvements to a Megrenn airship was all the proof he needed to add another name to his list for vengeance. It didn't matter that she was on a world he had no way to access; that was a detail for another time. That was a detail for if he survived his present predicament.

Breathing pained him with each inhalation, but Danilaesis stumbled across the deck to the stern. “Cut sail,” he ordered through gritted teeth. Shouting hurt worse than trying to breathe deeply. Fortunately he did not have to waste breath arguing, for the captain and crew found this order better to their liking than they had of the order to ram.

The Megrenn vessel was looping around, ready to make a second pass. Danilaesis crouched low, lest he take another coil-gun blast, and waited. He drew more and more aether, until the pain of it blotted the cracked ribs from his mind. For all the time he had spent among the Korrish, he knew little of how their machines worked. One of the minor points he had picked up on was the fact that machines running on spark *hated* getting too much of it.

He didn’t let the Megrenn ship approach too closely. He didn’t dare. After the pounding the ship had taken on the first pass, he didn’t want to weather another. Lightning flew from Danilaesis’s outstretched hand, slamming into the port side propeller. Crackling arcs spread to the surrounding hull; they lasted a fraction of a second, but that was long enough to set fire to the side of the Megrenn ship.

“Full sail,” Danilaesis ordered as the Megrenn ship twisted in the air, its remaining propeller pushing into a spin.

Danilaesis slumped against the ship’s railing as they got under way, retreating from the Megrenn and their new coil guns. “I’m going to kill her,” he muttered.

# Chapter 10

*"I cannot stress this enough. Do not attempt gene splicing or implantable prosthetics without proper facilities." –Traveler's Companion: Improvised Medicine*

Draksgollow felt out of place. There were so many eyes on him, eyes that didn't look to him as customer, employer, or owner. The assembly hall in Kupak Deep was packed with kuduk faces, showing mixtures of curiosity, disgust, and hope. Most of the time Draksgollow was able to brush aside the gaping looks he drew for the mechanical parts that had rebuilt his maimed body, but for the first time in as long as he could remember, he felt self-conscious. Maybe it was the suit he had worn for the occasion, its collar over-starched, its cut too close and restrictive. Maybe it was the fact that in this hall—at least nominally—he was not in charge. But more likely the cause of his unease was the fact that he needed the support of these people, and they found him freakish.

Few kuduks had ever been rebuilt the way Draksgollow had. The method was buried in moldering old books, and the practice undertaken by only the least ethical of physicians. Most of the ones who had metal grafted to their bones, their muscles, and their nerves were never quite right afterward. Some lurched around on tinkers' legs like broken clockwork toys. Others tore the limbs from their bodies in fits of madness, unable to accept that they were part *thing* and no longer just creatures of flesh and blood. Draksgollow had no troubles with his. It had taken getting used to, months in fact, but he was a tinker to his core. From taking lunches in the workshop, he imagined he had ingested more bits of steel and iron over his lifetime than most humans ate of real meat (excepting rats and other vermin). He was rebuilt in the manner he had wished—better in some ways, worse in others, but never so pathetic as the creature he would have been without.

Two of his men sat beside him at the witness table. Kep to his left, mostly for his steadfastness. General Bradet to his right, mostly because he looked respectable in a uniform. Both had been instructed to keep their rusting traps shut unless Draksgollow indicated otherwise. This was his show, his pitch, his chance to drive a spike into the stone of Korr and anchor himself there for posterity.

"Please rise," the bailiff said. Draksgollow waited until most of the room had stood before he followed suit. The councilors filed in and took their seats at the head of the chamber. They all looked in his direction, and he made a point of meeting the eye of every one of them. "This special hearing of the Kupak Deep Civic Council is now in session."

Councilor Gerkie Steelsmith rose from the seat she had just taken. "This hearing will determine our response to the recent human violence, and the appalling actions of the so-called Human Rebellion. We have two special guests today, Professor Ilvark Hargrick, senior lecturer of human history at Graines and Meddows University; and Mr. Ganrin Draksgollow, head tinker and owner of Draksgollow Metalworks in Cavinstraw Deep. Gentlemen, thank you for joining us this morning.

"For as long as we have kept humans among us, there has been violence. The mere fact that every slave-owning business is forced to employ overseers to keep their humans in line is a testament to that fact. Left to their own ends, humans will prey upon the weakest segment of our population, wresting what little the poor possess for their own greedy ends. But always has this violence been kept in check. The officers of Judicial Enforcement put the troublemakers in their places and excise the worst elements from among the humans. Even the occasional revolt has been dealt with swiftly and resolutely. Now … now we are faced with a graver threat. The humans have organized on a scale we have never seen. They are rioting all across Korr, and in greater numbers in any city than we have ever seen. Even slaves certified as docile have turned on their owners, betraying them after years of care and gentle treatment. Today, we will debate how best to put an end to this human problem. And though we may only speak for Kupak, we have a third guest whom I would like to introduce: Mr. Calamson Goldore, special liaison to the Ruttanian Central Defense Ministry. He will take word of today's resolution back to the Central Council, and they will take our actions under consideration for wider application."

Councilor Steelsmith took her seat and a well-earned glass of water.

A second councilor rose. "Professor Hargrick, if you would state your proposal for the council."

Professor Hargrick stood and teased out the end of his beard, worn unbound in academic fashion. "Esteemed councilors, I thank you for allowing me to appear here before you today. We have the great privilege, responsibility, and misfortune of standing at a crossing in history. Down one tunnel lies destruction and ruin; down another lies the peace and harmony that society must have as its bedrock in order to thrive.

"While I understand the intent of your opening statements, I would like to point out that there is in fact precedent for conflict with humans on this scale. We warred with humans once, long ago, not as rebels, but as rivals. We overcame them. There have been two great rebellions since then. First came the Loggers' Rebellion, some eleven hundred years ago, where humans from the Lumberlands' logging camps outnumbered their overseers by too great a margin and overwhelmed them. Those humans took control of a sizeable portion of the Lumberlands, shutting down the timber industry for nearly three years. Then there was the—"

"We gotta listen to this air?" Draksgollow said, leaning forward in his seat and sweeping a hand toward the professor.

A gavel banged. "Mr. Draksgollow, please contain yourself," said Councilor Steelsmith. "You will have your say. For now, Professor Hargrick has the floor."

Draksgollow slouched back in his seat. *Let him have all the time he wants now.* He glanced over his shoulder at the crowd. *They're all waiting for* me *to talk, not listening to him.*

Professor Hargrick cleared his throat. "Well … yes … then there was the Riders' Rebellion just three hundred sixty years ago, where rebellious humans used thunderails—which were quite new at the time—to get from deep to deep. They caused more property damage than loss of life, but estimates placed their numbers at upward of four thousand, their travels allowing them to spread strife and to rally humans to their cause from far-dug places." Professor Hargrick stepped in front of his witness table and began to pace in front of the council. He held a finger high. "Today! Today we face a new challenge, but an old problem: humans who have grown bold enough that they are willing to take up arms."

"What would your recommendation be, Professor?" Councilor Steelsmith asked.

"We must reform, and we must quell," Professor Hargrick said. "Like a rockslide, you cannot build a retaining wall while it is occurring. We must let it run out, shovel ourselves free of the debris, examine the origin of the problem, and put in place safeguards against recurrence."

"That's all very general, Professor," said one of the councilors who had not yet spoken. "Can you delve into more detail?"

Professor Hargrick gave a tight, smug smile. "I would be delighted, Councilor Lanbeck. The quelling is a Judicial Enforcement issue, possibly requiring military support. Of course, we cannot allow armed, rebellious humans to run amok. We take a methodical approach. One city at a time—starting here in Kupak Deep—we scour the city, take every human into custody, interview them to determine rebellious tendencies, and return the rest to their occupations. Those that resist are obviously rebels, of course, without requiring additional investigations."

"That sounds laborious," said one of the councilors.

"Each city will prove easier than the last," said Professor Hargrick. "We should employ the seeding method used in the quelling of the Loggers' Rebellion. Slaves believed to have participated in rebellious activities, or who aided those who did, will be punished by the removal of the tongue and breeding paraphernalia, then returned to their owners. If previously they were freemen, they are to be sold at auction for the public benefit. Once these chastened humans—pardon my pun—are returned to work, others will see the consequences of their actions, and become less likely to join rebellious factions."

"Thank you, Professor Hargrick," said Councilor Steelsmith. The professor sketched a shallow bow and returned to his seat.

"Mr. Ganrin Draksgollow, to address the council."

Draksgollow drew himself up to his full height. He wasn't tall for a kuduk, but he had a presence out of proportion to his stature, with his bald face and mechanical embellishments drawing fascinated looks. He nodded to the audience as he walked to stand in the narrow alley between the witness table and the councilors. "Now, far be it from me to question a plan that would result in a pile of human tongues and dangle-bits the size of a trolley, and result in gainful employ for a couple poor sots making that pile. But you're just cleaning up the problem with a greasy rag."

There were murmurs in the gallery as Draksgollow paced, imitating the professor with the addition of faint hissing and creaking sounds from his mechanical joints. "You see, you put them maimed and un-manned humans into mines and fields; they don't need to talk. Other humans will see them, then they've got to choose: do I put my head down and keep safe, or do I fight back like this poor rusted heap of a human next to me? You might think those humans would pick being safe, but you might just not understand how bleeding stupid they really are. It's too late; they've heard; they *know* they can fight back, and lookie there, it don't even get them killed. And humans always think it won't happen to them; it's some other poor ash-sop who gets ventilated, gets hanged, or gets his danglies tossed in a pile by Professor Hargrick over there.

"I got a real plan, a solid plan, a plan that we can sit down at the end, put our feet up, and say 'well, that's that.' It's the *only* plan I think we can count on to work, and I promise you, it's going to be *work*."

"What's that, Mr. Draksgollow?" asked Councilor Steelsmith. She knew already, but she wasn't letting on. All the councilors knew the plan. The whole show was pre-arranged. Only the audience and Professor Hargrick were ignorant, and that audience included the visitor from the Ruttanian Central Defense Ministry.

"We stomp 'em out," said Draksgollow. "Every last human if we have to. Maybe we let a few be exceptions, but they better be rusted rare exceptions. Make folks pay by the trolley-car if they want to spare one."

Professor Hargrick rose from his seat, eyes wide with shock. Draksgollow couldn't have found an actor to play the role like the Professor of Humans was playing it. "You can't do that. The economic tremors would shake us to collapse. We *need* humans. We depend on their productivity for our standard of living."

Draksgollow remained calm in the face of Hargrick's red-faced outburst. "Park yourself in that seat of yours, and don't sit on your head. I wasn't done. I've got a plan to *replace* all the humans we lose in the purge."

"Replace them?" Professor Hargrick scoffed. "You can't kill *all* the humans and replace them. You're missing a basic tenet of population growth: to make humans, you need to *have* humans."

"Now you see? That's your problem right there," said Draksgollow. "You're not looking to the future. You're just shoving your nose in a book for an answer. Me? I make my own answers." He pointed to the front of the room, behind the councilors' table. A world-hole opened, drawing gasps from the crowd. His own men were standing at the ready, marching a chained line of humans into the chamber, circling around to bring them in front of the audience. "There's other places out there. I won't get into details, but I tinkered up a way to get there. They've got humans there that have never heard of kuduks, don't speak our language, and enough of them that know a hard day's work that we won't have any trouble replacing our lost humans."

Draksgollow finished his speech at almost a shout to make his voice heard over the rumble of conversation that broke out when the world-hole opened. The banging of a gavel was a rhythmic undertone, like a metronome ticking as an orchestra rehearsed. Everyone ignored it, or pretended they didn't hear it. Draksgollow reveled in the moment, watching the chain of humans—many of them battered and bloody—shrink back with nowhere to hide. He let the chaos reign for a moment.

"Shut up!" he shouted when he decided that the crowd had enjoyed enough gossip and speculation. The voices still buzzed, but most of the room wanted to hear what he had to say. Professor Hargrick was forgotten, just five paces away.

"These here humans, they're mine. I went and rounded them up, and just like that, they're mine. They don't know spit about us, about what we want them to do. But they're humans. You beat them when they're not doing what you want, you beat them when they're being lazy, or sloppy, or proud. You stop when they're doing what they're told—no more, no less. Works on all of them, or if it don't, you cull them. I'm not going to pretend this won't be work. This'll be work like the thunderail tunnels. This'll be work like a war. But when it's over, we'll have humans that never heard of a rebellion, humans that don't know what's what and are scared of everything. These humans are going to be afraid any time they aren't doing exactly what they're told, and they're going to have that hang over them for the rest of their lives, and pass it on to their children. Our humans have got brave. They got stories from a hundred years ago saying things is fine. Makes them comfortable. Makes them feel like they've got the world figured out, even if they're at the bottom of the heap. We got these new ones, and it's gonna be generations before they even think of thinking they got the world sorted out."

The meeting was effectively over. There was no going back to mundane arguments after the show Draksgollow had put on. Debate over the plan had ended, even if there was no longer the proper forum for announcing a decision. Let the decision come later; Draksgollow was satisfied that he had won his case. As the room cleared, Draksgollow glad-handed a few spectators as he waited for the one person in the room he had been truly concerned about swaying.

"Mr. Draksgollow," said the representative of the Central Defense Ministry, holding out his hand, "I'm Calamson Goldore, liaison of the—"

"I know who you are," Draksgollow replied, shaking the man's hand and sizing him up. He had his beard woven into two long braids at the chin, the rest close-cropped—all grey. Soft skin on the hands, but a grip like a meat packer. He was a man who used to work, but had settled into a comfortable life. "You think we put on this kind of a display to drop the jaws of the trolley-riders?"

Goldore released Draksgollow's hand with a shrewd gleam in his eye. "That machine … what's it do, exactly?"

"Exactly?" Draksgollow asked. "It cuts a hole between two places, one end where the machine is, the other wherever the bloody bolts I please."

"And where *exactly* did you get those spare humans from?"

"That," Draksgollow said, "will take some time to explain. If you don't mind a trip through that machine, I'll be happy to sit down with you over dinner and lay it on the rails for you."

A metallic shriek echoed through the workshop over the thrum of machinery. Rebel workers manned the equipment, churning out parts for the various projects going on between the rebellion's tinkers and the everyday necessities that they replenished. In one corner of the workshop, Rynn had commandeered a lathe, where she was working on shaving a fraction of an inch off the diameter of a brightsteel rod for her next improvement. Her goggles kept brightsteel chips from her eyes; earmuffs kept the shriek from taking its toll on her hearing. But while the muffs protected her in the long term, in the short term they blocked out all but the loudest of sounds. It was peaceful. Everything around her was muffled. The goggles blocked most of her peripheral vision. There was just her and the workpiece. One thing to worry over.

A hand on her shoulder startled her. Rynn flinched away from the machine; her first worry was of getting caught in the whirring head that spun with enough force to rip her hand off. She twisted around. "What the—oh, piss off, Kupe! Don't you know better than to sneak up behind someone working at a machine?"

Kupe held up his hands. "Sorry. I called your name from the door and you didn't turn around."

"Rusted Eziel," Rynn swore. "Can't you read the signs? Get some goggles on at least, before something blinds you."

He shielded his eyes with a hand. "Sorry. I just needed to talk to you."

Rynn took him by the arm and marched him out of the workshop before he broke something or got himself killed. "What made you think this was a good time?"

"Well, because every other time I try to talk to you, you always find a way to get someone in my way, or you're too busy and I can't even get to you."

"Did you ever stop to think, 'hmm, maybe Rynn's time is pretty valuable? '" Rynn asked. "I can't drop everything I'm doing whenever someone wants my opinion on something. Bloody boots, it's not like I don't have enough people I *can't* get rid of … no offense."

"None ta—no, piss off!" Kupe shot back. "I was about to say I wasn't offended, but like an ox's ass I'm not. You parade me in front of your recruits because they recognize my face from that one bloody flashpop. I had come down here to thank you for letting me go with Hayfield on that liftwing heist. I want to get a chance to be a soldier."

Rynn pushed her goggles up onto her head. Kupe was blurry without them, but they were fogging from her sweat. "Kupe, you were a soldier before I met you. That's how you got your flashpop in the paper in the first place. You just aren't the hero you pretend to be."

"The hero you make me pretend to be. I don't want to pretend anymore."

Rynn sighed. "Fine. If your heart's not in it, you won't be any use as an inspiration. I'll get you put back on regular duties."

"No, you're not catching my toss here," Kupe said. "I don't want to pretend anymore; I want to a chance to *be* that hero. I want in on the big jobs, so that when those new recruits ask what it's like making a difference, I don't have to look for you, or Davlin, or Rascal for an answer."

"Heroes have a habit of dying young." Rynn said.

"Doesn't stop you."

Rynn stopped to really look at Kupe. He had changed. He wasn't joking about wanting to contribute. She could see the desperate longing in his eyes. *What have I put him through, making him the face of the rebellion? He's not much of a fighter, but then, who is when they first try?* He also hadn't looked below her jawline the entire time they had been talking, which was some sort of record for him.

"Report to Davlin tomorrow morning. We have a new initiative starting soon, and I'll get you in on it."

# Chapter 11

*"If faced with a communication barrier, revert to core languages. These have been found commonly in many off-world cultures, and suggest common ancestry or creation."*
*– Traveler's Companion: Contact with Indigenous Populations*

It had been two days. Kaia referenced the notes by the side of the console, checking the coordinates. It took her a moment to sift them through her head, deciphering the code Cadmus had devised to avoid ever writing actual, usable coordinates in plain sight. Kaia chuckled softly to herself. Cadmus was such an eccentric. Here they were, burrowed away in a cavern they had dug on the moon, of all places—Kaia could still hardly believe it—and he was still worried that someone might find them.

With the coordinates entered, Kaia turned on the viewframe. One of the more welcome improvements the Mad Tinker had made to the controls was a single lever for turning on the twelve switches that fed the machine spark. It was hardly an effort to bring the view alive now. The image showed the interior of a sitting room fit for a daruu, except that the nicer things were made of wood, not stone. Kaia had grown up in a freeman household, with a cobbler father and a baker's assistant mother; she had never seen anything lavish until she had joined the rebellion. Getting to see all the wonders of not just one world, but three, was worth everything she had done to join up.

The chair in the sitting room was filled to overflowing with an older man enjoying a glass of something golden brown. This was her target. With a nod to herself, she pulled the switch to open the world-hole. Normally, someone seeing one open next to them startled a person, even one who was expecting it. Anzik was different about it, and so was this Mr. Harwick. He just raised his glass to her with a wink and waited.

Kaia gathered herself, standing and smoothing the wrinkles from her shirt and trousers. "Mr. Harwick, my name is Kaia, and I am a representative of the Human Rebellion. I am acting on behalf of Mr. Cadmus Errol, who regrets—"

"Could you slow down a bit, my dear?" Harwick asked in halting Korrish. "Until a few days ago, I was aware of your language mostly in its written form."

"Oh … yes … I'm sorry," Kaia said with exaggerated enunciation. "I am visiting you to check on the books. If you have any completed, I would be happy to deliver them to Mr. Cadmus Errol."

"So, Errol thinks he's got me in his pocket now, eh?" Harwick asked. "I've half a mind to hold onto the translations until he comes in person to collect them."

"But sir, I—"

"Then again, how could I trouble a pretty young lass such as yourself," Harwick continued with a smile. "Please, come in. Have a seat and a drink."

"I … I don't think I'm supposed to," Kaia said, blushing.

"Nonsense," Harwick replied. "You're on business; I understand that. But I *am* the business, and I insist you join me." He waved a hand toward an empty chair. "And if you don't mind, turn that view aside first. I don't fancy a window into a bare stone cavern and a lot of clockwork trinkets while I drink."

"Um … all right. I suppose." Kaia turned the view around and stepped through. Harwick sounded like he was going to be trouble to deal with. It made her wonder if that was why Cadmus had given her the assignment instead of dealing with Harwick himself.

Once Kaia stepped through into Tellurak, Harwick rose and ambled around to the open side of the world-hole. In a flash, the hole closed. "What did you do?" she asked, her breath suddenly coming quick. She was stranded.

"Calm yourself, my dear," said Harwick. He went to the side table, which displayed an array of colored liquids in fancy glass bottles. "Let me pour you a drink. I just have some questions for you, the sort that I'd rather have frank answers to, without worrying who might be listening from the shadows."

"But how will I get back?"

Harwick shrugged. "All I did was lift the handle that turns the machine on. I can't imagine it will be long before someone happens by and pushes it back into place. In the meantime … brandy?" He filled a glass and pressed it into Kaia's hands.

She sniffed it and winced at the sting.

"Not much of a drinker?" Harwick asked.

"Mostly ale." She took an experimental sip and felt a stronger burn than she was used to.

"Can't say I keep much of that around," Harwick replied, settling into a high-backed chair with worn upholstery. "They often judge a man around here by the quality of the liquor he drinks. That sip you took cost more than a horse."

Kaia froze. She did a quick estimate and figured that there must be twenty or thirty horses left in her glass. She knew that Madlin had grown up rich, but Kaia could never get used to waste.

"Oh, have no fear," Harwick said. "Your company is worth every lost whinny. Besides, you can't spend all your money on horses, or you'd wind up neck-deep in horse dung. Now tell me, what does Cadmus Errol plan to *do* with what's in these books?"

"I don't know," Kaia replied. She chose a chair across from Harwick and sat down on the very edge of it. "Aside from wanting to know the details on the world-rippers—"

"Travel gates," Harwick corrected her.

"He doesn't know what's in them."

"And you believe him?" Harwick asked. He watched her with gun-barrel eyes. Kaia remembered then that Harwick was a sorcerer like Dan. He was too old and slow to pose a threat physically, but he had used magic to turn off the world-ripper, and he could probably turn her "off" as well.

"I don't see why I wouldn't," Kaia replied. "He's not much of one for secrets, really. I think it helps that no one knows what he's talking about most of the time anyway. I mean, Madlin and a few of the tinkers and machinists, of course, and the ones that see the other world."

"You're not like that, then? Twinborn?"

Kaia shook her head and tapped at her temple. "Just me in here."

"You're better off," Harwick said. "I was twinborn once, until an uncle of mine decided I was more trouble than I was worth. I'm really just half a man now. Better I was whole in one world all my life."

"Same thing happened to Mr. Errol," Kaia said. She called him Cadmus to his face, but she felt the need to make him sound important to an important man like Mr. Harwick. "Except it wasn't his uncle, it was a daruu trap that got him."

"Really?" Harwick asked. "He neglected that detail when we spoke."

"It's not much of a secret; just about everyone knows. He just doesn't like to talk about it. You'd probably understand better than most how that works."

"Indeed."

"So, you asking what he wants to do with the books makes me think you finished rewriting them," Kaia said. "How many am I bringing back with me?"

"I have two thus far," Harwick replied. "I didn't undertake them in order. I started with the one that details the workings of the transport gates. I consider myself a learned man, my dear, and I will admit that the breadth of it washed over me like the waves of a storm sea. I trust that the Mad Tinker has a better background in practical physics for deciphering it."

Kaia grinned. "I doubt there's any better, at least among our kind."

"The next book I chose at a whim, because its title intrigued me."

"What's that?"

"*Calling for Help*," Harwick said. "It presented such potentially enlightening questions as: 'help from whom?' and 'what sort of help?' I simply lost myself to my own curiosity."

"So did you find the answers?"

"To a degree, but not a degree with which I am satisfied," said Harwick. "The book presupposes certain knowledge on behalf of the reader. I don't know if it was simple oversight, or a means to denying that information to ignorant readers such as myself. But it does seem to indicate that with the device it describes, you can summon aid from beyond the barrier or worlds. It does not say from whom, nor does it specify the manner in which that aid might be supplied. It is also quite likely that even if such a device was to be made, there may no longer be anyone to answer the call."

"Wow."

"Indeed. This is why I questioned you in regards to Cadmus Errol's motives. I have a great deal of experience dealing with men of power, and sound judgment of the repercussions of their actions is not always prominent among their virtues. The Mad Tinker reputation of his doesn't help matters either."

Kaia nodded. Unfortunately, there was truth to what Harwick said. Cadmus's reputation was overblown, but that didn't mean he hadn't earned it.

"So you see, that's why I needed to speak to you alone," said Harwick. "And it's why you are worth every drop and more of that brandy growing warm in your hand. You are the one who is going to decide whether I can trust Cadmus Errol not to go building a device whose purpose and consequences cannot be foreseen. On your word, I will either send you on your way with both books, or I will withhold the second book, and you can truthfully report that I only gave you the one."

"But I'm not anyone important," Kaia protested. "I have no right to say whether Cadmus Errol can be trusted or not. He's the brains behind the rebellion. He's my superior."

Harwick leaned back and closed his eyes. "Have they told you much of Acardia?" Kaia shook her head, but before she realized that he wasn't watching, he continued. "King Gorden is the last of his kind, an old man who has seen the error not only of his own ways, but the errors of his father, grandfather, and all who came before him. His son will not inherit his title. We've spent years, he and I, setting up a government that represents the people, one that lets *them* choose their leaders, rather than mere heredity. Gorden is a good king, but that's just luck for we Acardians. His son would be a good king too, but that's not the point. The point is that wisdom is spread throughout the kingdom, not sequestered in the mind of one man by right of birth. People here have a say in their leadership, even now, and will only gain more influence with King Gorden's death. I believe in that. I believe that the best way to learn the heart of a man is by talking to those who he holds in his power. What a man does with power tells you everything you need to know about him. But much of what he does is done behind closed doors, where few see it. You're behind those doors. So tell me: is Cadmus Errol the sort of man I can trust not to do something reckless and astonishingly short-sighted with this book?"

Kaia sat still. *My choice? Why do I have to be the one? He's a good man at heart. It's all worked out, too. The world-rippers … where would we be without those? And the cannon? Maybe that was a bit much, but it did the job. All right, fine … if it had misfired or anything had gone wrong, it could have killed us all. But it didn't. That should count for something. Shouldn't it?*

"What's in those other worlds?" Kaia asked. "Does the book say?" She knew that there were twelve total; Rynn had explained that much to her. Out of curiosity, she had spun through the world dial on the console, but had never been able to see any but her own, Tellurak, and Veydrus.

"It doesn't," Harwick replied. "Who's to say what could be out there. The writers of these books would seem likely, or at least their descendants. Maybe the lost gods. Maybe something worse than kuduks. Honestly, I can only speculate."

"Maybe it would be best if I only took the one."

Kupe stood at the ready, along with a group of forty-nine other recruits. Davlin had told them they were part of Operation Potato now, but that didn't explain much. The uniform felt tight when worn properly. Kupe had never been fond of the top buttons of any coat or shirt he wore, preferring a more fashionably lax look. The ladies had always appreciated it. Davlin less so. It wasn't the first time he had stood waiting for Davlin to send him off into battle. He hoped it wouldn't be the last. Back in the tunnels of Cuminol, he had held a rifle, and only knew the basics of what to do with one. Now, Kupe carried a coil gun with what felt like a lifetime supply of ball bearings weighing down his pack. At his belt, he had four of Rynn's spark grenades, something that hardly ever got sent on raids, as far as he knew. A few of the rebel factions had been given some as last-resort defenses, but normally they seemed like a waste. Kupe assumed that Davlin was going to explain why he had them.

Pious Davlin looked out over Kupe and his comrades, eyes narrow as slits against the glare of sun in the plaza. "You all are now members of Operation Potato. We have word that our kin in Tellurak are being rounded up, killed or dragged off. We don't know where they've gone, but we know where they have been taking their victims. Across the Telluraki kingdom of Acardia, there have been reports of farms attacked. There have been no witnesses, but we know who is responsible. In Kupak Deep, the newspapers are calling it the Human Replacement Plan." Davlin spat on the deck. "We've searched Kupak, but none of the missing farmhands have shown up. They will, and when they do, we will make bloody sure they get home. Until then, we need to stop the kuduks taking any more of our kin.

"That's where you boys and girls come in. You are the hands of Eziel, holding both sword and shield. Most of our activities have weighed heavily to the sword hand, and I admit to being partial to the bladed solutions myself. But we must not reject Eziel's protection, and we must not fail to pass that protection to those who require it. You will be sent in squads of five, stationed at Acardian farms in a rotation that your squad leaders will go over with you prior to departure. Your job will be to keep out of sight, keep vigilant watch, and be ready to counter a world-ripper invasion at your designated farm, should there be one during your watch."

*I picked the wrong day to be a hero.* The prospect of days outdoors in a backwater world like Tellurak was enough to make Kupe wish he had a drink in his hand. He was a deeper to the core. There was no malice in him toward humans who preferred living in the skies, but he had no desire to join them.

While Davlin's speech wandered into details, Kupe's attention drifted off. It wasn't like he was in the front few rows. Kupe was all the way in the back, where Davlin's view of him was blocked by a bunch of fresh-faced soldiers, all hanging on everything the old priest said. With a subtle turn of his head, Kupe tried to get a better look at a few of the women in the new division. It was coats and trousers for everyone, but even with the uniforms, a practiced eye like Kupe's knew how to imagine the hidden details.

*What's Charsi doing here?* It was her. He knew it. She was at the far side of the crowd, one row ahead. Kupe had ogled her often enough that no pair of trousers was going to disguise her. She'd cut her hair short, showing off the milky skin at the back of her neck. He had barely seen her since coming aboard the *Jennai.* It wasn't until he had put two and two together that he realized that if Davlin was aboard, most of his followers would be as well. But Kupe had been living inside the moon most of the time since then. He hadn't seen her or talked to her since the flashpop. Why had she done it? He needed an answer, and not some slick-talk from Davlin about everyone having a job and doing it.

Kupe's musings were cut short when he heard the familiar litany and joined in midway. "Lord Eziel, grant us vengeance upon our enemies. Let us share our strength as comrades and become fearsome to our foes. I am your servant; teach me to kill in your name."

*Bloody Eziel. Grant me an hour alone with that girl, and I'll kill all the kuduks you want.*

# Chapter 12

*"Most large animals are edible, given proper processing. Refer to diagrams 7a. through 7h. for generalized diagrams of the edible portions of various classes of animal."*
*– Traveler's Companion: Hunting and Farming*

K'k'rt had been in larger caverns before. The underground complex below the human city of Raynesdark made this one seem miniscule in comparison. He had stood beneath the night sky and stared into the heavens, with stars so far above that the mind could not fathom. But nowhere else did he feel so small as a creature than standing beneath the looming gaze of Fr'n'ta'gur.

The summons had been perfunctory, which told him that the dragon was in a peckish mood. That was never a good sign. The priest who was sent to fetch him had been miserly with details, only willing or able to tell him that Fr'n'ta'gur had a problem that only K'k'rt could fix. That meant that K'k'rt had a problem. And thus he found himself before the mightiest creature he had ever met, wondering what he was going to be asked for.

"K'k'rt," the dragon boomed. "Were you aware of any problems with the human city prior to our invasion?"

K'k'rt chuckled halfheartedly. *Oh, that's not a good sign.* "Your Excellency, there were many deficiencies noted in the initial reports. Aside from the obvious infestation of humans, we were aware that the upper mines were in fact devoid of useful minerals, and that while the lower mines produced occasional diamonds, they were primarily a source of common ores. There were concerns about the stability of the repair work on the glacier wall, but those have since been allayed. Your Magnificence, I know of no other deficiencies that would warrant your notice."

"Indeed?" Fr'n'ta'gur said. He craned his neck to peer straight down at K'k'rt, who could imagine his own demise in vivid detail. "Then why have I received word that there is a geological issue that threatens the city's very existence?"

K'k'rt was dead. He knew it. Better to have taken his chances killing the priest who came to get him and running as fast as his old legs could carry him, rather than answer the summons of a peckish dragon. He couldn't even chuckle over his predicament. "That region has been stable during all recorded history, Great Fr'n'ta'gur. Perhaps this is a trick by the humans."

"This is no trick," Fr'n'ta'gur replied. "Goblins who have served me longer than you have confirmed that there is a volcanic pressure rising beneath the mountain."

"I am sure I had no idea—"

"I want a solution," the dragon said. "No excuses. Use the human girl, and have her create a solution. Her world must have seen this same problem. She will have an answer."

"Of course, Great and Merciful Fr'n'ta'gur. I will see to it at once." K'k'rt was bowing and backing away even before he finished speaking.

Rynn sat at a round table, crowded with ale tankards, coins, and cards. Heavy curtains blocked the windows, and a single spark bulb above the center of the table provided the only light. To either side, Rynn's top officers guarded their hands as they jested and cajoled one another. It was the General's Game, which had become a weekly ritual to keep relations among the rebellion's leadership friendly. It had been Vaulk's idea. He was the one who had pointed out the rivalry between Rascal and Davlin—Rynn hadn't even noticed. It wasn't that Rynn disliked Crackle, but it always felt as if they were betraying the trust placed in them by the rebels when they all idled at once.

"I fold," she said, throwing her cards to the middle of the table. Her tankard was a better companion than her cards had been.

"Me too," said Sosha. She gently deposited her cards atop Rynn's. It was lucky for Sosha that money was all but useless aboard the *Jennai*, otherwise she would have been mired in lifelong debt from her weekly losses.

"I'll take your coin," Rascal said, pushing a stack of coins forward to match Davlin's bet.

Vaulk, Hayfield, and Pick folded in turn. Despite his lack of rank, Rynn couldn't turn Pick away from a card game.

Before the next card was dealt to the middle, there was a knock at the door. At first, Rynn thought she might have misheard, but a second knock removed all doubt, louder and more determined than the first.

"Come on in," Rynn said. "But if you're not here to play, something better be on fire." Her fellow players laughed.

The door opened a crack. "General Rynn," Kaia said, peeking in. "Something's on fire."

Rynn pushed herself to her feet. It was still the most awkward motion for her tinker's legs to manage. "Deal me out for a few hands. I'll be back."

Rynn followed Kaia down a hall and into an empty side room. Her curiosity grew as she wondered what Kaia wouldn't say in front of the officers.

"I've got a dilemma," Kaia said.

"Doesn't sound like any sort of fire I've ever heard of," Rynn replied.

Kaia furrowed her brow and pursed her lips. “You weren’t being literal and you know it. This is a real problem. And for all I know it might cause a fire, depending what we do?”

“We? I thought you had the dilemma.”

“Well, it involves your father.

Rynn winced. “What has he done now?”

“Nothing ... yet,” said Kaia. “You see, he didn’t want to get dragged into another six-hour conversation with Mr. Harwick, so he made himself scarce and sent me to pick up the translation work he’s finished so far.”

“Sounds reasonable,” said Rynn. “That man could talk the paint off the walls.”

“Well, you see, he finished two of the books. One’s the world-ripper book. I brought that one back with me. The other’s a book that tells how to make a distress beacon. That’s a thing that calls for help for you.”

“Yeah, I know what it means.”

“Well,” said Kaia. “The book doesn’t tell you who it calls, or what kind of help they might send. Mr. Harwick was worried that your father might just build one to find out, and that maybe that wasn’t the best idea.”

“Sounds like something he’d do. After all, he wasn’t sure what the world-ripper would do when he first built it. And don’t let him tell you otherwise, either. He had guesses, and probably not as good a guess as what a distress beacon would do.”

“So … did I do the right thing?”

“That depends. Just what *did* you do?” Rynn asked.

Kaia looked all around, then leaned close. “Mr. Harwick still has it. He says he’ll save it for last if he has to, but he can’t stall your father forever.”

“Thanks, Kaia. Don’t worry about this. Just get back to the backup base and pretend nothing happened.”

Kaia let out a long breath. “Thanks, Rynn. You’re my hero.”

“Just get going before anyone notices you’re gone. Did you leave the world-hole open, or is someone waiting at the console?”

“Jamile. Just give her a nod when you get back to your game.”

“Will do,” Rynn replied. She watched Kaia sneak out into the hallway and shook her head. *At least someone around here can wrap her head around twinborn.*

Madlin was having lunch when K’k’rt arrived. Though the hour on her pocketclock mattered little, her days had developed a rhythm. Wake up. Breakfast. Lunch. Guard change. Dinner. Guard change. Bedtime. Overnight guard change. No one came to clean, and they didn’t let her out for bathing or her unmentionable business. Everything happened in the little suite of hers or not at all—and she’d be gutted and boiled before she cleaned her own prison cell. Breaks in the routine were always interesting, if not always welcome.

"What do you want?" she snapped. Even though K'k'rt had his change of heart, he had still provoked her into getting jolted by the guards. Plus, the guards didn't need to know she'd mostly forgiven him.

"I bring good news," said K'k'rt with a weak smile. "Fr'n'ta'gur needs you."

Madlin dropped her pencil to the floor and hopped to her feet, startling her guards, but not enough so that they used the jolt on her. "Well then, let's just run right down there and see what the fat lizard wants. Can't keep an ancient as rusted mountains dragon waiting, or it might finally keel over from age while it waits."

K'k'rt eyed the guards. There was no chuckle, which made Madlin worry. "He does not need to *see* you," K'k'rt clarified. "He needs you. This is good news. Your recent inventions have not, shall we say, amused him."

"Pardon me for bringing your tinkers into the Steam Age," Madlin replied. "It's hard to build modern equipment when you're practically whittling everything by hand. I'll draw up plans for a thunderail if you want, but without proper tools, good luck building one that isn't a rolling death trap."

"He needs something very particular this time, and I hope it will be an easy task for you," said K'k'rt.

"I don't like the sound of easy. Sounds suspiciously like anything *but* easy."

"There is a volcano at the heart of the mountain against which Raynesdark rests," K'k'rt said. "It is at risk of a rather spectacular eruption, according to the reports I've brought you."

"What do I know about volcanoes?"

"Presumably, how your own people stopped this same problem in Korr."

Madlin swallowed. *Worlds are the same. Makes sense.* "Oh, is that all?"

"Is there a problem?" K'k'rt asked, glancing at the guards.

Madlin forced a smile. "None at all. Give me about three days, and I'll have it worked out for you to start work."

"Excellent," K'k'rt replied, nodding to himself as he deposited a stack of documents on Madlin's desk. "That should be everything you need, I hope."

"I'll let you know if I need anything else," Madlin replied. *Three days to prepare to get myself out of this infected wound of a mountain.*

Cannon fire thundered, shaking the deck of the *False Profit.* Jadon Zayne did not flinch or wince, though he may have twitched just enough to keep his balance. The fog that surrounded them deadened the noise, not so much to muffle it as to snuff it out before it could echo. Their target was a ship they could only see by the fires burning along its sails. *He relies on me for everything now. I wonder if he even remembers how to pirate without magic to help.* It was a dilemma that cropped up in his mind often, and had preoccupied him for much of the morning. How much longer could he abide his father's behavior for the sake of the aid he gave the Megrenn Alliance?

Denrik Zayne was a puzzle to his son. Standing there beside him, he noted the resemblance to the reflection he saw in mirrors; his father was much older of course, and worn by wind, sun, and hardship. But the bone structure was unmistakably of common heredity, and the eyes held the same hue. Inside was the conundrum. The values that Jinzan Fehr—his father's dead twin—had fought and died for showed in scant evidence within Denrik. He still spoke the words when occasion demanded it of him, but nothing of his actions lent credence to them. Freedom. Equality. A better life for everyone, even the commonest of common men.

The cannons fired once more, the whole broadside punishing the prey vessel. They sailed northern waters, in the straits between Takalia and what had once been Tinker's Island. Jadon supposed that was still its name, but it was no longer home to the Errol Company. Those straits no longer clung to the iron protection of the Mad Tinker's smoking ships and their ferocious Korrish cannons. Denrik Zayne was making up for lost time and reminding the merchant fleets that the seas still belonged to him.

By his words, Denrik Zayne should have been everything he was not. He should have been a hunter of pirates, a man who rescued ships lost at sea. If he insisted on lawlessness, he should have been a smuggler, bypassing the Shippers' Guild's rules and bringing people the goods they needed and wanted, regardless of official sanctions.

The helmsman guided the *False Profit* in close to the prey vessel, which listed badly in the water, obvious even with only its burning sails to see it by. The crew threw grapples across, aiming at hazy outlines as the two ships finally drew close enough to see one another in the fog. Steel rang as cutthroats hacked their way through a pitiful defense by the merchant crew.

He had something important to tell his father, but for the first time, Jadon gave serious consideration to withholding his information. Was his judgment not superior to his father's by now? Was the benefit of Denrik's experience worth the risk of setting the two of them at cross purposes? Of course, there was only so wrong a conversation between the two of them could go.

"Father, we need to talk," Jadon said, raising his voice above the sound of men shouting and the clash of swords.

Denrik snapped a glare at him. "Now's not the time."

"Cadmus is bargaining with an Acardian lord, one who used to be twinborn."

"Scarlet tides, boy, you pick now to tell me this?" Denrik asked. He shouted an order to his men to mind the mainsail, which was ready to fall free to the deck, still ablaze.

"Well, I wasn't sure how you might take the news, so I had to decide how to approach telling you."

"Of all the … who is the lord, and who was … gut me, can we discuss this later?"

Jadon scanned the deck of the prey vessel. His aether-vision showed the flow of battle far better than his father could see in the light, through the haze of fog. "We've all but won. It's not as if you're over there fighting. The Acardian is Lord Dunston Harwick. I haven't discovered his Veydran identity, but I find it likely that he would have been Kadrin. Given how the population distribution trends between worlds, he should have been either Megrenn or Kadrin, and we would have been aware of notable Megrenn sorcerers well-placed in Acardian government."

A pistol shot cracked the air. Denrik swore and shouted for his men to return fire. Someone on the prey ship was better armed than he had realized. Generally his father did not allow his men to waste Errol bullets on poorly-armed vessels, now that the future supply of such ammunition was in question.

"You see," Jadon continued, despite his father's distraction. "There have been mass kidnappings in the Acardian countryside, which the Korrish rebels are blaming on kuduks. They have reports that humans are being wiped out in Korrish cities, and will be replaced with slaves from here. Cadmus Errol appears to be collaborating with the Acardians to put a stop to it."

"Very well," Denrik said over his shoulder. "But you don't seem sure of much. You're hedging this all as guesswork."

"Well, given that the Acardian is a sorcerer of unknown ability with Kadrin ties, I decided that discretion was the wisest armor. I haven't been near any of the world-rippers while they were opened to Tellurak."

"I thought you were confident in your illusions," Denrik said. He trained his pistol at the captain of the prey vessel, who hunkered behind the ship's wheel for cover.

Jadon's shoulders twitched. "Hence the unknown abilities. If he was the twin of Axterion Solaran—"

"That relic's older than the dragon."

"… or Dolvaen Lurien, I might very well be dead before I realized he saw through my illusion."

"Point taken," said Denrik. He fired, and a chunk of wood split from the wheel of the prey ship. "Just keep as close an eye as you can, given the circumstances. Kadrin or no, if he's helping save our kind in Korr, leave him be."

"Very well. Thank you for your time," said Jadon. "Enjoy the remainder of your battle."

# Chapter 13

*"Note: all listed formulae have mix ratios with a tolerance of 0.05% or greater. Do not attempt precision chemistry in backward worlds unless you have brought your own equipment." – Traveler's Companion: Chemistry without a Lab*

Kupe stood with his pack slung over one shoulder, waiting with the rest of his five-man—make that five-*person*—squad. Either through luck or someone flipping a few switches in the background, he had been lumped in with Charsi for the mission. He still couldn't get over the mission name: Operation Potato. Kupe had visions of impersonating a farmhand, spending days on his hands and knees in the soft, spongy soil, ripping potato after potato off the vine.

Davlin stood by the viewframe, which was just a web of copper strung every which way with no picture in it. His uniform was the same plain-spun robe he had worn as a preacher, except now he wore a sword belted at his side. Kupe had never seen anyone ever use a sword. They were decorations in posh houses and exhibits in museums, not actual weapons. The coil gun at his belt … that was a weapon. Knockers carried clubs to drub sense into lawbreakers, and soldiers carried rifles. A sword seemed like a half measure all around; there was no point getting up close to someone if you just wanted to kill them.

"All right, Squad Seven, listen up," Davlin said. "You will be assigned to the Kerrin Grove Orchard, which is seventy miles west of a city called Golis. It's the beginning of harvest season, so there will be a number of workers out there, and you will be watching over them in the event that the kidnappers visit Kerrin Grove. Your tour is three days, after which you will have three days back aboard the *Jennai* before your next tour. Your periscope is runed for nighttime vision, so I want it monitored around the clock. You are each carrying four runed grenades. In the event that your farm is raided by the kidnappers, your first priority is to get one of those grenades through the open world-hole to disable their machine. Do not—I repeat, *do not*—throw your last grenade. That last grenade goes off in your hand, is that understood?" Kupe joined a small chorus of affirmatives, though he didn't much care for the sound of that last provision. "We can't risk any of ours getting taken prisoner. Any of *theirs*, don't you hesitate a minute to grab one of them. And remember, no contact with the locals whatsoever. Sergeant Tipner, if you would open Squad Seven's hole please."

The world-ripper operator checked his log book and adjusted dials. When the hole opened, it showed a dark, soil-walled chamber. "Best of luck, and may Eziel guide your hand. Barring that, Tipner and the lads will be keeping an eye on all you potatoes."

Kupe frowned. He was obviously missing something. He leaned close to Charsi as they all crowded through the world-hole. "What's he callin' us potatoes for?" he whispered.

Charsi elbowed him in the ribs and shushed him. Their squad leader flicked a switch and a single spark bulb lit the chamber, which was an inverted T-shape of intersecting tunnels the same size as the viewframe—and the same size as the giant auger that had made the lunar base. Kupe realized how the chamber had been built and it started making sense. A ladder ran up to the top, where a steel-grate platform had been constructed, and a thunderail engineer's periscope was stationed. There were a few cushions spread around the floor, which had the look of fresh poured-stone, and three cots.

When the world-hole closed, Kupe's first impression was the smell. It had an odor like the inside of a boot, mixed with a whiff of the familiar scents of fresh poured-stone and welding gasses.

The furnishings were worse than sparse. Tunnel rats built themselves more lavishly appointed hovels than the little chamber of loose earth. There weren't even enough cots for the five of them. They would have to take turns sleeping or double up—Kupe wouldn't mind that, actually, now that he thought about it. But there was a distinct lack of both privacy and creature comforts that seemed to be designed to tell Kupe that he was a soldier, and he bloody well better be spending his time soldiering.

Of course, it wasn't all bad news. Kupe had expected to be out under the sun, disguised as a farmer. At least with a miniature deep, he would be safe from getting his skin burned, and no contact with the locals meant no farm work.

"Air's a little close in here," Kupe said, since no one else seemed eager to open a bottle of conversation. "They put enough vents in, you think?"

"General Rynn designed these potatoes," the squad leader said. Kupe wanted to say that the man's name started with a P … or maybe a B.

"Yeah, I keep hearing that. What's with all the potato talk?" Kupe asked.

Charsi let out an exasperated sigh. "Don't you ever pay attention?" she asked. "We're a big lump under the ground in the middle of a farm, just like potatoes. That's all there is to it."

It was the last thing Charsi said to him all day. The rest passed like a dripping faucet, an interminable annoyance until it was time for sleep. Kupe took his turns at the periscope, but there was nothing but little trees and folks plucking apples off them. Even seeing real live trees wore thin after long enough staring at them.

Kupe's second day as a potato was dampened by rain. He had imagined that tucked in the shallow deep he would be safe from the effects of weather, but he found that assumption to be mistaken. Soil wasn't stone, and they weren't even under that much of it. The rain soaked through the earth, and the hatch leaked; it had been built for a quick escape, not to be water-tight. The periscope hole leaked worst of all, with the pipe and handles trickling water into their hideaway. It made the already dank, sweat-smelling enclosure all the more inhospitable. Only General Rynn's foresight in adding a drainage grate kept them from a having to sit in puddles—though doubling as a latrine didn't help the odor.

The crazy, sky-dwelling Tellurakis didn't seem to care about the rain. They marched out to the fields with their woven baskets and plucked apples. It wasn't even much to watch, since they had moved on from the areas nearest the periscope. Watching distant farmhands was even less interesting than watching them up close. On his watches, Kupe kept hoping for a fight to break out or for a couple young lovers to sneak off into the orchard—anything to keep him entertained.

There was little to do in the potato except to gossip. Kupe learned more than he needed to about his fellow soldiers, their families, friends, and the officers in the rebellion. Half of it was guesswork, another half lies, the rest a combination of useless trivia and the eavesdropping of salacious busybodies. Kupe was used to hearing the same things everywhere he went. In Cuminol, people stopped him all the time to tell him pointless bits about their lives or someone else's. It went with the territory, being known and all, but back then it was his stock in trade. Part of being known was knowing everyone, or at least letting them think you knew them. It made people feel important, having someone known greet them by name, ask about their children, check on their health. Now, it just felt like he was spinning a gear that wasn't connected. The highlight of his day was figuring out that his squad leader's name was Barvy.

Night arrived by Barvy's declaration. The potato had a clock hung from a protruding root, and at 9:00 Barvy said it was lights out. It was a half-truth, since they didn't switch the spark bulb off. The two on night watch would need the light to work by, so they merely hooded it so it only illuminated the upper section.

"Charsi, Kupe, first watch tonight," Barvy said. "Wake up me and Barret in four."

"Yessir," Charsi replied with a nod.

"Gotcha," said Kupe, before hastily amending a "sir."

He and Charsi ascended to the grated platform. Kupe towed one of the cushions up with him so he had a choice other than standing or sitting on the cold metal when it wasn't his turn at the scope. The fabric was soaked and squished in his hands, but it was still more comfortable than his other options.

They took turns in half-hour stretches, watching nothing. It was an amber-shaded nothing, thanks to General Rynn's rune-work. It made it hard to tell whether it was daylight outside or the middle of a moonless night, but it made the orchard visible, so that was all that mattered. When it wasn't his turn, Kupe spent his time watching Charsi with her eyes pressed against the optics. She had thinned a little since joining up with the rebels. She was one of the few who had. Most of them had gotten their first taste of good food and ample leisure on board the *Jennai*, but Charsi had always eaten well, and her work at The Bearded Man was only ever as taxing as she wished. Kupe reserved judgment on whether he preferred her thinner until he saw her in a proper dress. The uniform fit, but it didn't flatter her figure.

"Ain't comin' tonight," Kupe said softly. He didn't want to risk waking the sleepers below.

"Huh?" Charsi replied, not taking her eyes from the periscope.

Kupe stood, feeling the hot, damp cling of his pants where the cushion had pressed them against him. He leaned close to Charsi's ear. "Them kuduks … you think they're gonna come in a rain like this? Most of them lot can't abide the skies in the first place."

"What makes you think kuduks who'd kidnap humans are soft on a bit of rain?"

"What makes you think they ain't?" Kupe replied. "Most of them prob'ly never thought of pickin' humans like they was apples, free off the tree, but I betcha most would take 'em. All a matter of opportunity. So if these is just regular everyday kuduks with a new line of work, why'd they be any less skittish over the weather?"

"Betcha there's a lotta money in it," Charsi replied.

Kupe ran a hand over his face. "Hmm, never thought of that. 'A day without work's a day without pay,' right?"

"You'd think." Charsi turned the periscope, stepping around to keep her eyes against it. Kupe took a step to follow.

"But it's still night, right?" Kupe asked. "They ain't likely to be up all night after a long day snatchin' up folk."

"How do we know what time they're on?" Charsi asked. "It's night here, but we don't know where the world-ripper kuduks are hiding."

"How's it?"

"Our clock's set to local time, high sun at noon and all that," Charsi said. "Who knows what time they're using. Could be Cuminol time, or Kupak time, or Deep Standard for all we know."

"How you know all this?"

"Kupe, maybe you never considered this, but I talk to five times as many people a day as you," said Charsi. "Mostly you hawk a paper at someone, they swap you a coin, and that's that. I bet hardly a kuduk says more than a 'good day' to you. Not nearly so many drinkers get by that easy. They hang around; they drink; they want someone to talk to."

"Someone who looks good in a low-cut dress," Kupe added.

Charsi's lip curled at the corner. "Girl's gotta make a living. If a few harmless eyes fatten the tips, all the better."

Kupe listened a moment, steeling himself to ask her a question. The dynamo for the spark bulb hummed softly. Water dripped from periscope to grate, grate to poured-stone, poured-stone to drain. Snores rose from below. "Why'd you do it, anyway?"

"Do what?"

"Take that flashpop. You know the one."

Charsi shrugged and took another step sideways to turn the periscope. "Davlin told me to get a flashpop for the papers, something that showed us getting' the kuduks good."

"But why me? Too many folks know this mug of mine. Most of Cuminol. Now, half the world's seen it."

Charsi took her eyes from the periscope and met Kupe's. "I had no idea that would happen. You just … well, you bloody well looked like you were posing for the shot. You looked right at the camera and stood there, so I took the flashpop. You're not the only one who knows people at the paper, so it was no trouble sneaking it to them for the evening edition. Besides, didn't you always want to be famous?" She returned to watch through the optics.

"I guess I never knew what real fame was like," said Kupe. Her back was to him. Even in the shadowed light of the spark bulb, he could see the smooth skin at the back of her neck. Kupe leaned close, letting her feel his breath a moment. When she didn't shy away, he brushed aside her hair and placed a gentle kiss just above her collar.

Charsi giggled, reminding Kupe of the old Charsi, when she was still running The Bearded Man. He circled his arms around her waist and kissed the side of her neck. She kept looking through the periscope, but there was a smile growing on her lips.

"Kupe," she said.

Kupe kissed her again and made an inquisitive noise.

"Kupe, there's a lot of ways to pass our shift without waking anyone. I guarantee this isn't one of them."

Day three in the potato bunker started out like day two, except drier. Unfortunately, there was limited ventilation, and the dank, cool air lingered despite sunshine above. Kupe had suggested looking for a time when none of the farmhands were watching, then throwing their clothes over a tree branch to dry. No one else had found the suggestion amusing.

"This is it, right?" Kupe asked. "We don't find nothing today, they come bring us back to the ship?"

"Yep," Barvy replied. "Next group'll come in. We get a few days in real beds and a chance to dry out."

"I'm planning to stand behind a liftwing prop for a few hours," Gandric said, cracking his neck. He was the bruiser of the group, and the one who seemed least suited to the cramped quarters.

"I'll just be happy eating something that's cooked hot," added Thurm from above, where he was on duty at the periscope.

"How's it, Charsi? What're you lookin' forward to?" Kupe asked.

She winked so that only Kupe could see it. "A little privacy."

"I hear that one," said Barvy. "Nice place to hide for a few days, but not fit for living."

Kupe managed a sly wink back at Charsi, ignoring his squad leader. He declined to mention what *he* was looking forward to, once he got back. He tried to imagine Charsi into one of her dresses, but found that his imagination had run dry. Living all his life in the deeps hadn't made confinement in so *small* a deep any more bearable. He just wanted ten miles of tunnels in front of him and no one to stop him. It would cost him a pair of boot soles, but that was just the sort of thing he didn't need to worry about anymore. A wink and a word to a world-ripper technician, and he could have his pick of the finest human-sized boots in Korr—or Tellurak or Veydrus, for that matter. Kupe found himself wondering what it would be like to own a pair of Telluraki boots—not the simple, floppy-topped boots the farmhands wore, but a pair with some flashpop appeal to them.

"World-hole!" Thrum shouted. The time for idle musing was at an end. The squad grabbed coil guns and buckled on belts hung with rune grenades. "One … two … three." Thrum counted off kuduks as they came through.

"How close?" Barvy asked.

"'Bout a hundred-fifty, maybe two-hundred paces."

"What do we do now?" Charsi asked.

"We wait," Barvy replied.

Kupe's heart sank. For a moment, he had actually relished the thought of going out beneath the sky to shoot kuduks, if only it meant an end to his confinement. *Of course more waiting. It's not like we haven't got our fill of* that *yet.*

"… eighteen … nineteen … twenty," Thrum counted off. There was a long pause, with all the squad waiting with just the sounds of their breath and the hum of the dynamo. "Looks like that's all of them. Clubs for sure. Too far to tell if they're armed proper."

"Lemme see," Barvy said, jostling his way in front of the periscope. "Bust me … those blighters are gonna pay for this. Them's women, half of them, and they're beatin' them like they was stuck valves."

Kupe nodded. "So, we go rescue 'em, right?"

"Not yet," said Barvy. "We gotta make rusted sure we ain't got surprises. Twenty to five ain't my favorite odds, but we got a job, and drain me dry if we ain't gonna do it."

The wait seemed like hours. Kupe hadn't thought to go down and check the clock to see. They all huddled around Barvy, waiting for the order to attack.

"All right," Barvy said. "You've all seen up there enough to know what's what. Charsi, Thrum, Kupe, you lot make for the low hill on the north side. Get behind some trees and start shooting kuduks. A few are pretty close to the farmers, so don't go killing kin—hold your shot if it's not a good one. Me and Gandric will grenade the world-ripper. With any luck, someone's watching from the *Jennai*, and we might see some reinforcements once their world-ripper goes down. They won't risk something getting through on their end."

Barvy counted down from ten, and when they got to one, Gandric shouldered open the hatch, throwing off a half foot of dirt, some of which rained back down into the potato. Kupe was the last one up, watching each of his squad mates climb the ladder ahead of him. The coward's voice in his head suggested that maybe it would be better to let the four of them handle things, but he ignored it and climbed after them.

The smell above was sweet with rotting fruit—the mislaid portions of the harvest left scattered in the orchard. Kupe struggled for a moment to identify things from higher than the knee-high periscope, and in full color instead of shades of amber. Thrum and Charsi were already on the run, ducking low to avoid being seen. Kupe dashed off after them, pulling his coil gun from its holster. *This is it. In the real line of fire again.* He had forgotten how scared he had been on the thunderail raid. Hayfield's trip to the liftwing factory had been all looting, no firefight, dulling the memory of kuduk soldiers pointing guns in his direction. The bile churned in Kupe's gut as he joined Charsi and Thrum on the far side of a low rise. He slid down to his stomach and peeked out into the orchard.

Kuduk thugs were rounding up humans, shouting at them in Korrish, though the humans seemed to understand better when they swung clubs. A few humans ran, but a perimeter of kuduks seemed to be hemming most of them in. Kupe, Thrum, and Charsi were outside that perimeter.

"What now?" Kupe asked.

"Pick one and shoot," Charsi suggested. She took her own advice and fired off three shots in succession. One of the kuduks went down in a spray of blood, and one of the fleeing humans got past.

Kupe fired at another, taking him in the shoulder. A second shot went through the chest. "Bleedin' knockers, they're scatterin'." There was a series of thunderous blasts—rune grenades detonating.

"What'd you expect?" asked Thrum, taking a shot at a kuduk who had taken refuge behind an apple tree. "That they'd just hold still while we shot 'em all?"

"Why's the practice range got 'em holdin' still, then?" Kupe asked, firing and missing as a kuduk dove for cover.

"We won't get them all from here," Thrum said. "Spread out and keep low."

Kupe watched as Charsi went one way and Thrum the other. He hesitated for a moment, then followed after Charsi. The ground was muddy from the previous day's storm, and the footing treacherous owing to roots and fallen apples. Kupe slipped and fell more than once, thankful that the ground was at least a safe place to be.

The click and spark crackling of coil guns firing was whisper quiet out beneath the sky. He could hardly make them out over the sounds of kuduks and humans shouting. The kidnappers were organizing their defense. Kupe risked a glance over the mound he was using for cover and saw bodies strewn in front of the world-hole.

One of the kuduks made a dash to escape through to Korr. Kupe swore beneath his breath and took aim. Before he lined up his shot, the kuduk jerked suddenly and fell limp. Either Charsi or Thrum must have gotten him, Kupe realized. When he looked closer through the optics on his gun, he saw that Barvy and Gandric were among the bodies lying by the world-hole.

*Bust me, they didn't get it closed!* Kupe ducked back down just in time to hear the crack of wood from a tree two feet from his head. Someone was firing at him. He needed to do something. "Gandric and Barvy are down!" he shouted. He hoped that was enough information for Thrum and Charsi, without giving away their plight to the kuduks.

By Kupe's best guess, seven or eight of the kuduks were down. Three of the remaining kidnappers held a string of chained humans as a shield. Somewhere, at least one of the kuduks was firing back with something quiet enough that it had to be a coil gun, and it was fool's optimism to think that was the only kuduk who carried one.

Kupe poked his head over the rise, and pulled it back down as a shot thumped into the turf beside him. He slid down into the valley—all of three feet deep—and slunk away. He needed to regroup with Charsi and Thrum, and get away. Missions had failed before; no shame in that. There was no point getting killed in the bargain. *"Some you win, some you just try to survive." That's what I'll tell 'em, next time someone asks what it's like being a hero.* Kupe tried to keep a positive outlook that there would *be* future recruiting trips. At the moment, the prospect was looking unlikely.

Kupe needed to get to his squad mates before the kuduks cut them off. There were twelve left, give or take a kuduk, and that left them outnumbered four to one. Kupe scurried on his hands and knees, coil gun getting muddier by the step. General Rynn had assured them all that the coil guns would fire when wet or dirty, or even when half busted. Kupe was going to have to find out for himself pretty soon, he realized. The shouts from the kuduks didn't tell him where all of them were, but it gave away the positions of enough that he could use them as a guide to where he didn't dare go.

"There's one!" a kuduk shouted.

Kupe looked all around, but he saw no one. The apple trees were heavy with leaves and unpicked fruit, blocking his vision everywhere but up and down the planted row. There could have been kuduks within a few paces of him without either of them seeing the other, but the voice had sounded farther off. He heard the trigger clicks of multiple coil guns firing, but nothing hit near him. *They found Charsi or Thrum, maybe both.*

Kupe plucked an apple from the tree, the branch coming with it until he twisted it free. There was a swish of leaves as the branch snapped back, but Kupe lobbed the apple into another row of trees making an even greater rustling.

"Over here!" came a shout in response. Kupe ducked inside the low canopy of leaves and peered through the branches as kuduks came to investigate.

Unhooking a grenade from his belt, Kupe recalled Davlin's instructions. It was one of the few bits of his longwinded speech that had stuck in Kupe's head. Twist the dial at the base. Five seconds later it blows. Tucking the muddy coil gun under his arm, he twisted the base, leaned out from beneath the tree, and repeated the same throw he had made with the apple. As soon as it left his hand, Kupe ducked under the tree and covered his ears.

He felt the concussion through the dirt. Scrambling to the edge of his leafy cover, Kupe aimed his coil gun at the vicinity of the thrown grenade. One kuduk stumbled away, disoriented by the blast. The optics were caked with mud, but Kupe lined up a shot by eyeball and put two steel balls through the kuduk.

Kupe heard three more concussions. One or both of his squad mates had taken the hint and brought out their own grenades. It was the best sound Kupe had heard since the battle started. *Eziel, if this is your idea of a battle, can you please show General Rynn something with a bit bigger boom for our side?* He could only hope they had good enough aim that they ran out of kuduks before they ran out of grenades.

Kupe spent the next ten hours of his life—or so it felt at the time—playing Rats and Knockers with the kuduk kidnappers. He'd scamper row to row in the orchard, quickly discovering that the kuduks couldn't navigate between the close-planted trees without shaking every branch in their way. He fired. He ran. He found a new spot to hide. Every so often, he'd get a look at the world-hole, still sitting open and unmoved. He knew enough about how they worked that he was surprised that the technician running it hadn't tried to use it to help swing the battle. Even on the simple raid of the liftwing factory, the rebel technician had kept the hole moving around to where it was most useful. It didn't seem right that the kuduks wouldn't know enough to use the same trick.

A rustling of branches took him by surprise. Whirling around with his coil gun leading, Kupe caught himself short. "Charsi!" he whispered fiercely. He wrapped his arms around her and held her for too brief a moment.

"Thrum's down," Charsi whispered back. "They tossed his grenade back at him."

Kupe winced. "How many left?"

"Dunno," she replied. "Not the easiest place to take a count. We've gotta get that hole closed. I know we're supposed to save one to keep from getting taken—"

Kupe snorted. "I threw all mine."

"But I'll toss my last one through to finish the job. Will you cover me?"

*No, I can't let you do that. Give it here, and I'll do it.* Kupe wanted to say something like that. It sounded brave and soldierly, the sort of thing he was here to be. "You can count on me," he said instead.

Kupe and Charsi kept under cover as long as they could, until they reached the last row of trees, their fruit picked bare. From there it was a run of nearly two hundred feet to the world-hole. If Kupe had been a great crashballer, he might have tried the throw from the tree line. But he doubted there was a newsman alive who had the arm to make a throw like that with a four-pound grenade.

Charsi holstered her coil gun and took the grenade in both hands, cradling it against her chest like a baby. She dashed across the open field, dodging the bodies of the fallen. There was no thought to stealth, just the element of surprise and all the speed Charsi's legs could summon. She was a thing of beauty. Mud-splattered. Short hair. Uniform cut like a man's coveralls. She was everything right about the rebellion. To the incinerators with the kuduks, the whole lot of them. They weren't going to stop her, not today.

Charsi stumbled. Kupe heard the click a split-second later, just as he saw the blood spray. She fell to the ground.

A kuduk crashed through the tree line at the far end of the row, heading for the world-hole. Maybe he thought he had finished off the last human. Maybe he was just hoping for a gap to escape through. The kuduk's run was nothing graceful, not the bounding, triumphant run that Charsi's had been a moment before. Kupe's first shot went wide. His second clipped the kuduk but didn't slow him. But Kupe was past worrying about conserving his ammunition. By the time the coil gun stopped launching a ball bearing with each click, the kuduk had been torn to shreds.

Kupe ran to Charsi's side. If he was making the same mistake as the kuduk, so be it. He was past caring. If he couldn't get to Charsi, he'd die trying. Everything moved like mud. He couldn't run fast enough. Beneath his feet, the ground grabbed at him, sucking at his boots. The world was blurry until he wiped at his eyes.

"Charsi!" he shouted as he reached her. She was moaning on the ground, still alive. Her left arm was covered in blood. Dropping his coil gun, Kupe pulled his shirt over his head and tore a strip of cloth free. He was no doctor, but he knew bad cuts had to be tied up tight to stop the blood. He did the best he could to patch up Charsi's arm where the kuduk coil gun had hit her.

"Kupe," she grunted out between gasps. "Close it."

Lying at Charsi's side was the grenade. They were close enough that Kupe could probably have made the throw from right there. Taking the grenade in hand, he twisted the dial.

"Do it," she whispered.

*Five* … Charsi needed a doctor, and soon … *Four* … they'd fought for too long without reinforcements to think any help was coming from the *Jennai* any time soon … *Three* … Kupe couldn't wait any longer. Reaching back, he threw the grenade as far as he could into the orchard, then shielded Charsi's body with his own until the blast shook them both.

"Why did . . ."

"I ain't lettin' you die here," Kupe said. He scooped Charsi up in his arms and headed for the world-hole.

The scene inside was a mess. There were the remains of a shattered glass wall and three kuduks on the ground; none was in good shape. They might have all been dead, but Kupe wasn't in the mood to check right then. They weren't moving, and for now that was enough.

Using his boot, Kupe swept a spot clear of broken glass and propped Charsi up against the wall. The world-ripper controls looked so much like the ones aboard the *Jennai* and in the secret base that Kupe felt familiar around them. But Kupe had never used one before. He had only watched, and he'd mainly been distracted by the image in the viewframe. The kuduks had log books, charts, and maps, but none of that did Kupe any good. Charsi needed a doctor, and there was nothing that said where to find one.

There was only one thing he could think to do. One dial on the console was labeled "world." Right now the viewframe was showing Tellurak. If he turned it to Korr, he could at least be a few miles outside Cuminol, where he might get her to a doctor in time. A dial only turned in two directions, so Kupe picked one and gave it a twist.

A howling wind arose, sucking everything toward the viewframe, as the image shifted to the swirling blue-white that lay between worlds. Kupe realized in a momentary panic that he had left the hole open as he moved it. Kaia would never have made a brick-headed mistake like that. But Kaia wasn't there, and Kupe at least knew which lever switched the viewframe back to a harmless image. He managed to revert it to that state before the swirling vortex ate all their air.

Kupe didn't know how far to turn the dial, so he went slowly, not wanting to zip past without realizing. Charsi moaned from the side of the room, prompting him to quicken his pace. After a few full turns, the image resolved itself into a landscape similar to the one they had left. Kupe hadn't seen much of the Korrish countryside, but it looked like a sky to him.

He picked up Charsi and carried her to the viewframe. *I should have saved that last grenade.* Swallowing back the guilty lump in his throat, he stepped through.

Had Kupe been thinking with a clear head, he might have realized how many more trees there were than any portion of Korr he had ever seen. Had he been in a positively clever mood, he might have realized that the relative setting to Korr *from* Korr ought to have been zero. But if Kupe needed proof positive that he had, in fact, not found Korr at all, the appearance of a twelve-foot, leather-skinned demon with glowing red eyes was enough to get through to even a befuddled Kupe.

The creature grumbled something, looking down at them with what Kupe's imagination told him was a puzzled expression. If Kupe hadn't wrung all the scared out of his system already, he might even have fainted. But Kupe's brain was too numb just then to properly assess the horror of his predicament.

"Sorry," said Kupe, "I was looking for Korr."

"You dundering imbecile," the creature boomed. "You just came from Korr. What is the meaning of this?"

"Them back there," Kupe said, jerking his head toward the world-hole, "they been taking humans from Tellurak for slaves in Korr. Replacements for killing off our humans. We set out to stop 'em. Me and her are the only survivors, but she ain't gonna survive long if I don't get her to a doctor."

The creature smiled, showing off a set of teeth like thunderail spikes. "You oppose those creatures?" it asked, pointing at the bodies of the kuduks in the world-ripper room.

"Yeah, doin' all we can," Kupe said. "You know 'em?"

"They have pestered me," the creature replied. "And you have given me a small opportunity for recompense."

"How's that?"

"Your mission appears to have ended in calamity," the creature replied. "How might it be resolved?"

"I need to get Charsi to a doctor, and we was supposed to blow up that there world-ripper. Um, if you're looking to really help out, all them papers could be a big help. So would a prisoner—you know, to interrogate."

The creature's grin broadened. "I declare that these creatures are responsible for a breach of my kingdom's peace. I will not set foot off my land, but I will send you on your way with what you need."

The creature took Charsi's arm in one clawed hand. Smoke rose with a sizzling hiss, and Charsi cried out. "I have not the skill to heal her, but she will not die quickly."

One of the kuduks in the world-ripper room drifted up from the floor, trailing a soft tinkling of broken glass as he floated through the world-hole and came to rest by Kupe and Charsi. All the documents joined the kuduk soon after. The creature presented a hand, palm extended, toward the open world-hole, and a ball of flame gathered there. It strained against an unseen barrier, roiling and thrashing, growing brighter and hotter until Kupe had to turn aside against the heat. Like a shot from a coil gun, the ball of flame leapt from the creature's hand, slamming into the world-ripper console. The hole was gone.

"Um, thanks," said Kupe. He looked down at the kuduk who was to become his prisoner. "I think this one's dead."

"A pity," the creature said. The corpse erupted in black flames, and in seconds there was nothing left but ash and a scar on the ground to mark where it had been. "Your people will be along shortly to collect you. I have alerted them to your presence here. I am Xizix, Supreme Ruler of Azzat. Warn your kind to keep clear of this place. Make it known."

# Chapter 14

*"Before eating an unfamiliar plant, either observe a mammalian creature eating it first, or irradiate it thoroughly—preferably both."* – *Traveler's Companion: Flora Safety*

The *Sudden Blade* wobbled over Kadris Harbor, fighting a headwind with the help of Danilaesis's magic. It was the long way around to the docks, but it spared the warlock and his crew the indignity of being seen returning in a derelict ship by half the populace of Kadris. It was not the worst return Danilaesis had suffered in his service to the empire. He had brought back one ship that drifted like a cloud; its hull carried on the breeze without so much as a single sail remaining. Twice he had returned on stolen horses, commandeered after finding himself afoot with no ship capable of lift.

When the *Sudden Blade* settled into its drydock berth, Danilaesis quit it at once without a word to captain or crew. He was done with them. Whether *Sudden Blade* or another vessel would next carry him into battle, not a soul among them would be by his side. The army and navy needed bodies, and the warlock would not deprive the Empire needlessly, but let other commanders suffer the fools, not him. It was a shame that Captain Waenrok had not survived the destruction of the *Falcon's Claw*; of all who had captained an airship for him, Waenrok was the one best suited to Danilaesis's service. Wily, quick-tongued, and with an air of bravado that suited a pirate, Waenrok never questioned Danilaesis, and when the warlock sought it, Waenrok provided sound advice.

*If he'd been born in Tellurak, he'd have been a pirate for sure, that one. He'd have been a better pirate than Zayne, make no mistake.* If only it were so simple. Madlin had done that sort of thing, taking people to places that they didn't belong, and using skills she shouldn't know. It was warfare Uncle Rashan would have approved of. Danilaesis would have taken a crew of pirates over the limp washcloths the navy sent him.

There was an idea somewhere in there. If Madlin ever slipped up, and he got a chance to steal a world-ripper from her, he might give serious consideration to recruiting among the pirates. His musings were short-lived, as a man in palace livery stood waiting for him. Few enough palace servants wandered outside those black marble halls, and rarely did those errands send them down to the docks. Even fewer people in the empire warranted such attention, but Danilaesis was among those—none of the crew could possibly have earned a palace messenger's visit.

"What do you want?" Danilaesis snapped before he had come close enough for the messenger to initiate a polite greeting. "I'm in no mood for the shit you're about to shovel in my path."

"High Sorcerer Axterion feared as much," the messenger replied with a bow. "He bid me inform you that he has pleasant news, news of a sensitive nature to which I am not privy. He did assure me that whatever inconvenience it may cause you shall be forgiven once you find out what it is."

"Oh, piss on that newly-young old codger," Danilaesis spat back. "What does he want from me?" He strode toward the messenger. The thin, weaselly creature had until Danilaesis reached him to explain.

"A fresh change of clothes, a bath, and an appearance in what was until recently a spice cellar."

Danilaesis stopped short. "Bloody winds, that old relic knows how to stir an imagination. Fine. Tell him I'll be there as soon as I find something to wear. I haven't magic enough to get all the blood out of this fabric." He held his arms out to his sides, smirking as the messenger blanched at the sight of his blood-stained sleeves. The black cloth hid the blood well, but having been forewarned, the messenger knew what he was seeing. Danilaesis wished that everyone else would have the same reaction without him having to explain.

Kezudkan sat waiting, his hand running idly along the underside of the table. The top surface was ground smooth and treated with polish, but the bottom was rough cut stone with a pleasant texture. It eased his mind as he waited to meet the newcomer human. It had taken days to acclimate himself to the idea that humans here were powerful, self-confident, and in charge of a rather large swath of the world. Even the Korrish rebels had a furtive quality to them, striking, running, and hiding. These Kadrins of Veydrus suffered him like a nuisance guest. Perhaps they thought that a daruu would not pick up on the nuance, but Kezudkan had owned humans since before any of them were born. The forced smiles, the lilting, patronizing speech that transcended the need for translation; they wanted an alliance, but they bargained from a position of power.

Now, there was word that High Sorcerer Axterion's grandson had returned. The Kadrin had kept coy about the whys and hows, but the boy had spent time among the Korrish rebels and learned their language—his language. There would be no more furtive side chats on the daruu side of the table once the boy arrived. The candid comments that conveniently went un-translated would boil away in the boy's presence.

The room was quiet, with a few hushed conversations around the periphery of the room. Everyone was there from the Kadrins' side except the High Sorcerer himself and Empress Celia—whose dignity did not suffer waiting.

The Pillar of Runes leaned close. "Anything you need to say before their translator arrives?"

"I'm not certain he's just a translator," Kezudkan replied. "Look at them all. You've been around these humans for four days of negotiations. Have you seen them this nervous even once?"

"I can't say I would have. You're the expert on humans here, Citizen Kezudkan."

Kezudkan snorted softly. *Expert. These humans are dripping with fear … except perhaps that General Varnus. Probably not a sorcerer with that kuduk brawn on him. Maybe he's just dumb as a crashballer and doesn't know what's good for him.* Kezudkan found himself caressing the stone of the table with more vigor, trying to summon his own peace of mind from its surface. The humans' fear was contagious, and he found himself envying the Pillar of Runes his obliviousness.

The door burst open. Axterion Solaran was preceded into the room by a younger version of himself. The boy's resemblance was unmistakable, from the thin, lanky build to the perpetual furrow of his brow. Even their black attire matched. The young newcomer spoke something Veydran over his shoulder and High Sorcerer Axterion replied in kind. An insipid smile spread on the boy's face. "Greetings, I am Danilaesis Solaran," the boy said. "I am Warlock of the Empire and blood-stained right hand of the empress. I think we have some common enemies."

Kezudkan could hear the echoes of Kadrin speech in the boy's accent, but the words were clear enough. It felt oddly personal to communicate directly, rather than waiting for the Pillar of Runes to repeat whatever was said. But Kezudkan was not the leader of the daruu delegation.

"I am pleased to greet you, Danilaesis Solaran, protector of your people," replied the king's successor as he rose from his seat. "I am Lunjak, successor to King Dekulon."

"That mean you're his son or something?" Danilaesis asked.

The successor smiled mildly, as close as Kezudkan had seen the man to poking fun at someone. He had to be twice the king's age at the least. "No, I have simply been chosen as the next king, should anything happen—"

"Yes, yes, I understand that sort of arrangement," Danilaesis cut in. This direct communication was going to prove *much* quicker. "Which one of you built the world-ripper?"

Kezudkan blinked. The boy had no grace or tact. Even Draksgollow had shown a modicum of civility as a businessman. The old daruu drew himself up in his chair. "Well, that would be me."

Danilaesis turned to Axterion and said something incomprehensible. Kezudkan spared a glance at the Pillar of Runes, but saw no sign of comprehension there; it must have been their own language, and not the common language of the rune-throwers. After a brief exchange with his grandfather, Danilaesis continued. "I want to see it."

"You mean now?" the successor asked.

Danilaesis shot a glare at the successor that had the daruu shrinking in his seat. "I wasn't talking to you. You're not king, and you're not the one with the machine I need. I've got a war to fight, and if I'm going to take time away from it, it's not going to be to shovel words down a pit with you diplomats. If we've got something you want, and you've got something I want, I can assure you we'll all be happy in the end. In the meantime, I want to see the gutted machine."

Kezudkan suspected the boy was mixing Veydran slang into his daruu, because the guts of the machine were staying intact as far as he was concerned, sorcerer or no sorcerer. He rose from his chair with an audible crackling of joints. Hefting his cane, Kezudkan gripped it and twisted it in mid-air, giving the day's prearranged signal to Gederon. The world-hole opened seconds later.

The boy sorcerer's eyes glazed over and a madman's gleam crept into them. His grin gave the old daruu a chill. "Excellent. Please … lead the way." Danilaesis stepped around the table and stood at the opening of the world-hole, sweeping an arm toward the controls beyond as if he were bellboy at the entrance of a hotel.

Kezudkan looked to the successor and the Pillar of Runes for guidance. He was leery of the boy sorcerer, and better understood the unease of the humans in the room prior to the boy's arrival. But the Pillar's eyes were unreadable, and the successor only gave a barely perceptible nod. With a twitch of a smile, Kezudkan stepped through into a different part of Veydrus—the daruu kingdom. Danilaesis followed on the daruu's heels.

"Much better," said Danilaesis, and with the flick of a finger, the sound from the Veydran council chamber ceased. "I don't need the rest of them. They can work out any deal they like with my grandfather. What do *you* want?"

"I … I …" Kezudkan looked through the viewframe, watching astonishment and outrage war on the faces in the room. He was in no position to bargain, and his cane seemed a paltry weapon compared to the sword slung across the boy sorcerer's back. At the control console, Gederon was a useless, gaping statue.

"Let's try this over," said Danilaesis. "My name is Danilaesis Solaran, and yours is Kezudkan something-or-other. You killed a man named Erefan."

"Well, yes, but—"

"Except you didn't," Danilaesis continued. He leaned forward, bringing his face level with Kezudkan's. "You killed his twin brother. They were in league together, but you killed the wrong one if you wanted revenge."

"What are you talking about?" Kezudkan asked, shuffling back a step. "Erefan had no brother."

"How would *you* know? You just owned him like a dog," said Danilaesis. "And don't you go getting any ideas that you're better than a human, because you're not. I've met Erefan. I stayed at his house. He tried to have me killed, and I barely escaped with my life. They betrayed me, and Erefan betrayed you. Now … can you think of anything you might want?"

"How about proof of your claims, for a start?"

Danilaesis took hold of Kezudkan by the collar and brought his face so close that Kezudkan could smell the alcohol. It seemed the Korrish vice took hold of Veydran humans just as well. "Proof? Do I look like the sort who dreams up lies to cover my motives? Those rebel humans from your world conspired with my enemies in this one. His daughter sold me into a trap to them. I have blood humming in my ears, a hunger for their deaths gnawing its way out of my guts. Do you even have a heart in that stony body of yours?" Danilaesis poked him in the chest. It was oddly incongruous, but the finger was soft and frail, which made the sorcerer's threats tarnish. *I could break him in two.* The thought came unbidden, some primordial pride as old as stone itself. "You should be half mad with rage at the idea that he's still alive. And you want proof?"

"Of course I want proof," Kezudkan replied. "I saw the man die. I outwitted him, he fell in my trap, and now he's dead."

"It's just like Erefan said," Danilaesis replied. "You're a blind idiot. He played you a fiddler's tune to get the world-ripper plans, and he just sang a song with you over his own grave. I bet he has a melody composed for the day he turns you into gravel. So let me ask you just one … last … time: what is it you want?"

"I want Erefan dead," Kezudkan replied. It was the answer the boy sorcerer wanted; that much was plain. Yet at the same time, it was true. Doubt had crept in. If what the boy said was true, he had been cheated of his revenge, and more importantly Erefan was still out there somewhere scheming against him.

"Then I think we have the foundation of a working relationship here," Danilaesis replied, an easy grin replacing the manic look. "I need three things from you: time to use this machine, instruction in its workings, and access to the books that you built it from."

Kezudkan looked away quickly—probably too quickly, he realized. He was caught. "I haven't even shown them to my own people yet."

"They're not your people," Danilaesis said. "They're just using you, same as me. The Korrish are your own kind, same as the Kadrins are mine. For my part, I can get you a good start on finding Erefan. I know where to look. What good is a nice comfy stone roof over your head and people who act nice to your face, when it can all be gone in an instant when Erefan opens a hole into your bedroom with a coil gun in his hand?"

Paranoia. Revenge. Suspicion. Down that path lay madness, Kezudkan knew. Yet in that moment he saw the easy trap and stepped in willingly. "Fine," he replied. "You win. You help me put an end to Erefan and you'll have what you wish. Confound it, I won't sleep worth salt until this is settled, now that you've dredged it up again."

"I'll have those books before we go back. We can detour with the machine to a little spot for safekeeping."

"Can you even read them?" Kezudkan asked.

"Better than I read your language, stone man."

"Anyone need a drink?" General Varnus asked. The question landed with a thud in the middle of the room. No one bothered to translate it for the daruu. It had been nearly half an hour since the world-hole had closed. The arguments that had followed in the immediate aftermath had cooled to mere simmering glares across the table. Axterion had not expected Danilaesis to do it. That mistake was on him. The boy was becoming too unstable to account for his actions. It should have been a joyful occasion, giving Danilaesis the weapon he needed against Megrenn. It ought to have occurred to him that the boy wouldn't wait for diplomacy to put that weapon in his hands in due course.

"They'll be back any time now," Axterion said to Zepdaan, the Pillar of Runes, and waited as the daruu translated the assurance in a dull monotone, not even looking at his companions. The daruu sorcerer watched him with a stillness befitting his heritage of stone. Zepdaan had a Source in him—that was certain. Most of the daruu were stout of Source, but few boasted such a formidable presence in the aether. If things went cowflop in the ensuing hours, Axterion was not looking forward to confronting the daruu. It wasn't that the High Sorcerer was timid, or uncertain of his own powers, but daruu thought differently, and were hardy as bears. Hardier, in fact, since a wounded bear might bleed to death. Daruu blood mortared a wound in seconds. It was one of the recent facts he had unearthed regarding the hermit race. The visitors from beneath the Cloud Wall Mountains had not divulged the peculiarities of their anatomy, but Axterion had dug among the libraries' vaults until he had found every scrap of information the Kadrin Empire had amassed on the creatures.

A tentative knock might as well have been a smith's hammer striking the door. A messenger poked his head into the room and beckoned to Axterion. "Excuse me a moment," the old sorcerer said as he rose.

"What is it?" Axterion asked as soon as the door latched shut behind him.

The messenger beckoned further, and Axterion followed him a short way down the hall. If they were not out of earshot of the meeting room before, they certainly were now. "I bring news from Empress Celia."

"You great buffoon," said Axterion. "I was the one who sent you to her, remember? Of course you bring news from Empress Celia."

The messenger took the verbal abuse in good humor. "She has given you leave to do what you must about the Danilaesis situation."

"You've shot two arrows into the hay bale," Axterion replied. "How about planting one in the target?"

"If you judge the daruu alliance to be a better choice for the empire than Warlock Danilaesis, you may take any measure you see fit to preserve that alliance."

"That's better. Pleasantly blunt," said Axterion with an insincere smile. "Empress Celia just gave me permission to murder my grandson. How wonderful. I'd like you to take a message back to her."

"Of course, High Sorcerer," the messenger said, bowing. "What message?" He looked up attentively.

"Go to the third floor sitting room, the one with the sunset view of the courtyard. There's a bookshelf, and on the second shelf from the top, third from the left, you'll find a book. Bring that book to Empress Celia, and tell her I suggest she read it well."

The messenger's brow crinkled, and he looked at Axterion with a question in his eyes. After a moment's restraint, the question slipped loose. "What book might that be? I … would not want to send the wrong message."

"It's titled *Procedures and Protocols of Imperial Succession.* It's not a long book, so she can probably have a go at it in one sitting. I've fairly well memorized it … you can mention that to her as well," Axterion said.

"That's the message you wish to send?" the messenger asked. He backed a step away. "Please, High Sorcerer. She'll kill me."

Axterion sniffed. "Look who's got a mighty opinion of himself. What would killing *you* accomplish? Now get out of here, and bring the empress that book. Maybe next time she'll keep her schemes locked in the dark recess of her mind where she's banished her heart."

The messenger bowed as he backed away, then scurried out of sight. There were lessons there, if you looked for them. The killing of a messenger was one of the first signs of a failing leader. Rashan was mad as monkeys, but he never fell so low as to take out his rage on an undeserving minion.

"It's the boy," Axterion muttered. There was no one in the hall to hear him. "He's got them all on edge. Rashan might not have killed messengers, but Danilaesis just might." Whenever Danilaesis returned, there was going to be a reckoning. If Axterion couldn't get through to the boy, then perhaps he knew someone who could.

# Chapter 15

*"The simplest way to find civilization is to follow running water. Do not attempt solar or astral navigation without localized charts."*
*– Traveler's Companion: Intra-World Navigation*

Under the shade of an enormous canvas tent, Stalyart ran his hand along the ship's railing. He felt the spots where the polish had worn through and bare wood lay exposed. Holes marked spots where the cleats had been removed; not all of them were gone, but the ship had so little rigging remaining that there was no longer any call for them. It was unnerving, like seeing a noble lady dressed like a dockside whore, baring too much skin. But it was a ship, and a ship unlike any he had ever sailed. While the sails had been stripped from it, the ship had gained two metallic wings, each fitted with a curious contraption. A spokeless wagon wheel arrangement of paddles faced forward from the mid-point of each wing. He had been forewarned, and knew that those were the wind-makers, the machines that would push the ship through the sky.

"Master Anzik, I must renew my protest," a voice behind him said. "This man has no idea what he's doing aboard an airship. At least Captain Illzarl has flown a wind-riding airship. He's clearly the better choice, even if we accept the commission of this … person." Stalyart ignored the speaker and continued his examination of the ship. It was no prize as a sailing vessel—fifteen winters old at the very least, and had been given only moderate maintenance. The wood was in need of polish, the hull in need of paint. It was best the sails were gone, for he could only imagine fraying and worn patches to match the rest of the vessel's threadbare state.

"Captain Stalyart was a friend of my father," said Anzik. "Councilor Fehr trusted this man with his life, and he is a better captain than any we have. As for Illzarl, the qualification you tout is merely the skill to crash softly and survive to be given another ship."

"Why has he not come forward before now?" the naysaying voice asked. "If he was an agent of Jinzan Fehr, where has he been all this time?" The voice rose and threatened to become shrill at any moment. Stalyart sauntered over to study the curious cannon that was mounted at the ship's fore. All steel, and a better alloy than he was accustomed to seeing. It looked like a swordsmith's craftsmanship, but on a piece of ordinance the size of which he had never seen.

"Captain Stalyart is no agent, Admiral" said Anzik. "He was a friend of my father."

"Where was this friend in the last Kadrin War?" the voice persisted. "I don't recall seeing his name on the—"

"I was a nuisance to Kadrin ships on the eastern coastline of the empire," said Stalyart. "I did small things, at the request of my friend Jinzan."

"Small things?" the admiral asked. He directed the question at Anzik. Stalyart was beginning to feel the part of a parrot, a mere talking distraction unworthy of the conversation. Of course, Stalyart was not a man to be put off by a difficult officer. "This is the man you want taking command of our new flagship?"

"These small things did not include sinking ships, but I am familiar with the process," Stalyart replied, continuing to inspect the Korrish cannon. It was wrapped in copper cord, which according to Anzik meant that it did not require powder. He looked forward to trying it. It was beyond unpuzzling right then, but he continued to give the gun the utmost scrutiny so as to avoid giving the petulant admiral the respect of his full attention. "They did include sneaking my ship into Kadris harbor in wartime, to move Megrenn agents into or out of the city. When the attempt was made on Rashan Solaran's life, it was I who delivered the assassins. When your spies were discovered, it was me they ran to for escape. When my friend Jinzan asked for my help, he asked only for these small things. He felt badly asking more, because as a very young man I helped deliver stripecats from Safschan during the Freedom War. I sneaked past a great many Kadrin ships during the blockade, a task that many lesser captains failed. I think maybe you would not have nice uniforms now, and a fleet under your own command, had the Megrenn rebels not possessed stripecat cavalry during the rebellion. It is an interesting question though, don't you think?"

"So," said the admiral, the bluster and fire gone out of him, replaced with a teeth-gritting coldness. "We become a navy of smugglers and spies?"

"We become a navy that doesn't get shot down every third time aloft," Anzik countered. "Captain Stalyart knows how to stalk ships, whether to avoid them or attack. Your navy has never adapted to the Kadrin dominance of the skies. You ruled the seas, and grew soft on tactics; you don't know how to deal with a superior foe."

"But Lord Anzik, if this ship lives up to all your claims, we're now the superior force," the admiral protested, gesticulating with his hands. Anzik remained impassive. For all the young sorcerer's skills, Stalyart thought it was his calmness that was his greatest asset. "I've a dozen men sharpening their harpoons to get this command. How am I going to explain this … transient to them?"

"However you like," Anzik replied. "You're their admiral. If this proves too difficult a task, I would assume that there are a dozen men sharpening their harpoons to get your position."

"As you wish, Lord Anzik," the admiral replied without once parting his teeth. He retreated with a bow and headed off in the direction of his own ship, which lay at dry anchor just along the beach.

The two airships were nowhere near Megrenn territory, on a tiny island just large enough to hold them both. The Korrish work crews—and Anzik himself—had met the ship there via world-ripper, the most singular device Stalyart had ever witnessed.

"He won't be any trouble," Anzik said. "We'll get more ships refitted, and his captains will get some of them. But I won't waste any more time with those dry, crusted minds while I have so few Korrish airships. You've always been my father's best man. Now, you're going to be mine."

"I will serve, of course," Stalyart said with the pantomimed tip of a hat he wasn't wearing. "But I am, as always, my own man."

"I've made the arrangements," said Anzik. "Rynn will retrieve me any moment, and I'll send Jadon along as your new ship's sorcerer in time for a sunset departure. Oh, and have you decided on a name for it? I'd like to have it for reports."

"I think I will call her the *Mirror's Trick*," Stalyart replied. It seemed fitting to follow Denrik Zayne's tradition and give his vessel a name with a double meaning. It seemed even more fitting for a vessel of Stalyart's to have a triple meaning.

In the hold of the *False Profit*, Tanner and Jadon sat side by side at a table that more commonly saw games of Crackle than quiet talks. As Tanner sat pondering, he traced a spot where someone had carved a name into the surface with a knife: Crawe. He didn't know any Crawe aboard, but it was a secondhand ship, and the table had probably come with it.

"If you're having second thoughts, you need to tell me," said Jadon. The boy was Anzik with shorter hair and skin that had seen the outdoors three hundred sixty days a year. "I'd rather have help, but I can do this myself if I have to."

"You sure Madlin's gonna be ready to snatch us up in that machine of hers?" Tanner asked. He pulled a knife from his boot and began scratching at the table.

"She's got someone watching us right now," Jadon assured him. "You've held your grudge long enough. You can finally bring yourself closure on that portion of your life. You can start over with Madlin's people. They need men with fighting experience. She's got incentive to help us."

Tanner sighed. He'd been dry for two days, waiting for word on Jadon's plan. Those two days had done more to tell him he needed a drink than any two he could recall. Rum and whiskey had an amazing power to make days slide by half-noticed—even ale could manage the trick, if there was enough of it. "Blade's not as quick as it used to be, but it's quick enough. Are *you* sure you're ready to go through with this?"

Jadon nodded. "I can't remain, nor can I let this go on in my absence. My circumstances have been tolerable only through increasing self-deception."

"Well, I'm not getting any younger," Tanner said, sliding out from behind the table. He made his way for the deck, while Anzik disappeared deeper into the ship's interior.

Under the sunshine, it was a mild and breezy day, the sort of romanticized vision of life at sea that had convinced Tanner to take up with Stalyart in Veydrus, and to go along with Denrik Zayne in Tellurak. A few stray clouds lazed across the sky, following the same wind as the *False Profit.* The crew had grown accustomed to Tanner's presence and worked around him. Deckhands gave him a wide berth, the bosun waved a hello, and Captain Denrik Zayne spared him a glance when he noticed the reaction of his crew.

"Mr. Tanner," said Denrik. "You're not up here to drag my men off to the card table, are you?"

"Day like this?" Tanner said, gawking up at the sky as if he had never seen such weather before. "Figured I'd get a sniff of what summer feels like up this far north. Rare as an honest banker, days like this." If there was one topic that was sure to pass time and do little else, it was to comment on fair weather. At least with a storm brewing you could make a pretense of it being precautionary, but no profit had ever come of belaboring the merits of a fair day. Tanner sauntered over beside the captain, a self-satisfied grin plastered across his face.

"Are you planning on being insufferable all day, or do I have some respite to look forward to?" Denrik asked. "This is a ship on the hunt, not some Kheshi prince's pleasure barge."

Tanner smirked but held his tongue. He didn't trust himself not to say something revealing. Instead he walked to the railing and stared out at the horizon. If anyone took note that he held onto that railing with a white-knuckled grip, or that he kept his balance well back from the edge, it would have been easy to pass the posture off as a dryfoot fearing the great Katamic Sea. Tanner was a reluctant sailor and everyone aboard knew it. When the ship shook, Tanner was the only one on deck who was prepared.

The explosion was the sound of a hundred cannons firing in a hellish chorus. But there was no barrel to shield the ship from the force, no projectile shot forth. The blast was the stored powder for the port broadside erupting. The *False Profit* rocked, first from the force of the explosion, then from the water rushing into the shattered hull. A good captain could recover a ship from many mishaps, but there was no saving a ship missing half its hull on the port side.

Of course, in any shipwreck there was a chance of survival if you were lucky. The wreck of the *Fair Trader* had provided floating debris for half the crew to cling to and reach landfall. Jadon hadn't wanted to take that chance. Tanner sprang into action. Men shouted and ran; others dove into the water without hesitation, fleeing the burning portions of the ship and the chance that yet unexploded powder for the starboard broadside might go next. Captain Denrik Zayne was neither a fool nor a neophyte on the seas, but even he could not have prepared himself for a personal attack with all that swirled around him. Tanner's sword was between the pirate's ribs before he could raise a hand to defend himself.

There was always a chance with a belly wound that a man would survive. Slim chance, but Denrik Zayne had tricks hidden beneath his tricks. Sliding a blade between a man's ribs on a titled deck amid the fires and smoke of a powder explosion was no small feat. But Tanner was a master swordsman—everyone in Tellurak seemed to keep forgetting that.

Denrik's mouth opened, but no sound came out. The final look in his eyes was bewilderment. "No offense, but you had it coming," Tanner said as he pulled his sword out dripping. Denrik fell away, tumbling down the sloped deck and into the Katamic.

Captain Denrik Zayne had survived the loss of two ships, and Tanner had made sure the pirate went down with his third. Sliding the wet blade into its sheath, he made for the ship's lower railing and dove into the water. If anyone had been paying attention to his confrontation with the captain, they were too preoccupied to do anything about it.

The breeze in the northern passage between Tinker's Island and Takalia had been unseasonably warm. The Katamic Sea was not to be fooled; it knew the season. The water bit into Tanner like a winter storm on bare flesh. He gasped a mouthful of water at the shock, and struggled to the surface, coughing and choking for air.

The sky above turned dark, or at least dim, in a circle of space just above him. In a dizzying sight, he saw people standing on a wall, the ceiling stretching off to a great height. The hole had opened facing downward toward him, Tanner realized, though he struggled to make his eyes believe him. A rope fell through with a loop tied at the end, pulling to one side of the hole, which Tanner guessed had to be 'down' where he was headed. Struggling to cough the water from his lungs, he pulled himself through the loop and hooked it under his arms. The ropes dug into muscle as someone on the far side of the hole hoisted him through.

A wave of dizziness passed through Tanner as the world decided to pull him in a different direction. He flopped to the steel floor and waited a moment for the room to hold still.

"Welcome to the rebellion, Tanner," said a voice from above him. He looked up and squinted. A face was backlit against an intense white light coming from the ceiling.

Tanner raised a dripping hand to shield his eyes. "Madlin?" he asked. Jadon stood beside her, his expression flat.

"Almost," came the reply. "I'm Rynn."

The room in which Tanner found himself was like no place he had ever been. Madlin had told stories of the world her twin came from. He had heard of the machine. Seeing the monstrosity of copper, brass, and a bunch of metals he couldn't name, Tanner realized his imagination had let him down.

"How're you dry?" he asked Jadon, who should have been dripping all over the room, but was not.

"I was off the ship before the powder blew," he replied. "It would have been foolhardy to stay any longer, since my part was done the moment the fuse was lit."

"Foolhardy, eh?" Tanner asked. "I'll keep that in mind next time you're lookin' for a favor."

"Don't worry," Rynn said, extending a hand and helping Tanner to his feet. "We approve of foolhardy around here."

The hum took getting used to. Stalyart likened it to a bassoonist who never ran out of breath. The deck buzzed, sending the hum right through boots and legs and into the gut. The Korrish must have been used to such sensations, but he could find no comfort in it. Time. That was all he needed. Eventually the *Mirror's Trick* would be like a piece of him—another leg or arm, another skin.

Tanner seemed less shy of the skies than he had of the sea. Perhaps the sky did not play such tricks on the stomach as the rolling waves. Perhaps the view so far below held some magic over him. Stalyart admitted he had a similar reaction to seeing the world spread below him in miniature.

"Fine day for sailing, is it not?" Stalyart asked when Tanner noticed him watching.

"You call this sailing?" Tanner shouted back over the wind and the hum of the machines.

Stalyart laughed from his belly. "I cannot say. Are we sailors, or some new thing? You should find me the word the Korrish use for those like us who sail the skies. I think this world lacks for a description that befits us."

"Slow us down," Tanner said, crossing the deck to where Stalyart manned the helm. "Machine's got sight of us." The crew was handpicked, each one of them Stalyart's man. It had been a shame that he could not take them all, but *Mirror's Trick* was a smaller ship.

A few shouted commands and crewmen brought the engines to a halt. They still flew as momentum and the air current carried them along, but they slowed. The wind rustled clothing and the wood of the deck creaked and thumped beneath booted feet. The rest of the sky had gone silent. Stalyart was reminded that nothing but Anzik's runes were keeping them aloft. It was easy to think that some Korrish mechanical magic had been responsible for their flight, but that told an incomplete tale.

Tiny arcs of lightning hopped in the air, preceding the opening of a hole into the world of Korr. Jadon was waiting beyond, along with a girl who had to be the Korrish tinker, Rynn, and several others whose names Stalyart did not know. He glimpsed the machine, strange and fascinating, far more complex than the flying devices that had been attached to *Mirror's Trick*.

Stalyart swept a hand to his side and bowed to those who stood beyond. "Welcome, and thank you for the gift of this marvelous vessel." He spoke Kheshi, which was a language Tanner had informed him the girl Rynn knew.

"We've got a chain set up," Rynn said. She was unladylike in her manner of dress, in sweat and grease-stained shirt and trousers, with spectacles like an old man, wearing boots fit for a miner. "You run into problems with the mechanicals, Jadon can get word to me via a few intermediaries." Jadon Zayne stepped through the hole in midair and onto the deck. Had Stalyart not known better, he would have sworn the boy was Anzik Fehr.

"How many?" Stalyart asked. He had been involved in such schemes before, and knew that each time information passed between twinborn, it involved delay. Messages could also become muddled in the passing—he knew this because he had muddied many himself.

"Three links and he's got my ear."

Stalyart gave Rynn a narrow look, but nodded.

"This is Veydran business," Rynn said. "You can do what you like with the ship. Payment for it is Anzik's business, one way or another. But I'd view it as a personal favor if you didn't go getting it blasted out of the sky."

Stalyart grinned. "My lady, I would be mortified to lose a ship. I am no Denrik Zayne."

That same night, back in the lunar headquarters, Anzik Fehr stopped by the small dining room to find Cadmus finishing a plate of basil-rubbed chicken in a cream sauce. Greuder had been cooking late meals for him again. Anzik stopped and sat down across from the Mad Tinker, waiting for him to acknowledge his presence.

Cadmus glanced up from his plate just briefly, then stabbed another piece of chicken. "Didn't think you had it in you."

"We are not so different, you and I," Anzik said.

Cadmus snorted as he chewed.

"We both endured circumstances that we viewed with contempt. Both of us remained despite the means for escape because we gleaned an extraordinary benefit from our position. I have seen your inventions. I find it difficult to believe you could not have escaped your daruu if you had wished."

"Cold-blooded, doing in your old man," Cadmus said around a mouthful of food.

Anzik shrugged. "Jinzan Fehr was my father, not Denrik Zayne. The pirate was unaware he had a son for most of my life. Jadon was abandoned by the whore who birthed him, who in turn was abandoned the moment my twin was conceived. Even with all that, I couldn't trust myself not to have second thoughts."

Cadmus grunted. "Not sure I like the look of that Tanner fellow."

"He bore a longstanding grudge with Denrik Zayne. I merely gave him an accomplice, and an escape. Your daughter seems to appreciate his martial prowess—most of your rebels are more eager than competent. Sosha seemed pleased to see him once more."

A fork clattered onto the plate, and Cadmus scowled across the table. "How's that now?"

Anzik sat back in his chair, surprised at the reaction from the Mad Tinker. "I only meant to imply they vouched for his character. I would hope that you might reconsider your appraisal of me as well. Your mistrust seemed rooted in my association with Denrik Zayne, which I have now ended. Please weigh this accordingly."

With that, Anzik stood and excused himself from the room, leaving Cadmus with an empty plate and a look of consternation.

# Chapter 16

*"Non-controlled biospheres have unpredictable weather. High winds and darkened clouds precede storms." – Traveler's Companion: Weather Awareness*

Rynn watched through the viewframe, blowing to cool her tea before taking a sip. She stood next to the viewframe, so close that she could read the words as Harwick transcribed them into a blank journal. It was the book on medicine that he worked on; she could tell by the anatomical diagrams. The terminology was torturous, with strange words that had no translation from the arcane language. Jamile might have better luck with it, but Rynn was out of her element. Humans were wet, sticky machines on the inside with too much plumbing and too little structural support.

Still, the work was only half done on the translation, and she had been through two cups of tea already while spying on the Acardian lord. He never touched pen to paper with his own hand. Through magical means, the quill dipped itself in the inkwell and set off to work, scrawling neat Acardian script across the page. Harwick merely flipped through pages and traced along the lines of runic text with a finger.

Though Rynn struggled to say what it was, there was something different about Dunston Harwick. Perhaps he had changed his hair, or maybe it was the fact that his spectacles rested on the table beside him instead of on the bridge of his nose. Wandering back to the control console, Rynn set down her tea and resigned herself to accomplishing something rather than wasting her night in speculation.

When the world-hole opened—she wondered if she could ever convince herself to call it a transport gate—Harwick perked up at once. "Ah, Rynn my dear! I was wondering when you'd stop peering over my shoulder and drop in."

Rynn felt her face grow warm. "You could see the viewframe?"

Harwick grinned. "Maybe. Or maybe you just confirmed my suspicion. Either way, I take no offense. Come in, come in. That cargo hold is so dreary and unwelcoming. Tell me, do you work in there all alone, day in and out, or do you just chase everyone away before coming to see me?"

Rynn stepped through into Harwick's study. The guards outside the cargo hold would be insurance enough that no one would shut her out of the *Jennai.* "I don't often work in there at all. We have enough competent technicians now that I can spend my time on other needs of the rebellion."

"Like building more of those peculiar limbs of yours?" Harwick asked. "I notice you've made a new set."

Rynn's tinker's legs were concealed beneath the fabric of her trousers. There should not have been enough evidence showing through for anyone to tell they were new. "You're bluffing again."

"Not so," said Harwick. He pointed to her legs with the stump of a pipe as he withdrew it from the pocket of his jacket. "New rune work. Similar pattern to the old, but a tighter structure and better formed runes. Either you had someone else do the work, or your carving has improved."

"I do my own runes."

"Neither here nor there, of course," Harwick replied. He ambled over to a side table and picked up a finished volume. "This is what you're here for. Chemistry."

"Anything worthwhile?" Rynn asked as she accepted the book. She would read it through later, but it never hurt to hear the highlights ahead of time.

Harwick tried to suppress a chuckle, but failed. "You really do lack the feminine predisposition toward noticing certain things."

"What?"

"Turn to page one hundred eighteen," Harwick replied. "You'll see."

Rynn flipped thought the hand-numbered pages—if a magically copied text could be considered handwritten. Starting from the heading at page one-eighteen, she read aloud: "If you should find yourself without a supply of age-stabilizer, this approximation can be concocted using only class two technology and class four magic. Most primitive worlds will have all the ingredients you need. Should you lack any, please consult table seven of appendix … Harwick, what is this?"

"Age-reversal!" he exclaimed. "I've de-aged five years in the past two days. I've been taking a dilute version of the formula it gives down below there, just to be safe. It's a gods-reborn miracle."

"It's magic."

"No, girl, that's the trick of it," Harwick replied. "It's neither magic nor your world's science. It's a combination, and so far beyond both our worlds' understanding that they make it seem a child's school experiment." He reached into his desk drawer and pulled out a stoppered vial. "I made a bit for Cadmus; figured it was only fair. You're still a bit on the young side to begin with." He eyed Rynn up and down.

"How are the rest going?" Rynn asked. She took the vial from Harwick and gazed into the liquid within. It was clear, but there were whorls and particles within that suggested impurities, but which were probably just the book's incomprehensible science at work. It seemed to have done little harm to Harwick, but she would hold onto it a while before deciding whether to pass it along to her father. She was beginning to feel the weight of being his keeper, deciding which wonders he could be trusted with.

"I copy the words, but medicine escapes me," Harwick replied. "I am neither apothecary nor physician, and my dealings with those who are have never delved into professional detail. People become ill; they make them well again. I've rarely given a thought to the 'how' of it."

"I can see why you and my father get along so well," Rynn replied with an edge of sarcasm.

"Indeed. Your father is cursed with a curious compulsion to be understood. I think that's why he moved to his own continent. Even if it was the sorriest barren rock in Tellurak, he could keep out layman clods like myself who didn't gawp over his clever machines."

"Hey now! I grew up there," Rynn protested.

"Then you should know," Harwick replied. "But then again, I think that you didn't. You're the Korrish one, if I'm not mistaken. You've fallen into the old trap of twin conflation."

Rynn shrugged. "We're really just parts of one whole person, when you think about it. I *remember* growing up on Tinker's Island."

"That's where you shortchange yourself, my dear girl," Harwick replied. "The Source is different. In almost all cases it splits unevenly between worlds. I bet Madlin doesn't have the same need of a machinery leg, either."

"One twin's misfortune," Rynn replied. "We need the same optical correction, have the same freckles, the same tastes in food and drink."

"What's she thinking, right this moment?" Harwick asked.

Rynn straightened and leaned away from Harwick. "That's none of your—"

"I don't particularly care," said Harwick. "My point is that *you* don't know. You'll know what she's said, what she's seen and heard. You'll remember it like you were there, but you didn't think it. I am keenly aware of the difference. Ever since the death of Caladris Solaran, I find myself missing the devious streak he had. It helped me sort through more political . . ."

Harwick droned on, but Rynn's mind blocked out the sound. *Caladris Solaran*, he said. It couldn't have been a coincidence. How many twinborn Solarans could there have been? There had to have been some relation to Danilaesis Solaran. Dan had mentioned his twin's name every chance he got, as if a Korrish twinborn like Madlin ought to have recognized it. The risk of him discovering the role she played in Dan's death made his possession of the books problematic. She was going to need to find a way to get them all back from Harwick and acquire another translator. The rebellion had thrown in fully with Anzik's people, and Denrik Zayne was dead. Perhaps Anzik or one of the sorcerers from among his people could be trusted now.

Harwick snapped his fingers. "You still in there? I didn't mean for you to go looking through Madlin's eyes. You're not going to unravel her thoughts, no matter how hard you try. Now, if you'll excuse me, I suspect that both of us have more important things to do than to toss words back and forth. While I don't understand most of this next book, the insight into the minds of these ingenious people is fascinating. They take for granted wonders that I can barely grasp, and I am sure there are concepts that are second nature to them that I am wholly ignorant of. It makes things patchwork at times, trying to translate them."

"Well, I'll pass your gift on to my father," Rynn replied, unsure as to whether she would do any such thing.

"Oh, and no offense, my dear," Harwick said. "But if you could send that girl Kaia, next time, I would much enjoy seeing her again." There was a mischievous gleam in the old lord's eye.

Rynn replied with a nod and a tight smile, then stepped though the world-hole back to Korr.

That evening, Rynn stared out at the stars from the window of her quarters aboard the *Jennai.* How many twists of a world-ripper's dials would it take to reach one of them? How long could she afford to stand on the firing range, dodging conspirators brought close by her own hand? The temptation to flee and leave the burden to someone else tugged at her sleeve. Chipmunk had known better than to get in over her head. When had Rynn lost that cautious, sly part of her that stuck to the tunnels when she went on her criminal errands? She had made herself a fulcrum, the wedge that drove one force against another, and she was feeling the pressure of that lever bearing down on her.

A tentative knock broke the quiet. "Come in," she answered at once. This time, she was expecting her visitor.

"You wanted to see me?" Sosha asked. She crept into the room as if a child lay sleeping in the bed. Rynn kept no light switched on. Only the moon and stars revealed them to one another.

"Yeah," Rynn replied. "You remember how I asked you to keep Cadmus from driving himself into true madness?"

There was a moment's hesitation. "Yes."

"Think you could do the same for me?"

"What do you … I mean, I think you … Rynn are you all right? What's wrong?"

Rynn sighed a long, cleansing sigh. It was like getting go of a rope you had been dangling from until your arms could take no more. "It's Harwick. He just let slip that his Veydran family name was Solaran."

Sosha clapped a hand over her mouth to stifle a gasp. "Does he know?" she asked when she took the hand away.

Rynn shook her head, still looking out at the stars. "It was offhanded. If he knew, I doubt I'd be here right now."

"Do you know how they're related?" Sosha asked. "The name has to be more than a coincidence."

"Of course it's more than a coincidence," Rynn replied, feeling the tide of panic rising. "But what do I do now? He's got the books, and he's only given back three of them so far translated. Do I keep my cards or throw them in?"

"Throwing them in is killing him, isn't it?" Sosha guessed.

Rynn put her hands against the glass and leaned against it. "Yeah. How do we risk him finding out about Dan, with so much at stake?"

"Are you sure he'd react badly? I mean … it's hard to overlook how Dan was."

"Consider Harwick's age. He's got to be a great uncle or something at the least, maybe even the kid's grandfather. Even if he doesn't hold it against the rebellion, you can bet your back teeth he's going to get revenge on *me* at least." Rynn gave a bitter chuckle and pulled the vial from her pocket. "He even gave me this for my father. It's supposed to reverse aging—one of the wonders of bookish chemistry. I leafed through the book, and there's a lot of weird substances in there. Acids that can melt through stone, artificial rubber, some disease cures you're going to want to read up on, a couple—"

"But that's all in Acardian," Sosha said. "I can't read the translations."

Rynn shrugged. "Least of our worries right now." She handed the vial to Sosha. "Can you at least take a look at this and make sure it's not poison or something?"

"Why would it be? Harwick has no way of knowing."

"He has no way that we know of," Rynn replied. "He's a clever old bastard, and he's happy to tell you about it. If he did know, this might be his vengeance."

"You're getting worse with the paranoia," Sosha said.

Rynn looked up to the moon, with her father tucked away inside. "I know. That's why I need you. Tell me, should I just open a world-hole while he sleeps, ventilate him, and start over with a new translator?"

"Who would you … no, forget what I was about to ask," said Sosha. She put a hand on Rynn's shoulder. "It's wrong. You can't just go around killing people 'just in case.'"

"I've been reading lately," Rynn replied. She pointed to a stack of books by her bedside, shadowed in the moonlight. "Histories of generals and kings. Korr didn't have what I was looking for, so these are all Telluraki. I wish I could read any of the Veydran languages; it sounds like they might be the most warlike. But they all seem to agree that killing people 'just in case' is good judgment. You have to know who your friends and enemies are. A known enemy can be a tool, but a questionable ally is dangerous. It cost Prince Artanchis in the Tea Wars, when he allied with Krangan pirates. King Gibani of Steth allied with the early Kheshi Empire against Takalish invasions, and there's no Steth anymore. What if I try to play Veydran politics in a Korrish rebellion, and end up costing us everything?"

"There's another option, even if you don't trust him," said Sosha.

"What's that?"

"You can just sneak in while he's asleep, take back the books, and never speak to him again."

For some reason that felt wrong. Some strategist in her told Rynn that it was worse to leave an ally questioning than to kill him as a traitor. She swallowed. *When did I start thinking it was all right to kill humans?* As a rule, Korrish humans did not kill one another. They fought, but it was the stuff of tavern fisticuffs and disagreements over crashball loyalties. There was always the underlying belief that harming a human helped a kuduk. All but the most ardent shavers thought that way.

It was the world-ripper. She had mixed the worlds, perhaps mixed them too much. Tellurak pitted humans against humans throughout history. Veydrus seemed little more than an arena peopled with armies and sorcerers, goblins and dragons. The creatures from there fought everything they could find. The Korrish thing to do—the human thing to do—was to take Sosha's advice. If she couldn't admit to the man's face that she had killed the twin of Danilaesis Solaran, she could at least spare the man's life in cutting him off from the rebellion.

"I'll sleep on it," Rynn said. "There's no hurry, if he isn't on to us. If he is … there's still two days until the next book is due. We have until then to decide. Madlin's got a big day ahead."

Sosha's smile twitched into place and vanished just as quickly. "Have you got a plan worked out yet?"

"Anzik's working on it."

Morning in the heart of Korr's moon was an arbitrary thing. On the world spinning below, it was always the break of dawn somewhere. For Cadmus Errol, it began when a clock at his bedside, set to Eversall time, struck 5:30 and set off a bell. Throughout the facility, every room had a clock that was within a second of matching the time Cadmus had decided for them. And so it was no surprise to Jamile to hear the bell through the door just before she knocked, and entered without waiting for a reply.

Cadmus stretched and twisted, his joints crackling as he threw off the covers and fumbled at the bedside table for his spectacles. A yawn preceded the first words he spoke on the day. "Where'd you run off to? Conspiring with Rynn again?"

"Sosha was," Jamile replied. She handed him a vial of clear liquid. "Here. This is from the latest book."

The light from the hall left the vial too much a mystery. Cadmus flipped a switch on the wall and a spark light flickered on. Holding the vial at eye level, he sloshed the contents around inside. "What's it do?"

"It reverses aging," Jamile replied, as matter-of-factly as if she had told him it was a salve for rashes.

"You don't say," Cadmus replied, continuing his examination. The only signs of his having just awakened were his rumpled clothing and wild hair. "Who concocted it?"

"Harwick," Jamile replied. "He's taken it himself, and he's already looking years younger."

Cadmus smirked. "I see. And you think it's worth the risk?"

"He gave a vial of it to Rynn, but that's not this one. I used the world-ripper and swapped it for an identical one in Harwick's desk. Rynn asked me to check it and make sure it's safe; I figured seeing how Harwick reacts to it in the morning will be as good a test as I can think of."

"Good girl. I'll get you thinking like a tinker yet."

"Rynn's also got a dilemma on her hands," Jamile said. "Harwick let slip that he's a Solaran."

"A what?" Cadmus asked with a squint.

"Dan's twin was a Solaran. They're sorcerers from Veydrus—enemies of Anzik's people."

"Wonderful," Cadmus muttered. "Does she have any thoughts on a replacement translator?"

Jamile threw up her hands. "You're just like her!" She looked around suddenly with wide eyes, then lowered her voice. "You can't just kill people because they might be enemies possibly maybe. You're helping save his people, and he wants to help us."

"And he made this …" Cadmus held up the vial to the light.

"And gave it to you freely."

Cadmus tilted to the side until a crackling sound emanated from his lower back. "I wouldn't mind forgetting what it's like to wake up every morning like a kinked chain. You ever wonder what I was like as a young man?"

Jamile smiled and glanced away. "Maybe. But you'd still be you. Just with a bit more vigor."

"And hair. I was blond once, you know. Aside from my build, folks would have taken me for full-blooded southern Kheshi."

"I'd like to see that."

Cadmus popped the stopper and raised the vial. "To Eziel, or whoever the bloody bolts wrote those books." He downed the contents.

Jamile waited in silence for a few moments as Cadmus sat with a bemused expression. "Anything yet?" he asked.

Jamile furrowed her brow and studied him. Taking him by the chin, she looked over the wrinkles at the corners of his eyes, and the edge of his hairline. "Nothing yet, but we should give it some time." She closed the door behind her. "Greuder's in the kitchen, but it'll be a while before anyone else is up. We should stay here and wait to make sure it's working."

"I'll be able to go on raids," Cadmus mused. "I won't need to waste six hours a night sleeping."

"I had more selfish reasons in mind," Jamile said. She wrapped her arms around him and they toppled to the sheets.

# Chapter 17

*"Who the blazes wrote these daft books?" – Lord Dunston Harwick*

In the cozy confines of his bedroom above the workshop he had worked in for years, K'k'rt packed away his belongings and said a quiet goodbye. For better or worse, Madlin had some plan tinkered together, and she was either going to take him with her, or he would be killed by Fr'n'ta'gur. K'k'rt snorted. Many of his fellow goblins would have found it a great honor to be devoured by their god. Most traitors and malcontents would be killed and thrown to the animals as feed. Fr'n'ta'gur was almost certain to kill K'k'rt himself, but somehow the old goblin could not bring himself to look forward to the prospect.

K'k'rt had not grown up among Fr'n'ta'gur's goblins. He had served another dragon, Ni'hash'tk, until her demise, and had lived among humans for a time. Just when he had become so different from his kin, he could not say, but he now valued his life more highly than his fellows seemed to. And there was so little left of it.

Just when K'k'rt thought he had every ache and malady of age his body could handle, it found yet another place to vex and torment him. For ten years, his back had ached each morning upon waking; for the last three it had never gone away. For five years, his fingers had pained him with their every movement. For the last two years, his spectacles had been the only thing keeping him from walking into walls, and even with them he could hardly read. And yet, for all that he was not ready to die, by dragon or otherwise.

A ripple in the aether caught K'k'rt's attention just in time for him to turn and face the world-hole as it opened. *Finally, they bring me word of the plan.* He had worried that he would be caught in the avalanche Madlin was no doubt about to unleash, struggling to keep up without knowing what was coming next. Secretly, he worried that he was not meant to survive with her.

But the world-hole revealed not Rynn, but Anzik Fehr, and Rynn's dark-skinned friend, who worked the controls. Anzik stood like his father, imperious and cold—though he lacked the edge of malice that Jinzan Fehr wielded like a dagger. The young sorcerer stepped through without preamble, and the world-hole closed behind him. It was a sound precaution, for as long as it remained open, it was bound to draw attention.

"I need to know about the collar Madlin wears," Anzik said.

"Welcome, Master Fehr," K'k'rt replied, injecting a greeting into the proceedings.

"The collar."

K'k'rt sighed and settled into a thick-padded chair. "I made it, you know."

"Then you should know how to remove it safely," Anzik reasoned. The human's head did not angle down to K'k'rt, the eyes merely glanced lower. It was as if the motion of the head was deemed unnecessary.

"Safely? There is no unsafe. There is no trick to it at all. Yes, the chains to the guards' bracers are unfortunate, but Fr'n'ta'gur insisted on some method of control over her. But merely scratching out a single rune on the collar itself will render the confining effect null. I wanted her escape to be as easy as possible, when the time came."

"So you could have released her at any time?" Anzik asked.

"Release her?" K'k'rt asked with a chuckle. "She didn't want to escape. Of course she hates it here, but she values the daily shipment of weapons for her rebels more than she values her freedom. She has the world-ripper, and she's even cleverer than she's let on. She could have gotten out of here any time she wanted."

"She bargained with me for her escape," Anzik said. "She wanted to be free of the runes that prevent her from passing through a world-hole. I think you've overestimated her."

"Bargained, eh?" K'k'rt asked. "What did you get in return?"

"Airships in Korrish fashion."

"Already delivered?"

"Yes," Anzik replied with a hint of a frown.

"Well, there you have it. She wanted your help, but not in escaping. You killed the Kadrin sorcerer for her, and she's worried that you might turn on her as well, so she tightened your alliance. You are too young for politics, it seems." K'k'rt chuckled. He liked being older than humans. "So when is Madlin planning her escape?"

"She has told me of no escape plan," Anzik replied.

K'k'rt stroked his chin. "Interesting. I had assumed her audience with Fr'n'ta'gur to fix the volcanic instability in Raynesdark was her deadline. There is no way that girl is going to solve a problem of that magnitude in just a few days. The dragon was a fool to think she could. You sure she hasn't left clues as to her plan or her time table?"

"Rynn isn't that subtle."

K'k'rt nodded. "Can you do me a favor?"

Anzik stared down at him, but said nothing.

"Can you take that pack, and the one on the floor by the bed, and bring them with you?" K'k'rt asked. "Whether Madlin chooses to honor our agreement or not, I don't think I'll be needing them *here* anymore."

Anzik nodded, then made a sign in the air with his fingers. The world-hole opened behind him. With a gesture, the two packs with most of K'k'rt's personal effects floated through to Korr. K'k'rt raised a hand and waved to the dark-skinned girl running the machine. She smiled and waved back just before she pulled the switch to shut the hole and leave K'k'rt alone in his bedroom.

There were things left that he had not yet packed. It seemed so pointless now. He lay back in the chair and fell asleep.

Madlin checked and rechecked her calculations. Across the page, diagrams and notations described in painstaking detail the method and means of venting and capping the volcanic conduit near Raynesdark. There was a fair to middling chance that some goblin would take the time to examine the plans in detail before she was allowed to present them to Fr'n'ta'gur, and she had to make sure they were believable.

Of course, Madlin held no illusion that the complicated series of piping and pressure vessels would do the least bit to stop the guts of Veydrus from vomiting forth and incinerating every goblin within miles. She rather fancied the idea that they would try. The whole project was thought out well enough that it could be used by the precocious creatures as a plan of action. She had even taught them enough that there was a chance they could build most of the components. With their primitive metal casting and their downright savage machining, she doubted they could build a residential steam heater safe enough that she'd stand anywhere near it.

But given the chance that the plans would come under scrutiny, Madlin double-checked her arithmetic. One of the key components of any lie was that it was consistent with itself. She could not recall who taught her that tidbit—lying was not on the list of courses for any tutor she'd ever had—but it had stuck with her.

The numbers swam before her eyes after hours of staring. It came as a relief when a knock at the door told Madlin that her escort had arrived. The jangle of chains and a tug at her neck was a reminder of the collar she was soon to be rid of. Whether her escape worked or the dragon killed her, she would not sleep with cold steel around her neck one night longer.

When her guards opened the door, she was surprised to find K'k'rt in the company of four priests. "Time to go," he said. There was a melancholy in his voice that carried a sense of dread.

*He thinks he's bringing me to my death.* Madlin had assumed that there was a strong possibility that the plans for Raynesdark's protection were the last thing the dragon felt he needed from her. She was a toy to him, a speculative investment that had proven more an annoyance than a profit. Or perhaps the dragon just didn't like the idea of having a human around. Since she didn't intend to hang around long enough to ask the question, Madlin accepted that she would never know for certain. That K'k'rt believed her lifespan measured only minutes long meant that he shared her trepidation.

"I get an honor guard today?" Madlin asked, gathering up the sheets of paper that described her plan.

"The chief geologist, his assistants, and the interim governor for Raynesdark will all be in attendance," K'k'rt said. "Of course, your shipment of weapons is ready as well."

*The bloody dragon wants my father to* watch *me get killed. Wonderful.* Of course, it was convenient as well. The dragon's spite would make the presence of a second world-hole that much less obvious. Rynn would be able to sneak her out as soon as Anzik destroyed the collar. The Megrenn sorcerer had assured Jamile that it would be an easy task for him. As she walked down the tunnel to the dragon's lair, Madlin wondered how many viewframes were following her. She resisted an urge to turn around and smile to them.

A nervous trembling welled inside Madlin as she entered the cavern of Fr'n'ta'gur. It was already lit, and there were goblins around the periphery. No doubt they were the officials and dignitaries that K'k'rt had mentioned. Madlin's guards brought her to the edge of the precipice overlooking the dragon's treasure hoard. The sea of gold coins disappeared into the gloom at the back end of the cavern, where Fr'n'ta'gur's breathing hissed like a bellows. The only point of solace in the room was the neat pile of crates holding her promised weapons.

K'k'rt announced her, calling into the darkness in his own language. She only made out the goblin version of her name: Md'ln.

Fr'n'ta'gur rumbled a response, his voice an earthquake. Coins sloshed and jingled as the great dragon approached. The chains at Madlin's neck rattled as her guards cowered and bowed. Bile rose in Madlin's throat, but she fought it down, gritting her teeth as she watched the reptilian head emerge from the darkness.

"Madlin Errol of Korr," Fr'n'ta'gur greeted her. "You have been given three days to show me the way your world has stopped the great volcano. Because of my infinite generosity, you had two days longer than you should have needed. Now, you will prove your worth and show the plan that will allow me to keep my new city."

Madlin realized that she had crushed the pages in a fist. She knelt and began smoothing the crumpled papers on the floor, turning each of them to face the dragon. Looking up at the maw looming over her, Madlin tried to slow her quickening breath before panic swept her away. *Not long now…*

What she had expected the dragon to do with the plan, Madlin couldn't say for certain. She had considered that she might have been required to recite the findings and explain the plan, or that one of the geologists might have been called forth to examine Madlin's work. One eventuality that she had not anticipated was that Fr'n'ta'gur would peer down and read the documents himself, but that was precisely what it appeared he was doing. The slit in his reptilian eye narrowed on the side closest to Madlin and twitched back and forth. Even with her spectacles on, Madlin would never have been able to read her scrawled handwriting from fifty feet up, let alone in the dim lighting of the dragon's lair.

Fr'n'ta'gur grumbled something and one of the goblins from the side of the chamber scurried over and scooped up the plans. "It shall be done as you suggest, Madlin Errol of Korr."

Madlin gaped up at the dragon. *It worked.* Once the dragon began his examination, Madlin was sure the creature would see her sham for what it was. Instead, she might have spared her own life. "Thank you, Mighty One. May my people have today's delivery now?"

"Of course," Fr'n'ta'gur said. Madlin thought she heard a hint of amusement, a suppressed chuckle, in that monstrous voice. "You may signal them. They are watching." The dragon's lips parted in a grin of obsidian-black swords.

Madlin held up a hand and flashed a series of numbers: three, three, two, four.

"That's not the signal," Kaia said from her seat at the world-ripper controls. The main chamber of the lunar headquarters was packed with all the residents, as well as a dozen soldiers that had been brought in for help during Madlin's extraction. They stood poised at the two auxiliary world-rippers that normally ran the river through the middle of the room.

"It is today," Anzik replied.

"Greuder, pull that lever!" Cadmus shouted across the chamber. He held a lever on the console of his own world-ripper at the upstream end of the river.

Greuder reached for a matching lever on the downstream control consoles. "What's this even—?"

"Now!" Cadmus ordered. The two men pulled their levers in unison. The workings beneath the dials clicked and whizzed as machinery took over the operator's function. "Open the hole."

"C-C-Cadmus, what are you doing?" Greuder asked. His world-ripper was aimed at the head of Fr'n'ta'gur. The dragon had brought its head level with the viewframe as soon as it had arrived.

Cadmus opened his own world-hole, this one aligned perfectly with the barrel of the World Ender Cannon.

Madlin ducked for cover as the dragon's head jerked forward. Peeking up, she saw a world-hole open in mid-air, level with Fr'n'ta'gur's head. Her guards were none too pleased with her sudden action, and jolts of spark wracked her body. Through the pain and spasms, she managed a laugh.

Right beside her, a second world-hole opened. On the far side, Rynn stood with a coil gun. Two clicks. Two dead guards. A squad of soldiers swept in and formed a perimeter. Just inside that wall of military humanity, a third world-hole opened, and Anzik stepped through. He hurried to Madlin's side and put his hands on the sides of her collar. With a sizzle of boiling steel, the collar felt away to clatter on the stone floor.

Above, there was a rush of air, an intake of breath like a sea storm. Fr'n'ta'gur's mouth opened, but it was Cadmus's voice that Madlin heard.

"That was my daughter you stole!"

The cavern shook before Madlin even realized what had just happened. Fr'n'ta'gur jerked backward, his neck wobbling. The ancient dragon toppled, his vast bulk dropping limply toward the cavern floor. Soldiers grabbed Madlin under the arms and hoisted her through the world-hole before she could think to protest.

A dragon is armored unlike any other creature. Its scales are harder than the finest steels, impervious to flame or heat of any sort. Arrows and swords turn aside without scratching it. The leathery hide beneath is sturdier than chain, tougher than an elephant's hide, and can dull a blade before it would slice through. But a three-foot diameter steel sphere, propelled faster than a rifle bullet, tore through Fr'n'ta'gur front to back in a fraction of a second. If there was time for one final thought to pass through the great beast's mind before it met its end, it would have been one of utter perplexity.

Madlin turned to watch as her rescuers piled through the world-hole, taking refuge aboard the *Jennai* from the cataclysm wrought by Cadmus's shot. She saw Anzik step through the other world-hole, taking another few of the soldiers with him and unleashing a blast of lightning from his fingertips toward foes outside her range of view. The last thing she saw before Anzik's world-hole closed was a lone, elderly goblin taking Anzik's hand and being yanked through.

Rynn's viewframe returned to just an image, so Madlin could not hear the great crash as Fr'n'ta'gur slammed to the cavern floor, his body hitting the sea of gold and his head slamming to the clifftop floor not far from where Madlin had just been rescued. The impact smashed the crates containing the day's delivery of coil guns, but that wasn't something that Madlin was going to worry about just then.

Across the *Jennai*, the word went out. The squads waiting at their world-rippers sprang into action. Human rebels swarmed into the goblin manufacturing site, coil guns clicking madly. The warehouse's magical rune defenses were blasted to rubble, along with the doors they protected. Workers streamed in and out of the world-holes, reclaiming all the goblin-made weaponry that had been stored. There were still hundreds unaccounted for in the hands of the goblin armies, but all other weapons were taken back aboard the ship.

In under an hour, the valley that Madlin had helped to build lay in ruins. The World Ender Cannon was reloaded and fired five more times, leveling buildings five or more at a time. The goblin penchant for order had laid the valley out in a convenient grid that the weapon tore into with an angry tinker's glee.

Madlin looked on from the main cargo hold of the *Jennai*, where the ship's first world-ripper had been sent to examine the dragon's lair. All the officers of the rebellion who were not at the lunar base were there. It was the sort of event that histories spoke of, and none of them wanted to miss it. The roof of the cavern had partly collapsed, but the majority of the structure remained intact. The goblin priests had all either fled or been killed. The dragon lay motionless, eyes gaping toward the viewframe. The hole where the World Ender Cannon's shot had exited its body was hidden on the far side of the corpse.

The world-ripper had enabled it all, but Cadmus's cannon had done most of the work. It was a grotesque, inefficient solution, but Madlin had to admit that it had worked. Seeing the beast dead on the floor of his own lair gave a hollow sense of satisfaction. If only all the kuduks could be lined up in one place and shot with a single cannon …

A horrible, sickening thought crept into Madlin's head. The world-ripper could be a better weapon than Cadmus had ever imagined. There *was* a place where all the kuduks were gathered together, a place where they could all be killed with a single shot: Korr.

A page in Madlin's mind drew the first lines of a sketch, a sketch of a device, a device that would kill them all. Pieces of concepts floated, yet to be placed: a river brought to a moon, a turbine turned by a waterfall, the carcass of a creature impervious to fire.

"Gather a work crew," Madlin ordered. She addressed no one in particular. "I want samples of teeth, hide, and scales, and I want them cleaned of blood and in my workshop by morning."

"What are you thinking?" Sosha asked.

"Creatures like this don't exist in our world, and I think we should learn what we can from it. Plus, I think I might like a trophy to remind folks what a tinker's vengeance looks like. Maybe we'll mount it's skull on the front of the *Jennai*."

"That's disgusting," said Sosha, aghast.

Madlin rolled her eyes. "I was joking. I just want to study it, that's all."

Rascal. She remembered at last. It was Rascal who had taught her to put together a proper lie.

# Chapter 18

*"Put two men who hate each other alone in a room and they might kill one another. Add a third that's done them both wrong, and they'll be best friends for as long that third man lives … which won't be long." – Rashan Solaran*

Jamile watched as Anzik crossed the main chamber of the lunar headquarters, exiting in the direction of his quarters. The sorcerer did not acknowledge her or Madlin as he passed, and did not give any indication of interest in the viewframe as it opened onto the Kheshi countryside of Tellurak's southern hemisphere. Madlin kept the dials moving, sweeping across verdant valleys and uncut forests. Khesh was heavily populated, but unlike the corresponding regions of Korr, there was still unspoiled land left to expand even further.

"What do you think?" Madlin asked. She kept her attention focused on the machine.

"I think he could help us," Jamile replied, staring down the corridor after Anzik.

Madlin frowned as she turned to Jamile, who stood behind her seat at the control console. "Forget him, I mean the land. The deep-dwellers will hate anything on the surface, but I think anyone from the skies would appreciate it."

Jamile shrugged. "Sure. It's pretty. But I mean, what if you sent Anzik to talk to Harwick? What's the worst that happens?"

"No, it's …" Madlin paused. Jamile saw it, the moment the question settled in and took root. The tinker's gears started turning and Madlin gave that simple question serious thought. She waited for Madlin to determine *exactly* what the worst case would be if the two met. "I suppose there's no harm if Anzik ends up killing him. There's no way of telling, but I suspect Harwick is no match for Anzik. I suppose the worst case would be angering both of them enough that they turn against us together."

Jamile snorted. "You really think that could happen? We have control of the world-rippers. We could do more damage to Anzik's people than those Kadrins could, I bet you. We're his best hope. And Harwick doesn't seem the type to … well, I take that back, I suppose he does seem like the type who'd ally with his enemy for some other reason. But I don't see Anzik going along with it."

Madlin pointed to the viewframe. "This is a real problem, one we've got right now. We have more refugees by the day, and not enough safe places to put them. If you want to go convince Anzik to confess to murder, be my guest."

"Why would I want to do that?" Anzik asked.

Jamile sat at the foot of Anzik's bed, looking up at the sorcerer as he stood regarding her with the most puzzled expression she had ever seen him display. "Because he's clever. He's going to find out sooner or later, I imagine. Better to tell him yourself and be honest about why you did it."

"I can only surmise that you have recently discovered his Veydran identity and that is what's causing your increased concern," Anzik said. He turned his back to Jamile, looking at the bare stone of the wall. "Who is he?"

"Kladriss Solaran," Jamile replied. "We don't know quite who he was, but he let his—"

"You mean Caladris," Anzik corrected her. "At the time of his death, he was one of the Inner Circle, the group of sorcerers that rules the Kadrin Empire behind their puppet empress. Caladris Solaran was also the father of one Danilaesis Solaran."

"Oh poo," Jamile swore softly. She hung her head. "So there's no way you could talk sense with him, I guess. Madlin's going to have to get those books back, then."

"Books?" Anzik's head snapped around. "What books?"

Jamile swallowed. "Oh, that's right. Double-poo. Madlin never told you about the books." Anzik stared at her, those oft unfocused eyes boring into her like the giant auger aboard the *Jennai.* "You're … not going to hurt me, are you?"

"No."

Jamile released a sigh that wasn't quite convinced by Anzik's reply. She drew herself to her feet. "Well, then I'll just—"

Anzik stepped between her and the door. "I would, however, very much appreciate you describing the books you mentioned."

Jamile sat back down. For a long moment, she stewed over just where to begin. Anzik waited, patient as ever. The impulse to call for help warred with Jamile's resolve to get Harwick and Anzik to meet. Madlin would come for her, she knew, but what would Anzik do to her in the meantime. Of course, if she relented and told Anzik everything, he might help her—but then what would Madlin do to her?

"They're old," she began. It seemed like something that had to be gotten out of the way up front. "No one even knows who wrote them. Madlin and Cadmus can't even tell what they're written on, but it's not any kind of paper anyone has seen. There are twelve of them in all, and they're written in a language none of us can read."

"But Harwick can."

"Someone told Jamile that it was all written in a language that Kadrin sorcerers can read," Jamile explained.

"Who told her that? Harwick?"

Jamile shook her head. "No, someone named Juliana. I have no idea who she was or …" She stopped. Anzik's eyes had gone wide enough to fall out of his face. "What?"

"She's alive?" he breathed.

"You know this Juliana, then?"

"She was thought dead, or so the Kadrins let us believe. There were rumors that Brannis Solaran survived his battle with Rashan Solaran and ran off with his lover. Neither of them has been seen since the last war. It was all speculation, as far as most credible accounts were concerned."

"Who is she?"

"One of their first airship commanders, widow of a failed warlock, none-too-secret lover of the most powerful sorcerer Veydrus has known since before that dragon you killed was hatched," said Anzik. "I met him when I was younger; at first I confused him for Tallax, because his Source shone brighter than the noontime sun—just like the Tallax in the stories."

"What's this got to do with Harwick and the books?" Jamile asked. She was put out, having decided to spill her mind on the matter and now being prevented from following through.

"Nothing," Anzik replied. "Everything. If those books came from her, they could be a trap, or a sign that she and Brannis have returned to help our cause. It could be a thousand things. The ways of deceit are a maze. Rushing headlong can lead to a dead end. I need to think … I need to think …" Anzik began to pace the room.

"Can you at least talk with Harwick?" Jamile asked. "If you two can come to an understanding, it might make it easier for us to get the rest of the books translated."

Anzik stopped in his footsteps. "What has come of them thus far?"

"Instructions for the world-rippers—it calls them transport gates—some chemistry things, including a youth cure-all, and a machine that calls for help." Jamile ticked them off on her fingers as she reported them. "Oh, you can't tell Cadmus about the call-for-help machine. He doesn't know yet."

Anzik furrowed his brow. "Why not?" There was something about talking with her that evoked actual emotive response from him. Jamile felt a pang of pride for bringing him a bit closer to being a normal boy.

"Madlin worried that he would use it," Jamile replied.

"Why is that a problem?"

"We don't know who it might call."

Anzik nodded.

"So … Harwick?" Jamile persisted.

"Very well, I'll meet with the man. However, his life will be forfeit should he try to avenge his twin's son's twin … which could turn out to be his actual son, now that I consider the matter."

The Harwick Estate was dark, save for a light in the sitting room. A lone sorcerer, not so elderly anymore, lounged in a high-backed velvet chair before a somber fire. The walls and furnishings were cast in flickering reds and oranges; the glassware on the liquor cart glistened. Anzik had already seen the study, with the stacks of books so clearly labeled, and the stack of translations which he could understand with some effort. The temptation had pulled at his soul, to fall into his father's own trap of betrayal and deceit. Take the books. Kill Harwick. Slaughter everyone in the heart of Korr's moon. It would have been so easy.

Of course, none of that accounted for Rynn. While she lived, vengeance would be certain, and Anzik doubted he could evade her for long. His magic was strong, his illusions convincing, but when boiled down to their essence, the tinkers vexed him. They solved problems they had no right to solve, and solving a lone sorcerer, no matter his strength, seemed well within their powers. Still, the temptation existed, and Anzik was forced to live with that as he pulled the lever that switched the viewframe to the active position.

Harwick's first reaction to the open hole was a long-winded sigh and the draining of his liquor in one gulp. It was not until after that he frowned at Anzik. "And who might you be? Have I become a way-watch for lost Korrish? No … you're not Korrish, are you?"

"No, I am not," Anzik replied. He stepped through into Harwick's sitting room and gestured to a chair. "May I?"

"By all means, and pour yourself a drink if you like," Harwick replied. "We don't stand on law and formality here. The age of accountability is a bit lower in Megrenn, especially for a sorcerer, is it not?"

Anzik's eyebrows rose a hair's width. "I'm not dressed in Megrenn style. How did you know? Did Madlin warn you?"

"That girl thinks the world is a game of Crackle. I swear if she played chess, she'd hide her pieces," said Harwick. "But I'm not blind, nor am I the fool some have taken me for. You look just like your father when he was your age."

"You knew Jinzan?" Anzik asked.

"Knew him?" Harwick replied. "Of course I knew him. He was schooled in the empire, or did he never mention that? We had allowed any fourth-generation occupied Megrenn to attend the Academy, and he was among the first. Supposed to have been long enough to breed out the memory of a free Megrenn, but by the look of it waiting for at least the sixth might have been more prudent. I taught there, like most of the Inner Circle did earlier in their careers. Your father was a brilliant, bitter bastard, stronger in Source than the others in his class, but that light haze of brown in his skin set them against him. In Tellurak, you'd never have known him from full-blooded Acardian, but he could never fool anyone in Kadrin into thinking he was a native."

"I knew he attended the Imperial Academy, but—"

"You know who I am," Harwick said, "and I know who you are. The question is: why are we both here right now? I have my answer. I'm here to rest my eyes, burn my throat, and let a warm, pleasant glow settle in my belly after a long day's work. What about you?"

"I came to tell you about your son's twin," Anzik replied.

"My what now?" Harwick asked, setting down his glass and leaning close.

"Danilaesis Solaran had a twin."

"Blast it and bugger all," Harwick swore. He stood to pour himself another drink, shaking his head. "All that time I watched for it, he had to awaken after I died. Who is he? Where can I find him? Blessed winds, who mothered him?"

"He went by a shortened form of his Veydran name: Dan. I don't know what name he was given here, or who his mother was. He's dead now though."

Harwick stiffened. The decanter in his hand stopped halfway to the glass. "Dead?"

"He worked with Madlin for a time," Anzik said. "He fell in with a twinborn named Tanner, and the two of them entered into an arrangement with Madlin and Cadmus Errol. Eventually, Dan's madness prompted her to end the arrangement."

Harwick set down the bottle and fixed Anzik with an unfocused glare. He knew the look; Harwick was checking his Source with his aether-vision. Anzik had hoped not to find violence on his visit, but knew it was possible, given what he planned to reveal. He had never before shied from battle, but rarely was a battle so personal, so intimate, as the one that brewed in Harwick's eyes. Anzik found that his stomach churned and clenched. Harwick was not so old and feeble as calendars said he should be, and he had decades more experience in magic. His Source was weaker, but not so weak that the prospect of facing him held any certainty of victory.

"You did it, didn't you?" Harwick asked, surprising Anzik yet again with his insight. "Madlin used you as her cudgel."

Anzik denied nothing. "Your son fell into the sway of Rashan Solaran. He became an obsessed devotee of the late warlock's philosophy, but without the centuries of control over his power. Rashan was a force of politics and scheming, backed by violence. Danilaesis Solaran is that violence ruled by whim and spite. Dan was a shadow of the Veydran twin, but just as mad."

Harwick slammed his glass on the table, sending up a spray of shattered crystal. "You dare show up in the middle of my sitting room, admit to murdering a son I never knew I had, then tell me he had it coming? What nerve, young sir. What nerve. You think you can get away with it because I'm just Telluraki? You can see my Source and assume I can't fight back? Well, you—"

"I came as a courtesy," Anzik replied. "You'd have found out eventually. I see that all the more clearly now, given your other surmises. I came to give you truth from the headwaters. I killed Dan because he is my enemy. I killed him because Madlin feared for her life even having him as an ally. I am responsible for the protection of Ghelk and all the Megrenn Alliance, and your son is the most destabilizing force in Veydrus at the moment. He is Rashan Solaran without the cruel, heartless cunning. He has nearly as much Kadrin blood on his hands as he has Megrenn. *You* failed him. He had nothing within him to resist the urge to destroy. My father was many things, but at least he taught me self-control."

"Danil was always a handful, but his grandfather did his best," Harwick said. "Blast me if I had the time to look after him. I was trying to keep the empire from collapsing in on itself."

"It seems it might have been better in collapse, and with a better disciplined warlock to defend what remained," said Anzik. "Now you are faced with an opportunity. I don't want this war; few among my people do. But *you* might be able to talk sense into them. Dam the flood your son has caused, and you might save the Kadrin Empire. You've seen what the transport gates can do. It's only a matter of time before the weapons the tinkers create are turned against Kadris itself."

"If you think that, why would you want my help?" Harwick asked. "Seems your tinker friends might just be rid of us for you."

"At what cost?" Anzik asked. "How many needless deaths will it take to stop Danilaesis Solaran's war? How much better to end it by him seeing reason? I abide my principles, no matter the cost. You hate me because I have killed your son's twin—who perhaps is the product of your own loose loins in this world. You probably think me a hypocrite, being the son of a pirate."

"I didn't know Zayne was twinborn until after it was too late to matter," Harwick replied. "I'd have made the navy send more ships after him, had I known."

"I killed him for you," Anzik said. "Well, not for you specifically, but I could not allow him to continue. I needed him when I was younger; he taught me much, and he protected me in his own way. But I was not blind to his nature. If Jinzan Fehr was a man who made questionable choices with good reason, Denrik Zayne was a man whose choices served no one but himself."

"Patricide doesn't typically vouch for one's character."

"What about my father was typical? How many men live in the shadow of a father who is a blight on civilized society, yet they follow him and defend him out of a misplaced sense of filial duty?"

"You're a strange one," Harwick said. Turning his back on the Megrenn sorcerer, he poured himself the drink he had abandoned moments earlier. Anzik found the resumption of Harwick's primary vice to be a positive sign in the negotiation. His odds of success seemed to have passed the break-even point.

"I have been told some variant of that same sentiment on more occasions than I can recall," said Anzik. "And in general, I have excellent recall. So what is your answer?"

"What are my options? Kill you here and now? Sadly, I fear that option passed me two or three glasses back," Harwick replied, throwing down the contents of a half-filled whiskey glass. "Tell you to go piss up a tree? I doubt you'd even find the humor in it, and it would get me nowhere. No, after all you've said and purportedly done, you still offer me the only chance I've heard to see my son again. Even Madlin didn't offer me that."

"You asked?"

"No, but I don't think she quite trusted me. Now I know why," said Harwick. He shook his empty glass in Anzik's direction. "I'm warning you though, boy. If my son has not wandered the dark, bloody path you claim, we're going to have a disagreement."

"I am not unaware of the risk that you will pursue vengeance for the twin's death," Anzik replied. "But unlike many of *your* people, peace is my ultimate goal."

Harwick filled his own glass, plus a second that he handed to Anzik. "To peace, then." Harwick threw back his drink, and Anzik raised his in acknowledgment and took a sip.

The workshop was dark. Strange machines were visible as vague outlines of shadow upon shadow in the faint light that spilled in from the corridor. Anzik felt along the wall and found a metal box with a finger-sized switch and flipped it up. Harsh yellow light burst forth from a series of glass bulbs along the ceiling, bringing color to the conglomeration of iron, steel, and brass of the machines. Though he had seen them in action, he was only passingly familiar with their workings. Unless he ever had need to work them himself, he could content himself with ignorance on the subject.

The pages scattered around the drafting table made more sense, but still painted an incomplete picture. The annotations were a language of their own. Aznik could tell that they depicted a world-ripper of some sort, because he recognized the general form of one from the diagrams that the annotations swarmed around like flies. He scanned other documents, finding familiar shapes of pieces of the larger devices that had transformed the war with Kadrin, and Madlin's own war on her world. Several were obscured by other sheets overlapping, but Anzik touched nothing. Any page that rested atop another was sacrosanct; even being in this room was an affront he knew, and he would not compound his transgression. He merely idled and took in as much as his magic-thinking mind could of the strange technology around him.

Footsteps in the hall quickened as soon as he heard them. They grew louder, so someone was on the way. Quiet yet insistent, the stomping feet of someone with soft-soles on her shoes and not enough heft to thump on the stone floor. Madlin. Kaia and Jamile were too meek. Greuder too heavy. Cadmus's shoes had soles like wood. Anzik turned to face the door and meet the verbal lashing he was about to take.

"What in Eziel's bloody footprints are you doing here?" Madlin snapped.

"I wanted to speak with you and I didn't wish to wake you. I knew you would come here soon enough."

"Wonderful. Now get out!" Madlin pointed to the door.

Anzik bowed his head and proceeded past Madlin into the halls. There were faint sounds from the kitchen, but Madlin pulled him aside into one of the storage rooms. It seemed she wanted to keep their meeting private. "I met with Harwick."

Madlin frowned. "What did she do to convince you? I figured you'd wall her off like you do everything else."

"She made a reasoned argument. At worst, I would have been forced to kill the twin of an enemy of my people. She made me curious." There was no need to specify who 'she' was. Both knew it was Jamile who had been intent on meddling.

"So, what'd you do with him?"

"He's quite alive and well," Anzik replied. "I believe you're confusing me with Dan. I don't kill wantonly or impulsively. Harwick wants to see Dan's twin, and I offered him the chance to end our war if he can talk sense into Danilaesis. He will continue his work on your books in the meantime."

"How do you know he's not going to give that information to the Kadrins?" Madlin asked. "You're as much handing them their own copies of the books." She shook her head. "I can't allow that."

"If you would grant me one thing, I think I can arrange that they do not fall into Kadrin hands."

"What's that?"

"I want to fire a shot from the *Jennai's* gun," said Anzik.

Madlin gave a single laugh. "Why would I let you fire it? Besides, it's Cadmus you'd need to convince."

"It's your army."

"People keep saying that, but he's got say here," Madlin replied. "What do you plan on shooting at?"

"You wouldn't know it. A place in the Kadrin Empire."

"I thought you wanted Harwick to help negotiate a peace," Madlin replied.

Anzik smiled. He had to force it, and he hoped it was convincing. He had been practicing. "Every negotiation has an opening offer."

The sun was low in the west, casting the city of Kadris into shadows. Among the few locations that stood tall above the sea of buildings was the Tower of Contemplation. Despite being the northwestern tower of the Imperial Palace, it predated the rest of the building by centuries. Its black marble was streaked with veins of green, carved with runes that kept it from aging, and unbroken by either seam or mortar. It was the very symbol of Kadrin magical might.

The air above it parted like a curtain, its edge crackling with a hint of lightning. A world-hole opened, and a second later, a sound like the sundering of a mountain split the air and shook the earth. Boats in the harbor were tossed on jolted waves. Glassed windows shattered across the city. Peasants panicked, screaming and seeking cover from a disaster whose nature they could not describe.

The ancient tower still stood, its runes holding it together when a lesser building might have crumbled. But a hole had been punched from roof to sub-basement and beyond. The hole in the sky closed, as if it had never been.

# Chapter 19

*"When in doubt, buy land. It will not spoil or rot. It never goes out of fashion. It will never wear out in your lifetime or those of any descendant you might imagine."*
*– Parjek Ran-Haalamar, trader*

Birdsong filled the air, and dawn's light glistened on the dew-speckled grass. There was an earthy smell, one that Madlin could barely recall anymore. It came to Tinker's Island a few days a year, and mostly while she was still abed. But Khesh was vast, and aside from the depths of winter, there was at least some portion of the empire that had such mornings. With Hayfield and Jamile in tow, she marched across the untamed grass, which snarled and tugged at her ankles while leaving them wet.

"Why doesn't anyone live here?" Madlin asked the fourth member of their group. He was a Kheshi of middle years, dressed more for a job of ink and paper than for a countryside jaunt. He wore his receding blond hair pulled back in a tail, and a pair of round spectacles gave him a superficial resemblance to her father.

"Lack of roads," the Kheshi official answered in excellent Takalish. For Jamile's benefit, Madlin had hidden the fact she spoke Kheshi fluently. He pointed to the north. "Three hours by horse to the Kurjin Trail, and that's if you know the marshes. If you don't, it's quite hazardous. Lord Stilvaar hunts these lands, but your offer has given him pause."

"It better have," Jamile muttered in Korrish. She proceeded to translate the Kheshi's comments to Hayfield.

"Are there any settlements that weren't listed on the maps?" Madlin asked, tromping through a patch of wild blueberry bushes. It was better to ask than spend hours or days scouring the land with the viewframe. Some tasks—a small number, by her estimation—still benefited from good old-fashioned human interaction.

For all his prim attire, the Kheshi official kept up well, and showed no hint of complaint about the cross-country hike. "Nothing so grand as that, but there are two hunting lodges, and there is a warden's farmstead down in the valley. He's looked after the lands and done his best to keep away poachers and squatters the past fifteen years or so. It'd be a shame to see him displaced."

"I don't mind him staying on the land, but he'll be out of a job. I plan on settling people here, not hunting it."

"There may be outlaws or poachers still," the official said. "We root them out when we find them, and tear down the hovels they build, but I cannot swear that we are free of them at the moment."

After getting the translation, Hayfield piped up. "We'll clean the place up, spit-shined and polished. A lot of this looks like pretty good farmland, and our folk can keep out the rough crowd."

"I can't help but notice the weapon you carry," the Kheshi said. "Quite remarkable. A new Errol Company weapon, I presume. Is there any chance of including a number of those—?"

"I'm already offering you ten tons of gold," Madlin said before the official could finish asking. "This place is nice enough, but it's not worth a third of that. I'm overpaying because I want this deal done quick. And since you seem like you're playing with your hand face up, let me lay this out for you. If you try to squeeze me on this deal, the next fastest way to get this done is to use these new Errol Company guns."

"Pardon my asking, Miss Errol," the Kheshi official replied with clasped hands. "It is my duty to Lord Stilvaar to get the best bargain for his land. Even yesterday, he was not expecting to sell it at all."

"Friendly advice then: tell him to start spending it quick. I plan on buying a lot more land around Khesh."

"How much more?" the official asked.

"Enough that there's going to be a lot of gold floating around the economy," Madlin replied.

Hayfield had wandered afield, and stood with Jamile at the edge of a precipice, looking down. Madlin ventured over and joined them, the Kheshi official trailing her like a puppy. The land dropped off sharply before leveling out into a forest of oaks and maples, old trees with a canopy that held room enough beneath for houses and roads. The sun was just touching the tops of the trees, and the valley floor still lay in night's final throes.

"Your call, Hayfield," Madlin said softly. It seemed somehow rude to intrude upon nature's awakening. "You think you can convince deepers to live here?"

"Deepers are going to be a problem anywhere we put 'em," Hayfield replied. "Forest's probably better than the open plains, and the sky-dwellers are going to love this place. Help from them world-rippers and we'll have this valley built up in a matter of months."

"You've always known how to deal with people," Madlin said. "I'm counting on you to sell this place as a home, not a hideout. This is a one-way trip."

Hayfield looked down into the valley and shook his head. "Leaving Korr … can't quite believe it, to be honest. You sure about this?"

"Hiding and half-measures aren't getting the job done. If everyone's counting on me to win this war, I'm going to fight it the only way I know how. And I don't want our people in the way when I do it."

Kezudkan stood with his hands clasped atop the handle of his cane. Beside him, the Pillar of Runes looked on as Gederon worked the controls of the transport gate. Ever since the Kadrin boy had read the book on its operation, he had insisted that they use the book's name for it. The pair of them watched in the target locator—once called the viewframe—as the countryside of human surface lands rushed by.

"Is this an appropriate use of such a grand machine?" the Pillar of Runes asked in a whisper, leaning close.

Kezudkan considered not replying. Muddy fools, the lot of them. The human boy Danilaesis was running amok, and none of them had the stones to stop him. But holding his tongue was never a course the old daruu chose easily. "Invite one rat, and they all move in."

"Stop there!" Danilaesis said, pointing at the scene. His Korrish was stilted, but clear, and Gederon obeyed without hesitation. The daruu lad was four times the warlock's age, but deferred to him as if he were an elder. "Move closer."

The target locator descended upon a village of cylindrical houses with conical roofs, interspersed with patches of farmland. Animals grazed in the pastures, and pale-skinned humans in hats that resembled the roofs of their houses worked the fields. They used primitive hand tools, doing work that a proper steam tractor would manage on the move at a walking pace. Savages, even by human standards.

Kezudkan felt a twinge of aether, and the switch to the machine snapped closed. The target locator became a gate—Kezudkan had to keep reminding himself of the new terms, lest he pique the warlock's ire by using the rebels' terms, even though he had minted those terms himself. A breeze wafted into the chamber, carrying with it the sickening odors of dung, sweat, and pollen.

A stronger pull in the aether made Kezudkan grab at the stone floor. The bare flesh of his feet clung tight, rooted to the essence of the rock. He could have held firm against a bursting dam. But it was merely a sensation in the aether, with no real ability to pull him loose from his footing. Swallowing back the dread in his throat, he watched the spectacle unfold before him.

Danilaesis Solaran was a rune-thrower, something that Kezudkan had heard in legend and myth until his world-ripper had opened a path to other worlds. He wished with every corner of his mind that he could stuff that knowledge back into the stories from whence he had first heard them. Sleep was growing harder the more he witnessed the power of unbound runes. The physical sciences fell apart at their touch. Lightning crackled forth from fingers instead of clouds, with thunder absent. Humans and lesser beasts were thrown by unseen hands. Fire belched in gouts that consumed buildings and crops alike, but had no proper point of ignition or intermediary fuel. It was madness that painted destruction, and if it was directed at humans, it took only a paltry flex of Kezudkan's imagination to see himself in the path of the flames.

Morbid fascination rooted him in place, as well as worry over Gederon's safety. What Kezudkan would do should the warlock's nitroglycerine temper fall upon the lad was a mystery to him. Were he not so old and feeble, he might get halfway across the chamber before the warlock struck him down. At best he could bear witness, and not hear about Gederon's death secondhand.

But the lad was fine—for now. Nothing of the sort could be said for the humans through the gate. They hadn't even managed to fight back, fleeing and cowering in the face of their doom. At the warlock's command, the gate was closed and the search began for their next target.

"How long until we can get him working on your world?" the Pillar of Runes asked.

Kezudkan sighed. "The successor negotiated five days of his use of the machine for five days of his help with Korr's half-breeds. I suppose we'll find out in four days what that bargain is worth."

"And what if he does not agree?" the Pillar is Runes whispered. The boy's eccentricities and savagery were apparent to all of them.

"He isn't unstoppable," Kezudkan replied.

"Or deaf," Danilaesis added, not turning from his vigil at the target locator. "I'll kill your kuduks. Don't worry. I'll get bored with this before long. What I really want to find is missing."

"What would that be?" the Pillar of Runes asked. As they spoke, Gederon continued to move the view across the Veydran landscape.

Danilaesis turned around, grinning lopsidedly. There was a glint in those eyes that Kezudkan had seen in one of his handymen, once. The man had killed two kitchen girls, and sat at the table with their bodies slumped across the chairs to either side of him, sipping soup. He hadn't flinched when the guards came and shot him. Same look.

"The one who killed me," Danilaesis replied.

The breeze from the Aliani Sea drifted past, languid with its own baking heat. Inland from the white sands, the tall jungle grasses shushed with the footsteps of unwelcome guests. Birds squawked from unseen heights, challenging the intruders, but the humans below had larger problems than the territorial rights of parrots and macaws.

"This is no way to run a war," General Kaynnyn said. She had shed her accustomed earrings and necklaces, resorting to simple garb without adornment, such as a humble islander might wear. Still a large woman, she had slimmed down amid the primitive conditions and unaccustomed exercise. "We're just hiding here."

"The airships are mobile," Anzik replied. He had shed his sorcerous robe in favor of a loose tunic and knee-length trousers that exposed skinny, pale legs.

"Anything that stays put in this war is forfeit. Hiding and moving are the only ways to survive."

"We need to mount an assault," General Kaynnyn replied. The two of them walked along the jungle's edge barefoot, within sight of the sea. "He's wearing us down by the day."

"I know," Anzik replied. "I'm the one bringing you the reports. Don't act as if I don't understand what's going on. Your army proved useless against the warlock. My airships only somewhat less so. The tinkers are our hope. Those guns of theirs can kill even a warlock, I think."

Kaynnyn shook her head and scowled down at Anzik. "Is that a way to protect your people? Just hope that a tenuous ally sees fit to rescue us?"

They came upon a secluded beach, tucked away in a cove and sheltered from view of ships by a stretch of rocks. A young girl knelt at the waves' edge, letting the seawater soak the skirt of her dress as she dug in the mud with her hands. She had wheat blonde hair and eyes like emeralds, with skin that had bronzed beneath the tropical sun. A number of guards kept a discreet distance with vigilant eyes on her.

"Princess Anju is safe here," Anzik said softly, so as not to let the girl overhear. She was a strange creature, ever growing. If he was away a month or more, he came back to see a different girl in her place, recognizable but certainly not the girl he left. He wondered what she would change into before she was of age to become his wife.

"For how long?"

"Long enough for me to put an end to Danilaesis Solaran," Anzik said. He took one final look at Anju, tucking away the image of her in his memories to compare when next he saw her. "I need to be getting back." He tromped off into the jungle, with General Kaynnyn in tow.

"We could use you here," she said to his back.

"Of course you could," Anzik replied. He held up a hand and flashed through a series of signs. "I could be a great use in many places. If there were a dozen of me, we would be faring far better than we are. If we had a hundred of me, we'd have won this war easily. But we must make do with the one of me we've got." A world-hole opened, with Kaia sitting just on the far side attending the controls. "And for now, the best place for me is with the Korrish rebels. They hold the key to our salvation."

Changed back into his proper attire and with his feet washed clean of the jungle dirt, Anzik felt more like himself. General Kaynnyn's objections weighed on his mind. The Megrenn Alliance needed him; that much was undeniable. But the general was an old cavalry soldier. She wanted to fight a war that looked like a war, and that wasn't what they were faced with. Anzik knew his mind held greater breadth than the rest of those in the Alliance. It was up to him to fight the war their enemies had brought them. It was up to him to know how best to do it.

The walk from his room to Madlin's workshop was eighty-seven steps. Long enough to come up with a plan of action for the near term. The fourth-dimensional geography involved was one of the key components of the war. Interconnected worlds. Indefensible fortifications. Impossible reconnaissance. It was chess with a million pieces and a board that folded in on itself. And it was everyone's turn. But even a seemingly infinite problem still consisted of a number of finite tasks, and Anzik needed to narrow those down, chop the problem into tasks he could accomplish. The first was clear in his mind before he stepped foot into Madlin's workshop.

The screech of metal always bothered Anzik's ears. The pitch was wrong, too shrill. He stuck fingers in his ears to dampen the sound, and heard his own voice echo weirdly in his skull as he called out. "Madlin, I need a moment of your time."

Madlin raised her head from the machinery. She wore muffled cups over her ears to deaden the sound of her own work. "What for?" she shouted back.

"My people are being slaughtered," Anzik shouted, still plugging his ears. "Too quickly, too erratically to be airship strikes. I think Danilaesis has gained access to a world-ripper."

"Piss on that!" Madlin shouted back. "That's the last thing any of us need."

"I was hoping you might allow me to evacuate my people along with your own. Tellurak has room enough for all of them."

"We've got enough trouble with logistics as it is."

"Please," Anzik shouted. "They're human too. They've done nothing. It's my job to protect them, and I can't do it without your help." There was greater than an eighty percent chance that the appeal to their common humanity would be enough to get Madlin to concede his point.

Madlin's shoulders rose and fell in a sigh that went unheard. "Fine," she shouted. "But you're going to have to teach me something to make a worthwhile trade, something I can use. Work it out with Kaia and Jamile; we don't need to tie up the *Jennai's* world-rippers for this."

"Thank you," Anzik shouted. Madlin nodded in acknowledgment and returned to her work. Once he closed the door behind him, Anzik unplugged his ears.

*She doesn't want the* Jennai *involved.* A jumble of thoughts jostled in Anzik's head as he meandered to the central chamber of the lunar facility. *The* Jennai *is where the Korrish rebels have their military power. She doesn't want it distracted from its primary mission. Its primary missions are to deal with the threats to the Korrish humans, and to keep the rebels safe and hidden.* A thought clicked into place. A second thought fell in beside it. Then a third.

*They need for Danilaesis to become a threat to the* Jennai, *then they'll deal with him.*

"Throw a rock or something," Danilaesis shouted through the transport gate. The farmers he berated were jumping one by one off an embankment that overlooked a pond. "Bleeding winds, you cowards sicken me. I'm burning your homes and killing you like hogs on a feast day morning. At least die like men!"

Of course, Danilaesis didn't speak a word of Ghelkan, so he swore and spat and raged at them in his native tongue. He doubted they would have heeded him even if they understood his words. They weren't soldiers or sorcerers, merely peasant farmers. That was all he found of late. The sensible ones, the tradesmen and the moneyed, had all scattered like dandelion fluff on a windy day. The only ones who clustered in numbers worth stopping the machine to slaughter were the farmers, enslaved by the land they worked, yoked to it until death.

It was sickening. Worse, it was unbefitting a warlock. Danilaesis was worth so much more to the Kadrin war effort. Burning the countryside was a siege tactic that might pay off in starvation if the war dragged on long enough. Danilaesis had always hated sieges, even when reading about them in histories. It was a quartermaster's way to defeat a general. Cut off supply caravans. Foul the water upstream. Poison the wells. Cluster your enemy in close quarters so disease might take hold among them. They were cowards' tactics. Danilaesis wanted a foe he could dull his blade against. None was to be found. The Ghelkan cities were mausoleums. The smaller towns all but deserted. Where the people had gone remained a mystery, but most likely they had fled any way they could, either hiding in the wild countryside or taking ships to lands across the seas. Danilaesis would get to those eventually. The missing armies were more of a worry. There ought to have been too many to conceal. He had not done so much damage to the Megrenn Alliance that their military had crumbled.

Danilaesis loosed a bolt of lightning into the pond, assuming that anyone in the water was as good as dead. Turning his back on the gate, he waved a dismissive hand and heard the sound of burning farmhouses end abruptly.

Reflecting for a moment as Gederon sought his next target, Danilaesis came upon an irksome realization: he was bored. There was no challenge in chasing villagers around with lightning and fire, even if they were technically enemies. The benefit to the Kadrin Empire was nil.

"Let's try something a little different," Danilaesis said, using the common tongue of the Korrish and daruu. "Switch this thing to look into Korr."

"Of c-course, sir," Gederon replied. The daruu had a stuttering voice that was going to get on his nerves one day. "Whe-where should I be l-l-looking."

"To the skies," Danilaesis replied, forcing a cheery smile. "I think it's long past time I found Madlin's flying barge. It took two of them to kill me, and if I can't find Anzik Fehr, I'll find Madlin Errol."

Axterion clung to the ship's railing with less dignity than he would have preferred to display in front of a bunch of navy men. The *Dragon's Kiss* drifted amid the trees, picking its way as through a patch of brambles. Podawei Wood was a blot in the heart of the Kadrin Empire, a forest deep and ancient that had defied exploration, logging, and even hunting beyond the nearest reaches of new growth at its edge. It was a place that made it seem the gods had fashioned it before deciding that trees should ever stop growing. The Kadrin airship passed among trunks that could have been carved out and made into towers, dodged branches that could hold three wagons driven abreast. There was a gloom of twilight upon the place, the midday sun held back by an ocean of leaves that formed the canopy above.

"We have no heading," Captain Mulrak reported. "We'll have to climb above again to check the sun."

"Just keep going," Axterion replied. "We're not here to find, so much as to be found."

The pieces all fit. Years ago, he had helped Brannis unravel the mystery of the demons' hiding place. Though he had never reported back about it, Axterion had long suspected that the boy had found them. Direct intervention was the only explanation for why the interior of Podawei could remain unknown to the Kadrin Empire despite history's greatest sorcerers and warlocks originating from within their borders. To think that mere happenstance or some natural phenomenon could keep so many curious eyes from learning their secrets defied logic. Many had never believed in the existence of demons; that was one great defense their secret had. But Axterion believed. He had known demons—by the winds he'd had tea with them. Now he finally had the impetus he needed to go looking.

Hours passed. The trees betrayed nothing. No stump marked a logger's work. No trail wove among the gnarled and serpentine roots that broke the forest floor. No cut or rope around a trunk marked a trail. The *Dragon's Kiss* flew low, for most of the branches started higher than the rooftops of Kadris, and posed the greatest threat to their flight—as far as the crew knew. Axterion held rank enough that he needed no justification for his orders. Being known as gruff, crotchety, and the only one who kept Warlock Danilaesis in line, kept most from arguing.

If only he *could* keep Danilaesis in line.

The mood of the crew was tense. It didn't take a captain's keen instincts to tell that much. It also didn't take a naturalist's study to know that the trees around them were obscenely old. The buildings in Kadris—some of them, anyway—dated back more than a thousand winters, but they were stone and all stone looks the same when runes preserve it through the ages. The mountainous trunks humbled the sky sailors, and it was not a humility that became them. They had become ants at the feast table, just noticing the gods that loomed above.

Several times more, the captain looked at Axterion with a question poised on his lips. A glare would shove that question back to where it came from. Let the men grumble and gossip and fret. There were more dangerous duties they could have been called to, and ones with far less urgency for the empire. Axterion had no patience for soldiers who didn't soldier.

The ship stopped. Axterion had given no order, and neither had the captain. But it was not the drifting halt that required an anchor. One moment the *Dragon's Kiss* had been drifting along, the next it was not. Glancing around for answers, Axterion noted that the sailors had stopped as well, frozen mid-action in whatever task had occupied them.

Letting his eyes slip into aether-vision, Axterion scanned the area. The Sources of the ancient oaks and pines blotted out most of the detail in the aether. But Axterion's eye for aether was keen. Though he had felt nothing, no disturbance of the aether at all, the ship and crew were all enchanted. It was the first part of their mysterious halt that had made sense. Now the question became: who worked such subtle magic that his sensitive Source had detected nothing at all amiss? There was one simple way he could think of to find out.

"Come on out and show yourself, you ghost-Sourced old bugger," Axterion shouted into the wilderness. He walked around the ship, looking for any sign of someone approaching. "You've as much as admitted you're around, now get over here and face me, before I go hoarse. I'm looking for Illiardra."

"You've found her."

Axterion spun to find the demoness behind him. Illiardra wore the garb of a peasant musician and carried a harp beneath her arm. It was a change from the fey dresses she wore when acting as Rashan's consort, but he supposed clothing tastes were fickle among her kind. "How'd you do that?"

"You're not as perceptive as you believe."

"I need your help."

Illiardra had a laugh life a child, bubbly and lacking self-consciousness. "What do you need *my* help with? I am no subject of your empire."

"Technically, your whole forest is inside the Kadrin Empire."

"No mortal creature has set foot in this forest and left alive," Illiardra replied. "How then do you think it yours?"

Axterion waved a hand between them, as if swatting away flies. "Forget that. I've got a warlock problem."

"Young Danilaesis?"

"We don't grow them in orchards," Axterion snapped. "Of course Danilaesis. He's got it in his head he's the next Rashan, and I'm losing my grip on his leash. I figured I needed the world's leading expert on taming madman warlocks."

"I failed with Rashan," Illiardra pointed out.

Axterion scoffed. "After a hundred winters. I'd be happy for a season or two of peace from the boy's tantrums."

"What do you expect me to tell you?"

"If I knew what you'd tell me, I wouldn't have come," Axterion replied. "You can talk to him though. He associates you with Rashan; he might take better heed of what you say."

Illiardra shook her head. "I have no association with the boy."

Axterion gritted his teeth and scowled. He was unaccustomed to dealing with his elders, nor was he in the habit of resorting to cheap tricks to get his way. Above all, however, he hated to lose. "He's as much a product of your failure as Iridan."

Illiardra rose, her delicate feet leaving the deck of the ship until she looked Axterion in the eye. "Leave my son out of this."

"Rashan pushed Iridan until he got himself killed," Axterion continued. "No denying that. Even Rashan admitted his fault there. Well, he put those same fool notions into the boy, and now Danil's grown enough to put those deadly notions into practice. Except he's not Rashan; not as strong, not as cunning. Imagine Rashan on his most bloodthirsty day, and you've got Danilaesis. He's headed down a mountain pass toward a bridge that won't take his weight. Except he thinks he's feather-light, thanks to that bloody warlock of yours. Tell me how this isn't your problem?"

"I was not Rashan's keeper," Illiardra replied. "In the end, his decisions were his own. I could not redeem him."

"Hope's not lost on the boy yet. He's crazed as a cat in a bathtub, but he's not so set in his ways. Rashan had a hundred forty summers before you met him. Danil's only thirteen. Humors do some strange things to a boy at that age, but he's got it worse than most. Set him to rights now, and you can spare everyone a load of hurt."

"He would not listen to me," Illiardra replied. "I am a woman, and no warrior. In the heat of youth, he would think of me as a conquest, to make himself a true heir to Rashan's legacy."

"A good knock in the head would cure him of that."

"And I am not the one to supply such chastisement," said Illiardra. "There is another though, to whom he might pay heed. You had another grandson … he could serve your need."

"Brannis?" Axterion asked, frowning in puzzlement. "He's been dead six winters now, ever since … aw, bugger all. You must know something about him that I don't, or you wouldn't have mentioned him. Brannis isn't dead, then, I take it? Where's that boy been? We could've used him all these winters, and who cares if the empress blames him for Rashan's death."

"He is blamed rightly, though by the wrong name," Illiardra replied. "I know you are aware of the twinborn, Axterion Solaran; your wife was one of their number. It was not Brannis, but rather his twin who possessed the magical power to end Rashan's immortality. If I do bear some blame for the state of your grandson, it is but a small measure. To atone for that small measure, I will bring word to your other grandson that you need his help with Danilaesis Solaran."

Axterion rubbed his chin. "I suppose. I wouldn't mind seeing Brannis myself. Blast it all, where's that boy been?"

Illiardra ignored the question as rhetorical. "I will return you to your city, along with your ship. The crew must remain with us."

"Pardon me?" Axterion replied. "I think I just misheard you. You're not kidnapping these men. I'll have this forest down around your ears."

"I am not the only one of my kind to take note of your presence," said Illiardra. "The warning spells alerted me while I was visiting another world. A dozen more of my kind are watching us right now. You blundered in, and only by the grace of my intervention are you being allowed out. Just you. Consider yourself honored by the exception."

"Now just you—"

There was a swirl of aether as Illiardra's magic grabbed hold of him, and Axterion was swept into the void between worlds, the place where aetherial transport was possible. Unseen forces tugged and prodded, but he knew his way in the space between worlds. Those forces tried to drag him off in the direction of Kadris. Axterion dug his mind's heels into the aether and held his ground. Time passed slowly there he knew, and so after a struggle that felt like minutes, he knew that hardly a blink had passed in Podawei Wood. When he reappeared in the same spot he had occupied a moment before, the shock on Illiardra's face was plain.

"—listen here," he continued. "You may have been born when this world was a ball of clay in the gods' hands, but I've been around a while myself. You won't shoo me away like some thick-tongued sorcerer garbling out his spells and waving his fingers in the air. You may have a subtle way with aether that you can work it without drawing it in first, but when I call the aether, it answers. Now, if you'd like to bandy spells back and forth to see if you can evict me by trickery before I cave in that demon Source of yours to find out what immortals are made of, by all means, let's. But unless you're willing to roll up those sleeves of yours and fight me over it, I'm leaving here with all the men I came with."

Illiardra drifted a step back, her feet dangling in mid-air. "Perhaps the madness in Danilaesis's blood is hereditary."

Axterion snapped his fingers. It was a showy gesture, and it had nothing to do with the exacting work of pulling apart the spell that held the crew of the *Dragon's Kiss* in thrall. But with a grunt of effort, Axterion freed them—and the ship as well. He gave Illiardra a glare he perhaps ought to have used on Danilaesis long ago—the look that demanded obedience and promised death.

"We're going now. If I don't hear from my other grandson in five days' time, I'll be back, and I won't be alone."

And he went.

# Chapter 20

*"When you take the short path through learning, you learn only the short path."*
*–Takalish proverb*

Cadmus and Harwick sat across a table next to one of the panoramic windows of the *Jennai's* finest dining hall. The room had been cleared except for a few guards near the entrance, and Vaulk, who was acting as both chef and waiter. A clutter of paper filled the space between them, along with a mug of ale for Cadmus, a wineglass for Harwick, and a platter of sugar-dusted pastries for them to share.

"This is all quite detailed," Harwick commented. "I'll need some time to pore over it on my own. If you don't mind me asking, did you put this all together since my agreement with the Megrenn boy, or did you have this all tucked away on speculation?"

Cadmus shrugged and took a swig of ale. The negotiation had gone well. Harwick was experienced in politics and needed no hand holding. "There was nothing to speculate over. I'd never thought of sending you to the Kadrins as an ambassador. That's not my fight. Far as I'm concerned, the boy was a consultant, not an ally. If getting peace in your world gets me more use out of him, all the better. Rust it all, I wouldn't mind *your* help once this matter boils down."

"I still have my responsibilities in Acardia. I've been remiss on that count as it stands."

"Well, don't you forget about finishing those books," Cadmus said. "There are some real diamonds in all that coal. I look ten years younger and feel twenty."

Harwick chuckled. "I look twenty younger and feel forty. Blazes, Cadmus, you weren't that old to begin with."

"I worked for a living," Cadmus replied. "I might have been able to buy and sell half of Acardia, but I got there working with my hands. Takes more of a toll than years alone would account for."

Vaulk stopped by the table with a pair of pitchers, refilling both men's drinks. "Anything else I can get you gentlemen?"

"Nothing for me, thanks," Cadmus replied.

"You wouldn't know any Veydran confections, would you?" Harwick asked. "I might as well get my palate acclimated to the food."

"Sorry," Vaulk replied. "I mostly do Korrish and Acardian. I can bake you a batch of spiced crescents if you like."

Harwick waved him away. "Fine, go bring something distracting." He waited until Vaulk had left the dining hall. "Do you know I once thought that man's twin was a Megrenn spy?"

"I'm the one who got him out of Acardia before your people hanged him for treason."

Harwick snorted. "If we didn't hang Denrik Zayne, why would we hang a disloyal baker?"

"He wasn't disloyal," Cadmus replied. "He was finding Korrish twinborn for me. And he's good enough with politics that he helped me put together our agreement. All but that one letter that Anzik wrote in your language."

"It bothers you, doesn't it?" Harwick asked, smirking over his wine glass.

"I'd like you to read it aloud before I send you off with it."

Harwick raised an eyebrow. "You know, I hated dealing with you as a businessman. You knew when you had a man pinned by his purse strings, and you never let him forget it. But you'd have made a fair politician with a bit of polish. Bit ham-fisted, asking me outright, but the distrust is well-placed. I don't know what the boy is playing at either, but I'll take the opportunity to see my second home again."

"And your son …"

Harwick paused, lips pursed. "Not sure I'm going to like what I see. Whatever that boy's twin did to get his own allies to turn on him, I hope it hasn't taken root in Danilaesis. Unfortunately, I fear you might have only heard the echo, not the scream."

Cadmus pushed a page across the table. It was written in a more delicate hand than the treaties and notes penned by Cadmus and Greuder. "Aloud."

Harwick sighed and took the letter in hand, adjusting his spectacles. After a moment's struggle, he took them off and chuckled. "Haven't any need of them, it seems." He cleared his throat and began to read:

"Greetings and so forth. On behalf of the Ghelk, Megrenn, Safschan, Narrack, and all the other peoples of the Megrenn Alliance, I extend the following offer of peace. I propose a redrawing of borders … he goes on in some length as to a proposal … I would also propose a reduction in standing military forces to no more than one active soldier per eighty citizens … Kadrin had one per twenty-four, last I knew … and a moratorium on airship travel over one another's territory until such time as trade relations are established, which may be negotiated in future treaties. I would also propose regular summits between sorcerous officials of all treaty signatories, and the designation of a neutral third party for arbitrating disputes … by the winds, I think the boy's been reading my Acardian legal framework for the post-monarchy era. He goes on for a while on the particulars and gives some tentative suggestions. Oh here's a bit near the end: and should you decline to accept the premise of negotiations, the Megrenn Alliance is prepared to reach farther afield for allies, and expand the conflict until such time as we are able to overmatch the Kadrin Empire. I hope that with reason ruling our actions, we can avoid the needless loss of life that would ensue. Signed, Anzik Fehr."

"Looks like more is written than just a name at the end," Cadmus said, pointing to the bottom of the page. He had followed along as Harwick read, watching for signs that the former Veydran twinborn was making things up instead of reading them, but he had found none.

"Oh, just the boy's formal title," Harwick said. "Similar to Kadrin titles, it's a fire that belches more smoke than it should. He claims to be elder sorcerer of the Megrenn Alliance—certainly not by age—protector of the Ghelkan people, betrothed to Princess Anju, and heir of Loramar. That last bit's puff if I ever heard it. My twinborn spy network has withered in recent years, but I know that it was his father that unearthed Loramar's tomb and took up the title of heir. I don't think that's the sort of thing that's hereditary."

"Who's Loramar?" Cadmus asked.

"The last one to seriously threaten the Kadrin Empire," Harwick replied. "A necromancer—that's a sorcerer that brings the dead to semi-life and makes armies of them—he had a grudge with Rashan's conquest of Ghelk, and nearly succeeded in wiping us from the face of Veydrus a hundred winters—er, years—ago."

Cadmus took another swig of ale as he pondered something. "Is that boy one of those necromancers?"

Harwick smiled in reply. "Probably."

Kezudkan ambled along at the head of a procession through the tunnels of the daruu city. It had no name; it was simply "the city" in their tongue. That was going to change, he assumed, once word spread of Veydrus. The Korrish daruu that followed him gawked and questioned, exchanged greetings with Veydran natives, and just generally enjoyed the feel of bare feet on the stone. All of them wore cloth, but he could see the envious gleam in their eyes at the precious metals worn by the upper class daruu of Veydrus.

Taking the low road through the market quarter, Kezudkan fielded questions of every sort. How did they get their water pumped in? How did they get by without humans or kuduks to do the ox-work? Did the daruu of Korr ever live like this? Kezudkan answered all the questions he could, but deferred others for when they dined with their hosts that evening.

"Do they accept payment in tenar?" his cousin Ilgadru asked, eyeing a suit of silver chain.

Kezudkan grinned. "No, but if you like, I can put it on my credit. It turns out I have quite a tidy fortune at my disposal, thanks to the use of my machine."

"That beast of a contraption ought to fetch a price and a half, that's for certain," said Olumaruk Steelspinner, an old business acquaintance of Kezudkan's from when they were both young men. Olumaruk pursued too many projects involving the thunderail for Kezudkan's taste however, and the amount of time Olumaruk spent under the sun had led them to part ways a century and a half ago. "*You* must still take tenar. How much would you want for one?"

Kezudkan laughed in earnest, the infectious sort that had a few of his normally dour fellow daruu joining in, though they didn't know the root of the jest. He had them in a positively jolly mood, exploring the wonders of their kinfolk's land. "Tenar are the currency of the past. Kuduk money, if you will. I plan on liquidating the remains of my Korrish fortune."

"You're not planning ever going back, are you?"

Kezudkan spread his arms. "Look around you. You haven't even seen a tenth of the wonders this place holds. You'll see all that was lost, corrupted, or replaced by our kuduk 'friends.' I have only one piece of business tying me to Korr, and one civic duty."

"What might those be?"

Kezudkan clenched his jaw and frowned, but could not muster the effort to maintain his resolve. He had to tell them. He had to show them that he was the foremost among them—a leader, not a mere tour guide. "One is to get the world-ripper machines out of the hands of the kuduks. The other is to get them out of the hands of a human."

Harwick lounged in his shipboard accommodations. He had the night and the next day to familiarize himself with the proposals, to arrange his arguments, and to prepare himself for a meeting with Danilaesis. It was the last that worried him most, but above all those worries was a puzzlement. He glanced at Anzik Fehr's proposal once more, only sparing the corner of his eye for the task. There was the risk that someone was watching him through one of the target locators of a transport gate. Despite his hedges to make the Korrish wonder whether he could, Harwick was blind to their looming presence. A lesser man might have gone mad with paranoia under such ever present scrutiny, but Caladris Solaran had lived in a nest of subterfuge, rumor, and gossip, where spies were dinner guests, stable hands, and children playing in the streets.

He reread the last line.

*I will bargain the airship's location for peace.*

It was not quite the wording he had conveyed to Cadmus. To give the Mad Tinker credit, he was suspicious of the Fehr boy's motives. But he was no match for Harwick at the chess game of backroom politics. Caladris Solaran had told more lies in a daily Inner Circle briefing than Cadmus Errol told in a year. The tinker was clever, but his mind trod different paths, ones paved in steel and copper instead of lies.

It was sorely tempting to throw the offer into the fire—assuming there was a bloody fireplace aboard the airship. But if there was reason for Anzik Fehr to believe Danilaesis would trade peace for the *Jennai's* location, there was the chance he might need to barter that same information for the boy's obedience. Clearly it was meant as a means of enacting vengeance, but he had to puzzle through the Fehr boy's logic for the betrayal.

On the surface, it seemed a straightforward matter. At the cost of some itinerant allies, the Megrenn would gain peace with the Kadrin Empire. But there must have been some way to negotiate peace otherwise. Why not simply trick the girl and strand her in Veydrus? Was Anzik Fehr that frightened of Danilaesis that he would not even enter so closely into the plan as that? And for that matter, he had far more to do with the twin's murder than Madlin had. Why would Danilaesis satisfy himself with vengeance upon the lesser actor?

Harwick was not a man prone to rash decisions. If he were going to show the letter to Danilaesis at all, it would only be after he discovered Anzik Fehr's game.

"*Indresio ananakne ubtaio wanuzar pronetook,*" Madlin mumbled.

"*Indreithio anamakne ubtaio wanuzar pronedook,*" Anzik corrected her. "Try it again."

"*Indreithio ananakne ubtaio wanuzar pronedook.*"

"*Anamakne,* not *ananakne,*" Anzik said.

"*Indreithio anamakne ubtaio wanuzar pronedook.*" Even thinking the strange words was tiring, and her tongue was twisting itself into knots.

"Better. Again."

Madlin repeated it ten times more at Anzik's insistence. She counted them, forcing herself to push through the cramping in her mouth. At the eleventh time Anzik told her to speak the words, she held up her hands. "I'm done."

"You wanted to learn magic. You're learning magic," said Anzik.

"I'm not learning magic; I'm learning to repeat gibberish. Nothing happens when I say it, and nothing happens when *you* say it, so it's not as if getting it right or wrong is the problem. Can we just skip to the actual magic part? I'm a quick learner."

"No."

"But I—"

"You already wanted to skip the spell primer, and I agreed. If you wanted this to be easy, you'd have started with the most basic of spells and learned to form proper thoughts in your head," said Anzik. "But you wanted spells with immediate applicability, so I'm starting you as far in as I dare. Nothing is happening because I am teaching you the words and gestures separately. Trying it all at once would get you hurt."

Madlin gave him a long-suffering grin. "I'm not *that* bad … am I?"

"It's not a matter of being good or bad at it. You're inexperienced. Imagine me blundering into your workshop and trying my hand with the machines."

"That's different," Madlin said. "There's a lot of power in those machines. Even something as simple as a drill press can tear a finger off if you get it caught in the wrong place."

"A simple light spell, misspoken and without proper safeguards by the caster, can leave you a charred husk with ash for blood."

"Oh?"

"Yes. Having second thoughts?"

"Are you just trying to scare me?"

"Yes, but everything I've said is true. I want you to understand the seriousness of this undertaking. Being exposed to Dan and to my own magic has given you a false sense of ease of what is going on. For all his faults, Dan was a virtuoso of combat spell-casting. Part of his mania was a single-minded focus on a particular result he wished to achieve. You have a mind like a magpie's nest, filled with useless shiny objects. I need you to practice the words until you can speak them without stray thoughts intruding. Then I will teach you the path each finger must take while those words are spoken. Then I will help you learn to do both at once."

"And there isn't a shortcut?"

"This *is* the shortcut. If this was a traditional education, you'd start with creating candle-sized balls of light, then move on to levitating feathers."

"I can already levitate things with runes," Madlin said.

"An entirely different craft, I'm afraid. If you have the time to carve runes and empower them, it is the safer course. It would be years before anyone would teach you a shielding spell such as you are learning."

"And this is the easiest spell I can learn that would help me in a fight?"

"If you want to fight, the first thing you must do is survive. Now, repeat …"

# Chapter 21

*"Never force a man into a corner. It's harder to put a sword in his back."*
*– Rashan Solaran*

"It's like a blast furnace out here," a kuduk soldier complained. Draksgollow ignored the comment, but privately agreed with it. He walked down the rows of unfamiliar, stalky plants, a club in one hand, pistol in the other. Like his troops, he wore a wide-brimmed hat to keep away the worst of the sun; he could only imagine how much worse it would have been without it. It would have seemed like a mistake ever coming here, if it weren't for the fact that the land was overflowing with humans. If they could take the heat of this sub-tropical backwater, they would thrive in the fields of Korr.

"Hey now, another group over yonder," Draksgollow said, pointing with the end of his club. The optics over one eye were set to a five times magnification, making walking awkward, but letting him spot distant humans with ease.

The nearest troops quickened their pace, shouting at the humans to stay where they were and kneel. It must have been some mental deficiency, Draksgollow decided. The soldiers knew that the humans didn't understand a word of their language. Still, the vain effort to save themselves a chase made them try. Draksgollow wasn't even sure it would have mattered if the humans understood them. Any free human with sense would know better than to let himself get rounded up and collared. It wasn't as if he was running a subtle operation.

It was stupid things like the shouted warnings that compelled Draksgollow to continue going along with the raids. One day he hoped for a sense that affairs were in good hands without him, and he could put up his feet and read reports. Humans looked a lot better as columns of numbers. One column for culled, one column for captured; simple as that. He didn't like dealing with the faces, the curses that needed no translation, the whining, the begging, the crying, the fluids that dripped and gushed and leaked. They were low, primitive creatures, obstinate for the sake of it, and dumb as a rubber hammer.

A shushing of the crops alerted Draksgollow to someone cutting across the planted rows toward him. Kep trampled a row of the stalks and pulled up short, panting. "Got about thirty of the rat-herders rounded up to the south. Had to send for more troops if we're going to bring this lot in whole." He took off his hat and fanned himself.

"What's that bring us up to for this run?"

"Eighty-eight. Maybe eighty-seven if one we had to club senseless doesn't come around," said Kep. He took a flask from his belt and tipped it back, chugging the contents noisily.

Draksgollow nodded to himself. He gave Kep a squint and sized him up as if he had never seen him before, or was seeing him anew. "Hey Kep, think you can oversee the rest of this roundup?"

"Me?" Kep asked. He held the flask near his lips, frozen between gulps and a gasp for air.

"Yeah, you seen what's what with these runs. Just keep the boys from doing anything too stupid. They know their bit."

"I dunno …"

"Aw, it's just like being shop foreman, except it outdoors and the parts put up a bit more fight," said Draksgollow.

"I've seen brightsteel put up a good fight."

"Now I know you're just blunting my tools. Get out there and watch those clods. If you can manage to get me out of having to come do it myself, there's a pay raise in it for you."

"How much?"

"Mercenary bastard. Listen, I got a meeting I gotta get ready for tonight. You keep me from having to worry about some loose-bolted mix-up while I go over my speech notes, I'll bump your pay … twenty-five percent."

"Make it fifty."

"You're fired."

"Oh, fine, twenty-five."

"Good," replied Draksgollow. "I'll want a full report on my desk tomorrow morning."

The clang of armor plates and the pounding of booted feet echoed down the tunnels. Sickly spark light flickered in a coal dust haze that threatened to clog the breather-cloths around the rebels' faces. Kuduks shouted, trying to rally a defense, but the rebels had taken them by complete surprise. Many of the dead kuduks in their wakc wore their night clothes or were half dressed, weapons having come to hand quicker than shirts in the rush to respond to the attack.

Cadmus bore the unfamiliar weight of his tinker's armor with a sense of childlike glee. It almost didn't seem real, taking part in a raid. It had always been the province of younger men, men whose contribution to the rebellion lay in their muscles, not their brains. But Cadmus had a fire burning inside him, a restlessness that he could not recall even from when he was the age he now appeared to be. His body *was* twenty-five again, and he had the mind of a fifty-three year old tinker to guide it. But along with the youthful body came youthful urges; along with the renewed vigor came a sense of invulnerability.

"Rescue! Rescue! Humans, call out!" one of the soldiers at the fore shouted in Acardian. All of them had either been Acardian born or had been taught a smattering of Acardian before being allowed on the raid. The kuduks of the Human Replacement Project might steal humans for their nefarious ends, but Eziel damn them before the rebels would let the kuduks keep them. And so long as the HRP kept making newspaper headlines, they wouldn't be able to hide their captives.

A distant shout carried over the sounds of the kuduk defenses. "Down here!" The cry echoed from somewhere ahead, but the tunnels branched and twisted. It took a deeper's ears to sort them out.

"This way!" Hayfield shouted, pointing with his coil gun. Rynn had given him command with the explicit instruction of keeping Cadmus safe. The Mad Tinker outranked anyone but Rynn—or perhaps Davlin, depending on their strength of faith—as far as most rebels were concerned. But Rynn had given Hayfield unambiguous authority over him until he was safely home from the raid. She had wanted to come personally, but even the need to protect her father was not enough to overrule the thought that both of them should not go together. Too much at risk for the rebellion. Cadmus smirked at the thought—he was in no danger.

The rebels thundered down the tunnel in the direction Hayfield had indicated. Rounding a bend, they ran into a trio of kuduks with scatterguns. Rebels shielded their faces with the armor plates on their off-hand arms as the scatterguns fired. Dull metallic *thunks* sounded from the runed steel that protected the humans. As the double-action clacking of the scatterguns signaled a reload, the rebels opened fire. In seconds, the kuduks lay in pools of blood, and the rebels were past them, trailing crimson footprints. A few of the rebels dug in pouches as they hustled along, loading more ball bearings into the ammunition chambers at the backs of their weapons.

One soldier glanced down at his left arm and saw a glow in the warning crystal near his elbow. He had taken two of the scattergun blasts, and his runes were all but depleted. The soldier raised his arm for the world-ripper technician to see, and a world-hole opened to fetch him to safety. A reserve soldier—with freshly empowered runes on his armor—came through to replace him.

Cadmus figured that three of his shots had hit. He replaced the four balls he had fired, wanting his weapon loaded to full for any encounter. He had read the reports of all the rebels' previous raids. With a vivid and detailed imagination, he had constructed stage plays in his mind showing what those raids must have been like. But no amount of imagination could get his heart to pump like a thunderail piston, nor could it bring the smells and sounds so close and ubiquitous. He had never imagined the desperate disarray of the kuduks, the shoulder to shoulder jostling with his squad mates as they careened down the tunnels, the slick footing of fresh-spilled blood on stone.

The two kuduk guards on the humans' sleeping barracks dropped their weapons and put their hands up when they caught sight of the rebels. Cadmus didn't see who it was, but someone at the front of the squad dropped both of them with a quick pair of coil gun shots. When one of the pair survived the initial shot and lay moaning on the floor, Cadmus was the one who put a second shot into the kuduk to silence his cries.

"Stand back!" one of the Acardian-born soldiers shouted through the locked steel door. One of the guards likely had a key, but this wasn't a search-for-a-key sort of raid. Hayfield swung a backhand fist at the bolt side of the door. The rune and compression spring device on the back of his glove became momentarily as heavy as a shot from the World Ender Cannon. The bolt snapped and the door slammed open.

Inside the room, fifty or so Acardian farmers huddled on blankets piled on the bare stone floor. The men were chained together along one wall, women along the other, with just enough slack that neither group could reach the other. Hayfield raised a hand in a series of signals, and a world-hole opened in the room. The squad took up defensive positions at the door as crews from the *Jennai* poured in with bolt-cutters, freeing the slaves. A few Acardian speakers offered hasty explanations of the need for haste, and that everything was being taken care of—that they were safe.

*My people.* From his position at the door, Cadmus watched over his shoulder as the Acardians were ushered through the world-hole in a daze. *This is bigger than me, bigger than any of us.* He was responsible. Without his help, Kezudkan might never have assembled a working world-ripper. A plan that had started out with the goal of rescuing the twinborn of Korr had gotten a great many one-worlders killed in Korr and enslaved in Acardia. While it didn't change his mind, that realization added weight to the guilt he felt that what he really wanted was to see his former owner dead.

As the squad finished clearing the mine, more humans taken from Acardia were rounded up and ferried through world-holes to the *Jennai.* Every time they came to a new room in the mine complex, however, Cadmus found his hopes rising that on the other side would be one of the world-rippers that Kezudkan had used for the attacks on Acardia. Every time, he was disappointed.

When the squad finally returned to the *Jennai* themselves, they had freed two hundred eleven Telluraki humans and killed thirty-five kuduks, most of them guards. When the mine was deemed clear of human occupation, they fired the World Ender Cannon and collapsed the tunnels.

It was cathartic, fighting back in person rather than letting Rynn and her underlings do all the work. But at the same time it felt hollow. Kezudkan and whatever associates he had among the kuduks would be back to slaving in Tellurak before long, looking for replacements. They needed to find and shut down the daruu's world-rippers. Until that happened, any victory was temporary.

Draksgollow stood fidgeting in his newly tailored suit. Minute by minute, spectators filtered into the cavernous lecture hall of Klockwerk University. The lectern was piled with notes and reminders, points he would have to remember along with facts and figures for the question period that would follow his speech. The front row of the hall remained empty, flanked by ushers with flat-combed beards and tidy red uniforms that looked as if they had been ironed into place while being worn.

While Draksgollow's mechanical appearance drew curious eyes, he was not the spectacle he once was. For months his face had been appearing in newspaper flashpops. He was a public figure now. More eyes were drawn to the easel standing to one side of him. It was covered with a drop cloth, making what lay beneath seem more mysterious than it had any right to.

Once the student seating had been filled by newspaper reporters, local business owners, the politically well-connected, and anyone else lucky enough to have gained a ticket to the event, the final spectators filed in. Entering through a side door, the members of the Central Council walked past the lectern and took their places in the front row where they had an unobstructed view. A bailiff followed behind them, closing the waist-high door that separated the seating from the area where the lecturer was free to roam.

The bailiff stood before the gathering and rapped his wrists against one another, the stone bracelets he wore sending a sharp crack for all to hear. "Order. Order. Be seated and silent. Tonight our speaker is Mr. Ganrin Draksgollow, head of the Human Replacement Project. He will enlighten us on the details of the project, his progress to date with Kupak Deep's human problem, and his proposal for wider adoption of the Human Replacement Project's goals and policies. Mr. Draksgollow …"

The bailiff swept an arm toward Draksgollow and bowed out of the way.

Draksgollow cleared his throat. "Ladies and Gentlemen of the Central Council, citizens of Ruttania, fellow Korrish." There were titters and muttering from the crowd, who weren't used to being referred to by world. "I am a tinker by trade, a smith of steel and copper, not of words." He flipped the card with that opening line out of the way on the lectern, feeling like a fool. "You all read the papers. You've read about the troubles across Korr, of humans who have turned violent, and worse … turned organized. Human violence has touched every one of you. Maybe you've got relatives in the mining business, or know someone whose slaves up and ran off with the rebels. The rest of you have felt it too, in higher prices at the market because thunderails get boosted, or because crops rotted in the fields with no slaves for the harvest. Most of you grumble about it, wondering when someone's going to put an end to it. Up until me, nobody has. You see, you can't just wrestle a bunch of rebels to the ground, take their stolen guns away from them, and stick them back in the fields and mines. It don't work that way. You try that, and you've got killer humans everywhere, telling stories and steaming up the blood of the docile ones. You might even get them taking a pick or a hoe to the head of one of your overseers."

"No, that's not the way," Draksgollow said. He fumbled beneath the lectern for the water pitcher and poured himself a glass, never taking his eyes from the audience. It felt like an hour before he had poured his drink and taken a sip to wet his throat. He wasn't the sort who talked for long stretches, and it took a toll. "You need a purge, same as with a fouled engine. Clean out the dirty grease and oil, put in new." There were murmurs in the audience again, and the bailiff clacked his bracelets again, continuing until order had been restored.

Draksgollow smiled his best flashpop smile. "You wanna know how, huh? What're we gonna do if you do what I'm saying and we get rid of the humans? Well, let me explain." He pulled down the drop cloth, revealing a placard beneath, large enough to be seen from the back row. It was a diagram of three worlds: Korr, Veydrus, Tellurak. "You see, this ain't the only world. I already proved that much to the Central Council before they let me up here to talk. That ain't the point. The point is that these other worlds have got humans, humans who haven't got all one language, who can't possibly manage to organize on the scale our rebellious humans have. These worlds look just like ours: same rivers, same mountains … we know our way around them. On a trial basis, I've been rounding up humans from these worlds and putting them to work."

Draksgollow tipped the placard and let it fall to the floor, revealing the one behind it. It showed a diagram of two humans, side by side. He had hired out for the fellow who illustrated *Meadefeld's Medical Journal*, and the detail was spot on. Draksgollow pulled out a slender brightsteel rod with a blunted tip and pointed to the diagram on the left. "This is a Korrish human, average in every way, right according to Slave Welfare census data. This other one is a specimen taken from one of the other worlds. Three inches taller, twelve percent more muscle mass, a bit of fat on him, but that won't last him long." There were a few chuckles. Draksgollow felt he was getting through to them. "Already acclimated to sky work and with a good understanding of manual farming. Put this one to work in the fields, and you'll get more work out of him and less grumbling about rebellions."

Draksgollow flipped to the next placard. It showed graphs of projected human purge rates and human capture rates. As he began explaining the details of the plan, he was already anticipating the reveal at the end: the opening of the world-hole. The Central Council had already seen it, but they needed public support for the plan. Once the spectators got to gawk into another world—even if it was really just a spare workshop with a world-ripper in it—that would tighten the final bolt. The Ruttanians would pay. They would give him all the resources he needed to field armies, to construct world-ripper outposts. Best of all, they would put his name atop it all.

A newspaper slapped down onto Rynn's desk. It was the Eversall Deep Herald, evening edition. The headline read: "HUMAN REPLACEMENT PROJECT GAINS COUNCIL APPROVAL." Below was a picture of Ganrin Draksgollow and an open world-hole behind him. In the background, through the world-hole, was a world-ripper.

"Charsi, glad to see you up and about," Rynn asked. "Kupe's been moping around and acting like a proper gentleman lately. This ought to—"

"Look at it!" Charsi insisted, jabbing a finger at the page.

Rynn adjusted her spectacles and picked up the paper, holding it up to the light and looking close. The technician at the controls was standing and posing for his flashpop with an imbecile look on his face—a lot like Kupe's famous flashpop, now that she considered it. Finding nothing else unusual about the picture, she began scanning the accompanying article. "Looks like they're going to scale up their efforts. We're going to have our hands—"

Charsi snatched the paper out of Rynn's hands and pointed again. "Look right there. You can see the controls!"

Rynn shrugged. "It's a newspaper flashpop. It's too grainy to read the numbers; that was the first thing I checked. I appreciate your enthusiasm, but—"

"It's a flashpop," said Charsi. "There's a negative somewhere, probably at the print room of the Herald, or at the home of the newsman who took it."

Rynn's eyes widened. She leapt from her chair and wrapped her arms around Charsi, careful of the bandages where her left arm ended. "This could be it, the break we've been looking for! Charsi, you might just win us this war."

Charsi glanced down, toward Rynn's legs. "After the war, any chance I could get a tinkered arm?"

"After the war I'll make you anything you want," Rynn replied. She grabbed the paper and rushed for the door. "I've got to get Kaia on this right away."

Dunston Harwick had never traveled much. Caladris Solaran had traveled, if possible, even less. It was the way with important men that they developed a gravity all their own, with people and events drawn to them. So it amused Harwick that the Korrish airship was parked low in the skies just high enough that the waves could not reach them, with no land within sight. It was as if Cadmus Errol thought he was some great trader, who knew the world so well that he could draw maps of it by memory and know where he was by the shape of a hill or a shoreline.

"Can't say I got to see much of Korr while I was here," Harwick remarked as he followed Cadmus to the transport gate. "That is, unless your world flooded and no one mentioned it."

"You know how it is," Cadmus replied without looking back. "Anything you don't know, they can't get out of you."

"You really ought to learn at least the basics of political evasions, Cadmus," Harwick said.

"It's not that I don't trust you," Cadmus said, the first bald-faced lie he had caught the Mad Tinker in. "It's just that I lost my twin to a daruu who got clever with a world-ripper and trapped me."

"I had thought it too rude to ask how your twin had perished," Harwick replied. "So I got the story out of your daughter's friend days ago. Ghastly business, but I understand the sentiment. I was done in by an uncle of mine, and I still quite haven't gotten over it going on six years."

"I hear there are daruu in your world," Cadmus replied. "Well, the one we're sending you to, anyway."

"Generally my people refer to them as the stone folk, but the old term still exists."

"Any idea where I might look for one?"

Harwick saw no harm in letting the tinker spy on the stone folk's business. It might occupy him for weeks. "Far beneath the Kadrin city of Raynesdark, they have their city. If they have others, I don't know of them. They aren't the most sociable of peoples, though the empire has gotten on well enough with them that we've traded on occasion."

"Raynesdark?" Cadmus mused aloud. "I know where that is."

"Has your Megrenn associate been schooling you on Veydran geography, or did my son deign to convey scholarly information?"

"Something like that," Cadmus replied.

They reached the hold of what was once the Grangian airship *Sulfurous*, according to the brief history of the ship he'd been given. It housed one of the adjunct world-rippers used by the rebel raiding squads. Harwick's luggage had already been piled next to the target locator, ready to carry through. A fresh-faced young soldier sat at the controls, while Cadmus kept himself between Harwick and the console, blocking the Acardian nobleman's line of sight.

"I can't convince you to set me down any closer, can I?" Harwick asked. The target locator showed a road some miles north of Kadris. He would either have hours of walking ahead of him, or have to debase himself before a wagon driver to allow him aboard.

"Your people sniff out the viewframe a bit too readily," Cadmus replied. "Sorry."

"Better safety than haste, I suppose," Harwick replied with a sigh. "Very well, send me through."

Cadmus gave the technician a nod and the gate opened. An attending soldier helped the now-middle-aged sorcerer haul his belongings through to Veydrus. Just before the gate closed, Harwick leaned to the side, trying to look past the Mad Tinker to catch a glimpse of the console. Cadmus leaned as well, shaking his head. The view vanished, and Harwick was left at the side of the North Road out of Kadris with his luggage at his side.

Harwick sat down on a trunk filled with clothes and waited for a likely-looking wagon to happen by. He was in too good a mood to spoil it with a long, sweaty walk. *Really Cadmus, your people spend too much time underground or bottled up in ships.* Dunston Harwick was no traveler at all, but he was a scholar of the highest caliber. The night sky was a vast map that stared down upon the land, and sailors had been using it for navigation since before the invention of the compass. To those who enjoyed astronomy, knowing the date, the time, and the location of a constellation or two was all it took. Harwick had calculated the location of the *Jennai* the night he arrived.

# Chapter 22

*"Judge a man not by what he has, but by what he seeks." – Kheshi saying*

The chamber was too dark, lit by just a pair of spark bulbs overhead. Madlin would have to do something about that, but it could wait. The quiet was isolating, with only the single room and no companions. Of course, only someone from the deeps of Korr could find quiet with the dynamos running constantly and the hum of paired world-rippers. This was Madlin's refuge.

Hollowed out of Tellurak's moon, it was a place only she and Rynn knew of. Rynn had carved it out using the *Jennai's* auger under the guise of expanding the facility on Korr's moon. For some time, Madlin had been pillaging supplies and parts coming out of the airship's workshops, and had managed to shrink the design of the world-ripper to table-top size.

Bolted to the stone wall was a pair of world-rippers as wide across as her forearm, just a few inches apart from one another. Like the pair in Korr's moon, they were set into river water, submerged halfway. But Madlin's system was compact, contained. A short length of pipe matched the diameter exactly, set with spigots in the bottom to siphon off water and pump out waste. The top had ventilation piping and a fan.

Her real achievement had been the second pair of reduced-size world-rippers, set flat on their sides and sealed together watertight. One end was set at the bottom of the Katamic Sea, the other near the surface. In between the two she had set a turbine, and that turbine was strong enough to power the whole facility, world-rippers and all. In theory, it violated the physical law that prevented machines from perpetual motion, but Madlin knew that the world-rippers probably violated a lot of physical laws.

On the workbench in front of her lay the most recent and ambitious project she had undertaken with the world-rippers. Like the others in her secret lair, each viewframe was small enough for her to lift by herself. The unique thing about these was the lining of dragonhide. It stretched between the two frames without a seam or gap; having been flayed from one of the dragon's digits as a single piece. It was macabre to think where it had come from, but Madlin had worked with leather before, and knew it for cowhide. Then again, she had never spoken with any of the cows whose leather she had used.

Another of Madlin's innovations was the secondary viewframe. With the technical manual, she had been able to dissociate the viewing function from the hole-opening function, and via a selector switch, she had linked all of the moon's world-rippers to a single control console. Flipping the selector to one of the new world-rippers in the dragonhide frame, she prepared to test a theory.

The view was set to Tellurak, the location a remote mountain in the unpopulated northern portion of what was once Tinker's Island. Madlin supposed that mapmakers would still call it that for some time, but for her it had always been The Mad Tinker's Island, and had lost that name when he left it behind—perhaps for good. She aligned the view until it was inches from the ice-crusted face of a granite peak, and turned the world-ripper on. A chill breeze wafted into the room through the open end of the dragonhide tube, out the inert world-ripper.

Madlin put on a coat and switched the selector to the other world-ripper of the pair. Turning the world dial, she ventured into Korr. Though she was sure she could find what she needed in Tellurak, she knew exactly where to go to find it in Korr. Industry demanded steel, and steel demanded smelting. Smelting took heat. The auxiliary view-frame whizzed through the frozen northlands and across the Sea of Kerum. There was no sign of the *Jennai* as she passed; the world was too vast for such coincidences. Eventually she found Eversall Sky, and from there it was no trick at all delving into Eversall Deep, the part of Korr Madlin knew better than any other, despite *technically* never having been there. Eversall wasn't a major steel-working city, but Drendath Brothers' Fine Alloys produced specialty brightsteel alloys prized in chemical plants. They had a smelter on site.

Madlin found the facility with ease, located in a remote corner of Layer Three, with its own ventilation straight to the surface. It was off hours, but the furnaces were never allowed to go cold. Night watchmen were stationed to prevent anyone getting in and causing mischief, and to alert the owners if anything should happen in the night while the furnaces were only lightly attended. Those watchmen could do nothing to stop Madlin's intrusion, and any report of her activity would sound peculiar at best.

Stopping the view-frame over one of the furnaces, she adjusted the view until it was not quite touching the sizzling hot surface. Pulling on a pair of protective goggles over her spectacles, Madlin pulled the switch to turn on the second world-ripper. There was a muffled hiss, like an air leak inside a machine's guts. Madlin shut off both world-rippers and pulled off her goggles.

*What had gone wrong?* She had expected something more dramatic. Flipping the selector to the Acardian peaks and resetting her view-frame with the flip of a toggle—a time-saving device that matched it to the world-ripper's settings—she inspected the mountain peak.

The ice was gone. It hadn't been a thick layer, but Madlin could see bare rock where once there had been a crusted layer of ice at least the width of her finger. With her heart quickening, Madlin rushed over to the world-ripper to inspect the dragonhide. It was damp with condensation, but completely unaffected by the heat.

Over the course of an afternoon, Madlin performed a number of follow-up tests. The paired world-rippers, which she was thinking needed a name of their own, held up to open flame and to the heat from a magma chamber, but stretched dangerously when exposed to pressurized steam. Hours of rune carving into the tough, leathery surface made the dragonhide tough as the walls of Raynesdark, after which the device could hold the pressure from even industrial chemical storage. In northern Acardia, there was now a blackened peak that had been blasted with acetylene gas where Madlin had placed a candle. The resulting fiery explosion had done nothing to the dragonhide tube.

Satisfied with the day's work, Madlin sat back and put her feet up on the workbench. Reaching over, she idly turned the view-frame until it looked directly at the sun. The dim lunar cavern brightened as if Madlin had pulled back the curtain of a south-facing window. There wasn't much for refreshment in the tiny hideaway, but she had a bottle of Kheshi wine she had been meaning to try. No one was around to raise an eyebrow at her highbrow choice. Pulling out a pocket knife, Madlin jabbed the cork and wiggled it free. The wine went down smooth, and a warm, relaxed feeling filled her belly. She settled in for some quiet time alone.

A pile of books lay in a corner, stolen from the finest libraries across Korr. Most of them were ancient daruu tomes on the subject of runes—a welcome diversion into a form of magic she had some skill with—but others were chosen specifically for her current project.

Madlin selected a book published just months ago, a scientific text on solar physics, expounding on the latest theories of what goes on inside a star. Stripped to bare bolts, it said that the sun and other stars like it were the hottest things in the known universe.

Madlin was going to find out just how impervious to heat dragonhide was.

Everyone else was asleep. With a mug of strong tea, Cadmus kept the tides of slumber at bay. Finding the daruu city had proven remarkably easy with Harwick's simple explanation of where it was located. He already had the coordinates for Raynesdark in his notes from Madlin's goblin-led assault on the city. But far below, the tunnels changed. Gone were the rough-hewn mines of human excavation. In their place were tunnels like a Korrish art museum, with walls polished smooth and flowing with sculpted murals. The signs were written in plain Korrish, with even simple tunnel signs carved in a master's steady hand.

Cadmus had no inkling of whether Kezudkan had found his people or not, but he suspected the crafty old daruu would have known where to look. In the absence of any clue where in the city to begin his search, Cadmus started at one end near the top and worked through the whole of it methodically. It was tedious work, the worst sort of task to toil at alone the middle of the night, fighting to stay awake.

Cadmus had renewed youth in his favor, but he could have used someone to talk to while he searched.

For a moment he considered waking Jamile. Like most twinborn, she slept soundly, and she hadn't noticed when he slipped out of bed to return to the control consoles in the main chamber. He used to sleep that way, when he had Erefan's eyes to look through at night. Now, the great dark void behind his eyes was as much a reason to stay awake as his work. It was half a death, a preview, he imagined, of what awaited Cadmus when he died as well.

That death would come all the sooner if he couldn't find Kezudkan and put a stop to him. That Draksgollow fellow was the one making headlines, but he was just a face to allow the daruu to remain safely anonymous. The kuduk tinker and his horrific Human Replacement Project might even be a trap. The daruu knew nothing of twinborn—or at least hadn't before exploring the other worlds, Cadmus had to consider—but there was the rest of the Human Rebellion to consider. Even if he believed Erefan was dead, Kezudkan had to realize the rebels would want to put a stop to him. What better way to draw their attention than a scheme that promised to wipe out them and their families.

And so Cadmus stayed up long into the night, taking in the sights of a city built by Veydran daruu. As he scanned, he sketched a rough map, occasionally noting a coordinate (in code, of course) to make up for the deplorable lack of proper scale. He was able to add names to the tunnels from the helpful signs the daruu posted at each crossing. Even on a first visit, Cadmus imagined it hard for anyone to get lost if they knew the language. But none of the signs hinted at a world-ripper, or anyplace that one might erect dangerous machinery, or housing for guests from other worlds. Cadmus just kept going, yawning between sips of his tea, trips to the lavatory, and refills of his mug.

At length he stumbled across it. There was a stretch of unadorned stone wall, which was a rarity from what he had seen. He guessed that meant it was new—no one had gotten around to embellish it yet. Following it, he found a simple hemispherical chamber dedicated to a single device: Kezudkan's world-ripper.

Cadmus had never suspected that when Erefan fell to the daruu's trap, the search to hunt him down would lead to Veydrus. But it was clearly the daruu's work. Kezudkan had not even made improvements to the design since delving into constructing them on his own. Drifting the view close to the console, Cadmus noticed a number of lingering old flaws that he had eliminated from the current design: improved dial layout, single-switch activation of the viewframe, fuses to protect against surges. With a smirk, he reminded himself that he had been the brains of the collaboration between daruu and human, owner and slave. Kezudkan liked to ponder and dabble, not get his hands greasy.

The room was unoccupied, with a pair of stout daruu guards posted outside. As much as Cadmus might have wanted to catch a glimpse of his nemesis, at least he now knew where to find him. With a twist of the world dial, Cadmus sent the viewframe into the swirling miasma between worlds, then shut off the machine.

He headed back to bed with a sense of contentment tinged with excitement. He would sleep better now.

"I feel like we're breaking a law or something," Vaulk whispered.

"Oh, you're just being a worry-worm," Sosha replied softly. The two of them sat side by side at the controls of the world-ripper in the rear left quadrant of the *Jennai*, near the liftwing hangar. "I'd do this myself but Mr. Harwick wrote the book in Acardian."

"I'm glad to hear you think of me as a confidant, and not just a purveyor of delectables."

"Well, you lived in Acardia and Cadmus trusts you," Sosha replied. "He can't get mad at both of us, right?"

"You might be underestimating him."

Sosha scrunched her nose at Vaulk. "I know he *can* get mad at two people at once, but I mean, he can't think *both* of us are wrong."

"What if we are?" Vaulk asked. "What if we find something horrible?"

"Now, don't let's tie our laces before the boot's on," Sosha replied. "We haven't even found them yet."

She pushed a sheet of paper in Vaulk's direction, covered in handwritten notes. Vaulk skimmed over it. "That's it? I thought it would be something complicated."

"It didn't need to be complicated," Sosha replied. "Just being written in silly-talk was enough to keep me from understanding it."

Vaulk drew back, scowling. "There's nothing wrong with Acardian!"

"I meant what Mr. Harwick translated it from. I'm sure written Acardian is very nice."

"You sure about this? You said Madlin was against it."

"Cadmus doesn't want us bringing the other worlds into this, because they're too far away and they're not like our worlds. He says we've got enough gears in the works as it is."

"Well, Veydrus certainly seems to have been more trouble than help."

"We just got unlucky," Sosha replied. "Dan and the dragon didn't work out, but Anzik's been a big help."

"I'm no gambler, but one in three doesn't sound like great odds." He set the notes down and pushed them in front of Sosha.

"We couldn't find any negatives for Mr. Draksgollow's world-ripper flashpop, and we don't have another way to pull up the Human Replacement Project by the roots. But if we build one of those beacon things to call for help, it would probably come from one of those other worlds. The people who wrote these books ought to be able to find them."

"Maybe …" Vaulk said, drawing out the first syllable.

"Well, I think it would stand to reason, wouldn't it? And … well aren't *you* curious? Madlin and Cadmus can claim they've got too much to do, but unless people are getting shot—and thank Eziel we haven't had much of that lately—I've got time to wonder who else is out there." Sosha paused a moment and caught her breath. "Well?"

"Well, what?"

"Are you going to tell me how to aim the view-frame to find them, or aren't you?"

Vaulk grumbled beneath his breath and took up the notes once more. "Which one did you want to try?"

"Olara," Sosha replied. "It's the nearest one by the look of it."

With Vaulk's assistance, Sosha made the adjustments for a world that was not aligned with Korr. The step-by-step instructions made finding Olara simple, but it would not have been possible without reading the long-form explanation. The writer of the books had included no diagram to explain the procedure.

With one final twist of the world dial—which the book recommended leaving for last—Olara sprang into view.

"What the—"

"Blessed Eziel," breathed Sosha.

They found themselves looking upon a city of steel and glass towers, stretching off into the sky. Sunlight caught in the glass gleamed a brilliant orange, but left the ground level completely shadowed. Spark lamps more than made up for the difference, bathing the crowded streets in stark blue-white light. Steam wagons of every sort streamed by, with the sides of the road packed with pedestrians. Tiny glassed-in tunnels connected some of the buildings to one another at the higher stories, and they could see people walking through those as well.

The two of them stared for uncounted minutes, awed by the scene. If Korr made Tellurak look backward and primitive, Olara made them both look like lands of cave-dwelling savages.

The steam wagons parted, and the pedestrians scattered as other steam wagons topped with rotating blue and red lamps pushed their way through. The spinning-light steam wagons stopped not far from the viewframe, and uniformed riders exited.

"At least they're all human," Vaulk muttered.

Sosha leaned closer to Vaulk, not taking her eyes from the viewframe. "You don't suppose they can see us, do you?"

Sosha surmised that the uniformed men were Olara's version of Judicial Enforcement officers. They set up little posts and connected them with yellow ropes, blocking off the area and keeping the pedestrians at bay. More steam wagons arrived, allowed in by Olara's head-knockers. People in long white coats, carrying strange machines approached the viewframe.

"I … think they might," Vaulk replied. He wandered closer to the viewframe. "Keep a hand on that switch." Sosha did as he asked, and watched the response of the men in white coats—actually two of the five were women, she noticed.

Vaulk stood just an arm's reach from the view of Olara. He waved his arms overhead. He leaned one way, then the other. He shook a fist at the white coat people. There was no response, no sign that any of them could see him.

Or was there? One of the women in white seemed to be staring through the viewframe. She had a nervous tic, jerking her head to one side. On an impulse, Sosha gave one of the fine adjustment dials a slight twist, sliding the view a few feet in the direction the woman seemed to indicate.

The men with the strange machines seemed not to notice, but the woman with the nervous tic nodded and followed the viewframe. She held no machine, but had a clipboard and pen. When she held the clipboard up, angled away from her companions, it had a message scrawled on the back in Korrish:

NOT HERE. NOT NOW. GO.

Vaulk stumbled back from the viewframe. Sosha slammed the switch open, and Olara was gone.

"That was spooky," said Sosha.

Vaulk nodded. "I don't think we'll be asking for help from them anytime soon."

# Chapter 23

*"Never allow surprises to divert you from duty." -Anonymous*

It had been too long since Harwick had been home. He supposed he ought to think of himself as Caladris Solaran while he was in Veydrus, but it would take getting used to. The Solaran Estate was dark, save for lights showing through the curtains of two rooms in the servants' wing. The wagon driver helped him unload his belongings at the main entrance; he should never have gotten so close unchallenged.

Letting the wagon driver free of the magical compulsion that had gained him a free ride across half of Kadris, Harwick strode confidently to the door. He was still a sorcerer, even if he was only a pale Source next to the twin who had died here. He was still a Solaran. The giant iron knocker tempted him for a moment, but he wasn't about to come home as a beggar or a guest. With a push at just the right spot in the aether, the ward on the door gave way and the door swung inward.

"At least no one changed the lock," he muttered as he wiped his road-stained boots and stepped inside.

The foyer was well kept, but had an empty feel. The whole place reeked of a museum. "Hey, how about someone gets down here and helps me with my things?" Harwick shouted, using that special volume that toed the line between wanting the whole household to hear and being boorishly rude. The Kadrin language still felt awkward on his tongue. He spoke it infrequently when he still had a twin, and since Caladris's death, he had rarely had cause.

Footsteps approached from the second story, two pair by the sound of them. When one of the servants emerged onto the landing atop the foyer stairs, he shouted down. "Now, just who do you think you … Sorcerer Caladris? What sort of trick is this?" A second servant poked his head over the railing and ducked back.

"Werthen, Faudrick, if you'd be so good as to fetch my belongings up to my room and rummage up a late dinner, I can explain everything," Harwick replied. Not that more than every third word would be true—mostly articles and conjunctions—but he had enough of a story prepared for the servants to chew on.

"But how did … but where have … is it really you?"

Harwick sighed. "Yes. If you're not yet accustomed to Solarans showing up when everyone thinks they're dead, you're just going to have to set your jaw and get on with your duties."

Werthen flashed a nervous smile. "Of course, sir. Right away." He jerked his head and Faudrick reemerged from the shadows on the landing.

"Where can I find my son these days?"

"Warlock Danilaesis prefers his accommodations at the palace."

"I'm sure he does," Harwick muttered. "What about my father? Is the old relic still knocking around someplace? Suppose he's probably in bed, what with the sun being nearly down."

"High Sorcerer Axterion has been faring much better of late," Werthen replied. "And he stays at the palace at the behest of the empress."

"At the behest, eh?" Harwick asked. "There's not any … you know …"

"Blessed winds, no, sir," Werthen replied.

"Fine, then," said Harwick. "In the morning, send someone to make me an appointment to see the High Sorcerer."

He had heard through his few remaining contacts that had access to Veydrus about Axterion taking up the position of High Sorcerer. It was amusing, given his father's age, but Axterion had actually been High Sorcerer for most of Caladris's life, so it seemed even more a trip to the past than six winters would have credited.

The next morning, Harwick found himself at the door of the High Sorcerer's office in the Tower of Contemplation. He had been curious about the hole in the very ceiling of the structure, which allowed rainfall down the open central shaft all the way to the entry hall. It had to have pierced the wards in the Inner Sanctum itself. As much as he would have liked answers as to how it had happened, Harwick knew he was walking an icy pond on a warm day. The less he said the better until he spoke with Axterion.

Just as he was about to knock, a voice from inside snapped: "Just get in here."

Harwick let himself in, and saw the years peeled back from his father. Axterion looked like a man in his hale mature years, just as the last hints of boyishness had left him. His hair was dark, his skin unwrinkled, his eyes sharp and alert. "What are you gawking at, dead man?"

Harwick shut the door behind him. "Fair point. I know this is going to take quite some explanation, but I'm sure I can convince you that—"

"You're Caladris's twin. You've still got the Acardian slur in your Kadrin," said Axterion. "Now, skip the boot polish, and tell me why you're here."

Harwick blinked. The old man he had left behind in Kadrin had been feeble, senile, and one breath from death at any given moment. "So you were twinborn?" He assumed the past tense, since no one in Tellurak lived as long as Axterion had.

"Caladris—and I don't intend to bother muddling things up with your Acardian name—I am a busy man, so let's make this brief. I was never twinborn, but your mother was; I know all about it. We're in the middle of a war right now because your son got himself one-worlded and decided to go kicking hornets' nests until he found the one who did it. I imagine he's got something horrible cooked up for the poor sot, but I'd settle for Danilaesis just killing him and getting it done with. So, since I've taken time from my busy day running the Imperial Circle, a war, a fragile new alliance, *and* trying to keep our young warlock from running amok, what did you need to speak with me about?"

"I'm the new ambassador to the Kadrin Empire."

"Oh, really?" Axterion replied in a mocking tone. "Ambassador from where?"

"From the Megrenn, specifically the one who killed Danilaesis's twin."

Axterion gave a single guffaw. "Doesn't that beat all? Does he even know what he's done? He's pitched himself right into a trap."

"Unfortunately, no. He hasn't," Harwick replied. "He's using these devices, machines built by a twinborn from a third world—"

"Korr. The Mad Tinker's machine. The boy's filled me in on the details. Quit wasting my time with things I already know."

"Anzik Fehr is hidden away in some remote location underground. They were able to keep his whereabouts secret, even sending *him* to meet *me* when he made me the offer: the location of the Korrish rebels' airship for peace with Megrenn."

Axterion harrumphed, the most he had seemed like his old self since Harwick had arrived. "Some deal for him. He loses nothing and gains a peace treaty for a war he can't win."

"He seems convinced he can win with the tinkers' help," said Harwick. "He claims to want to lessen the toll on his people."

"Noble, if you believe him. Which I don't."

"I don't either, but I didn't come here to get you to accept the offer."

"Oh, why then?"

"I came to see if what they're all saying about Danilaesis is true."

Axterion sighed and slouched back in his chair. "It would be hard for them to come up with things to say about him that aren't true. I'd rule out cannibalism, necromancy … probably copulating with animals, but just about anything else you can go ahead and believe."

"How could you let—" Harwick began.

"How could I have *let* anything?" Axterion leapt from his chair and shouted the question, placing his hands on the desk and leaning across at Harwick. "I was at my wits' end trying to keep up with that boy. I taught him right from wrong. I taught him to love learning. I taught him how to work his spells as best I could. Then Rashan showed up and tore every moral fiber I'd stuffed into that boy to shreds. I'm still holding hope that he'll come around when he matures, but it's a flickering hope, and the winds of war blow mighty strong."

"Maybe if I talked to him?" Harwick asked. "I at least have to see for myself."

Axterion slumped back into his chair and waved him away. "Fine. I've got other matters to attend. Best of luck with that demon you sired. He should be back around dinnertime."

Harwick felt his face warm, and he was a man unaccustomed to shame. He backed out of the office and let himself out. Just before the door shut behind him, Axterion called out one final thing. "Oh, and it's nice to see you again, son."

"That was harsh," a voice called out a moment after the door shut.

Axterion glanced up and saw his second ghost of the day. "Brannis! You're here! I scarcely believed that demon woman when she told me you were alive." Taller than any among the Solarans, Brannis had always stood out. First as a failed sorcerer, then a knight, then again as a sorcerer of untold might. Anyone who had lived in Kadris six winters ago knew that face from parades and feast-day functions. With young eyes, Axterion could finally see his grown grandson as everyone else had.

"I've actually found that Illiardra is a poor liar," Brannis replied. "Strange. You'd think ten thousand summers would give a demon plenty of practice."

"What happened between you and Rashan? The official story was you betrayed and attacked him, but both of you perished in the struggle."

"Who made up that load of dung?" Brannis asked. "That paranoid maniac attacked *me*, and he paid the price for it."

"But where have you been all this time? We could have used you around here."

"I took Juliana and we left," said Brannis. "I can traverse worlds without those machines. But I came here for a reason, and it wasn't to correct the fictions you're writing into history. You wanted to see me about Danil?"

"I wouldn't call him that to his face anymore," Axterion replied. "It's Danilaesis … preferably *Warlock* Danilaesis. And he's sliding down the path to becoming the next Rashan."

"I heard he already got his twin killed, by friends no less, for the way he's acted."

"That's the rough size of it," Axterion replied. "He's not so far gone that he doesn't know what others think of him, but he doesn't seem to care."

Brannis grinned. "I'll work on that."

Danilaesis rubbed his eyes as he stumbled into his bedroom. The room was dark save for a sliver of starlight that peeked between the drawn curtains. He had spent most of his days staring into the viewframe as that clod of a daruu wandered the skies above the Korrish sea, looking in vain for Madlin's airship. There had been no way to save face after the search had begun; he had to continue on until the day's end or until they found something. The day had ended. As irksome and repetitive as it had been slaughtering farmers and lighting wheat fields aflame, that had been a festival dance compared to staring out over the trackless waters for hours at a stretch. Of all the bloody annoying traits the daruu had displayed, a stoic patience for menial tasks had proven the most vexing.

Unslinging the sheath of *Sleeping Dragon* from his back, he tossed the weapon across the arms of a chair. The down-stuffed mattress of his bed called out to him, its draw stronger than the want of food that snarled within his stomach. He collapsed onto his back, letting the softness envelop him.

"You'd think a boy your age would have more energy," a familiar voice called from a shadowed corner of the room.

In an instant, Danilaesis rolled from the bed and dove for his sword. As he moved, he switched to aether-vision to discover where his foe was hiding. There was no one. The wards around the room glowed in the aether, as did the runeforged blade of *Sleeping Dragon.* Backing himself against a wall in a crouch, Danilaesis kept the blade out in front of him against whoever might be hiding even in the aether.

"Who's there?" he demanded of the darkness. All traces of fatigue fled as aether surged within him, ready to be unleashed.

A light flared, drawing Danilaesis's attention out of the aether. Standing before him was the image of Brannis Solaran. A trick. Brannis was dead.

"It's me," the apparition claimed, smiling insouciantly. Whoever had created the illusion had done well, perhaps *too* well. Brannis looked just like the Brannis of six winters past. He ought to have aged. His hair ought to have edged back from his brow. There should be a grey hair or two by his temples.

Danilaesis looked around the room, ignoring the false Brannis. "Nice try, whoever you are. But I'm no fool to be taken in by your illusions. Show yourself."

"I wouldn't believe it if I wasn't seeing it with my own eyes," said the false Brannis. "You have completely lost yourself to paranoia."

Danilaesis loosed a bolt of fire at the apparition, hoping to send it back to raw aether in shreds. It struck a shielding spell instead. His eyes widened. There had been no shield a moment before; he would have seen it clearly in the aether.

The apparition of Brannis approached. "I've had about enough of this nonsense, Danil."

Danilaesis swung two-handed, aiming to remove the arm that reached for him. Moving faster than any human could manage, even with aether-sped muscles, the apparition grabbed the blade—a blade strong enough to bite into stone—mid swing and tore it from Danilaesis's grasp.

"What are you doing with this sword?" the apparition demanded. "This was Iridan's. I helped make it for him."

"If you're really Brannis, you'd know who empowered it." Only three other people knew that secret, a blacksmith, the empress, and his dead cousin.

"You did, you little slackwit," Brannis snapped back at him. "Now, why are you playing at being a warlock instead of finishing up at the Academy."

"You're … you can't be him."

"They told you Rashan killed me."

"You killed each other."

"They guessed. They didn't know."

"You're not dead?"

"Do I look dead to you?"

"Yes."

"Look closer."

Danilaesis knew that Brannis meant in the aether. He closed his eyes to the light and looked once more. The shielding spell evaporated as he watched, leaving nothing to protect. There was no Brannis, no Source shining in the aether. Brannis had displayed a Source visible from across town, but this person who claimed his name was as invisible in the aether as … as Rashan had been.

"You're a demon!" Danilaesis exclaimed, backing away. "What happened to you?"

"Rashan had the fool idea that I wanted to kill him, so he attacked first. In so doing, I was forced to prove him right. But before I finished him—and for selfish reasons I won't be telling you how I managed that—I forced him to reveal the secret of his immortality."

"Some good it did him," Danilaesis muttered.

"Indeed," said Brannis. "He could have lived out his days, had he resisted the lure of blood, the call to war, the whispers of paranoia. He died because for his own peace of mind, he *had* to kill me."

"Sounds like he died because you wanted to be a demon."

"Listen to yourself. You're starting to sound just like him. He second-guessed everyone. He killed because it was safer than letting an enemy live, even if he killed a few allies by mistake. He saw everyone aligned against him."

"I *want* to be just like him," Danilaesis countered. "He is the greatest hero the Kadrin Empire ever had."

"He's dead."

"Fine, everything but that."

"Dead is what being just like Rashan is going to get you. No one can charge headlong and take on the world. Not for long, anyway."

"I've got a war to fight."

"A war I hear you started," said Brannis.

"He *killed me*!" Danilaesis shrieked. How could people not understand that? The call of vengeance for a lover or a father was the stuff of stories. But how could that compare to the desperate need to avenge one's own death?

Brannis looked at him with pity in his eyes. *Pity! How dare he?*

"You ran off, you coward," Danilaesis said. "You're Kadrin. This is your fight, too. With your help, we can leave Megrenn in ruins, find Anzik Fehr and make him suffer, pay back those Korrish rats for helping him."

"No."

Danilaesis clenched his teeth. "You're worthless, then!"

Brannis took a step forward, and some reasonable part of Danilaesis's brain dumped ice water on the fires that burned in his heart. "Now wait a minute … I didn't mean you're *worthless* worthless, just that if you leave us during wartime, you're worthless to the empire."

"Danil, if I was going to put an end to this war right now, I'd do it by wringing your neck. You're trampling across the continent, ruining lives, destroying families. You've aspired to follow in the footsteps of a madman, and I fear you've already followed them too far."

"Now Brannis—" Danilaesis backpedaled until he bumped against the wall.

"This isn't my war. I've kept the other immortals from interfering, and I won't play the hypocrite any farther than coming to talk sense into you. All I can promise is that if you continue following Rashan's path, you'll meet the same end."

Brannis picked up *Sleeping Dragon* and handed it hilt-first to Danilaesis. Then he was gone. Danilaesis was left alone in his bedroom, holding a sword. He waited for some sign that Brannis might return, then slid the blade back into its sheath and returned to bed.

After five attempts to unravel Brannis's light spell, he gave up and fell asleep beneath a noonday glow.

Though the door was fashioned of polished oak, it might well have been cast in iron with a barred window. Inside waited a monster. Harwick had heard the exchange inside, scarcely able to believe his ears. One voice he only knew as his son's because the room belonged to Danilaesis, and because the second voice called him Danil. That other voice … he had not expected to hear that voice ever again.

But Harwick had come with a purpose, and it was a purpose that grew no less needful with waiting. The room had gone quiet, and it seemed certain that Brannis had departed. If only Harwick had stopped for a drink before coming, his hands might not have shaken as he reached up and knocked.

"Go away," came a reply muffled by the door.

A heat rose from Harwick's chest and spread until it reached his face. That tone—that lazy, disdainful tone—had hardly changed in six winters. *That spoiled, arrogant … I'll show* him *who isn't going away.* Slipping into aether-vision, Harwick inspected the wards that protected the door. Like any sorcerer of worth, the boy had formed the wards himself. It was sloppy work, with runes looking as if they'd been carved with a weapon rather than a tool. It was a simple pattern, empowered nearly to bursting to make up for the shoddy craftsmanship. Even though he was not the sorcerer that Caladris Solaran had been, Dunston Harwick had more subtlety to his magic than Danilaesis. With an expert application of aether, he collapsed the ward and shoved the door open.

Danilaesis was lying atop the blankets of his bed, but rolled to the floor and grabbed for his sword before Harwick could even pass the threshold. The sword pointed at Harwick drooped as realization dawned in the young warlock's eyes. "You! How … bloody blazes, I get nothing but dead people visiting me!"

Harwick shut the door behind him. "You loathsome clod, I raised you smarter than this."

"Grandfather raised me," Danilaesis shot back. "You were never around."

"Then I *sired* you smarter than this," Harwick replied. "Caladris is dead. I came here from Tellurak."

"Sure you did, dead man," Danilaesis replied. The sword tip raised once more, aimed at Harwick's chest. "I've got enemies who could tell me that tale. Prove you're him. My father never mentioned being twinborn."

"Do I need to bring your grandfather in here to vouch for me? I've already spoken with him since I arrived."

Danilaesis's eyes unfocused, a sign that he had switched to aether-vision. After a moment, he returned the sword to its sheath. "You've got nowhere near the Source my father had."

"True enough. From what I hear, your Telluraki twin was the weaker as well."

A scowl came on like a summer storm, arriving in fury and with no warning. "I wouldn't bring that up too often, if I were you. I'm no fool. If you're here, you came through one of the transport gates, which means they got to you. Father or not, you're with them. What do you want here?"

"They sent me as an ambassador. I'm supposed to trade you the location of that airship of theirs for an end to the war."

A soft snuffling sound issued from Danilaesis. His shoulders shook, and the corners of his lips curled. The sound grew until it escaped as a burst of helpless laughter. "You can't be serious. Why would I settle for that? I'll find the bloody ship myself *and* burn Megrenn to ash."

"Sit down, boy, and put that thing away," Harwick said. "It seems I left them to stuff you full of spite and boiling anger. Spite is a fool's indulgence, and vengeance is a cold road, best walked by a patient man—the kind of man who can stand barefoot in the snow and study his enemy through a frost-covered window as he sits by the fire."

"You want me to make peace with Megrenn, and save my vengeance until I'm an old man?" Danilaesis asked with a sneer. "Not likely."

"Bloody idiot," Harwick muttered. He pointed to the sword. "Quit thinking with that thing, stow that arse of yours in a chair, and listen to me a moment. Anzik Fehr thinks to bargain the location of the *Jennai* for peace. That's an obvious ruse. He's not stupid enough to think you'd take that offer. The ship's location has value, but not *that* much. He's the one you want dead; the girl was a mere accomplice."

"Fine, so you're an ambassador with nothing worth offering," Danilaesis grumbled, slouching into a chair. The sword dangled from a loose grasp, but he had neither set it aside, nor returned it to its sheath. "Congratulations."

"Has it not sunk into that …" Harwick sniffed the air, "… wine-soaked brain of yours that my mere presence here is of aid to you? My absence in Acardia won't go unnoticed, but I was an old man; my time there was going to be short, or grow suspicious. I've returned here to stay. Whatever cleverness the Errols possess, it ends with their machines; they're no good with politics in either the light or shadows. They've made a mistake, and they're going to pay for it."

"No offense Father—if that's really you—but you're not exactly the strongest sorcerer around. I've got a dozen better than you."

"But none of them have worked out the location of the Errols' airship."

Danilaesis's eyes gleamed and he leaned forward in his chair. "Where?"

"All I ask in return is that you wait for the right time," Harwick replied.

Danilaesis threw his head back until it hit the cushioning of the chair, staring up at the ceiling. "I'm going to start making sacrifices to Eziel if I don't get my hands on someone soon."

Harwick waved a dismissive hand. "Forget that dried old rubbish the Korrish dug up. All I need is time to coordinate with an agent of mine. I've got a man on the inside."

# Chapter 24

*"All that is old will be new again. I think whoever said that meant music and clothing, but apparently it works for people, too." – Lord Dunston Harwick*

Tanner stood at the railing of the *Mirror's Trick*, looking down at the countryside far below. Long shadows stretched to the west, as trees and hillsides fought back the dawn's light. Tanner had never cared for sea travel, despite having spent far too much of his life traveling the waves. But airship travel was growing on him. His twin aboard the *Jennai* would go on raids through the machine and find the feel of solid ground beneath his feet strange. The engines had a hum to them, heard by the ear and felt by the soles of the feet. It never went away during flight, merely changing in tone, and its absence was louder than its presence.

"Have you stolen a pocketclock?" Stalyart asked. Tanner flinched at the voice, but relaxed immediately. Stalyart was among the few who could still sneak up on him unheard—he supposed it was easier due to the engine noise.

Tanner glanced around, finding the two of them relatively alone. Only a few crew members were topside; most still weren't accustomed enough to the air to seek the skies for leisure. "Yeah, couple raids ago."

Stalyart pressed a timekeeping device into his hands. "Well, here is one to go with it. My man has reported back. The time is set. When the small hand reaches eight, it begins."

"How many of them have you got?" Tanner asked.

"Pardon?"

"Twinborn spies? How many have you got spread around Tellurak and Veydrus."

"Never enough, it seems," Stalyart replied. But it wasn't a true reply. Tanner knew he wouldn't get a proper number out of the cagey pirate.

"Just feels like I'm getting hung out in the wind on this one."

"My dear friend," said Stalyart. "You were a coinblade for many years. This is far from the most danger you have faced. And in return, an airship, a pardon, and vengeance for your friend."

"You got a drink by any chance?" Tanner asked.

"Jadon slumbers still," Stalyart replied. "Perhaps afterward, we will drink in celebration. Until then, perhaps it is best you remain alert."

Everything was too tall. For a goblin, it was the plight of living among humans. But for all the inconvenience of tabletops above eye level and forks that barely fit into his mouth, there were advantages as well. The *Jennai* had the greatest workshop K'k'rt had ever seen, and Rynn had apologized for it being small and crowded. If only she knew what crowded was really like. K'k'rt had shared a space the size of the *Jennai's* workshop with no fewer than fifty other goblins.

Using an upturned packing crate as a stepstool, the goblin tinker surveyed the plans spread over the workbench. He had learned the Korrish style of draftsmanship from Madlin during her stay among his people, and was soon able to puzzle out that the device simply called a "lift," was actually an arrangement of pulleys that lifted a box with doors up a shaft. Apparently the *Jennai* was in need of such a device. Stretching across the table for a sheet of the schematic that was barely within his reach, he winced in anticipation of the pain the act would cause in his shoulders and side.

No pain came. K'k'rt chuckled, unable to get over just how much help that little potion had been. When Madlin had told him it would make him young again, he had hardly believed her. It was the lie of the legend, as his people would say. A great many old stories contained a pearl of truth at the core, but had been surrounded with lies too extravagant to be possible. Yet here he was, with the color returning to his hair and the aches all but gone from his joints.

The opening of the workshop door drew K'k'rt's attention from the plans for the lift. With hearing better than he'd had in years, he picked up the subtle squeak and squish of spring-stabilized legs. Rynn had arrived for the day's work.

"You're here early," she remarked upon entering. There was a tingling in the air around her.

"Time shift," he replied. On a hunch, he let his eyesight drift into the aether. "I wake up at odd times since I've been here. You've ... been playing with magic."

"Anzik taught Madlin a couple tricks," Rynn replied. "I've been practicing for her sake. I can barely rub two aethers together to make fire."

K'k'rt chuckled. "That's not how it works, you know."

Rynn scowled down at him. Even standing atop the crate, she was a head taller. "I got it working, didn't I?"

K'k'rt took a moment to inspect the shielding spell she wore more closely. "Aligned to lightning. Are we doing something dangerous with one of your spark devices today?"

"That's what Anzik worries about, anyway. You can tell that by looking?"

"It takes practice," K'k'rt said. He muttered in the arcane language and weaved his fingers through the air. A shielding spell similar to Rynn's sprang to life around him.

"I see you've got the touch back."

"I don't feel the bones in my fingers grinding together anymore when I move them," said K'k'rt. "You'd be amazed how much that sort of thing gets in the way of spell-casting."

"Anzik and Dan always seemed to be able to manage without moving or speaking."

"Freaks, the both of them," said K'k'rt with a sneer.

There was a brief shudder in the ship, a tremor that worked its way from the steel floor through the crate, into K'k'rt's feet and up into his belly. He looked to Rynn. "Does the ship do that often?"

Rynn's mouth hung open, as if she was waiting for an answer to form there before she spoke. Her eyes drifted to the wall nearest where the tremor seemed to have originated. "No. Never."

Without another word, she sprinted for the door. K'k'rt followed, wondering what it was about youth that made one prone to rashness. He supposed it was the lack of pain when moving.

The daruu in their resplendent armor lined up like statues, awaiting orders. Danilaesis had never had troops quite like them. Though the armors they wore varied wildly in color, decoration, even material from one to the next, they all shared a similar glow in the aether. Runeforged. Not the tawdry runed weapons carried by the likes of Tanner, the daruu had hammered the runes right into the heart of the metal—or as in one case, dragon scale.

"It is as you say, Warlock Danilaesis," King Dekulon said. They all stood before the transport gate, looking through at the *Jennai*, where some lowly underling sat at the controls of one of the rebels' machines. "Just as with the kuduks, we cannot allow these enemies of the daruu people to maintain possession of such dangerous devices."

Danilaesis glared sidelong at Kezudkan, the daruu who had built the machine, daring him to contradict the king. His time among the rebels had furnished him with Kezudkan's name, as well as the knowledge that these humans hardly gave any *other* daruu a second thought. Put Kezudkan's head on a serving platter for Cadmus Errol, and they'd have an alliance done within the hour. But so long as neither he nor Kezudkan came down with an unfortunate case of honesty, there was no need for that ever to become public knowledge.

"My troops are ready when yours are," Danilaesis said with a military bow to King Dekulon. The Kadrin soldiers looked shabby by comparison to the daruu Iron Guard. Not a single knight of the empire numbered among them. As far as Danilaesis was concerned, he was bringing them along as fodder. It had been a courtesy to their daruu allies to bring regular army troops instead of conscripts, but that was as far as he was willing to go. Had someone laid odds for him, he might have bet that a few of the Iron Guard might survive the assault. But as it was planned, he was likely to be the only survivor from either side.

The king turned to Kezudkan and his other advisors. "Let us adjourn somewhere comfortable to await the results."

"Once we're through, shut it all the way down," Danilaesis replied. "One of our enemies can see the target locator even when it's not open. I don't know whether he can see *through* or not." Danilaesis knew that nothing could be seen through from the far side when the transport gate was closed, but there were certain events about to take place for which he wanted no witnesses.

"Yes, sir," Gederon replied. Danilaesis found much about the daruu people to both like and dislike. Gederon never objected to anything he was ordered to do, and rarely asked questions.

"When we get through, you're going to find at least four machines like this one aboard the ship," Danilaesis said. "These *must* be shut down; otherwise, they can use them to bring in reinforcements. You just need to break them enough that they don't work. If we recover any that can be repaired, fine, but that's not the goal here." Danilaesis repeated the instructions in Korrish. It was bloody inconvenient that neither side had troops who understood a common language.

Danilaesis had chosen their first target, the one that would put the rebels on the defensive the quickest: the main transport gate. More importantly, once all four were destroyed, it would trap Anzik Fehr aboard with nowhere to hide.

"Open it," Danilaesis ordered. He drew *Sleeping Dragon* and stood at the fore, ready to be the first one through. As the transport gate opened he charged through, releasing a blast of lightning that took out the operator of the machine as well as the control console. "No survivors!"

Silverware clattered as a plate thumped down on the table. Greuder looked down at his early morning guest with a narrow gaze.

"Since when do you take a breakfast anywhere but at that gutted machine of yours?" Greuder asked.

Cadmus grinned, sizing up his eggs and bacon and making a quick estimate as to how hungry he was in comparison. He took a gulp from a tankard filled with coffee to brush aside what little remnants of sleep his excitement hadn't scrubbed away. "Big day today," he replied. "Can't afford any distraction. Once I get to work this morning, I'm pushing through until I'm done."

"Oh?" Greuder asked. He set down a plate bearing his own meal and collapsed into a chair beside it. "Making any improvements? Or is this something to do with the hush-hush project Madlin's been off working on."

"Blast me if I know where that girl's gone. Only Rynn and Eziel know for sure. No, I've got something else planned. Something I've waited a long time for."

"Just spit it out, Cadmus. What've you got cooked up?"

"I found Kezudkan."

"Where's that daruu bastard been hiding?" Greuder asked with a mouthful of bacon.

"He found daruu in Veydrus. They've got a world-ripper. All I've got to do is watch the machine, wait for him to show up, and …" Cadmus patted the holstered coil gun at his hip.

"So you haven't actually *seen* him?"

Cadmus shrugged. "I see his footprints all over this. It's the same model we built in his original workshop. Anyone building one fresh from the books would have made it differently. This had to be his work."

"How do you know he'll show up at it? Maybe he sold it. Maybe he has a dozen or so, like we do now, and only comes once a month."

"You trying to sour these eggs?" Cadmus asked with a glare. "I'll wait as long as I have to, but I don't expect that to be long. You're welcome to come watch. I wouldn't mind a steady set of hands by the controls if I need to go through."

"What about Kaia?" Greuder asked. "She's the best technician we've got."

Cadmus lifted a palm. "I'll ask her if you're not up for it. But we've been friends since before Kaia was even born. Figured you've earned it. Not like I expect this to be a multi-axis mid-air chase. The blasted daruu can barely walk."

Greuder bobbed his head, considering. "All right then. Right as soon as I clear up the dishes."

Half an hour later, Greuder entered the main chamber of the lunar headquarters. Cadmus had already dialed in the coordinates and begun his vigil, watching as a familiar young daruu sat fidgeting at the controls of an idle world-ripper.

"This the daruu machine?" Greuder asked.

Cadmus scowled in reply and pointed to the daruu sitting at the controls.

"It was polite, that's all," Greuder said. "Forgive me if I've picked up the habit of asking easy questions to pop the cork on a conversation. I used to have a hundred customers a day or more at the bakery. Here I've just got you lot."

"That daruu there is Kezudkan's nephew," Cadmus replied. It had taken viewing the lad from a few angles before Cadmus was able to recall where he had seen the daruu: it was Gederon. He was the only one in the room, and kept checking a pocketclock every few minutes. He was waiting for someone. Cadmus had a good guess as to who it might be.

"So what now? We just wait?"

"We just wait," Cadmus replied.

However, waiting was more painful than Cadmus remembered it being. His foot tapped of its own accord, and his leg bounced beneath the console. Time passed more slowly than his pocketclock claimed; he was tempted to take the device apart and check its innards for slipped gears or a defective spring. Every fiber of him wanted to be moving, to be doing something. Normally he would have blamed his anxiety on having drunk too much coffee, but he knew better. It was the youth serum.

A fifty-three year old Cadmus—in mind and body—had puttered away for years in servitude he could have escaped at any time. He had stayed to finish the world-ripper and then to steal it. With a body as fit and vigorous as he'd had in thirty years, there were too many impulses to ignore. He had energy to work all day, but also enough that he could not sit idle. Contingency plans began to form in his head, plans that didn't involve a wait of indeterminate length.

"I bet you that nephew of his knows where Kezudkan is," Cadmus said, staring at the daruu lad in the viewframe. It was a strange parallel seeing Gederon checking his pocketclock as often as he was. Were they waiting for the same thing?

"You're thinking of grabbing the technician?" Greuder asked.

Cadmus shrugged. "Just speculating."

A moment passed in silence. Greuder's patience seemed better intact than his own. The baker had been judicious with his own supply of the serum. A few of the older rebels had held onto theirs for later, waiting to see how the others reacted, but Greuder had chosen moderation.

"But if I wasn't speculating …"

"I'll work the controls," Greuder replied. "You're not some hot-headed Veydran boy. I trust you know what you're doing."

"Thanks."

Cadmus was up and ready at the viewframe, coil gun drawn and ammunition checked—all before Greuder settled himself into his seat at the console. His heart was working double-time; his mind at half-crew. At the last moment, he remembered his runed armor, but decided that he could handle a single daruu without the help. After all, an unarmed daruu was no threat beyond arm's reach, and with a coil gun in hand, keeping one beyond arm's reach was fool's play.

"Ready when you are," Greuder announced, reaching up for the switch.

"Now or never," Cadmus replied.

The world-hole opened, and the fidgeting Gederon spun in his chair, showing remarkable agility for a daruu. Cadmus hopped through and leveled the coil gun at his head. The world-hole closed.

Gederon held up his hands. "Please don't—"

"One more word out of you and I will," Cadmus snapped. "You answer what I ask, nothing more. You understand?"

Gederon nodded vigorously. "Yes."

"Do you know who I am?" Cadmus asked.

Gederon shook his head. "You c-c-can't be … Erefan. He's … d-d-dead."

"I'm surprised you even recognize me," Cadmus admitted. Of course, it had been many years since Gederon had visited Kezudkan's estate, and he looked a similar number of years younger now. He gestured with the coil gun toward the chamber's only door. "Who you waiting for? Your uncle?"

Gederon nodded, but said nothing.

"When's he coming?"

"I don't—"

"You keep looking at that pocketclock of yours. I think you do."

Gederon's breathing quickened until Cadmus feared the daruu might pass out. He wasn't even sure that was possible for daruu; he had never heard of one succumbing to something so innocuous. "He's late. He should be here already."

*Stalling. He knows something.* "Where is he now? Where was he going to be before he came to you?"

Gederon shrugged and shook his head at once.

"Listen to me. I need to talk to your uncle. It's not going to be a pleasant conversation, since he made a rather unsporting attempt to kill me, but it doesn't need to involve you. If you can't get me to him in the next few minutes, I might just have to leave him a message. *You* would be that message, left in the wreckage of this machine. You following my tracks here?"

Gederon swallowed. "Yes."

"And you're going to take me to Kezudkan?"

"What are you going to do to him?"

Cadmus sneered. "Not a question you're in any position to be asking. But for starters, I want answers out of him. The only choice you need to worry about is dying right here, or taking your chances."

Gederon raised his hands and stood away from the console.

"Good lad," Cadmus said. He waved the coil gun toward the door. "Now, let's go find that uncle of yours."

A blast of lightning left Danilaesis's fingers before the first of the Iron Guard piled through the transport gate. The technician's flesh sizzled, freezing a shocked expression on his face as he died. Something within the machine sizzled as well, emitting a gout of smoke with a foul, metallic odor. Just to be safe, Danilaesis slashed *Sleeping Dragon* through the side of the target finder, just in case anyone was able to repair the damage done to the controls. It would be just like those tinkers to take two broken machines and salvage a whole one from the remains.

"Fan out," Danilaesis ordered. "If it moves, kill it. If it hums, break it. If it shoots, duck." Elaborate tactics were for grand wars fought across rolling landscapes or at the base of city walls. This was to be an avalanche, an unstoppable offensive that struck with little warning and no means to fight back.

Though he had eagerly led the initial charge, Danilaesis followed now. His shielding spell had been cast such that it was better suited to fast, physical attacks like the shots from those coil guns, rather than a general defense. Still, he would rather someone else take the shots than test those defenses. They poured through the ship: twenty Iron Guard, doughty and mighty, sturdy enough that one shot was unlikely to kill them; twenty Kadrin soldiers, mean and bloodthirsty and chosen for just those reasons, but ultimately expendable; and one warlock, intent on ending the life of everyone aboard.

The Korrish rebels were outmatched. Unprepared for the sudden attack, they fell to spears and axes as they scrambled for safety. Here and there, a pocket of resistance formed, but as soon as his troops called out the locations of these, Danilaesis made short work of them. The metal armor some of the rebels wore was well protected against physical attacks, but drew lightning like a spire. Time and again, the same trick worked. It wasn't that he could even blame them. The only ones who realized their mistake died before they could warn anyone else of the folly of trying to fend off a sorcerer's lightning with steel.

As he made his way through the ship, he would stop at particular locations, places he knew he would need to visit before he was finished with the *Jennai*. There must have been a thousand people aboard the *Jennai*, and with just forty warriors along, it would take forever to kill so many. As *Sleeping Dragon* hacked through the first of the *Jennai's* levitation runes, the ship lurched. It wasn't enough to bring the ship down, or even put it in serious jeopardy, but the weight of the huge vessel settled differently, the metal creaking in protest. And he was just beginning.

It sounded like a riot had broken out aboard the *Jennai*. There was no question that they were under attack of some kind, but it wasn't until Rynn saw an axe-wielding daruu that she knew what had happened: Kezudkan had found them, and now they were under attack via world-ripper. It had taken three shots from her coil gun—plus a fourth that had glanced off the daruu's shield—before the invader stopped advancing on her. A fifth and sixth ended the writhing on the ground. Rynn had never killed a daruu before, and was surprised that their blood wasn't actually muddy. In fact, they barely bled at all, though what they did bleed was as red as human blood.

K'k'rt kept up with her pace. For a creature with such short legs, she had expected him to be slower. Then again, dogs have short legs, and she couldn't think of outrunning those, at least not without upgrading her tinker's legs. Rebels swarmed in every direction throughout the ship, some advancing toward the battle, others away from it. Many who lacked a clear plan just ran without direction, keeping their heads down. Rynn shouted orders in passing, but in the chaos, she was barely heard and rarely obeyed. Ambushes weren't the time for rallying the troops; they were times for an army's training to kick into gear. Soldiers should be reacting, not panicking, and certainly not conceding the battlefield to their foes.

There were non-combatants, and no soldier ought to place his life above those. Rynn managed to think of this as she herself fled the battle, heading for her quarters.

Along the way, they encountered a group of four human invaders, dressed alike in chain with loose red shirts thrown over. Rynn had worried that they would get within spear's reach before she could put shots into each of them, but K'k'rt muttered something and the four froze in place. Even after a coil gun shot through the chest, none of them toppled to the ground before she and K'k'rt left the area.

When they reached Rynn's quarters and the door slammed shut behind her, Rynn found that K'k'rt had ended up on her side of it. "What do you think you're doing?" she demanded.

"Keeping as close to you as I can," K'k'rt replied. "My life might not be worth much here if you die."

"Well … turn around or something at least," Rynn said. She didn't have time to argue, already pulling off her shirt and squirming into the under-padding for the runed armor she had made for herself.

"Those were Kadrin uniforms, you know," K'k'rt observed. Rynn spared a glance and saw that he was watching the door, not her change of clothing.

"So does that mean Dan is behind this?"

"Could be," K'k'rt replied. "Could also be that your father's daruu friend made some allies."

Rynn slipped the armor plates over her front and back, quickly buckling them into place. She had researched history books on armor making before designing them, and had been appalled that knights couldn't get into the stuff on their own. She had left no such glaring deficiency in her design. Buckling on the straps for the arm plates was tougher, mainly because one arm couldn't help, but she managed that in short order. The helm snugged into place with a single chin strap, and she was ready for battle.

"You look ridiculous," K'k'rt observed, gawking up at her.

Rynn pulled out her coil gun. "It's not a formal dinner down there; it's a war. You coming?"

K'k'rt chuckled. It sounded odd without the gravelly rasp to it that had been a product of his age. "I wouldn't mind waiting things out up here."

"Up to you. If this isn't your fight, we can send you home when this is over."

K'k'rt's eyes widened. Home was the last place he wished to be, and she knew it. "But—"

"If you want this to be home, you're gonna have to fight for it."

K'k'rt glared at her, but after a seething breath, he relented. "Fine. Let's go."

Jamile rushed down the hall of the lunar headquarters in her nightclothes, with her shoes tucked under one arm. The lunar stone was rough and cold as her bare soles slapped against the floor. Cadmus had been gone when she awoke, but he snuck away often enough that it was not cause for alarm. She already had alarm to spare, to donate, or to sell at a loss. She just needed to get to the world-rippers.

"Cadmus!" she shouted as she approached the main chamber. "There's been an attack!"

She stopped short when she saw that it was Greuder at the controls of the world-ripper, not the Mad Tinker. "Where's—" but she stopped herself short. There in the viewframe, Cadmus was walking down a stone tunnel lit by a soft blue glow, pointing a coil gun at a daruu a few paces ahead of him.

Greuder spared a glance over his shoulder. "What's this about an attack?"

Jamile spread her arms wide, inadvertently letting her shoes tumble to the floor. "It's an attack. We're under attack!"

Greuder turned his attention back to Cadmus on the other side of the viewframe. "Gut me. What're we going to do now?"

Jamile pointed to Cadmus. "Bring him back. We need to help them! Help us. How did Vaulk not notice the *Jennai* shaking like a runaway trolley?"

"We're sound sleepers, Vaulk and I," Greuder replied. "And I can't just bring Cadmus back. He's found his old owner and he's about to get payback for Erefan's death. I'm not sure that he'd come willingly, even with the *Jennai* at stake."

A sleepy voice called from the side corridors. "What's going on?"

"Kaia!" Jamile shouted. "Get over here. Cadmus is gone on some vendetta, and it's down to us to save the *Jennai*."

"Huh?"

"They're under attack!" At least with Kaia it was forgivable, not being twinborn. "Go wake up Kupe and Anzik."

Kaia fought back a yawn. "I sent Anzik to the *Jennai* last night."

"Well … just get Kupe!"

"What are you thinking?" Greuder asked.

Jamile rushed to the controls of one of the river's world-rippers. "First I'm going to bring Sosha here; then, we're going to start evacuating the wounded." Beneath her breath she muttered. "Blast it, Madlin. Where are you?"

Madlin sat with her hands in her lap, staring at the small array of world-rippers she had constructed. She had wanted to create a weapon smaller and more versatile than the World Ender Cannon, but so far she had failed. Connecting one end to a volcano was nice, but the heat was hardly an effective long-range weapon; she would be better off just opening a world-hole and firing a coil gun through. If only she had a coil gun with her. In the isolation of her hidden lair, it had seemed redundant to bring one.

The one thing she had yet to try with the device was the one thing she most feared. Connecting one end to the heart of the sun ought to devastate anything on the far side. But Madlin, in reading up on stellar theory, had found reason to be cautious. Some scientists theorized that a star was the entry point for energy into the universe. More practical ones had calculated the temperature required to warm Korr from so far away, and the numbers had a frightening number of zeroes in them. Yet others claimed that traditional physics broke down, and that stars exhibited behaviors that defied current understanding. In light of those claims, the little tinkered arrangement of steel, copper, and dragonhide seemed a paltry defense. She would test it with a timer, and make sure that no one was in the hideaway when it went off. If it worked as she hoped, there would be ample evidence in the aftermath, even without witnessing the event as it occurred.

But there was no time. The *Jennai* was under attack now. And without access to a world-ripper that she could fit her shoulders through, Madlin was stuck. Her own paranoia had left her stranded while Rynn fought for her life.

With proper armor on, Rynn felt invincible. The feeling lasted until she saw the first pack of Kadrin soldiers advancing on her. With K'k'rt clinging to her shadow, she was rounding the corner heading toward the front-portside world-ripper, hoping to secure it, when four spear-wielding Veydrans caught sight of her.

They shouted something in their own language. Two of them crouched low, spears presented against a charge. The other two used the soldiers in front as cover and hurled their spears. Rynn stumbled over her tinker's legs trying to back out of the way and get behind the corner for cover. One spear thumped harmlessly against her chest plate, the other glanced off the side of her helmet.

As she hit the ground on her back, Rynn spared a thought for K'k'rt, hoping she hadn't crushed him in her fall. But the old tinker wasn't acting so old anymore; he was already around the corner Rynn had been retreating toward. The Kadrin soldiers did not waste their advantage, rushing forward to finish off their downed adversary. The two who had disarmed themselves drew stubby swords from their belts, pushing past the spear wielders as the latter worked to stand while being jostled.

Rynn tried to scramble to her feet, but as accustomed as she was to the tinker's legs, they weren't built for such contortions. As the four Veydrans barreled toward her, she pictured them falling upon her, overpowering her, and sliding one of those ugly little swords through a gap in her armor. Propping herself up on an elbow, she took hasty aim and fired. And fired. And fired.

"They're good and dead," K'k'rt said, poking his head around the corner.

Rynn nodded, her breath coming too quick to easily form words. She climbed to her feet and stepped around the gore and the growing pool of blood. One Kadrin moaned, not yet dead from his wounds. He muttered something in his own language. Rynn took aim at his head and looked away. When she pulled the trigger, there was a click, but no shot. She had emptied the coil gun.

As she dug in a pouch for more ball bearings, K'k'rt retrieved one of the Kadrins' swords. The weapon was ludicrous in his hands; it could have been a sharpened shovel for the goblin. Taking the hilt in both hands, he spoke something to the Kadrin and slit his throat. Rynn was caught by surprise and didn't manage to look away before watching the light go from the Kadrin soldier's eyes.

"What did you say to him?" Rynn asked.

K'k'rt chuckled, dropping the sword to the deck plates with a clatter. "I told him he'd be seeing the rest of his friends soon."

Davlin crouched by the viewframe of the rear-starboard world-ripper, with his coil gun aimed for the door to the rest of the ship. Through the other door, the one that led to the protected control console, a technician's hands flew over the dials, rounding up a raid team that had been sent to hold off local authorities that had been party to a dispute in Khesh. Keeping order amid border and cattle ownership disputes was an acceptable use for soldiers—in peacetime. Now was the time for a soldier's true duty: the defense of his people.

Already, two Veydrans lay dead at the door. Davlin had only two soldiers with him when he had arrived, and now had six more who had been retrieved from Tellurak. Davlin had killed both Veydrans himself, before help had arrived.

"Forgive me, Eziel, for I have turned my weapon upon my brothers. I killed with neither vengeance nor anger, but only forgiveness. In your light may they find peace and camaraderie in the next life. In your wisdom, send me the enemies of my people, and not the wayward souls whose hearts have been led down the path of fratricide. Give us the strength of one people, to stand against the foes who come against us. So we implore."

"So we implore," the soldiers around him muttered.

There was quiet following the prayer. The soldiers fidgeted, and breath came heavy. The reek from the two fresh corpses by the door turned Davlin's stomach. There had been nothing in the old texts about the smell, but he remembered it well from his days working for the militia. Korrish or Veydran, a dead human smelled the same.

Sounds of battle seemed muted and distant. It might have been Davlin's imagination, but the ship seemed to be tilting. If he didn't worry that he would need every last one before this was all ended, he would have taken one of his spare ball bearings and set it on the floor to see which way it rolled.

Footsteps sounded in the hall. They weren't the trampling stampede of a charge, nor the tentative steps of someone whose skulking had failed to go unnoticed. It was a brisk stroll. The footfalls were neither hard nor heavy; someone slight of build in soft-soled boots approached. Davlin hoped that it was Sosha. He worried for the safety of the only doctor aboard.

The footsteps stopped short of the door. "I see you in there, waiting for me."

Davlin's blood went cold. It was Dan's voice. "Eziel, forgive us and grant us the mercy of your intervention …"

"I bet you have those guns of yours all pointed and ready for me," said Dan. "Well, let's give this a go."

As soon as a figure appeared in the doorway, Davlin and his men opened fire. Shot after shot thudded into flesh, but the human in the doorway didn't fall. It was one of their own men, a corpse hung in the air by foul magic. A crunch and shriek of steel drew Davlin's eyes to the wall. Stuck through was a foot of blade, piercing the bulkhead like an awl through leather. As soon as it disappeared back through the wall, Davlin fired, counting on the coil guns to puncture the steel and still be lethal on the other side. But it was too late. The hole where the sword had been belched fire. The last thing Davlin heard was a spiteful laugh at his expense.

"He's going to be here any time now," said Tanner. He crouched behind the control console of the rear-portside world-ripper, alone with the *Jennai's* best hope of stopping Danilaesis.

"Of course," Anzik replied. "He knows he cannot control the ship so long as the world-rippers are in Korrish hands." He sat cross-legged on the floor beside Tanner, his demeanor no different than ever.

Tanner shook his head. "I don't get it. How can you be calm? Dan's gonna be here any minute, and you've got the same old trap laid out for him. Ain't you worried he won't fall for it twice?"

"Not very," Anzik replied. "The variation is minor, but the juxtaposition of weaponry will be unexpected." Anzik twisted the coil gun in his hand, looking it all over. "He won't expect the same trap, simply because he expects that I would know better. Thus, the appearance of the same trap will distract him momentarily, and a moment is all I will require."

"And we're hidden back here? Completely?"

"Danilaesis will be blinded by the obvious." The false Anzik paced the room, muttering to himself and flexing his fingers to limber them for spell-casting. Tanner spared the decoy a glance, and had to admit that it was convincing.

Tanner drew his blade, the soft scraping against the leather of his scabbard quieter than their voices. "Don't mind if I keep this out, do you? Just in case?"

Anzik twitched a smile. "It is unnecessary, but I welcome the sentiment. Should anything go wrong, I don't expect you will stand much chance against him." He perked up, turning his head in the direction of a blank wall. "He's coming."

Tanner had never been gifted with aether-vision. Just being able to scrape a shielding spell together had pushed him to his limits. Anzik had shown time and again that he was ever alert to the aether. Danilaesis had a brilliant Source by all accounts, and Anzik could see him coming through the bulkheads.

It was minutes before Danilaesis arrived, minutes spent with a quickening heart and a sweating brow. When the warlock entered the room, Tanner could hear the strut in his walk. He looked down and checked the time on his stolen pocketclock.

"I can't believe this," Danilaesis said. "You're going to fight me yourself? Just like that? I would have thought you'd—" something must have occurred to the warlock just then. A blast of lightning in the room made the hair of Tanner's arms stand on end. "Gut me! Where are you, you rotten, lying illusionist?"

Anzik didn't answer with words, but sent a shot from his coil gun in reply. Danilaesis was thrown against the wall by the force of the shot, but his shielding spell prevented the ball bearing from piercing his flesh. The blow dazed him, however, and the blade-tooth sword fell from his limp grasp. Before the warlock recovered his wits, Anzik emerged from hiding and took careful aim.

"This ends your war," Anzik said. But before he could pull the trigger, he stiffened. Whirling, he turned toward Tanner, mouth agape and a look of complete bewilderment on his face.

Tanner was already moving, he batted the coil gun out of Anzik's grasp and ran him through. There was a brief flare of resistance from the Megrenn sorcerer's shielding spell, but the runed blade Tanner wielded pushed through it. As Anzik collapsed to his knees, Tanner slid his blade free and cut off the sorcerer's head. Though the chest wound would have been fatal in short order, there was no killing too quick for a sorcerer. Even as he swung his blade, Tanner noticed smoke rising from Anzik's body as he tried to fight back, but failed to concentrate to control his aether.

"Tanner, what the bloody blazes are you doing here?" Danilaesis asked, rubbing the back of his head as he retrieved his sword. "And you just stole my revenge."

"Kick him or something, but get moving," Tanner replied. "I can't be seen talking to you. As far as anyone knows, this is Kadrin blood." He held up his reddened blade to make his point.

"I don't understand."

"Your father had a plan," Tanner said. "It involved a free airship, an imperial pardon, and paying back that inhuman sorcerer for murdering you."

"Madlin played a part in that," Danilaesis said. "I've still got to—"

"She's not aboard right now, and I don't know where Rynn is. But she's not important. We finish up, and we get out of here alive."

"Let no enemy live once he has offered violence," Danilaesis quoted. "Or in this case, she."

"And look where that got Rashan in the end. Go on, move."

Another Tanner, in another world, leaned with his back against the wall of the hold of the *Mirror's Trick*. The weight of the blade in his hand was familiar, as was the blood that dripped from it. Jadon lay dead in his bunk.

Footsteps pounded down the stairs from the deck. "I heard the commotion," Stalyart said. "Is it done?"

"Almost blew my shot," Tanner said. "Got to him a few seconds early, put Anzik on his guard. If he'd been a proper warlock, I'd be dead over there. But I saw the smoke; he tried to burn me and got himself instead."

"So, we have ourselves a ship," Stalyart said. "With Kadrin blessings and no one in Megrenn the wiser. Excellent."

"I ain't feeling too excellent right now," Tanner replied. He wiped his sword on a clean part of Jadon's blanket, then returned it to its sheath. "I'm gonna go find me a drink, and it's nothing to do with celebratin'."

The other Tanner, aboard the *Jennai*, was on his own now. He could get drunk enough for both of them.

Cadmus kept his feet quiet as he could on the floors of the stone tunnels. Strange rumors persisted about the daruu, that they were so in tune with the stone that they could know a man by his footsteps a mile away, simply by feel. In all his years with Kezudkan, Erefan had never been able to say for certain if they were true. But in this place of daruu legend, he gave those legends fair consideration.

Gederon was less careful, leading the way. They had been going for far longer than Cadmus had expected. Despite not finding Kezudkan, neither had they run into any other daruu. He had warned the lad not to run them into anyone, but it surprised him how long they had gone unnoticed.

"Stop," Cadmus ordered in a harsh whisper. "I recognize this tunnel. We've gone 'round in a loop."

"What? N-n-no!" Gederon protested. "We're al-almost there."

Just then a world-hole opened behind him. Cadmus turned to see Greuder at the controls, beckoning urgently. Kupe and Charsi were watching from near the viewframe. "Come on Cadmus! There's been an attack. We need you!'"

"I trust you all to handle things," Cadmus snapped. "I'm just one man, and no warrior. I'm so close now! Close that thing before I put a bullet through it."

Greuder gave a nervous chuckle, despite his obvious distress. "You couldn't bring yourself. Kupe, go drag Cadmus back here. His brake lever's snapped off."

Kupe gave Greuder a nod and hopped through the world-hole without hesitation.

Cadmus didn't hesitate either. In one smooth motion he took aim and put a shot through the spark line that fed the viewframe.

Kupe spun and looked back, but there was no world-hole any longer. "What'd you do that for?"

"Kaia can fix that in under an hour," Cadmus replied. "That ought to be plenty of time. Stick close, and don't hurt our guide. His life is what he's getting in return for a meeting with his uncle."

The *Jennai* was listing dangerously. It had grown worse progressively as Rynn and K'k'rt waited by the world-ripper. A few of the rebels had reported in. There had been world-holes opening around the ship, spiriting away the wounded to the lunar headquarters. She was far past worrying that it was no longer a secret. Madlin had an even more secret locale, and look at the good that was doing them. She had outsmarted herself with her preparations, with the assumption that having only Rynn able to retrieve her would be security enough.

Now, Rynn's life was measured in minutes. Danilaesis was loose somewhere on the ship. The reports of magic being flung about and a boy with a sword spotted among the invaders removed all doubt of that. He would be looking for Anzik—who by fortunate coincidence was aboard and able to help defend the ship—and for Madlin. On the one hand, Madlin was safe from the rampaging madman. On the other, he knew full well that Rynn was her twin, and would treat her accordingly.

K'k'rt cleared his throat. Rynn briefly confused it for the goblin muttering to himself in his own language, before he continued in Korrish. "You don't suppose it might be time to evacuate ourselves, now, do you?"

"And leave whoever is left to their fates? We can't save everyone in time, even with the help from our other base."

"I'm not sure we can save ourselves, if he comes for us," K'k'rt replied.

Rynn nodded. Maybe they couldn't save themselves. She didn't pray often, but if not at a time like this, then when? "Holy Eziel, defender of my people, lend me strength in my time of need. I am technically about to violate your tenet about not killing my own kind, but I would submit to you that Danilaesis Solaran is an inhuman monster, and thus exempt. So if we could both look the other way this once, I think everything will work out for the better. Thank you."

"Nice god you've got there," K'k'rt remarked. "Does he ever show up to help?"

"Nope, not yet," Rynn replied. "But he's never tried to eat me, either, so I'm still scoring him a goal up on your dragon."

K'k'rt snorted. "If we had a dragon here, this warlock would be dead already. One fiery breath would be all it would take."

*One fiery breath. If only he knew.*

Rynn rechecked the count of ball bearings in her coil gun. Six. Same as the last time she counted. If she needed more than six shots—if she needed more than one or two—it wouldn't matter whether she had any more than that.

The ship shook. There was a long, agonized groan of steel being stretched in directions it was not meant to go. Rynn put her hands out to steady herself as the floor shifted, tilting at a new, steeper angle.

"And what if he drops us from the sky instead of coming to us?" K'k'rt asked. "How many runes do you think still hold us up?"

"Enough," Rynn replied, thought she wasn't so sure of that. They were in a room with no windows to the outside. It was possible that they were drifting down already. It wouldn't take anything as dramatic as freefall to kill them. The *Jennai* would likely break apart even hitting the water at a moderate speed.

The main dining hall had once played host to the wealthiest kuduks in Korr. They ate pastries dusted with powdered gemstones and drank from crystal that cost more than a human at auction. During the rebel's custodianship, it had seen plundered coin passed back and forth over games of chance. Humans who had never put twenty tenar together in the same place drank exotic liquors from another world. Now, it had become a battlefield.

Hayfield hunkered down behind the bar along with four of his fellow soldiers. They'd had luck, but their supplies of ball bearings had run out. Eight Veydrans and a pair of daruu in fancy armor sprawled out on the dining hall floor, along with a dozen rebels. Not everyone carried coil guns aboard ship. Only a few officers and raid leaders made a habit of it. No one wore their assault armor except squads on assignment. Who could have guessed that the worst battle in the rebellion's brief history would be fought on the defensive, aboard their own ship?

The wind whistled through the broken windows, letting the cold outside air into the ship. The clouds in view beyond the glass were rising, or at least it looked that way.

"This is it, boys," Hayfield said, despite one of his soldiers being conspicuously female. "We're down to cutlery. Stick to loading kitchenware. Most of the spoons and forks are brightsteel and won't shoot worth piss."

"Want me to go scrounging?" one of the soldiers asked, hooking a thumb at the scattered bodies throughout the room.

"Ain't gonna find much," Hayfield replied. "Those steel balls don't stop for much. Most of 'em probably gone clean through the ship and out to sea."

"Piss."

There were murmurs of agreement with the sentiment. Hayfield wished he had better news to share, but truth was truth. He could lie to his superiors when the situation called for it. He could lie to a kuduk without blinking. But he couldn't lie to men (and a woman) about to die with him.

A shockwave tore through the room, ending idle conversation. Hayfield's makeshift squad was sheltered from the blast by the bar, but every bit of glassware in the room shattered, from the chandelier, to the drinking glasses, to the bottles behind the bar. The squad was doused in liquor amid a rain of broken glass.

"Fire what you got," Hayfield ordered. He followed his own command and stuck his coil gun over the bar, peeking just enough to catch a glimpse of the crazy young Veydran with the black sword. Pulling the trigger, he fired a paring knife across the room and ducked back behind cover. Peeking again to see if he had done any damage, he found the Veydran still coming. His squad mates fared no better, and there was a moment's panic when the Veydran giggled.

*Whoosh.*

A plume of flame rolled across the bar, forcing those stealing glances across at their foe to duck down. But there was no safety in that. The liquor caught fire, and being soaked in it, so did Hayfield and his comrades.

Frantically, Hayfield tried to tear off his clothing, but he was soaked to the skin and alcohol burned quickly. He had heard that alcohol fires burned cool, but when it came to being aflame, fire was still fire. The giggling laughter turned to cackling and faded. The Veydran had left them to die.

As soon as their foe was gone, a world-hole opened. Hayfield was screaming when the bucket of water hit him, followed by others for his companions.

"Get them through, quick!" Jamile ordered. Rough hands grabbed him, but Hayfield didn't care. He was dimly aware of being hauled through the world-hole to someplace that wasn't on fire. That was good enough to let go and let his mind drift into unconsciousness.

It was time to go. Actually, it was well past time to go. Tanner slunk along the corridors of the *Jennai*, avoiding both sides in the conflict. He was in less danger than perhaps anyone on board the ship, but that would only last so long as neither side saw him consorting with the other. His destination was the liftwing hangar, which he could only hope had survived the airship's violent jolts and shudders as Danilaesis snipped the strings that suspended it from the heavens.

Keeping a bloody sword in hand was an excellent way to avoid confrontations with either side. A nice, clean, shining sword might mean you were still looking around for someone to stab with it. A man with a clean sword was prone to get orders shouted at him from the first green-eared sergeant that crossed his path. Drench one in someone's blood, and you took on the look of someone engaged in serious business. In Tanner's experience, that told most people you were fine on your own.

Of course, few people seemed to carry swords in Korr. It was sad. Tanner had purloined a coil gun from a fallen rebel, and he could see the appeal. Punching holes in brick walls with the tug of a finger had its charm. But Tanner had grown up with a blade in his hand—in two different worlds. There were few in his own world who could match his skill, and he doubted that Korr had anyone worthy of crossing blades with him, let alone besting him. He was a relic in a world where guns ruled the battlefield, and every hole-riddled corpse he passed reminded him of why he didn't belong in Korr.

The liftwing hangar was a shambles. The tilting deck had let the individual airships slide into a pile at one side of the room. Tanner couldn't let that stop him, since he had no other plan at the moment, and Danilaesis's plan seemed likely to get him killed if he didn't do something soon. The young warlock had every confidence that his father would get them both out before it was too late, but Danilaesis had a habit of thinking of himself first and last, and if there was time after things were settled, then maybe someone else. Tanner wasn't in the mood for a maybe. He climbed into the pilot's seat of the least entangled craft and buckled himself in.

Rynn's people had never let him actually fly one of the liftwing airships, but he had talked to the pilots at length about how they worked. Pilots were like sailors; get them started talking about their livelihood and you could hardly shut them up. Tanner had everything he needed to know that didn't come from practical experience. He pressed the switch and grinned when the engine roared to life, twirling the propeller into a blur at the nose of the liftwing. For a moment, he forgot the war going on throughout the ship and basked in the childish glee of commanding something big and powerful.

The noise in the hangar was horrific. Normally, the liftwings were towed into the plaza with a winch, but there was no time or manpower for that. The engine's echo reached deafening levels as Tanner threw the throttle to full power and the liftwing forced its way free of the tangle of wings and chassis. His airship lurched and tugged, finally pulling completely free. It shot forward, and Tanner jerked the control stick back and forth, oversteering in both directions until he managed to aim it through the hangar door.

The plaza was deserted but cluttered. Supplies that had been stowed along the outskirts of the massive strip of steel had spilled across the runway. Tanner throttled back, steering drunkenly around the worst of the debris, hitting some of the boxes and a pile of rope. Someone at a window in one of the converted vacuum tanks shouted down, asking where he thought he was going. It seemed a stupid question: *anywhere but here.*

Tanner hit the end of the plaza runway well below the speed the pilots recommended, tumbling over the edge rather than lifting gracefully by virtue of Korrish science. As he fell nose-first toward the sea, Tanner hammered the throttle to full once more and pulled back on the control stick. The little liftwing pulled out of its dive and flew level.

Tanner left the throttle at full, not caring about his heading. Danilaesis could send someone for him later, but he wasn't going to risk his life on waiting.

"He's coming," K'k'rt said in a hushed tone. "I can see him in the aether. Last chance. We can turn on your machine and be gone before he gets here."

"We're staying," Rynn replied. She crouched behind a corner of the control console and took aim at the doorway.

"Turn it on anyway," K'k'rt said. "It glows in the aether. We'll be harder to see for him."

Rynn nodded. "Go ahead. Do it." She never took her eyes or her aim from the doorway.

*This is it. It's him or me.*

When Danilaesis appeared in the doorway, Rynn pulled the trigger. He was already ducking for cover, but the shot traveled too fast to avoid. It caught him in the shoulder and spun the warlock to the ground out of sight of the doorway.

"Well, hello Rynn," Danilaesis called out from the hallway. She could hear in his voice that his teeth were gritted as he spoke. Her shot had hurt him. "You're a better aim than most of your men, but then again, most of them were pissing themselves at the time. Must be a real distraction. The problem all of you keep running into is that none of you can take a punch."

Rynn replied by firing two more shots, aiming at the wall where she guessed Danilaesis hid on the far side. With a shaking hand, she loaded replacement shots into the back of the weapon. Six shots total. She needed a full complement.

"Fine, no need to be terse about it," Danilaesis called around the corner. Clearly her shots had missed.

When Danilaesis peeked around the corner again, he was crouched low. Her shot went wide as an unseen force tugged at the barrel of her coil gun. Danilaesis grinned, staring right into her eyes from ten paces away. Then he unleashed the lightning.

Rynn fell back against the wall, twitching, watching spots swim before her eyes. The force tugging at her coil gun vanished, but her arm was limp. Smoke rose from the world-ripper machine, which must have shared the blast with her.

"You idiot tinkers and making everything metal," Danilaesis said. Rynn closed her eyes, listening as he approached. "I can't even miss with lightning if I tried."

A guttural phrase, filled with clicks and glottal stops, came from the corner of the room. Rynn heard the rush of flame and felt warmth on her face. She peeked one eye open and saw a wash of fire wrapping itself around a shielding spell that protected the warlock.

"You sniveling goblin scum," Danilaesis said with a sneer. He turned and flung another blast of lightning; she couldn't see where it connected.

But Danilaesis was distracted. Rynn raised her arm, still tingling from the spark's aftereffects. Her first shot glanced off Danilaesis's shielding spell. He turned to face her. The second caught him square in the chest, launching him across the room to strike the wall with a hollow, metallic thump. The third caught him in the forehead and went through. The fourth, fifth, and sixth were just for good measure.

Rynn drew herself unsteadily to her feet, buoyed by the mechanical stabilizers in her tinker's legs. She walked across to Danilaesis's body and looked down at the horrifying mass of burst flesh she had caused. She held her coil gun trained on him, on the chance it was all some trick of light and magic.

"I think he's dead," K'k'rt said. The goblin tinker wobbled as he made his way beside her. "No need to reload."

Rynn nodded. "We've got to get out of here." She turned toward the world-ripper, but stopped short. The machine had been on a moment before, idle but humming with spark energy. Now, it was lifeless—just like she was about to be.

Just then, a world-hole opened, free from any viewframe on her end. The hole shuddered in the air … as if someone were trying to hold it steady as the *Jennai* dropped from the sky! Rynn had been right, they *were* losing altitude.

"Grab hold," Greuder yelled from the far side, extending a hand. The scene beyond was a mass of miserable humanity, with wounded soldiers and refugees crowded in throughout the main chamber of the lunar headquarters. There was a story there, but one that would wait for less pressing times.

Rynn wrapped one arm around K'k'rt, and reached up to take the offered hand. Her coil gun clattered to the ground as the old twinborn baker pulled her to safety.

Madlin let loose a long sigh, and eased her hand away from the switch. In the little viewframe of her hideaway within Tellurak's moon, she watched Danilaesis's body drift down, along with the rest of the *Jennai.* The airship passed through her field of view until she was looking down on it from above. It hit the Sea of Kerum with a force the World Ender Cannon might have envied if the weapon were not the first part of the ship that hit. The splash must have launched a hundred feet into the air. It took time for the hull to sink below the water, folding up and breaking apart as impact damage and the might of the sea itself wrecked the rebellion's months of work.

Switching inputs on the viewframe, Madlin turned her head lest she be blinded by the light. With the twist of a dial, she sent the view to the harmless void between worlds. It was no longer set to watch Korr's sun from the inside. Rynn was safe. Danilaesis was dead. She had not been forced to flip the switch and find out what would have happened if she brought the sun to the *Jennai*.

# Chapter 25

*"My greatest worry in this whole rebellion business is that Madlin's going to do something brave and stupid, and get herself killed." – Cadmus Errol*

The tunnels looked different, which Cadmus took as a good sign. But there was still no Kezudkan, which limited the extent to how pleased any tunnel could make him. He had long suspected the daruu had some sense of innate navigation, some feel in the stone that was akin to constellations or the position of the sun for telling north from east. But he was no daruu, so his suspicion that they had not traveled far at all from the world-ripper room remained nothing but speculation. It was time to put the premise to empirical test.

Still holding the gun pointed at Gederon's back, Cadmus pulled out his pocketclock and opened the face with a flick of the wrist. "You've got five more minutes," he said. "After that, I kill you and take the chance that I can find him quicker without you leading me astray."

"I'm n-n-not misleading you."

"Four minutes, fifty-six seconds."

"B-but it's going to take m-more than five m-m-minutes to get there," Gederon protested.

"Then pump those stubby pistons of yours faster," Kupe snapped. "He's running out of patience with you." He winked at Cadmus while the daruu wasn't looking.

Gederon quickened his pace, and before long he was breathing hard. Cadmus sneered, marveling that his younger body was holding up to the rigors of the search better than a lazy daruu.

There was no door, when they arrived, just an opening in the side of the tunnel. Gederon stopped and pointed silently, but Cadmus could already hear the voices within the chamber. He waggled the gun in Gederon's direction, indicating that the daruu lad lead the way.

As they approached, Cadmus could pick up the conversation. "I just think that we'd be better off if—Gederon, what are you doing down here?" Kezudkan asked as Gederon appeared in the entrance.

Cadmus stepped up behind the young daruu, still training his gun at Gederon's back. "Hello, Kezudkan. Surprised to see me?" The room was filled with daruu, dressed in strange, metallic clothing made of fine rings. They looked important, though he recognized none of them.

"Erefan," Kezudkan breathed, his eyed widening. "You're … you can't be here."

"But I am, and it's time for—blast it, none of you move." Cadmus aimed the gun at a brawny daruu reaching for an axe that dangled from his belt—the only weapon he could see in the room besides his own. "I'm here for Kezudkan Graniteson. This doesn't involve the rest of you."

"I don't know what you're trying to accomplish here," Kezudkan said. "Just put the gun down and we can talk. Just leave the boy alone."

"I've got no quarrel with your nephew—yes, I remembered him," Cadmus said. "But I just want everyone here to know why I'm here, and that this doesn't have to end with a lot of bodies to clean up."

"You're a thief, a runaway, and a murderer," Kezudkan said. "Why should any of us believe you?"

One of the younger daruu in the room, the one dressed most extravagantly, stepped between Kezudkan and Cadmus. "I am Dekulon, king of the daruu people. I cannot allow you to harm one of my subjects."

"Even a criminal?" Cadmus asked.

"He had broken no laws among our people," King Dekulon replied. "If you have a pre-existing quarrel—"

"Quarrel?" Cadmus scoffed. "He tried to kill me!" He wanted to shout that Kezudkan *had* killed him, but that would have muddied the waters more than cleared them. "I'm going to have my justice, whether it's given to me or I have to take it. Now, step aside."

King Dekulon shook his head. "I cannot."

"Erefan," Kezudkan said. "Let's be reasona—"

*Click.*

*Crack!*

The shot went through King Dekulon and Kezudkan both. So did the second shot. By the third, the two daruu had fallen in separate directions, and Cadmus only cared to ensure that Kezudkan was dead.

The room erupted into chaos. Cadmus's attack had shocked them all—probably because no one had ever dared attack their king before. Two of the daruu rushed to the king's aid; the one with the axe took the weapon in hand and rushed for him; the eldest daruu began muttering something that had a suspicious sound to it—magic.

Cadmus dealt first with the threat he best understood, planting a shot in the head of the daruu with the axe and dropping him to the ground with a thump just a pace away. He fired another shot that took the rune-hurler square in the chest, but it struck a barrier that flashed blue and flattened the steel ball bearing. The rune-hurler seemed unharmed, but flustered, stumbling over his words and feet at the same time as he backed away. Not to be deterred, Cadmus fired a second shot at the rune-hurler, and a weaker flash from the barrier was not enough to turn aside the shot. The rune-hurler collapsed against a wall, not dead, but no longer a threat.

The surprise was Gederon. The stutter-mouthed daruu lad had stood bolted to the floor to that point. But something inside him must have snapped free. He whirled on Cadmus with a speed seldom seen in daruu. The Mad Tinker fell back and fired again.

*Click.*

There was no shot left. In the excitement, Cadmus had not kept count. He should have dealt with the threats before him and reloaded to finish off Kezudkan. It might even have been a chance to gloat; he had felt so clever disposing of his nemesis without bothering with melodrama, but pure ruthlessness had an impractical side to it as well. Kezudkan had been no real threat.

Gederon was. The daruu lad closed the two-pace distance to Cadmus in a heartbeat. He struck like a trolley with no brakeman, bowling Cadmus over and driving him to the ground. The Mad Tinker slammed to the floor, his head cracking against the unforgiving stone. He blinked out of consciousness for just a second, coming around just in time to see a heavy fist bearing down toward his face. After that, there was no waking up.

Kaia and Greuder made frantic efforts to direct the two working world-rippers around the *Jennai* as it sank into the Sea of Kerum. The main chamber of the lunar headquarters was splashed with seawater and so crowded with people that rebel refugees were stumbling over the wounded. The able-bodied stood stationed at the viewframes, ready to haul survivors into the crowded confines.

Rynn found herself, for the first time she could remember, surrounded by rebels who weren't looking to her for answers. They jostled and pushed, trying to keep out of her way as she made her way to the main world-ripper, which was the only one of the three that was idle. Most people who ended up beside her asked after her health, or expressed relief that she had made it.

"Why isn't this one on?" Rynn shouted over the general commotion.

"Blame your father for that," Greuder shouted back, though Rynn had lost sight of him at the control console of the upstream world-ripper. "He shot out the spark line, and we haven't had a chance to fix it."

If that wasn't a call for Rynn's services, she didn't know what was. "Why would he do that?" she called out as she moved to inspect the damage.

"He was after that daruu, hot for blood. We sent Kupe to drag him back, but the lad got stuck on the other side with him."

"Eziel, you rat bastard," Rynn swore. "You'd better not have …" she didn't finish the thought. "Greuder, let Kaia finish the rescue from the ship. I need that world-ripper."

"But Rynn," Jamile shouted. Rynn couldn't see her, but imagined that she must be with the wounded. "There are still people trapped on board."

Rynn gritted her teeth. One life—two if Kupe counted—against however many might still be alive and trapped in the sinking airship. How could she ask that? How could she demand that? She could order it. She was still in charge. They would understand.

She still couldn't do it. "Fine. Keep up the search."

Rynn shoved her way roughly through the crowd, which couldn't part fast enough for her liking. "Any mechanics around, get over here. I've got a machine to repair."

Kupe huddled with his back to the tunnel wall, coil gun pointed at the entrance. He had heard it all and was no fool. Cadmus Errol was probably dead. A bunch of daruu were likely dead as well, but not all of them. The coil gun shook in his hand. He couldn't go look.

"Stay back!" he shouted as a daruu stuck his head out to look down the corridor. "You all stay right where you're at. I'll stay out here. Don't you come closer or I'll blow so many … I'll shoot you up good."

Kupe squeezed his eyes shut and swallowed. What he wouldn't have given for a drink right then. He'd shoot straighter with the tunnel a bit wobbly than with his hands shaking like he was holding a steam hammer. Some hero he was. The tinker that had helped set the Human Rebellion to boiling had needed him, and he was stuck to the floor with his own glue.

"Put down your weapon and surrender," a steady, bass voice called from within the chamber.

"Ain't gonna," Kupe replied. "They're gonna come for me … well, come for him at least. I'm gonna get rescued, and you're in a heap of scrap when they get here."

A thump rumbled through the floor, accompanied by a scuffing sound. The thump repeated, became a rhythm, but not a steady beat. One of the barefoot daruu was stomping a signal. Kupe wasn't sure if it was paranoia or if he was smarter than he gave himself credit for, but he was in no position to run. He needed them to find him. If he ran off, there was no telling whether the rebels would get to him before the daruu, or even if they would keep looking once they found Cadmus. Kupe had to be realistic—he wasn't that important.

To his surprise, when the world-hole opened, it was right beside him. Rynn was standing there with a look of fury in her eyes. "Grab him," she ordered.

A pair of soldiers hooked Kupe under the arms and pulled him through to safety. The area just in front of the viewframe was packed with soldiers, all armed, all with their weapons pointed out into Veydrus. Kupe was dragged out of the way, but he had as good a view as anyone of what was about to come.

The viewframe moved, advancing at Rynn's command into the room where her father had died. Kupe saw the body, face bloody and misshapen, lying on the stone. The young daruu Gederon knelt over a daruu body, shoulders heaving in silent sobs. His hands were bloody.

There were plenty of daruu bodies. It looked like Cadmus had taken four of them down before they got him. Kupe didn't recognize any of them, nor had he expected to. These weren't Korrish daruu, the sort of folks who made the newspapers with flashpops at the opening of museums and the fluff pieces about quadricentennial birthdays. These were foreigners, otherworldly, only their language familiar.

"Who are you people? Who are you to have invaded our home and attacked our king?" one of the daruu asked, stepping forward.

With enough coil guns to add a screen door to the chamber, Rynn must have felt safe enough to parley. "Kezudkan Graniteson took my father as a slave, buying him in return for my mother's freedom and mine," she replied. "You harbored him. I don't know what happened here, but if you involved yourselves in my father's conflict, it is your own doing. Which one of you is responsible for *this*?" Rynn pointed at her father's body.

"He killed my uncle!" Gederon shouted, turning his attention from the elderly daruu's corpse. "Shot him, clean through the king, who'd done an honorable thing to shield him. He was a madman."

Kupe watched Rynn's face. The knit of her brow, the clenching in her jaw, that raw hatred in her eyes. She didn't want to shoot the daruu, he realized. She wanted to bash his head in with her bare hands.

"We want no war with your people. I am Lunjak, now king of all daruu. What would more loss of life gain either of us?"

Rynn turned to her soldiers. "Bring my father's body."

She watched the new king as six rebels gathered up the broken man who was once the Mad Tinker. The daruu's eyes were fixed on her as well. King Lunjak must have noticed her eyes wander to Gederon, because he stepped in front of the young daruu, just as Gederon claimed the prior king had done. "An act in grief, and against the killer of a king, is no crime."

"Maybe you haven't noticed," Rynn replied. "But war isn't a time for trials and laws. You attack us, enslave us, then try to claim innocence? I ought to pour lava down the halls of this whole kingdom of yours."

"We have done nothing to your people," King Lunjak said. "We have merely—"

"Draksgollow," Gederon cut in. "He's the one stealing you humans. He's the one who took this whole mess off the rails and made a war of it. My uncle just wanted to mine gold on a world where no one knew about it. Until your father ran off and started a rebellion, he didn't give a sandstone brick about humans one way or the other."

Rynn adjusted her aim, but the king kept himself between her and Gederon. After a long, slow, shuddering breath, she lowered her coil gun. "Where can I find him?"

# Chapter 26

*"Warning: the transport gates can create some rather unusual side effects when paired. Please use extreme caution when activating two in close proximity."*
*– Traveler's Companion: Transport Gates*

The rolling green hills of Khesh were dotted with new houses. The sweet smell of wildflowers was tinged with coal smoke and the raw, fresh scent of cut lumber. The refugees from Korr mixed with repatriated slaves and the survivors from the *Jennai.* The Human Rebellion was in the past for most of them, though a few still hung on in ancillary roles.

"Are you sure this is going to work?" Jamile asked.

Madlin filled her lungs with country air. It felt good to stretch her legs. "No," she admitted. "But I only get one try, most likely."

"What if it goes wrong?"

Madlin sighed. It was hard to be pessimistic looking across at new construction. She didn't have a sense of the Veydran people, knowing so few of them. Most of the Tellurakis she knew took pains to get someone else to do their work for them; her father had recruited those less prone to that vice. But the humans of Korr were workers, and by grace of Eziel, they were working for themselves now. Everything they built was theirs, and they set to the task with fire and zeal.

"Then we keep trying," Madlin replied. "That's why we win. We just keep trying until something works."

Across the three worlds, messengers dispersed. They came by world-ripper and departed likewise. They visited kings and empresses, goblin priests and kuduk councilors. Every major faction known in Korr, Tellurak, or Veydrus was invited. Each received a message, written in their own tongue, which said the following:

*You have been invited to the remaking of the world. You may attend in person, or send a delegation of your choosing. This is a meeting of peace, to end all wars, if not for all time then for all foreseeable time. Those who attend will bear witness to history. Those who abstain will still be held accountable to its resolution. Those who defy its edict will perish from these worlds. You will be summoned.*

With each copy there was a listing of a time and place where the delegation would be gathered and brought to the meeting. None of the messengers were lost.

The few who encountered resistance in their appointed delivery found themselves with a world-hole filled with ready coil guns at their back, ready to defend them. The Human Rebellion had taken no chances.

As twilight darkened, they gathered. One by one, group by group, world-holes opened, delivering the delegates. From Tellurak came the Kings of Acardia and Hurlan, with their retinues. The Emperor of Khesh sent his eldest son and three advisors. Takalia sent three governors. The kingdoms of Krang and Silk Waves came together with their delegation of diplomats. Sak Qual sent no one, but the land of Feru Maru boasted the largest delegation, with the entire royal family attending.

From Korr came the politicians: the governors and prime ministers, the councilors and mayors of the great cities, the peacemakers and warmongers. None came without attendants, using them to fluff their reputation among their peers. The prime minister of Braavland brought a professor of history and five secretaries. Tollopland came with a poet laureate. Grangia's delegation consisted of secondary officials from nearly every government agency, but no one of principal importance. Ruttania sent their entire Central Council, and at special request, one Ganrin Draksgollow.

Veydrus boasted the smallest number of delegates, but the most diverse. The goblins sent priests of the dragon gods who remained; all were wary of the slayer of Fr'n'ta'gur. The Megrenn Alliance came as one, with the regent of Ghelk and a tiny girl who was heir to that kingdom. Azzat had one ruler, and one delegate: the demon Xizix. He chuckled and snickered, and assured the other delegates that though they were but vermin to him, he had but one intention: to witness the promised history making. The Kadrin Empire had three delegates: the Empress Celia, High Sorcerer Axterion Solaran, and Sorcerer Caladris Solaran (or Dunston Harwick, depending whom you asked). The daruu's lone delegate was their new king, Lunjak.

They gathered beneath clear skies on the night of a full moon, with the stars winking into sight as the night grew deeper. A tropical breeze wafted from the nearby Aliani Sea, masking the potpourri of odors from every major culture of three worlds. The hushed crash of waves from beyond the leafy palms surrounding the clearing conveyed a sense of calm. Three massive stone tables had been placed in a triangular arrangement. Each was round, surrounded by chairs, and carved in the center with runes that spelled three names: Tellurak, Veydrus, Korr.

Rebels of the Human Rebellion milled among the delegates, guiding them to seats amid an atmosphere of tension and mistrust. Every war that could be fought, every war that had been fought, had its participants present. The rebel ushers had been chosen for the languages they spoke. As the delegations finally took their places, the ushers fell into place behind them, ready to translate.

A world-hole opened, and a lone figure stepped through. There were murmurs, but the delegates were too wary of the power gathered around them to draw unwanted attention to themselves. "My name is Madlin Errol, the Mad Tinker, as my father was before me. I have gathered you all here tonight to deliver a message. The time for vengeance is at an end. We have warred, and through ingenuity and cunning, we have devised a means of plunging three worlds into perpetual war, with no hope of safety, with no peace of mind without the annihilation of our foes. We gather beneath the Veydran night by means of this very device." Madlin raised her arms to the sky.

"What safety is there, when an army could be camped in your bedchamber? What peace when a lone soldier with a gun can kill a king? What hope does victory hold when all that you hold dear dangles by a thread? Tonight I offer peace."

Questions erupted then, as the translators caught up with what Madlin had said. She understood a few, but most were garbled by the din of voices or by dint of language. "What peace can I hold forth, you ask? Why should there be peace at all, when you have at your disposal the means of such effective war? I offer you the warden's peace. The tinkers have out-thought you this time. We hold the upper hand and we intend to play it. Those who would think to kill me here and now need only remember that it is not my hand that holds the gun to your heads."

Rynn stood at an open world-hole, the control console of the secret base's world-rippers within her reach. Madlin had made one key modification before her departure: a timer. With the flip of a switch, the machine would activate thirty seconds later. But Rynn was not watching the world-ripper; its controls were already dialed in, its target ready. She watched through her twin's eyes, waiting for the right moment in Madlin's speech, and it had arrived.

Taking a deep breath, she closed the switch. An arrangement of gears set into motion, a motion that would take precisely thirty seconds to complete. Rynn glanced to a corner of the secret base, where Cadmus Errol's body lay covered in linens.

"Goodbye, father," Rynn whispered. It harkened back to the ancient traditions of the Korrish humans, spoken with reverence in the teachings of Eziel. The funeral pyre was an extravagance in a world with little wood. Even the rebellion, so enamored of Eziel's reborn elegies, had not taken up the practice. But Rynn and Madlin had one fit for the Mad Tinker.

Rynn shut the world-ripper that allowed her to reach into the secret base. She found herself once more in a lunar headquarters that had long since stopped being a secret among the rebels.

"I don't know if I hope it works or not," Jamile said quietly.

"We'll find out soon enough." They were both there in Veydrus: Madlin speaking, and Sosha translating for a Takalish governor.

Amid curses and threats, kept under tight control by rebel soldiers with coil guns, Madlin shouted over the cacophony and managed to continue. "You ask what right I have. You ask who am I to tell you what you can or can't do. You boast of your magic, your armies, your entitlements. I ask you to look to the sky, and witness the wrath of science unleashed!"

Madlin raised both hands to the sky, hoping that her estimate of thirty second had made for proper dramatic timing. She hoped there would be something worth seeing at all. This whole mess could have gone very poorly if not …

There was a flash, and Madlin felt a wave of relief. A tiny orange plume jetted forth from the surface of the moon. *It worked! Let them see that I can blast a crater in the moon, and see what they …*

But that wasn't all that happened in the night sky. A shadow slashed across the surface, irregular and jagged, but thin. It spread like cracks in broken glass, and Madlin's breath caught in her lungs. The moon above Veydrus had shattered, and the pieces were drifting apart. She stared up in mute horror at what she had done. The world-ripper had been positioned a hundred feet below the lunar surface on the visible side. It ought to have been enough for a spectacular show if the machine worked as she had envisioned.

Most of the audience was struck dumb as well. A few muttered prayers were heard, and more than one delegate was brought to tears. Madlin had some expectation of what was about to occur, and even she needed several moments to collect herself.

"That could have been the homeland of any of you," Madlin said, hoping no one noticed the tremor in her voice. "That could have been the whole of Korr, or Tellurak. If you persist, this is the weapon you will face. These are my terms: The humans of Korr are free from this moment. They will be evacuated via my machines, to the destination of their choosing. There will be no further use of the machines known as world-rippers by any other than my own organization. We will find violators and they will be eliminated. There will be justice for the Human Replacement Project. The kuduk tinker known as Ganrin Draksgollow will oversee the dismantling of the project he had created. He will be under constant surveillance for the remainder of his days, and will take part is no further activity relating to the development of world-ripper technology. All existing machines will be turned over to Errol Company or destroyed utterly."

Madlin looked out over the stunned delegates. Only the demon appeared amused. "These are my terms. There is no negotiation. You will be returned to your homes, except for Mr. Draksgollow, who will be coming with us. Good evening."

A world-hole opened and the new Mad Tinker vanished through it.

# Chapter 27

*"The clearest message we have from Eziel is this: the preservation of mankind. Do what you must, whether fight or flee or hide, to give our kind the best chance to survive."*
*– Pious Rascal*

The engine of the steam wagon chugged and puffed along. Madlin had been thinking for months that she ought to replace it with a fully rune-powered model, but she had grown fond of the little mechanical beast. Its iron-studded wheels bit into the turf as it climbed the hillside. As she crested the rise, Madlin pulled down the binocular attachment for her spectacles and surveyed the area. It seemed decadent, owning land that she had never seen. Most of Tellurak was populated by common folk who would never rub two stones of their own together.

The valley was overgrown with tall, wispy grasses and thorny bushes, but it was still easier than dealing with tree cover. At her side, Jamile looked through a spyglass—one of the ones they had brought for the delegates of the Final Peace meeting but never needed. "It's pretty down there. Seems a shame to disturb it."

"Everywhere's pretty to you," Madlin replied. "But we've got a thousand people a day coming through from Korr, and no place to put them. Well, plenty of land, but no places in it. Blast it, you know what I mean."

There were chuckles from the back of the steam wagon, where the surveying crew rode. There were six of them, a mix of Korrish and Kheshi. The Kheshis were locals, who knew the land. The Korrish knew how to measure it properly.

"Go on," Madlin snapped, "Get to work." They knew she wasn't cross with them; they had worked with her on five city sites previously. "I figure we'll run the new thunderail line down that valley pass, cutting the hillside back. We'll cross the brook over that way. Base the layout sketches on that and measure accordingly."

"Yes, tinker," they replied in rough unison. Madlin had cured everyone of calling her "ma'am" as soon as decorum allowed, following the war. She had retired officially, though officially only Rynn had held rank. Madlin's new title was Mad Tinker, which was less an epithet than an honor, as far as she was concerned. The title had passed down from Cadmus, but she had no idea who she would pass it on to. She was not yet twenty, though she felt at times that her life had run twice that long. A side effect of being twinborn, she supposed. There would be time one day for home and family. For now, she had a country to build.

"You coming?" Madlin asked as she hopped down, her boots sinking in the soft soil.

Jamile smiled. "I'll watch from here, if you don't mind." Jamile had been keeping off her feet more and more of late. The swell of her belly was all the reason she needed. Madlin had been surprised when she realized that Jamile was carrying a child. Never had she noticed Jamile taking an interest in men, or at least none in particular. Wartime passion, she supposed—ill-considered and fleeting. The father was a mystery, and one Madlin felt better left alone. She had a strong suspicion that the child was Kupe's, and a scandal was the last thing Prime Minister Kupe and Lady Charsi needed. Kupe was swimming upside down as it was, trying to lead where everyone showed him.

"Well, you take it easy, then," Madlin said. "We'll be a couple hours. I'll try to stay in shouting distance in case you need anything."

"You're not nervous at all?" Jamile asked, wringing her hands.

"Why would I be nervous?" Madlin said. "This place is tame as a milk cow."

"Not *that*," Jamile replied. "The other thing. You know."

Madlin chuckled. "I'll be fine. It's science like we've never seen. Trust them."

Rynn heard a beeping sound—rhythmic, steady, and oddly comforting. She opened her eyes and saw white. A white ceiling overhead, with a soft white light shining down. White walls with white panels, scrawled with words she couldn't understand. She was covered in white sheets, and wore a white smock as soft as kitten fur. White wires snaked out from under that smock, running to white-painted machines with glowing displays—one of which made the beeping noise.

She was not alone in the room. She had three visitors. One was Sosha, her dark skin contrasting with the stark white all around, including the toothy smile that she gave. Another was dressed in a loose, pale blue outfit of matching pants and shirt. He carried a rectangular panel like a clipboard, but one face glowed with that same incompressible writing, along with some graphs. A loose cloth mask hung around his neck, a pair of laces dangling loose from it. Rynn's impression was that he looked like a stage actor, with his perfect smile and coiffed hair, but it didn't seem out of place for a doctor. The third in the room with them was a translator. The grey-haired woman had a kindly face and alert eyes, the sort of eyes that looked at things, not just passively taking them in.

"How do you feel?" Sosha asked.

"Thirsty," Rynn replied. There was a peculiar taste in her mouth that she could not identify. Reaching for the bedside table, she drank from a little white cup they had left there for her.

The doctor said something. His language was lyrical and mysterious. "Do you have any feeling?" the translator asked.

Rynn shrugged. "Yeah, but that never meant anything. Let's just have a look." After waiting for the translation, the doctor nodded. Some things, it seemed, needed no translation.

The doctor pulled back the blankets and Rynn looked down. There, just below the knee, the skin turned fresh pink, like her tinker's legs had been a scab that had just been removed. With an effort of concentration, Rynn wiggled her toes.

"They work!" Sosha squealed. She clapped her hands together.

"What else would you expect?" Rynn asked. "These people have medicine figured out. Blast it, they seem to have everything figured out."

After an exchange back and forth in the local language, the doctor replied via translator. "Not everything, madam emissary. I've been fielding calls from the Ministry of Science, the Ministry of Defense, and no fewer than a dozen research universities, all wanting to study those runes of yours. The Ministry of Foreign Relations has been keeping them at bay, but they've been wanting to study your prosthesis."

Rynn smirked. "They must think I'm some sort of witch."

The doctor nodded. "You're in little danger, of course," he replied via translator. "Your activities will be monitored, both for the populace's peace of mind and for your own protection."

"As long as I can learn the science of your world," Rynn replied, "you're welcome to anything I know about mine."

She felt like a card hustler. These poor folks of Olara didn't know the shabby end of a bargain when they saw one. Tellurak would get the benefits of science a thousand years ahead of its time, and Olara would get floaty runes and mechanical replacement legs. But as long as they were happy with the bargain, who was she to argue. It wasn't as if she had real magic to show them.

# Chapter 28

*"The distress beacon is only to be used as a last resort. Traveler's Companion will not be held responsible for the consequences of frivolous use."*
*– Traveler's Companion: Calling for Help*

In a forested grove, the immortals gathered. They had taken their leisure among the mortal races, but one of their number had called them home. Now, beneath the stars and under the light of the cracked moon, they waited.

"You have to admit; I was right," Kyrus whispered, grinning at his companion.

"Yeah, I feel *so* much better now that the Errol girl knows how to blast a planet to bits," Juliana replied.

"But those kuduks never managed to wipe out their humans or replace them from Tellurak," Kyrus replied. "They got the tinkers who knew how to build the machines and rounded them all up."

"So now only one group controls inter-world travel."

Kyrus chuckled.

"Fine, so we can do it too," Juliana said. "But they've still got a weapon that could kill us. The mortals might not have realized how she did it, but we know what we're up against. Do *you* think you could survive the sun?"

Kyrus shrugged. "I don't expect I'll ever have to. What quarrel have they got with me? Besides, I know a secret."

"Oh?" Juliana asked. Kyrus wasn't in the habit of keeping those, as far as she knew.

Kyrus leaned close and cupped a hand over her ear. "They don't have a machine to do it."

"But she said—"

Kyrus grinned. "They don't need another. Sure, they could build one, but they blew that first one to ash and nearly cracked Tellurak's moon in the process. But I like it, the threat of that thing will keep the peace, and since no one can find it, no one can ever be sure it's gone."

"Then how do *you* know?" Juliana stuck her tongue out.

"A good magician never reveals how he does his tricks."

Juliana raised an eyebrow. It was a worse threat than anything she could have said.

"Fine," Kyrus relented. "Illiardra told me. And don't ask, because I have no idea how she knew."

There was a small commotion among the immortals. The absent member of their order had returned—the one who had called them together in the first place. At first it was difficult to recognize Viyax, looking as plain and common as a Korrish human. But when he spoke his voice was the same as ever.

"Thank you all. You honor me with your attention," Viyax said, projecting his voice to the far reaches of the assembly. He was dressed in coveralls stained with grease, and beside him was something about the size of a wine barrel, covered in a grimy cloth.

"Since when have you cherished anything else?" a voice called out from the crowd. There was good-natured laughter at the prankster demon's expense.

"We gather tonight beneath a wounded moon," Viyax continued, unable to prevent a smile from turning up his lip. He could not resist a good joke, not even when he was its target. "It made me think we are not so invulnerable. We have a new Tallax watching over us."

"You overstate matters," Illiardra said, her voice carrying clear across the grove.

"Do I?" Viyax asked. "When Tallax died, his threat died with him. This girl has left us in the hands of science, a force which bows to no single master. When the new Mad Tinker dies, some other will take up her cause, and if she is like the Korrish I have met, it will be a score of someones, not a lone successor."

"What's under the cloth?" Bvatrain asked. He had returned reluctantly from his visit to a land that had become a stranger to him. He made no secret that he wished to return.

Viyax grinned, his smile impossibly wide for his otherwise human face. "I built one!" He pulled the cloth away to reveal a curious contraption beneath. Despite never having seen one before, any immortal who had read through the twelve books recognized it from the descriptions contained therein: a distress beacon.

"Really, Viyax, you think we need help from some unknown source?" Illiardra asked. "From the same ones who wrote of age elixirs and makeshift transference devices. From the ones who told me the names of plants and animals I knew from their first appearance in the world. From the ones who worried that they would get lost exploring. We need no help from the likes of them."

"Aren't you curious who would come?" Viyax asked. "If they are weak and foolish, they are harmless. If they are not, then we might ask succor of them."

"You have to admit he has a point," Kyrus said. Juliana elbowed him in the side, but didn't speak against him. She ought to have been proud; Kyrus so rarely instigated trouble.

"Thank you," Viyax said with a bow in Kyrus's direction. "So good to see the youths among us looking for the novel solution. I don't relish waiting out five hundred years of domination." He pulled a lever and the machine sparked to life. It cracked with energy, whirring to a high-pitched whine. When the whine steadied, the machine warbled a series of gibberish sounds, like spark-powered birdsong. Then it went dark and silent.

The immortals waited. Patience was a trait widely admired among them. It became a test of wills to see who would weaken first and make some comment. Before the first of them broke ranks, the skies grew clouded. The stars vanished. The crippled moon disappeared behind a wall of heavy black stormclouds. Lightning struck the ground in their midst, and a man appeared as if carried on the bolt.

"What is this?" he asked. He had a deep, melodious voice, and spoke the arcane tongue that all present understood. He appeared human, though tall for the species. He wore a long, sleeveless white tunic, trimmed in gold and belted at the waist, leaving muscular arms and calves bare. His face was … familiar.

"Eziel?" Juliana asked. She knew the face from the statue in the Acardian city of Golis, where the ancient gods stood in sculpted form, watching over a plaza.

He frowned, but it carried no hint of anger. "You are too young to know me," he said.

"But not I," Bvatrain said, drawing the god's attention.

"Nor I," added Illiardra.

"Why have you summoned me?" Eziel asked. "I had no idea these worlds still held life, so long had they been dormant."

"Dormant?" Illiardra asked. "Your brethren cleaved them loose in fear of Tallax."

Eziel scoffed. "Not fear for us, but fear for mortals of the other worlds. The daruu of Tellurak died at his hands. He drove the Korrish dragons to extinction. All because he was unable to find the answer to the one question he cared for."

"He has been dead for thousands of winters," Illiardra protested.

"And the worlds have drifted back together once again," Eziel replied. "You could have contacted us long before now, if you were in no further danger. I'm surprised you turned to science instead of magic though. I did not expect it of a pastoral world."

"Does this mean you're going to return?" Juliana asked. She had prayed to Tansha as a child—the blink of an eye ago, to the ageless creatures around her. There was still a part of her that longed for proof that the goddess was real.

"Return?" Eziel asked. "Why would we return here? Our work is done—long since done."

"You still have worshipers here," Bvatrain said. "Some few in this world, many more in Korr and Tellurak. The humans of Korr just fought a war in your name."

Eziel's face wrinkled in disgust. "I taught them the means to defend themselves, not to wage war. I suppose I must shoulder blame for letting that message erode in the winds of time. But it is not for me to disabuse them. Let them believe of me as they will. They are not my problem any longer."

"But what of the Korrish weapon that broke the moon?" Viyax asked. "What if they turn it against us? We need your help."

Eziel threw his head back and laughed. "Is this why you've called for aid after all this time? Because some class three or four world gained access to class seven science? You mighty magicians are afraid of technology that can barely toddle across the floor, and you cower in the corners from it?"

"Yes?" Viyax ventured sheepishly.

"Come to me when their civilization expands to the stars, and they threaten to collapse the heavens upon themselves. That day they might inconvenience my current works, and I might come to stop them for you then. Those of you whom I remember, you disappoint me. You are so much as you were. Grow. Begin anew. Explore. Do not fritter away your vast lifespans. Even your so-called immortality is not without end."

"What would you have us do?" Illiardra asked.

"Have you do?" Eziel asked. "I would have you tend to your own affairs. You want the gods watching over you, but to whom do these mortals turn? They pray to memories, listen to echoes, read shadows of old beliefs. Steer them. Guide them. Protect them as we once did, as we once needed to. This world is old enough; it no longer needs us. It has its guardians."

With that, lightning struck where Eziel stood, and he was gone. The skies cleared and the broken moon stared down at them once more, accusingly. In the silence that followed, the immortals looked to one another, each trying to decide what to make of Eziel's admonishment.

"I guess no more non-intervention," Kyrus said with a wan smile.

"If there are no other volunteers, I'll be the goddess of war," Juliana offered.

# Other Books by J.S. Morin

If you enjoyed World-Ripper War, why not go back to the beginning, and experience the journey of mundane scribe Kyrus Hinterdale who discovers what it means to be Twinborn—and the dangers of getting caught using magic in a world that thinks it exists only in childrens' stories.

The **Twinborn Trilogy** is available for sale on Amazon

**War-Bringer**
Prequel

**Firehurler**
Book 1

**Aethersmith**
Book 2

**Sourcethief**
Book 3

# About the Author

Born in New Hampshire in 1977, J.S. Morin found himself captivated by the wonders of fantasy novels at a young age. He was introduced to the genre via the works of R.A. Salvatore, Ed Greenwood, and Margaret Weiss and Tracy Hickman. He loved exploring other people's worlds, from Shadowdale to Hyrule. He also quickly found Dungeons and Dragons to be a creative outlet for stories, characters, and new worlds of his own creation.

His other passion was for building and designing things, and when it came time to choose a career, he went down that road. A Mechanical Engineer by day, he spends his evenings with his wife in their New Hampshire home, enjoying the simplicity of life in a quiet state.

By night he dreams elaborate dreams of visiting fanciful worlds, performing acts of heroism, and solving intriguing puzzles, which inspire him to craft stories that he hopes will help shape the lives of the next generation of fantasy readers. He hopes to avoid finishing growing up.

Tanner scratched at a week's beard, weighing the risk of trying to shave with a runed sword. He had never been fond of beards, but he had never been fond of beaches either, yet here he was. The liftwing was perched not fifty paces away at the edge of the sand and the tall grasses. One wheel was broken, having given out when he made his first landing. For someone who never took a lesson, he considered it a victory.

He took a bite of a fruit he couldn't name, the juices running down his face amid the unaccustomed hair. The first day, he had counted himself lucky for having found a grove of trees laden with the fruits not far from shore. By now he was sick to death of them, but had yet to find anything else that looked safe to eat.

Tanner looked up into the bright blue sky. "Dan, I know yesterday I swore I'd have your spleen out for leaving me here. I take it back. You get them to open a gate and we can call it even."

He took another bite, and waited.

17966959R00144

Made in the USA
Middletown, DE
17 February 2015